revival

kate vine

Revival

Kate Vine

Copyright 2016 Kate Vine
All Rights Reserved

Published by Kate Vine

Except the original material written by the author, all songs, and song titles contained in this book are the property of the songwriters and copywriters holders. The author concedes to the trademark status and trademark owners of the products mentions in this fiction novel and recognizes that they have been used without permission. The use and publication of these trademarks is not authorized, associated with, or sponsored by the trademark owners.

This book is a work of fiction. Any references to real events, real people, and real places are used fictitiously. All the names, characters, places, and incidents are product of the author's imagination and any resemblance to persons, living or dead, actual events, organizations or places is entirely coincidental.

All rights reserved. This book is intended for the purchaser of the e-book ONLY. No part of this book may be reproduced or transmitted in any form or my any means, graphic, electronic, or mechanical, including photocopying, recording, taping, or by any information storage retrieval system, without the express written permission of the Author. All songs, songs titles and lyrics contained in this book are the property of the respective song-writers and copyright holders.

WARNING:

This book contains sexually explicit scenes and adult language and may be inappropriate or offensive to some readers. It is intended for readers over 18+

Editing by Cassandra J. LaPorte
Formatting by R. Shenk
Proof Read by Lexi Brodie of Book Reviews by Lexi
Cover Design by Cassy Roop of Pink Ink Design
Cover Image by Cassy Roop of Pink Ink Design
Cover Model Robert Simmons
Final Edit and Proof Reading by Patricia A. Essex

Dedication

This one is for you,

I believe you have your heart broken in one way or another.

Remember, there is always hope and second chance is right around the corner.

There is no saint

Without a past

No sinner

Without a future

~Augustine of Hippo

Prologue

The last couple of months have been nothing but survival.
Literally.
If you were to pull out Webster and find the definition, I'm spot on.
Remaining alive.
Sustaining myself.
Pulling through.
Getting through.
Holding on.
Making it.
Keeping body and soul together.
Oh well, maybe not that last part, as I lost my soul at exactly the same time she left me, when I let her go.
So, yeah I'm soulless, an empty corpse walking around, drinking whatever is offered to drink and fucking whatever is around to fuck.
I know what you will say, and trust me, I know what you are thinking right now. What a piece of shit, soft hearted, worthless motherfucker I am. And you are totally right, I'm not even going to argue with you on that subject. I'm nothing.
I'm nothing without her.
I'm totally aware that everything I did since New Year's Eve is a calculated path of destruction.
The destruction that is impossible to escape.
The destruction that I DON'T want to escape.

The destruction that is something I devour, something I seek, something that gives me a peace for my fucked up mind.

Yes, I'm that deep into that shit.

Grief.

Is a bitch.

Dylan

I know my breath is nothing but Scotch, my eyes are bloodshot and my face doesn't resemble the youth it should.

I know.

And I also know that all those stupid shit, rich pricks around me don't care about any of that. They only care about one thing; to get the deal sealed. To get their money flowing and to sign those damn papers as soon as they can, so they can leave and head out for the next deal. I know all of that. That's why I'm not trying to pretend that I'm here for anything different.

I sign the last sheet of paper with a shaky hand, and close the folder with way too much force, causing all the bald heads turn in my direction.

"That was nice and easy gentlemen." I take my time to look into each set of tired eyes, letting them know that, indeed, I'm glad how easy this deal went. "See you on the other side of the ocean." I manage a wink as I lift the glass of water to my mouth.

They all start talking at the same time, and it's all muffled to me, I don't hear it. I'm gone the second my mind stops focusing on the contract I just signed. I stand and shake dozens of hands mechanically, nodding my head to what I suppose are congratulations and hopes for a great partnership in the future.

Yes, sure, yes, we will do great, yes, we will

probably work together again soon. Same shit every time I close the deal. Same words. Same reactions.

It used to bring me satisfaction. It brought me a high.

Not anymore.

Not since she's been gone.

Nothing makes sense since she's been gone.

And nothing ever will do.

Ever again.

Even when she wasn't mine, when she wasn't by my side, I knew she was around. I knew she was there, and now, nothing. Emptiness. The black stone of her grave left behind. Fuckin' A!

I need a drink; I need a fucking drink at this very second. So I shake all those remaining hands faster and nod my fuzzy head rapidly thanking them for the pleasure of doing business and head straight for my office.

Once the doors are closed behind me, I rush to my not-so-secret cabinet and pour myself a good double dose of amber liquid. I sit, and take a long sip that burns my throat and slides down to my stomach, warming its path. I try to push away the image of the brown eyed beauty that is with me no matter how much I try to let her go, no matter how much I drink, and no matter how many pussies I fuck in order to forget.

She is still everything.

She is still very much alive in my head, even though I know there is nothing left of her. Literally, there is nothing left of her. Five months later, she's buried in the ground. There is nothing left of her. Nothing. Not even her ashes. And how do I know that? I checked, I read this stuff like it is the fucking Bible just to know what is going on with her. Every word, every fucking word on that shitty Google page made me spasm, made me convulse and gag at the

revival

thought of my love, my only love going through that horrifying shit of death.

I know people say that life goes on, that I'm still very much alive and I should keep going, but honestly, to me that's the saddest fucking part. Sure, life goes on, but it goes on without her by my side. Without her generous eyes looking at me, without her sweet mouth covering mine, without her raspy voice whispering in my ears. That's not life; without any of this, that's a fuckin' vegetative state. Survival. Getting from point A to point B without thinking about anything in between. Although my in between is numbing the life, numbing everything that is making me feel. Feelings equal pain, and pain is something I try to forget about.

Because the undeniable truth in all of this; was that it was my fault. My fucking fault. If not for me, she would be living her simple, happy life, unaware of my existence, unaware of the destruction I brought along with my presence.

I am the murderer. I am the person that brought the death upon her and there is nothing and no one that can tell me otherwise. I know better. I am the only one who knows what happened before that accident, what triggered it. If only she hadn't read the stupid piece of paper lying on my table, inviting her to the path of death. She would still be here, breathing, talking, standing next to me. If only...

I down a fourth glass of whiskey and head out of my office, downstairs to where my car is waiting for me. I know I should go home, I know I should sleep it off. Tomorrow I'm heading overseas for a couple of weeks. I also know that jerking off will do nothing, neither will fucking a random chick, but having my dick deep inside someone is way better that having it in my hand, so I text Cassey. Yes, the good ole Cassey who fills the space when needed. Normally I would visit The Club and have my taste of the night, but I'm too hammered. I'm too wound up in my own fucked up mind to go and bring the game on, the game that is hanging by the thread anyways, as I lost it a while ago.

I look at the lit up screen and I don't even crack a smile at the response that comes right away. Of course she will be there, no questions asked, no answers needed. My kind of whore. And no, I don't feel bad for using her like that, she strives for it, she lives for it, and any other way would be a misunderstanding.

I'm lying next to the familiar yet strange body next to me. It feels like I fucked a blow up doll. Seriously. Not that she wasn't enjoying it, oh, trust me she was, but I heard nothing. I just saw her puffed up mouth, forming the letter "O" while she was underneath me.

Tell me right now that I'm normal. Tell me right now that I'm not losing my mind, and I will give you anything. You know you can't. You know I'm losing it. And I know it as well. I know it better that anyone else. Every pussy I fuck is hers, it doesn't feel like her, it doesn't taste like her, but I block those senses out and make it be her. I need it to be her.

I tell myself that I will start another day with a different approach, but I fail.

Every.

Damn.

Day.

I fail.

And even though I'm saying the same thing tonight, I know that tomorrow won't be any different. I miss her. I miss her terribly. I miss her like a fish misses water, like a plant misses the sun; I miss her like you have no fucking idea.

I still have so much left to say to her. So much we thought we could say to each other later. There will never be a later. This is it. That was it.

I stand up and go straight to my kitchen, head for the bar, take a beer out of the fridge, and down it in a two big gulps; slamming the bottle on the counter.

The memory is floating, coming at me like an unexpected thunder, and this one, this fuckin' one in particular strikes straight into my heart, breaking it into a million pieces.

I bawl next to the counter, hands on my head. Animalistic sobs go through my vocal cords, loud, rough and painful. Ripping my lungs out and cutting my air supply to the point that my mouth is fully open, trying to catch air, trying to breathe.

I cry for her, I cry for me and I cry for everything that I lost and everything that hasn't come yet. I can't live my life without her. I can't go forward without her presence by my side. And knowing that all of this, all of this is my fucking fault is making it a thousand times worse.

I could have stopped it, I should have stopped it, but I didn't. I was this selfish motherfucker, thinking that leaving out facts would ease things. If I only called her right away, talked to her, told her what I knew...

Things could have been different.
Things could have been a lot different.
Better.
A life would have been saved.
One would have been saved. The other one would end. I would die slowly, suffering from not having her close, not having her as mine.

But at least she would be alive.
She would breathe.

The air feels warm as I exit the jet and pull my sunglasses over my eyes to block the annoying rays of the morning sun. Combine seven hours of drinking and about forty-five minutes of sleep and you'll get the idea. I don't actually remember waking up sober in the past couple of months. But on the other hand I like that I'm constantly reminded. That every morning is a reminder of why I drank in the first place. It keeps me sane in a wicked, twisted sense.

My car takes me straight to the scheduled meeting to go over the project I finalized a few days ago. I go over the papers while sitting in the back of my limo and put some redness reducing drops in my eyes, because I'm sure they look like hell. Hell I've been living in for some time now.

Just two weeks, two weeks and I will leave all of this behind and get the hell out of my own life. I will get far far away, to fall even harder. What's left of my pathetic life? Nothing. So I will keep sinking and sinking until I can't sink anymore.

Nina

I knock three times then stop for a second, then knock two more times. I fidget nervously while waiting for the door to open. I hear some movement, steps getting closer and closer to the door. I look around the narrow hallway, not because I'm afraid, but because it's a habit of mine to get in and out unseen. The locks open one by one, the bottom one makes a quick noise of metal sliding over metal, next a key turns twice, then comes the chain, and then the squawk of the upper bolt.

The door opens and I get in and search the room for the little person I was missing terribly the whole day. I scan the small play area designed just for her, it's already been cleaned up and organized. My eyes move slowly around the small space that combines the kitchen with the living room and they land on the couch where the big blond halo of curls is sleeping. I come closer and lean over to give her a kiss, a kiss that I was craving the whole day. Moments like this keep me going, they keep me going forward.

"Gran, are you feeding her chocolate all the time?" I ask while wiping her sweet mouth that is coated in brown sugary sweetness. "You can't do that, she needs regular food once in a while."

Grandma waves her hand in the air as if trying to make me go away "Oh please, I did the same thing with you and look at you, you turned out just fine."

I smile at that, what can I say? I did turn out all

right after all. When I recall those sweet moments when she was feeding me sweets and nothing but sweets, I can't keep my face straight, those were the happiest memories of my life.

"You don't mean those years of dieting, do you? I still have a few pounds to lose and they seem stuck to me; like they depend on me." I grab the fold on my stomach and she twists her face in a disapproving expression.

"Stop complaining child, you are perfect and there are far worse things people need to worry about, just stop." She moves to the kitchen and takes out the container of soup from the fridge. "I made chicken soup, just heat it up and you will have dinner ready in no time."

"Thank you Gran, you are the best." I take the soup and place it carefully in my oversized bag, smiling at her, grateful that she takes care of us like that.

"Damn right I'm the best, so don't you dare accuse me of not feeding my only great granddaughter properly."

"Yes you are." I bring her little body into a gentle hug. She is so tiny that I'm afraid if I show her how much I really love her, I might break her. I take a minute to drink in the comfort of her arms, smelling the familiar scent of her powder and chicken soup. Always comforting. Always makes me feel safe.

"Ok, get that little creature off my couch so I can watch my show." She pushes me off gently. I turn around and walk to the sofa where my little angel is sleeping.

She is an angel. Her bright, blond halo of curls falls around her face, sticking to the chocolate covered mouth. Her long lashes rest peacefully on her slightly pink cheeks. How did I manage to create such perfection? I ask myself that question every day and I remind myself that I am, in fact lucky, no matter what that stupid life is trying to throw at me.

"See you tomorrow," I whisper over my shoulder while heading to the door.

"Goodnight child," Gran is standing behind me, patting me on my back. "Goodnight."

I walk out the door and head for a short flight of stairs, eight to be exact. The reason I know how many steps my stairway has is something I would like to forget, but every time I walk those eight steps the memory flashes before my eyes.

Punch.
Step back.
Punch.
Another step back.
Punch.
Going down eight steps.

I move my jaw right to left and the slight discomfort that I was told would never go away is definitely there.

I was never lucky in choosing my boyfriends. No, scratch that, I was terrible in choosing whom I was seeing and the choice was always made by me. Calculated even. I never aimed for those handsome, popular boys walking around the school. No, I was always going for the losers. You have all the rights to ask me why. Why on earth would I make that choice?

Well, let me tell you why. Even though everybody was telling me I was pretty as a child, with my strawberry blond hair always falling over my shoulders, narrow blue eyes that resemble the eyes of a cat, big thick eyebrows and full as hell lips, my parents thought otherwise and their nickname for me was Weirdo. Yes, you read that right. WEIRDO. So, after a while I felt like one and I was frightened about bringing any attention to myself. Petrified even. So, of course, I was hiding myself in the background for most of high school, satisfying my sexual expedition through losers and drug addicts.

Oh God, even losing my virginity wasn't glorious at all. Somewhere in the beginning of my junior high, I ended up at a lame party. After one too many beers, I gave myself up to Johnny Bruschwick, the biggest ass loser you can think of and my long time neighbor. I still recall his stinky breath and rough hands on my body, not to mention his pencil sized dick trying to take what I should have kept sacred for someone special. It wasn't glorious; it was far from it. It was painful as hell and as I kept my eyes shut the whole time, I wished it were over already. Yep, that's how I was deflowered. Painfully, drunk and young. And that's how I became popular amongst a circle full of losers and I rolled with it for a few years until I decided to leave my home town and start afresh.

And that's how I ended up here. New Orleans, Louisiana. Why here? I don't really know, I just bought a ticket at my local bus station and that was the farthest ride I could afford.

I open my third lock and lean against my door, as this one needs a little push to work. I try to be careful not to wake Ellie as I bump my body on the door a few times, but she is out for good, despite all the sweets she probably consumed during the day. I smile to myself as I enter our one-bedroom apartment. I head for the bedroom and put her under the cool covers of my bed, our bed that we've shared from day one. And I can't imagine any other way. The last five years I have had the most peaceful nights in all my twenty-six years of existence. Night, where I was able to listen to those calm breaths, breaths that were reminding me that my life is not about me anymore. That I gave up ME

revival

for something better, something that is far more precious, far more important. And those little hands reaching for me every morning and caressing my face to wake me up, tickling and making me laugh in the process, those big grey eyes sparkling in the morning like they just discovered the most hidden secret of life. Love. And that is what I feel every single morning when I open my eyes and see those sparkling eyes staring back at me.

Love.

Nothing can beat that.

Nothing and no one.

I tug the sheets around her little body and head to the living room, well, technically the kitchen with a sofa and coffee table that I made into the two rooms. That is the best I can do for now and I'm not complaining about any of it. Not that I knew any better before. My parent's house was the size of a big apartment, two bedrooms to be exact. One of which I shared with my elder sister, a sister whom I haven't see in a seven years. The sister that took off right after she graduated high school and never looked back. I was just entering my junior high, and secretly I was counting on her sisterly advices. Yes, the ones I never received. So much for having a sister if you ask me.

I take the soup container out of my bag and transfer the liquid to the pot, putting it on the stove on a low heat before heading to the bathroom to take a quick shower. My stomach growls like a hungry monster, reminding me that I haven't eaten anything today. I jump in and out of the shower in exactly four minutes, as the smell of the chicken soup is calling me with such a force, I can't resist.

The hot soup burns my lips and I have to open my mouth and breathe in air to cool it off before I swallow. Once the first spoon is down, the comforting, warm sensation makes me shovel the rest in as fast as I can. Nothing like Grandma's chicken soup. Soup that warmed my empty stomach for as long as I can remember warmed my heart and gave me hope. How pathetic that a cup of warm, chicken broth can give you such peace of mind.

I walk fast to the Omni Royal. I'm late as per usual, nothing new as I couldn't fall asleep until I did the laundry, got Elli's clothes and toys ready for the next day and got myself ready for another long day. Every day is a long day. First an eight-hour shift at the hotel, then a six-plus hour shift at the bar, depends on how long the customers are planning on partying. And today is a Friday, so I'm sure they will be around well after three A.M. We don't have a closing law, not a good thing, but I will take all the tips I can. They bring me closer to my dream, and that's all that matters. That's all that keeps me going forward day by day.

As soon as I enter the hotel and push my cleaning cart into the elevator, I turn off all my human emotions and all my human reflexes. Believe me, that is more than necessary in my job. I thought I saw everything before I started cleaning hotel rooms. Oh, how wrong was I, how very wrong. There is much more to human nature, so much more. Toilets that are not flushed and full of weird unidentifiable matter, trash full of way too personal items, condoms next to the bed, often in the bed. Tons of dirty, stinky underwear next to the bed, a bunch of crap around the rooms that you would refuse to touch with your bare hands. And I don't touch it without putting on my thick, rubber gloves.

revival

They have been my number one safety item from day one.

———•●•———

"How are you doing?" Kelly asks me as she fills the round of shots for my table.

"Not bad, not bad." I rub my temples as I try to relieve the headache that I feel is building. "Long ass day at the hotel, so I'm praying we close up early tonight," I say as I look around the bar. The tables are full, and quietly I'm hoping that the party will end soon so I can head home to rest and cuddle with my girl.

"We need those drunken asses to be here, don't fool yourself Nina." She puts the numerous glasses on my tray and slides it my way. I know she's right, without the drinking, loud crowd, I'm not making any money. So yes, we do need those drunken folks to drink until they puke, but I'm tired of this crap. I wish I could finish work at five p.m. and head home to my baby, not work my ass off until morning hours to make ends meet. *Hang in there Nina*, I tell myself as I grab the tray, plaster a fake smile over my face, and head for the table.

"There you go boys." I say as I put the alcohol on the wooden table. "Have fun!" I add while turning around and heading back to the bar.

"Number six is yours as well." Kelly nods in the direction of a table that is right across from the bar, and there is only one person sitting at it. I take the menus in my hand and walk straight to the costumer.

"Hello, anything to eat?" I ask politely scanning the rest of the bar to see if anyone is in need of anything.

"Ten shots of vodka." The sound of the sexiest voice I ever heard hit my ears. In all the years of working here, I've heard many sexy sounding males passing by, but this one right here is something different.

"You mean a bottle?" I stifle a laugh as it's not often you see a single person order such a large amount of alcohol.

"I said ten shots, you need a fuckin' hearing aid or something?" His voice came out rusty but not angry, and I swear it sounds familiar but I can't place it. I look down at the guy, but all I see is a baseball cap and dark stray pieces of hair sticking out of it.

"I'm sorry but we can only serve one shot at a time for each person, would you like that?" My patience is leaving me as I see a few people at the tables are waving in my direction. Hell no, I'm not losing a good, table packed to the fullest for this prick.

"Does Ritchie still own this shit-hole?" He asks keeping his eyes down on a napkin he is folding over and over.

"Yes, as far as I know, he does." I reply as a matter-of-fact, rolling my eyes, hoping he can hear the boldness in my tone. I've heard it a million times, guys thinking they are the shit cause they think they know the owner, we laugh at it all the time while we clean the club. Nothing new.

"Call him over." It doesn't sound like question. I swear he just ordered me to call Ritchie over.

"He's busy right now sweetheart, I can bring you a shot and you call me when you ready for another one, is that good?" I itch to finish this order as numerous hands are waving at me, and I send them polite smiles to let them know I'm on my way.

"I said call Ritchie." His voice came out growly

revival

and I swear if I hadn't lived in this scary neighborhood for so many years, I would be pissing my pants by now.

"Yeah, sure, whatever." I walk to the office and knock on the steel door. "Ritchie the guy on six is asking for you, don't even blame me for it, he's scary as shit and insists on seeing you. I'm gone."

Even though I'm already annoyed with that moody costumer, I can't deny the weird feeling that was taking over me when I was standing close to him. That sense of being next to someone familiar. That little, tiny tingle that can be easily overlooked. Except, I don't get that tingle. Not anymore.

I head straight for table number two, as there is a party of 12 and their bill is sky rocketing, so I'm hoping for one of those kick-ass tips that makes the night worth it.

As I come back to the bar I see my boss talking to the guy in a friendly manner, and I frown. I've been working here for five years and he never was friendly with anyone. He usually gives the customers a friendly pat on the back, reminds them about the rules, then leaves them to it. But right now, he is talking with this stranger for way too long; laughing and smiling like the happiest person on the planet. Weird, the guy doesn't look local to me at all and my boss doesn't have many friends from out of town.

I place the next order with the kitchen as I eye them both. I would be lying if I said that he doesn't remind me of someone. There is something in his presence, in his posture that looks familiar. His big muscular arms are resting over Ritchie's shoulder as they both laugh over something.

"Not bad huh?" Kelly nods in their direction. "If his face is as good as the rest of his body I'll take it. Heck that, if he's got an ugly face I'd just put a paper bag over it and ride that muscle." I just shake my head, Kelly would ride anything that is available, this girl has no shame and God only knows how many guys she's slept with. I'm sure she can't keep track.

I scan my eyes over her skimpy top that reveals way too much cleavage, something she is definitely proud off. Her tight black shorts fit perfectly over her butt. There is not one man that doesn't notice her while she's working here. And I don't blame them. She is hot without even trying. She always wears her auburn hair in one of those messy buns that I don't even know how to make. Mine always ends up resembling a weird nest on the top of my head. Her face is covered in lots of makeup, but not in a slutty kind of way. Yeah, she is pretty, without even trying hard.

"He is an ass." I say while grabbing a tray, but when I turn around Ritchie is standing next to me.

"Whatever he orders, you give it to him," he says slapping his hand over the bar and heading back to his office. I turn around and grab ten shiny shot glasses and fill them with vodka.

"There you go." I put the whole tray on the table and walk away. He doesn't even say thank you, nothing. I watch him grab a glass of the clear liquid and down it one by one until all of them are empty.

"Another one!" He calls me while I'm half way to the bar. I sigh, repeat the round knowing that he will definitely be shit faced before we close. And I won't be the one to drag his drunken ass out the door. No, definitely not. I will leave that honor to Rich. Let him deal with the craziness he allows.

I think it was my third trip with another round of shots when he finally lifts his head and looks at me. And once I see those eyes, even though they're glossy and hazy from the amount of alcohol, I feel a jolt of electricity coming out from them. They look so

revival

familiar. They look like one of those places you visited before, so long ago that you forgot where it was, but you knew it was great.

While I stand and try to remember that place, I feel a hand grab my wrist and another one wrap around my waist, bringing me closer to him. My heart is racing and pounding in my chest while I see his eyes blaze with something I'm actually scared of. I try to free myself from his grip and I lose my balance. I feel the tray sliding out of my hand the second I land on his lap, and all of the glass shatters on the floor, all eyes are on us. I feel something on my neck and I realize that his mouth is sliding up and down my exposed skin. I try to wriggle myself out of his firm grip but I'm failing miserably, he is strong as hell.

"I will take you to my place sweetheart and I will fuck you to oblivion. You will never forget this night, I can promise you that." His mouth is on my ears now, the breath that smells of nothing but alcohol circulating around my nostrils. "No thank you." I hiss while jabbing him hard in his abs with my elbow.

"What the fuck?" He mumbles under his breath and he pulls me a little tighter to him. I feel trapped. Panic goes over me. This brings a bad memory and one moment in particular that left me trapped just like that. I feel my eyes burning with the tears that will come at any second. The moment I see Ritchie heading our way with lightening speed, I try to free myself once again using my whole power to jab him in the ribs. It works. He loses his grip and I fall into Ritchie's arms. I can feel the hot tears stinging my eyes and I do my best to keep them in. I'm not going to cry. I'm not going to show that this drunken asshole shook me up this much. I'm mad, scared and humiliated to the point where I could beat this guy to death.

"Dylan, leave her the fuck alone, what the fuck is your problem?" Ritchie is standing next to me, his arm folded around me, breathing heavily, checking if everything is ok.

Dylan...

Dylan...

As Ritchie loosens up his grip over me, I try to compose myself, and even though I should run away from this mad stranger, I turn around as the blood drains away from my veins. For all I know I could be dead right now.

Dylan.

Dylan...

That can't be. It can't be.

I try to take a look at his face but he puts his face between his hands and just sits like that, saying nothing, obviously realizing that he fucked up big time.

"You ok?" Ritchie eyes me carefully. I nod, even though I can feel my arms aching where his strong hands where holding me. I keep nodding my head staring down at him, trying to take a better look at his face. That can't be him. There is no way he is the Dylan I knew.

"What the fuck is...?" I hear Kelly behind me, but she shuts her mouth as soon as our boss raises a finger at her to stop her filthy mouth.

"Just take her away and give her a glass of water," his voice is clipped. "Come on boy, I will give you a ride, you've had enough."

Ritchie walks towards the exit and he follows him, head down, shoulders slumped, stumbling as he is trying to keep a straight line. His black hoodie is now pulled over his head, hiding his face. But as I match the name with that posture my heart starts to beat faster and faster. It can't be him. It cannot be...

Dylan

The morning sun is drilling a hole straight through my eyeballs, my mouth feels like a desert and my tongue is stuck to the roof of my mouth like someone used super glue or something. I try to wet my lips but I fail, the moisture in my mouth is non-existent. I turn around in bed to shield myself from the rays and I realize that I'm still in my clothes and my heavy as fuck biker boots. I bring my feet closer and untie the laces, throwing my boots on the carpet with a heavy thud. I swear I hear someone singing in my living room. I open my eyes slowly and take in the hotel suite I booked last night. My duffle bag is sitting in the corner, reminding me that I didn't even unpack when I arrived here late last night because I headed straight to the bar. That, I remember. The rest is coming back in a total blur. I get up and look around for something to drink. Not even a single water bottle in sight, great.

Yep, there is definitely someone in the other room, singing. If I brought someone here last night I don't remember shit. Judging from the clothes I still have on, I either took care of her and her only, or she just gave me a blow and was kind enough to zip me after so I wouldn't wake up with my dick dangling out in the morning. Fuck. That's not how I wanted to start my get away time in New Orleans. Or maybe I did, what the fuck do I know anyway?

I push myself out of bed and head to the en-suite

bathroom. Just one look in the mirror confirms that I look exactly how I feel. Like shit. I splash some cold water over my face and rinse my mouth with the tiny bottle of mouthwash provided by the hotel. I run my wet hands over my hair, and head over to the door to see who is naive enough to come here with me last night.

I open the door slowly and search for the source of that sweet voice that is singing some love song.

I see her standing in the small kitchenette, cleaning the counter while swaying her hips side to side to the beat that I can faintly hear even though the headphones are on her head. *Jesus, is she deaf?* I crock my head to the side and take a better look at her. Her blond hair is up in a high ponytail that swings in the same beat as her hips. Left to right, right to left. Her hips, yes they are quite something to look at, especially in those skimpy shorts she's wearing. Shit. I guess I was lucky to find a hot piece of ass. I run my hand over my hair trying to remember anything from last night, a name maybe? There is nothing but a blank space that leaves me clueless. I walk closer, and I'm about to touch her shoulder to let her know I'm up, when she spins around, her eyes the size of saucers, her mouth is forming the biggest "O" I've ever seen. The "O" I wish I could fill with my dick right now, as I'm definitely starving for some morning hangover sex. She reaches for her headphones and in a split second they are around her neck, music blasting on full volume.

"Didn't mean to scare you sweetheart," small smile creeps on my face as I feel my dick twitch in my pants. I like what I see and he must like it to. Her face is angelic; her features are soft and innocent. Her thick eyebrows, even though they are pulled together right now, frame her big blue eyes

revival

beautifully. Her full as hell mouth is now pressed tight together, but still looks tempting. I slide my eyes down her body and I must say she's a fine piece of ass. "Sooo... " I stretch the word as I step closer to her. "So, did we have fun last night? Because to be honest darling I don't remember crap about last night." I smirk as I reach for her body, but never touch her as she ducks under my out stretched arms and takes a few steps back. Her face is white, like she just spotted a ghost. I have to say that I'm the one that is confused here.

"I didn't know that someone was here... There was no sign on the door..." She rumbles while she picks up cleaning supplies that are scattered all around the room and gets ready to leave.

I'm confused.

I'm more than confused to be honest. It would help if I would remember some shit from last night. Before I can ask her anything else, she's gone, door slamming behind her.

I stand in the same spot for a couple more minutes, my mind racing while I search for the answer that never comes. The only thing that I know is that I saw those eyes somewhere before, the color of the sky at night, deep and mysterious. If only I could remember who they belong to.

———•●•———

I stand under the stream of a cold shower, trying to erase the headache that reminds me that last night must have been crazy. The second I close my eyes I'm hit with the image of brown eyes and long chestnut hair. My chest tightens and once again I feel like fish out of the water, struggling to breathe. And like the sadistic bastard that I've become, I keep my eyes shut and let the image and memories float before my eyes, remembering her, remembering us. The very first time that I spotted her in the crowded bar, the almost animalistic beauty that was pulling me in, pulling me into my destruction, my happiness. We both knew that we were no good for each other, somewhere down deep our gut was telling us to stay away. And we should have considered the warning, but we both pumped the same stubborn blood in our veins.

We should have stopped.

We should have listened to our inner voices for once.

Life would have been so much easier.

Different.

She would be alive.

Fuck!

The guilt eating me alive will never go away, and to be honest I don't want it to go away. I want to feel it as a reminder that it was me that put her underground. It was me that ended the life of such a beautiful soul.

I'm the murderer.

The ring of my phone wakes me up from the dark thoughts. I slide the shower door and peek at the screen and see an unfamiliar number with Cali area code on it. *It can wait*. I tell myself while I finish the shower.

I hear the message alert beeping and grab the phone putting it on speaker while I dry myself. The second I hear her name being mentioned I stop. I stop breathing. Again.

I hear some woman talking but I don't hear what it is she's talking about. All I do is concentrate on breathing, in and out, in through my nose and out of my mouth. In and out. In and out. Once I'm positive I won't pass out I hit replay and keep the breathing going.

"Hi Dylan, I hope I got the right number, all I got was your name so I searched for Dylan Heart and you're the only one that came up in our state, so I hope, God, I hope I have the right one. Well, I'm Dina, Mia's psychologist, shrink or mental coach if you like. Anyways, I'm calling as Mia left a letter for you, on the envelope it said specifically to call you four months after ...God, this is harder than I thought" I hear the sharp breathing on the speaker and I swear I'm doing the same. *"After she's gone for some reason, so I'm doing what I was asked. You have my number, so if you are you, and you know Mia call me so you can stop by and pick it up, or we can arrange something else. Ok, take care now."*

The message ends and the phone goes quiet. My mind goes into an overdrive. What? When? Why? She left the letter for me? Why would she do that? When would she do that? What's in it? Fuck! That is insane. Why would she write a letter to me while we were still together? What was going on in that beautiful head of hers? I feel my pulse galloping and my heart pounding in my chest like it's looking for its way out. Tiny sweat beads drip down my nose, hitting the sink that I'm still clenching hard to. *I can't take it! I swear I can't!* I grab my phone and throw it with all my force to the opposite wall, watching how it shatters to pieces. I look in the mirror and the face I see is foreign to me. My eyes are empty, dark circles have formed underneath them; my lack of expression became my signature look. I'm definitely not the person I was. I'm full of anger, my eyes are an evident mirror of that. My face is hard, stone-like with no expression as I keep my feelings to myself, hidden, under the armor I'm wearing. Somewhere deep down I know I have to let her go, let everything go, but thinking about this only pulls me farther, deeper, farther into the darkness. And I see no fuckin' light. The light is long gone.

Time will heal, they say.

Time will make you forget, they say.

Time will nurse the wounds, they say.

Fuckers don't know shit.

I dress quickly in clothes that I pull out of my duffle bag, run downstairs to the parking lot, and jump on my bike, pressing the gas to the fullest. I don't care. I don't fuckin' care what happens. I can be dead in seconds, but for all I know I'm already dead. Shit doesn't matter now. And my own death will only reunite me with her. Maybe that's what I really want, without even realizing it.

I run every red light that there is to run, I hear cars honking at me and people waving their hands in panic. I keep going and going until I reach the beach, blocking out the images around me.

The beach.

Another place that was mine, and mine only until she came around.

There is no escape from her. Everywhere I go, anything I do is connected to Mia. And it will always be that way.

I park my bike and walk on the white sand until I reach the water. I know I look like a freak, wearing jeans and bike boots walking on the sand. *Let them watch the freak show*, I think as I take my boots off and walk into the warm waters of the ocean, folding my jeans up to my knees.

Dina.

I knew Mia was seeing a shrink, she told me all about it few times, but the call about the letter really throws me off. Why would someone like her, someone as free and as strong as her write the final letter? I won't lie that I'm dying to know what's in it. I'm dying to feel the connection to her once again, even if it's only through paper and words. Maybe I could feel her close to me once again. Maybe I can get her back for a minute or two. Maybe.

Fuck! I would give anything to bring her back. I'd even trade my own life just so she could have hers. So she could smile with that smile that lightens up the room. So she could dance in the middle of the club like nobody is watching. So she could whisper her sweet dreams into my ears.

There was so much waiting for us. There was so much we didn't do together. Too much.

Life has a wicked way of showing you that you are never the boss, that you are never the true maestro in this whole play that's called life. You only get the illusion that everything is under your control. That everything will be the way you planned. Until the big BOOM strikes and you are left with nothing. Starting from scratch only with much heavier baggage. And it's only up to you, how much you can carry, it's up to you how long you are going to carry that baggage.

Decisions - the hardest part is on you.

The sound of loud giggles brings me out of my train of thought. I look around and see a big halo of blond curls bent over the water next to me.

"Ellie, get back here!" A tired voice is calling behind me. I turn around and see who I assume is her grandmother standing with her feet deep in the warm sand, watching the little girl carefully.

"Oh, come on Gran, just a sec, I found another one." Her sun-kissed face lights up as she picks up a white shell from under the water. "See, now I only need ten more and I can make the frame for mommy," she squeals.

I smile and look under the clear water myself to see if there are indeed, any shells. I dip my hand in and pick up the ones that are around me. "Here, I found some," I hand a few small shells to her. She stiffens immediately and turns around looking at the old lady, like she is looking for approval. I don't turn around to see what her grandma has to say about that, but I assume she gets a go ahead as she stretches her little hands in my direction and takes the tiny shells from me. I watch her scan them one by one, before throwing two of them back in the water. She must have noticed my surprise, as she is looking at me funny, as if I don't know what's going on and I missed the whole reason that she is doing this.

"Mommy only likes the white ones, they come from the moon you know." Her chin is lifted higher and her grin conveys that she knows something I don't know.

"They fall from the moon huh?" I ask, and I swear I'm the one being curious right now, I've never heard anyone besides my mom state that about white shells they've found in the ocean. It was something my Mom told me when I was about five or so, and it stuck with me forever. Every time I saw white shells I knew they were from the moon.

"They do." She states with a stoic face and puts the shells carefully in her bucket.

"I believe so," I said looking in the water.

"You only pick the white ones Dylan."

"Why? I like the other ones as well"

"White ones are from the moon, they are special, they bring you luck and they keep your spirit pure. They're meant only for you to find, it's like they are looking for you, not the other way around."

I lift my eyes up to the little girl who is still fishing for the seashells in the water and as I take her little frame in, I smile. I smile at the memory of myself doing the same thing years ago, believing that I'm looking for the greatest treasure of all.

"Are you going to help me or what?" She lifts her head up and meets my gaze, for a second there, I feel like I'm looking at my own childish eyes staring back at me. I shake that feeling quickly, not sure if it is the effect of the crazy-ass night I had, or the morning call that I'm trying to forget. "I need nine more, so dig in." She orders me, and I chuckle walking farther in the water to begin my search.

"Ellie," I say her name while stretching my cupped hands towards her. "I have seven white ones for you." I watch her pick them up from my hands and inspect each one before she puts them in her basket.

"That's ok, I have four so that makes..." She nods her head like she's trying to do the math. "We have one extra." She digs in her orange plastic bucket and hands me one little seashell. "Keep this one, that's for helping me out." Her little hand puts a tiny shell on my callused one. I look at it and smile, a truly genuine smile. A smile that hasn't been on my face in quite a while.

"Thank you," I say as I close my hand and slide the treasure into my back pocket.

"You are welcome." She says seriously, heading in the direction of her grandmother. I stand with my feet in the water, looking at the horizon, feeling somehow happy. I swear, that was the most normal conversation I've had in months. And it was with a little stranger.

I walk into the dark pub and immediately I'm hit with the smell of smoke and beer. I stroll up to the bar and take a seat in the far corner, next to Ritchie's office. I look around the club and scan the crowd.

Nothing really changed from the last time I was here, considering that I don't remember much of last night. Last time I was here was about six years ago. I took an innocent bike trip and spent my summer here, escaping the bullshit that I couldn't take any more. Just like right now. I'm escaping, or trying to.

I motion for the hot redheaded bartender to take my order, but as soon as she sees me, she's goes right past me, straight to the office, ignoring me completely. A few seconds later, Ritchie is standing next to me slapping my back in a welcoming gesture.

"How are you kid?"

"Could be better." I look between him and the redhead.

"You remember anything from last night?" He takes a seat next to me and turns around, watching me carefully.

"Honestly man, I think I had way too much to drink." I force a fake laugh because I know that something is not right. I must have fucked up pretty well last night if he is giving me this talk.

"Hmmm," he rubs his grey beard with his right hand while narrowing his eyes on me. "You basically assaulted one of my waitresses, you are lucky she's a good, kind girl and that I like you. But that's not ok, and honestly, Dylan, starting today you need to follow the rules. I'm not giving you any special treatments 'cause you can't handle it right now." His eyes turn sad and I know I must've told him why I'm here, because I see pity. Pity I hate, but I will suck it up and take it from him, like the big man I am.

"Noted." I raise both my arms in the air. "Not happening anytime soon."

"Not happening fuckin' ever Dylan, I'm serious and you better apologize to her once she gets here." He stands up from the chair and as he walks to his office, he turns around and points his finger right at me. "I mean it, apologize."

"Sure thing Ritch," I say as I turn around and ask for a beer.

While I lift the cold, bubbly beverage to my mouth I look over the walls, scanning the familiar place for anything new. There are numerous photographs of the staff hanging on the walls. Some of them with Ritchie, some of them with the bands that have played here over the years. Some of the pictures were here years ago, when I first visited the place, and others are new to me. I look at each of the photos and I stop at one. It is a photo of me standing next to a petite girl with black pixie cut, surrounded by four guys. I frown and walk closer to the wall to get a better look at the pic. Yep, that's definitely me, smiling from ear to ear while placing a kiss on the cheek of the pixie girl. She's beautiful with her big blue eyes staring straight into the camera...those blue eyes. Those dark, navy eyes. The eyes I saw this morning.

Holy shit. I run my hands through my hair, the realization hits me and I connect the cleaning girl that I saw this morning with the one standing in front of me, frozen with a wide smile on her face.

Holy fuck.

I go back in time and try to recall the moment when that picture was taken. Hazy memories are flashing through my brain. All I know for certain is that I remember those eyes, as I've never seen that kind of deep blue ever again.

Dylan

Six years earlier...

I come in well before the club is supposed to open. A little privilege I get from Ritchie after countless nights of talking and bonding over our life stories. As I push the back door and step inside, a confident, powerful voice hits me. It is strong, it is power, it is screaming I'm the queen of the world and you stay away.

    I stay hidden behind the swinging back door and listen while I watch her fill salt and pepper containers. She makes sure there are enough napkins in the holder, inspects the ketchup bottles by lifting them up and scanning them, while still singing with this incredible voice.

    I would be fucking lying if I said that my dick didn't react to the perfectly shaped hips, or the over the top breasts that are slipping out of the black shirt, which is tamed by the black skimpy waitress apron. And if you add that angelic, innocent face to the picture, then FUCK ME, she is perfection. I take a step forward and am ready to pull my best game, when Ritchie steps out of the office and starts talking to her. The emotion I see in his eyes, the love and respect I see between them, makes me step back, to tame whatever animal was just screaming inside of me.

I respect Ritchie, I would never cross that line. She is probably his daughter, and he would fucking kill me if I pull anything on her. He knows my tricks better than anyone else here. He was watching me for two months after all, and saw me leaving with a different girl every night. So yeah, I'm definitely not taking any steps towards her like that.

I walk up to the bar right after Ritchie disappears in the back. Seconds later, she resumes her musical concert. As soon as she sees me she stops singing, looking embarrassed as hell, her face a crimson red. She lowers her head trying to hide herself from me and I chuckle as I look for the bartender.

"The usual?" Brandon asks, even though he has my favorite brand of beer already sliding my way. I just nod while I lift the bottle to my lips and take a long sip of cold, bubbly liquid that slides down my throat, cooling me down a bit.

"I never knew Ritchie had a daughter." I point in the direction of the girl, and he looks at me with confused eyes.

"Who? Nina? Ritchie's daughter?" He slaps his hand on the bar and laughs loudly. I look around. The awesome singer, Nina, as I found out, is looking in our direction.

"Yeah, what's so funny about that?"

"Nothing man, nothing. It's that she's not his daughter. She started here few weeks ago, and our old man took her under his wing, that's all."

"I see." I smile because the gate to whole new possibilities just opened for me. She's not off limits after all, she's very much within reach. I look at her once again, as she gracefully moves between the tables. Still humming something to herself, but no words escapes her mouth. And the fucking predator that I am, I know I will bang her before I leave this place in two short weeks. That's on my to-do list and I always complete the tasks I put on it.

The fact that she's been here for a few weeks makes me frown, as I never noticed her before. I'm here every night, and only today do I see her. But that would make sense because she doesn't look like the flashy, skanky kind of girls that I'm usually after so, yeah, no surprise there. And honestly if not for her voice, I wouldn't even notice her at all.

A few hours later, after I down few more beers, she's standing on the other side of the bar putting some orders in the computer. Even though I have my hand sliding up and down over the knee of the girl sitting next to me, who I'm sure will end up in my hotel room, I can't resist talking to her.

"Nice voice," I wink. As soon as the words leave my lips, she snaps her head up at me and squints her eyes, like she's trying to take a better look at me. And holy shit, those eyes! I have never, ever, seen such a blue – unless you count looking a night sky filled with sparkling stars. That's exactly how they look.

For a second, I think I see a challenge cross the features of her face, but that quickly vanished.

"Thanks," she says, and walks away like it was fucking obvious that she's good, that she has an incredible gift that not all of us possess. I smile and turn back to give my attention to whatever her name was.

I get to the bar early the next day. Not because I have nothing better to do, but because I want to see her again. See her in that raw, free version of herself. I get in quietly, making sure the back doors don't hit the bell while I open them. As soon as I step inside I hear it. The voice. The power. The incredible emotions I can feel right through me while her voice wraps around me. I stay hidden behind the

revival

swinging door and watch her, like a fucking stalker. Like a hunter that watches its prey get in the right place to be struck and become a trophy. Only I never get the guts to attack.

I listen to her as she pours her heart out; unaware she's not the only one in here. I listen to her sweet voice and minute-by-minute, I become more and more fond of her.

I like simple, I like easy, but she's none of that. Being shy and not even acknowledging me while I'm around her is new to me, considering the fact that every pussy is always interested in me. So this, her not giving me a second glance is quite intriguing.

I step out of my hiding place and take a few long, quiet steps toward her. With her back to me, and the semi-loud music sounding out through the speakers, I'm sure she can't hear me. I stand right behind her when she turns around, a frightened expression on her face.

"Oh, it's you." She takes a quick glance at me and turns around again to resume whatever shit she's doing. "You scared me there for a second," she says, not looking at me.

"Come on Golden, I'm not the one you should be scared of," I say while stepping closer to her, being careful to not touch her. She's like a little bird, and I want to do nothing to scare her, so I keep my itchy hands to myself.

"Golden?" She cocks her head to the side while furrowing her brow at me.

"Yeah, Golden. Like, one of a kind. The kind you know you will never find, but you search for anyways."

Her mouth opens and closes like she has something to say, but decides to keep it to herself. I smile at this, and to my surprise she does the same, and help me God, her smile is the most beautiful, the most honest, genuine smile I've seen in quite a while. It's like sun shining right through the stormy sky. You know it's not possible, yet you are in awe that you were lucky enough to witness it.

"So when are you singing on stage?" I ask as I take a seat at the table she's currently working on. I watch surprise register on her face as I pick up the saltshaker and begin to fill it.

"Don't know what you're talking about." She picks up a bottle of pepper and fails miserably in her attempt to refill it, spilling a fair amount on the table. I chuckle at her clumsiness, or maybe nervousness. Girls are never nervous around me. If anything, they're always ready and giving, so this is totally new to me and I have to say, it's flattering in a way.

"C'mon you are good, like no shit good, get to the stage, let people judge if they want to listen to you or not." I fold the napkin into a square, and then into another and another. "Let them see the real you." She doesn't respond. She just keeps her head down with a slight frown like she is thinking about it. Good.

Sometime later that night, I hear her sweet voice behind me.

"You really think I should?" Her voice is quiet. "You know, go for it?"

I smile before I turn around and face her. "You definitely should." I swing around on my bar stool and I bring her between my legs, not too close, so I don't scare her, but close enough to have her trapped. She looks uncomfortable at first but as I bring my hands to her shoulders and rub them slowly in a friendly gesture, she relaxes under my touch. Even though this is not the reaction I want, and this is not the kind of touch I've envisioned with her, this is satisfying. It's comforting. Her whole presence is comforting in a weird kind of way. I've never felt this way towards a girl. There was always a want, a need, a rush to get it done. But with her it's different. She's like this little, scared soul that I don't want to hurt. Even though she has a killer body, her innocence is showing through, telling me to take a step back, to behave. And I do. Fuck, I do.

"They want me to perform in two weeks with the band but I don't know..." she trails off, lost in her thoughts.

"Go for it." I slide my hands down her arms and rest them on the sides of her waist while I watch her eyes go wide. The questioning look in her eyes is evident, obvious even. She scans my face and I smile a lopsided grin when her eyes land on my lips. I lick them on purpose. Knowing that she probably won't be able to resist them. The simple, yet erotic move will get me what I want. God, I want it! There is nothing else that I want more at this moment than to taste her perfectly pink, moist lips. As I watch her eyes go wide and follow every millimeter of my tongue, I swear I get hard, like my mind is playing tricks on my imagination.

But that never happens. She steps away from me and nods her smart little head up and down, weighing my answer.

"Thank you," she says while backing up towards the bar. I just watch her, because there is nothing left that I can do. All I can do right now is watch. Watch as she walks away. For now.

Two weeks later...

She steps off the stage and all that I feel is pride. Pride that I've never felt before. Honestly, I haven't banged any chicks in a week. I've spent all of my energy on her, helping her get over her doubts, her fears. Letting her know that this, the stage, is where she belongs. And trust me, she does belong there. With her perfect, heart-gripping voice, that is the only place she belongs.

As I look at her hugging Ritchie, I can't be more proud and excited for her achievement. The moment she turns to me, all I want to do is to bring her close and touch her the way you touch a lover, not your friend. Oh, trust me, she's not a friend to me, even though we played the friendly part well for two weeks. There is nothing in me that wants a friendship from her.

I want more.

I want her body.

I want all of her.

I want to be buried balls deep inside her and hear her call out my name while she is lying underneath me.

I want her lips all over me. This is the night I will make that happen. I swear I won't fail, because the energy, the electricity that is traveling between us is undeniable. It is not something you can hide or run away from. I will go for it, head on, and I know I won't hit a wall. All that I will hit is a high she can give me. And from the lusty, dark look of her eyes, I know she wants the same thing. Too bad I don't have much time. I will be gone this time tomorrow. Then in a few days, once I get to Cali, I'm sure I will forget her and I will go back to my usual habits. Habits that don't include her.

Habits I know I will never break.

Nina

I walk in the bar and stop in my tracks when I see him standing right in front of the pic we took six years ago. Right after I had my debut with Thunder. The band will be here in about thirty minutes to set up for our weekly play. Awesome.

Now he will connect the pieces, and I will have no excuse to pretend that I don't know him at all. To pretend that he never existed.

I regain my composure and walk straight to the bar, grabbing my little black apron and punching in. I glance at him and breathe in a sigh of relief that he didn't see me walking in at all. He is still standing next to the wall, scanning the picture, like he is looking at some famous painting. Sipping his beer slowly, his eyes focused on the image in front of him.

"Your pretty boy is here," Kelly says while leaning on the bar next to me. "I have to say, he's a super fine piece of ass. If you are passing on him girlfriend, I'll take him." She wiggles her eyebrows and waits for my response.

"He's all yours Kels," I say while trying to hide my trembling hands, and keep my eyes away from her. "All yours," I repeat. Knowing her ways, he probably will be hers by the end of the night.

A tiny stab of jealousy pricks inside my heart. Unexpected, unwelcome, just like the very reason that caused it. I ignore it. I learned over the years that a heart is tricky like that. It tricks you to feel things that you shouldn't feel. And this is exactly that.

I turn toward him once again, and goddamn, he hadn't changed at all. Still the same muscular build, broad shoulders, the powerful stance that says nothing but "back off". The stupid power that I found so amazing years ago, still makes my legs wobble after all this time, along with the familiar electricity of his grey eyes, even though they seem a little clouded, covered by the fog of either fatigue or pain.

Crap. I shouldn't be thinking about him that way. I hate him. I do. With all my heart, with every cell that is a part of me, I hate him. For what he's done, and most of all for what he didn't do. I know it's stupid and childish to blame him for something he has no idea about. I know, but there is this part of me that has become pure hatred towards him. And the first sight of him in such a long time should easily erase all of those feelings that I have.

But...

Goddammit. I feel the same need when I look at him now that I felt years ago. The same energy running between us, even though he is standing a few feet away from me.

I should stay in the shadows and never let him get close to me. I should lock up every emotion and never let him slip in. He will only destroy them. He will only ruin everything that I've worked so hard for.

Lock it up, Nina. I repeat to myself as I try to focus on my work.

I walk over to the table that, Jen, our daytime waitress left me with. When I turn around to head back the bar to put in the order, I see him standing with his elbows resting on the wooden bar. His eyes are pinned on me.

Crap.

I walk past him, trying to look as relaxed as I can be at the moment, when his low, husky voice speaks behind me.

"Care to explain?"

This voice. This sexy yet nonchalant voice is what got me at first. I swear I will not let it get to me this time.

"Explain what?" I bark as I turn around and see his eyes looking straight into mine, brows pulled in together. I can't help but roam over his chiseled face, and stop on his full lips, which are currently pressed into tight line. *Oh.My.God!* Those lips didn't change a bit. It's the same full, inviting mouth that I swear I can remember the taste of.

Pull yourself together.

"Besides the insult you pulled on me last night, there is nothing to explain" I throw at him, then round the corner heading directly to the computer to punch in the food order. My fingers working way too fast, punching the screen way too hard, making quite few errors in the process. I can feel his eyes on me the whole time, and I feel the blood rising all the way up to my head, making me dizzy and unable to finish this order correctly. That itself is a very strong sign that he is not welcome around me.

The goose bumps covering my whole body right now serve as a lie detector while I try to convince myself that he doesn't affect me at all. They are not lying. The only thing that is lying is my practical brain. I should hate him with every fiber of my being, just like I've hated him all these years. Damn.

I see his eyes narrow even more as he walks past me and into Ritchie's office. I breathe a sigh of relief. The less time I spend around him, the better. For both of us.

"Ah Nina, you like this guy," Kelly is making a drink, standing next to me and giving me a sideways glance. "That's a first."

"I don't. Cut it out Kels." I snap at her and she stops what she is doing and looks at me, eyes wide open, her drink hanging in the air.

"Listen, I've known you for what? Five years? You brush them all off like the dust on your fuckin' shoes, but honey, you definitely don't look like you mean to brush him off." She winks at me and walks to the other end of the bar.

I don't even have time to process her comment because he is next to me. He came out of nowhere.

"I'm so fucking sorry about last night. I was intoxicated as shit and I want you to know that I'm not that guy." His eyes hold mine, and I see way too much in them. Too many memories, too much pain.

"What kind of guy are you then?" I challenge him. "Because last night you definitely came off as THAT GUY."

He searches my face a tad too long and I shuffle on my feet, feeling uncomfortable.

He is standing inches from me and I'm too aware of the heat of his body. Sensing him so close makes me shiver. His cologne hits me and I inhale deeply through my nostrils. I don't care that I might look like a dog sniffing around, all I know is that I recognize it as the same cologne he wore back then. Back when I was stupid enough to be caught in his sticky web of sweet words and promises. I take a step back and blurt out, "No worries, it's ok."

I try to sound as casual as I can, but I can hear my own voice tremble, so I walk away to the tables, to keep myself busy. For once I wish we were packed tonight and I was running around like a maniac, too busy to answer any of his questions. *God, please help.*

I try to keep myself occupied I see my band setting up on the stage. The fact that I will have to

revival

perform in his presence paralyzes me. Damn. I never get the jitters before I go up on stage, but him being here is making me uncomfortable. I know I have about an hour before I go on, so I focus as much as I can on erasing him from my mind and try to block out the fact that he's going to watch me on stage.

Every time I round the bar, I see Kelly standing close and flashing her famous smile right at him. From what I see, he is buying it, even though his eyes are carefully watching my every move.

"And now Thunder will take the stage, so give a round of applause to Nina and the rest of the band!"

I walk on the stage and the bright light instantly blinds me. I tune out, forgetting everything and everyone.

Him.

Life.

Everything.

All that matters right now is me, pouring my heart and soul out, in hopes that someone can relate to that. Relate to the pain and sorrow that occupies my body and soul.

"Hello there," I bring the microphone close to my mouth and listen to the loud welcoming applause from the crowd. "Welcome to all of you, I hope you will enjoy the show." I turn around to Michael and give him a nod to start. The moment I hear the guitar come to life, my whole body relaxes and everything washes away. Everything and everyone.

It's just me and my music. Nothing else really matters. Standing on stage is like magic. A pure, unknown experience that surprises me every time. I swear there is nothing like it.

I become a totally different Nina when I stand in front of the crowd.

I'm fearless.

I'm brave.

I'm free.

And I love that Nina. Once a week, when I become her and I get lost in how phenomenal I feel, I don't think about the problems that are chasing me. I don't think about the fact that I can barely make ends meet, and that I'm clueless about what tomorrow will bring me.

I close my eyes and feel the music flow through my veins, reaching every tiny cell in my body. The music becomes my oxygen. As I sing the first verse of the new cover we are doing tonight, I hear the crowd cheering and clapping their hands along with the music. I know I'm doing this right.

After about forty minutes we take a break. I step down off the stage and run to the corner of the bar, only to bump into Kelly wrapped in *his* arms. I eye both of them quickly. I see her happy, flushed face contrasting with his dark eyes, filled with anger and focused on me.

I can't believe this. He looks angry all of the sudden, although it's me that should be going bat shit crazy. Isn't it?

"Great show." He says in his husky, low voice. He keeps his eyes on me while he brings the bottle to his mouth.

"She's always great, aren't you Nina?" Kelly says over her shoulder while heading to the other side of the bar leaving me alone with him.

"Dylan," he stretches his hand toward me. In this moment, in this split second I'm paralyzed. It's like all of my muscles froze. As if I was standing for way too long on cold Alaskan snow. I'm at the point where I think I'm moving my body, but nothing is happening.

"My hand doesn't bite, I can't say the same about my mouth though." He keeps his hand in the same place, hanging in the air, palm turned inward, waiting for my hand to join.

"Nina." I practically whisper, not sure if he caught it, though honestly I couldn't care less.

He should remember my name. He should know who I am. He should remember the time we spent together. He should.

Obviously he doesn't. I think as my cold, stiff hand reaches his warm flesh. I would be lying if I said that this little skin-to-skin contact did nothing to me. I would be lying if I said that the memories didn't run through my mind like a kaleidoscope. Those would all be lies because I do feel the warmth and mysterious tingle right where our hands join. I do see long forgotten images flashing before my eyes.

"I have to get back on stage. Nice to meet you Dylan," I take my hand back, and I'm about to walk away when his strong arm grasps me gently by my elbow.

"I'm so sorry about last night, I wasn't myself." He says like he means it. I just throw a quick "It's ok," and get back to my band, as it seems this is the only safe place for now. For him and for myself.

Nina

Six years earlier...

I step down from the stage and I feel happy tears streaming down my face. I did it. I can't believe that my lifelong dream actually came true tonight.

I sang with the band. *My* band on stage. And by the sound of applause and amount of hands that congratulate me right now, I think I did well. Awesome, in fact.

Singing is something I have loved since I was little girl, and even though I only sang covers, tonight I feel like I've completed the first step. The biggest step – to perform onstage, a real stage, with a real band, for real people. The next step is my own list of songs. Songs I will write. Then I can truly call myself a singer.

I round up the bar and Rich and Dylan are standing there, looking at me with so much pride it makes my heart jump and my eyes water, in the good way, the happy way.

"Congrats Nina I knew you had in you!" That's Ritchie being as fatherly as he can be, even though there is nothing that connects us by blood. He's been caring and loving towards me since the day I stumbled through the front door asking for a job.

He brings me into a close hug and I do the same.

revival

I wrap my arms around him, squeezing him tightly, letting him know just by this one hug how grateful I am. How I am forever grateful for everything that he has done.

"You did awesome Golden," Dylan's raspy voice cuts through the loud music blasting from the speakers. I break the connection with my boss and take a step to be closer to him. The look in his eyes is telling me that I, indeed did awesome. The pride, the sparkle of excitement that twinkles like the North Star, is telling me everything words cannot say.

I nod my head slowly as a big grin spreads across my face. He pulls me closer to him and his steel grey eyes dance all over my face. My eyes, right, then left, my nose, my mouth and back to my eyes again. And before I can say anything, before I can react to that powerful, electric current that is traveling through me, his mouth presses to mine and I feel his soft, sweet lips on mine; I'm high. High on everything that he is offering me. Our tongues play a frantic dance inside our mouths. My heart is beating so hard and so fast I'm sure I will die any second. Die of happiness, if you ask me, that's the best way to die.

I pull away to catch my breath and I mouth a silent "thank you", letting my emotions take control over my facial expressions. I'm smiling from ear to ear now. I never knew this kind of smile was possible, but considering the fact that my soul, my whole body is humming with excitement, I know it is. Just another look into his eyes, and I know that today will definitely top one of most incredible nights of my life.

"We need to celebrate." He's calling Brandon, our bartender. In a matter of seconds I'm holding gin and tonic in my hand, my current favorite.

"Cheers." I say as I clink my glass with his and

take a sip of the tangy cocktail.

"Cheers," he says as he lifts his beer to his mouth. I look at his lips wrapping around the brown glass bottle. I wish those lips were on me right now. I swear I can feel how soft they would bel on my skin, even though he's never put them anywhere else but my lips. Actually, the very first kiss we shared was just an hour ago, before I went on stage. He wished me good luck while looking at me with his hungry, dark eyes. Holding my hand in his while the other was wrapped around my waist.

I knew what he wanted and I wanted the same thing, so I didn't run away. I didn't shy from the situation. I did the opposite, and that's a very unusual thing for me. I leaned in first, brought my hand to his cheek and caressed his tiny stubble, hoping that he would get the cue and that he would proceed.

And he did. He did proceed with power I hadn't expected. The power that forced a loud moan out of my soul, straight into his mouth. I dove in like a drowning person looking for a tiny, invisible string to hold on to. I failed miserably because he pulled me in with all he had, the current that you have no chance to escape from.

And I drowned.
Completely.
Not even fighting to stay afloat.

Yes, that was a hell of a kiss if you ask me. But the one that I just received was nothing less, maybe even better.

"You are quite something Golden." His voice hits my earlobe while he leans down to me, making sure I hear him over the loud music in the bar. I shiver; clenching my glass tighter and praying he is not paying any attention to my snug grip on the glass.

"It felt incredible. I never knew that I was

capable of doing something like this." I shake my head at the realization that just hit me. I did it. I did accomplish my biggest dream and he, the one standing next to me, had a huge part in that. If not for his constant blabbing about how good I sound and his daily questions that included: *When are you going to sing live?_When are you going to get on stage? You can do it.* I would have never, ever had the guts to do it. I would still be singing to myself while cleaning tables, dreaming of the stage and the mic that had been within reach. I would... but now this just happened for real and he played the main part in its occurrence.

"Thank you." I say while scanning his hard yet handsome futures with my starving eyes. I know he can feel the heat coming from my own. I know he can tell what I want, what I'm wishing for at this moment.

"Lets go, you are done here anyways." He pulls my hand and guides me toward the exit and I follow. I follow because I have this unexplained need to feel him, to touch him, to be one with him, and I'm sure he feels the same.

We step outside and the heat of the New Orleans summer night hits us right in the face. I'm not sure if I'm hot and sweaty because of the weather, or because this hot, incredible man is next to me, or because my body and mind are perfectly aware of what is coming.

He puts a hand around my waist and guides me through the wave of people walking around us and I feel like I'm floating in the air. Floating between the bodies that pass around us but the only human being I see, is him.

Once we get to the hotel and get into the elevator, his hands roam over my hips, my ribs, my shoulders and stop at my face. He cups it with his big, strong palms. The thrill that travels through every single cell in my body is too much, way too much. I can't contain the raw need rising in me and I push my body closer to him. His every touch, every tiny stroke over my sensitive flesh feels like fire. Fire that I want, I need to burn brighter. His every touch wakes up my muscles, bringing them alive.

I'm so close to him that I can feel his fast breath on my neck as he puts gentle yet powerful kisses on my exposed skin. I moan and beg for more, and he does what I ask for. Giving me more, sliding his hands under my loose shirt, caressing my breasts over my silk bra.

The ping of the elevator brings us both back to reality. We step out and I follow him to his room, holding his hand tight. As soon as the door shuts behind us, he turns around and pushes my body flat to the hotel room door. I bring my hands to his head and run my fingers through his short hair as his lips explore my collarbone, moving down to my breasts before going lower, down my stomach. To the place that no one has been before. I stand there, my breath fast like I'm about to suffocate. All I want is for him to take my breath away. I can only imagine what he will do next. When he finally goes lower he lifts my skirt over his head, putting his hot mouth all over me. I'm lost. And I never want to find the way out.

He lifts my left leg over his shoulder. His lips exploring the most intimate place imaginable, sending jolts of ecstasy through my core. I reach down and run my numb hands over his hair and bring him up to my mouth, kissing him hard. Tasting myself all over his mouth. I'm ready for more, ready for all of him.

"You taste like fuckin' heaven." He breathes out while pulling his jeans down. As soon as they are off,

revival

he presses his body to mine, letting me know he wants the same thing right now, at this moment. His hard shaft digs into my thighs.

He pulls me up without much effort as my legs wrap around him. He walks us to the bed that is going to be our love boat for the rest of the night. I feel his hot body pressed to mine, and just the thought of him sliding inside of me gets me all worked up. As I feel him position himself at my entrance, I open my eyes and search his. I find the exact same need that I'm sure mine show right now. I relax and let him in. Inch by inch. Slow thrust in and slow out, one by one, in and out.

"You like that babe?" His voice brushes over my neck.

"Yeah," is all I manage to say as his mouth slides over my clavicle, down to my breasts.

"You feel incredible, wrapped around my cock like that... there is nothing better to wish for." He breathes into my mouth placing a deep kiss as he pushes farther into me.

I don't known how many "Oh's" and "Ah's" escaped my mouth that evening, but all I know that it was the most incredible night I've ever had, and Dylan was the most incredible guy I've ever been with.

Too bad he was gone the next day.

Nina

"Mommy, mommy look, I'm done!" Ellie is holding a frame to my face while I lay on the old, faded couch in our living room. I smile and take her project in my hands and my heart skips a beat, maybe two, before it stops completely. Like a rushing train when you pull the brake all of the sudden.

It's an old frame that was lying around, used, but never filled with any pictures. An old used frame that now has white shells glued all over the edges. There is nothing out of ordinary about it until my eyes land on the picture inside, and I see myself, *him* and Ritchie standing in the bar; right after I stepped down from the stage after my very first performance. I freeze for a second, trying to rearrange my face so I look happy rather than surprised.

"That's beautiful honey, where did you get that picture from?" I ask, trying to control my voice so it sounds stable. Not angry, not surprised, but normal.

"You don't like it?" She pouts her little mouth while scanning my face. That little person is like an emotion detector; she will feel even the smallest lie, the smallest hesitation.

"No, honey, I love it," I say while I bring her closer to me. "You know I love the white ones." I trace the shells carefully, gently with my fingers and remember what someone once told me.

"That's why I made it for you!" Her pride could

revival

beam for miles, and all I can do is smile. Smile at how genuine and big her little heart is. "That was the only picture I like from the old shoe box I found in your closet." Her declaration takes me aback, I totally forgot about that little, dusty treasure box I had hidden in the back of my closet. Far enough to never reach for it, but not deep enough to completely forget about it. The one that held more than this one, old picture. I stiffen at the thought of what else she could possibly find there.

"What else did you find there, love?" I ask as I toy with the frame in my hands. I would be lying if I said they didn't tremble, and I reassure myself that she can't read yet. There is no way she will know what is in the letters I wrote years ago to someone I missed terribly, someone I was hoping would somehow run back into my life and make it all better. The letter I wrote but never sent, simply because I never found the address to where it could be sent.

"Some papers," she shrugs. "That was the only picture I found." Her big, grey eyes look up to me and I lean down to kiss her cheek. God, I love this child, and even though she may never know the truth and the fucked up circumstances she was conceived in, she's a miracle. The biggest miracle I could wish for.

"I love it," I touch the shells one by one, dipping my fingers in the little edges and going back up again. "They are all white." I state after a minute, a small, sad smile touching my face.

"You like the white ones." She answers, putting together the puzzle she has scattered all over the floor.

"I do." My eyes water slightly and I push my head back so I can hold them in place. Don't let the tears slip. Don't let them trace my cheeks. Don't let them mark my skin with another path of sadness.

They are from the moon, someone once said. *They are there to find you, not the other way around.* I know that all of this was made up. I know that such a thing doesn't really exist and all of this beautiful talk was just to get in my pants, to make me want to follow him to that hotel room and give away part of myself.

Still, I passed it along. I couldn't help it, and it was a beautiful tale, full of hope.

Holding that frame right in front of my eyes I look at the picture that I thought I would never see openly see in my own house again; even though the exact copy is hanging at the bar. Not that I look at it, no I don't, it makes me uneasy. Uncomfortable even.

"Thank you love." I say, and put the frame on the side table next to the couch. I will put it back in my closet right after she goes to sleep. She won't remember it, I'm sure.

"What kind of cake do you want for your birthday?" I ask to change the subject, or rather, take the subject off of my mind.

I watch her pause with a puzzle piece in her hand and I smile knowing I just asked a million dollar question. Her birthday is in a month and she is super excited about turning six. It's like a magic age for her, knowing she will go to school next fall. I smile to myself at the thought of how old she is getting and I'm a little sad about how fast time flies. Reminding me to hold the best moments for as long as I can remember.

I'm fully aware that the theme may change numerous times before she settles on one, but I can't resist the fun of watching her face go through the thinking process. Just like she's doing right now.

"I want Dora, no wait, I want princesses, like all

revival

of them you know, Sophia, Ariel, Cinderella, Rapunzel, Frozen."

"Ariel wasn't a princess, she was a mermaid," I do my best to contain the laugh and try to keep my face straight.

"Ok, then I want a mermaid party." She put the piece into the puzzle and looks around for the next piece, acting like she already made up her mind. I know better. I know not to order the cake until the day before, as God knows what she will come up with before then.

I turn my attention to the photo standing within my arms reach and I look at the girl with short pixie black hair, smiling wide, her arms stretched around the two men by her side. One is still her favorite man on the planet, but the other one is my least favorite, and there is no doubt that he will stay that way for the rest of my life.

Looking at a photo of myself from years ago puts a small, sad smile on my face. I was so different back then, it's hard to believe that person can change so much in a few years. Yet again, life can crush you when you least expect it. Push you into a tight corner without giving you a chance to choose the direction in which you want to escape.

I know I shouldn't be bitter about something that was out of anyone's control, well, sort of, as I was taught as early as middle school to protect myself in situations like that. And there is no one to blame for my stupid action but me, not even him.

I want to feel you, right this second, please....

My own words will haunt me until my last day. My own words, spoken in a moment of weakness, in a moment of pure passion will follow me everywhere I go. They felt good, they felt light on my mouth, wet from his kisses. They sounded good between my moans and his deep growls. But now, sitting here all alone, not sure what the next day will bring, they feel stupid, foolish even.

And foolish I was.

"I want to go to bed Mommy." Ellie's face is right next to mine, interrupting my little pity party.

"Let's go." I say, and stand up from the couch, forgetting about everything. I head to the bathroom so we can brush our teeth together, like we do every night. Our little time together before we dive into our dreams, then wake up in a new day, a new chapter.

Dylan

I step out of the Verizon store and my new phone goes bat shit crazy. Beep after beep, notification after notification, text, after text. I know exactly what these calls are all about, the fucking investors not being able to reach me, my assistant going ballistic over my silence.

Fuck! It's not like I will have to explain myself, but I've never abandoned my business, even in my darkest hours. I was always on top of it, doing everything I should. It kept me sane. It kept me alive through my miserable days, my saddest hours.

I run over my missed calls, my mother's cell number shows among the others. I press the call button right away. If anyone, she's the only one that deserves an explanation.

"Dylan?" Her stoic, always calm voice hits my ears.

"Hey Ma, I lost my phone on the road, just left the store with a replacement." That's the best I can do. The best lie I can pull off at the moment.

"I was worried son, you haven't called in a few days and then Austin called saying that he couldn't get a hold of you... Oh, God, worried is not even close to what I felt." She goes quiet and I can hear soft whimpers, probably covered by her little wrinkled hand so I can't hear it.

"I'm ok." I take a deep breath and I know I have to give her the reason why I left so unexpectedly.

Leaving everything behind like it didn't matter. "I had to get away Ma." I take a profound breath and push the words out of my mouth. "I had to."

"I know love, I know," she pauses for a second, "I wish you could give me a heads up, so I wouldn't be so worried. I know you still blame yourself, I know you..."

"I'm ok." I cut her off. I don't want to hear the next words she will say. I don't want her to say how she understands things; how she wishes everything went differently. It couldn't and it went the way it did. It went the high, fucked up road straight to fucking hell. The Hell I'm living right now. Hell I'm not sure I will ever be able to escape. Ever.

"Where are you?"

"New Orleans."

There is a second, two, three of pause before she finally says, "Watch out for yourself." Her tone is worried, motherly, the exact tone you wish a parent to have while you're on the thin line of falling.

"I will Ma, I will call you soon." I swallow the gulp of guilt that suddenly is blocking my throat. I know I should have called her, to let her know that I'm taking some time off. I didn't want her to think that I ran away, not that I would ever do such a thing, but worrying her like that was never my intention. How fucking selfish of me. How fucking immature, to leave without giving notice to anyone.

"Ok, you do that." She hangs up the phone before I can say anything else.

I turn the corner and walk to the Deli. It has a few round tables set up inside, so I take a seat at the one closest to the window and call Austin.

"What's up?" I shoot right away, that short sentence is our code for so many things. Things like: *Did they buy it? Did they go for it? When are we starting the new project? Is everything Ok with all the deals?*

So many things can be said in two words, it's amazing if you think about it.

"We are good so far, the Germans are all set, and they signed with no problems. There was a slight misunderstanding with the Russian's but we got that resolved right away, so I would say that we are good. Better than good, actually. The only problem is that they both want to start building at the same time, they are both eager to finish the construction by the end of the year. I know you like to place one hotel at the time, so I didn't really give them a 'go'."

"It's fine."

There is a long silence on the other end, and I smile. Fuck yeah, I smile. I would probably not smile if I were in Cali right now. I would probably flip and yell at him to make them to come to an agreement about how they are going to split the dates. Now, sitting in a quiet deli that is playing some old tunes from fried speakers, I'm more than ok with them competing against each other. More than ok with my two new hotels hitting the market at the same time.

"It's fine?" Austin repeats my answer and I smile at the thought of his mouth hanging open, eyes bulged out of their sockets, complete shock.

"Yep." I take a sip of my coffee and swallow it, letting the hot liquid burn my throat, scorching a path down my chest. " Anything else?" I ask as I point to the ranch omelet on the menu to let the cute chubby waitress know what I want. She bobs her head in understanding and I go back to my coffee... oh, and Austin.

"I guess we are good," there is a moment of silence and I wait for him to ask the question I know he wants to ask. "So when are you coming back to the office?" There it is. How predictable he is, or how predictable my life is, either way, maybe we are all predictable after all.

"No idea." I take another sip of the black liquid, "If you need me, call me, but as far as stepping into the office I honestly don't know." I look through the window, my fingers tapping on the white coffee cup, trying to follow the rhythm of the Zeppelin song playing through the speakers. Who in their right mind plays *Stairway to Heaven* while serving breakfast? Only in NOLA.

"Ok, take care then, and talk to you soon."

"Austin?" I take another sip of coffee before I say, "You goddamn well know what to do, so don't call me with little shit, will you?"

"Sure," as soon as I hear that, I press the end button and relax in my chair. My mind drifts to the night sky-eyed girl that thinks I don't remember shit about her.

I frown when I recall her pathetic introduction of herself to me last night. She really thinks that I don't remember her. And the truth is I didn't, until I saw the picture on the wall. The moment came back to me so clearly when I laid my eyes on that black and white photo. The wheels turned in my mind and everything seems like it was yesterday.

But she acted like she doesn't remember anything about me, or rather like she doesn't want to remember anything about me. I remember how I pushed her too...

The beeping on my phone lets me know that I have a new voicemail. I break my train of thought as I open the window. I scroll and see a call from the number that I wish would never call me again. Dina. Mia's shrink called me again. My fingers tremble as I keep them hovering over the green button that will play her voicemail. I know what she will ask me, and to be fucking honest, I'm not sure if I want to make that decision right now. Hell yes, I want to know

revival

what she was thinking, writing the letters while she was still alive, while she was not even suspecting that her precious life would end in such a stupid way. Not knowing I would be the one to end it.

My omelet arrives and as soon as I smell the food, I'm no longer hungry. I get up and place a twenty-dollar bill on the table to cover the food and the service. I'm fucking nauseous. I'm disgusted with myself and the first thought that comes to my fucked up mind is to get wasted, right here, right now, drink myself to oblivion and forget everything.

Forget why I'm trying to forget.

Just forget.

Everything.

I walk the busy street and I try not to think about her. I try to push all the memories aside and focus on today, on this very minute that I'm living in.

I already tried bargaining with God about giving her back to me. Didn't work. I told him I will give up everything, will give anything.

Every.

Fucking.

Thing.

To get her back. To have her next to me. To save her. None of that worked and I finally gave up on the idea that God will make any deals with me.

He disappointed me once the night I let her go. I begged him to have her back. I told him I would change every single habit of mine if she would simply open her eyes and look at me in the hospital bed the night I had to decide to pull the plug on her life. He didn't listen. He let me do what I thought was the best; letting her go and setting her free by disconnecting a bunch of tubes that had kept her alive for months. Seven fucking months. I sat beside her every day, hoping that she would open her eyes and look at me with the love we shared. That she would wake up and forget about the cause of her fucking coma. That she would forget about the stupid letter she found on my table, stating in black and white that she is my sister, half-sister, and that I could pretend that I didn't know that shit as well. I was ready to pretend. I was ready to forget if she didn't remember. I know how wrong that sounds but my feelings were much deeper than my standards, any standards. I was ready to sacrifice everything. And still I got nothing in return. I buried my half sister, the love of my life a few days later. Even though I act like I'm ok, I'm not. And I'm not sure I ever will be.

That was the first time I opened myself like that for someone.

That was the first time I trusted someone like that.

That was the first time I loved someone.

All that love and trust got me to the darkest place I ever been. Loneliness. The worst feeling you can experience.

I enter the lobby of my hotel and I head for the elevator, pressing my floor number a few times, hoping it will speed up the closing doors and get me faster to where I'm going.

I rush up to my room and an aggravated growl escapes me when I see the cleaning cart right in front of my room. The door is wide open and a deep, troubled voice is coming from inside my suite. I slowly walk to the door and look around so I can locate the source.

And there she is. The waitress, the memory, standing next to my bed, wearing jean shorts and a tight, faded blue top that rides up as she bends down to put the fitted sheet in its place. I move back a step to keep myself hidden behind the thin wall, the only thing that keeps us separated, a piece of sheetrock and paint. Very thin separation if you ask me. I listen to her singing while watching her hips sway.

Go ahead and let me go,
Out there and off alone,

I suddenly remember how my hands felt on her body years ago, traveling up and down, hair, breasts, hips, thighs.

Go ahead and take your time,
Try to get me off your mind,

Her body arching under my fingertips like a perfect bow ready to shoot, her moans quiet, yet so loud in my ears.

Fuck, my dick is definitely agreeing with that memory. I rub my jeans as I try to calm the fucking bastard down. How fucked up am I? I was just mourning the love of my life seconds before, and now I'm getting hard looking at the ass of a girl that is standing in front of me. Well, not exactly. She is not facing me directly, her butt is, but still. My dick is a fucking moron, reacting to everything that moves.

I back out slowly and head for the exit, grabbing my sneakers that are by the front door and exit quietly. Once I'm out in the hallway I put on my gym shoes. I don't want to get noticed and I definitely don't want to get involved in any conversation. Not today. Not right now.

I hit the gym hard. Going all out. Welcoming the burn in my lungs and all over my body. I push myself harder than I have in months, burn, pain, the voice inside me tells me that it's enough, that I can't do any more; but it's ignored, faded by my fanatic, angry self.

When I step into my hotel room two hours later I don't find an open door, the beautiful voice is gone. Instead, freshly laundered sheets, fresh towels in my bathroom and a vacuumed carpet welcome me.

That's it. My memory of blue, night sky-eyes. The sapphire is gone.

I put my cell on the nightstand and will my twitchy fingers to not call Dina. No, I'm not ready for this, I don't even know if I will ever be ready for a letter from her.

Holy shit I need a drink, like right this second. My eyes fall on the small fridge that is placed strategically next to the TV. Even if you try to miss it you can't. There. Right in front of your eyes. Hell yeah, I open it and grab a little vodka bottle and down it, keeping my eyes closed, focusing on the deadly taste of the venom I'm consuming, the venom that will keep me going until the next morning.

Nina

I step out of the bathroom with a towel wrapped around me and see Gran standing next to the coffee table, holding the picture frame covered in white shells. Crap, I meant to hide it last night but I guess I was too tired.

"Good morning to you too." I say, passing her on my way to the bedroom. The look on her face is as blank as an empty canvas. Nothing, absolutely nothing that I can read. This is not good. She flicks her eyes from me to the picture and I know, I feel deep in my bones that she is forming the question right at this moment. A question I'm in no way capable of answering. Not now anyway.

"Would you mind taking Ellie for her six-year-old checkup?" I step into my room and leave the door slightly open so I can hear her answer. "I tried to take a few hours off, but no luck." My voice is cracking a little and I clear my throat quietly while hurrying to dress, I want to get out of here and escape the questions she is about to throw at me.

"She's not six yet, so how can she have a six year old checkup?" She is still holding the picture in her wrinkled hands while I walk past her, grab my handbag and sprint for the door.

"Don't do that Nina," her eyes narrow as they hold me to the ground. "Don't leave before we talk about this."

"That's how it goes nowadays, it doesn't have to

be right on her birthday. Plus I need the paperwork for the Kindergarten. I left the form on the counter. Thanks Gran," I brush her off, not really knowing what else to do. "See you later." I manage to say before turning around and closing the door behind me. I lean against the cold wall of the hallway. I push my head back. *Shit*, I can't even think about anything at the moment. I know she will grill me about it very soon; she is not one to let go of anything once she sets her mind on it. I can only avoid her questions for so long, but the day will come and I will have to testify. And God help me she is going to kill me. How am I going to do this? I have no idea; I never thought this day would come. To be honest I intended to keep it to myself and bring it with me to my grave. I don't really know what she is thinking actually, and what she wants to ask me in the first place. But the look on her face and her surprised, angry eyes were pretty much self-explanatory. She must know. She must see the obvious. She must see what I've known for the past five years.

I turn the corner of my street and head inside the deli to get my morning coffee fix. I've been stopping at that little heaven since the first day I arrived here. They have freshly brewed coffee and kick ass pastries like éclairs and chocolate croissants.

I can't count the calories I've eaten here while pregnant, or during my darker days. Hector and Lila have been like a family to me since I met them, and I swear to God they were trying to make me die from a sugar overdose every time I was feeling down.

I look around as I stand in a small line, checking out people sitting at the tables. A habit of mine, to scan the faces, see if there are any regulars sitting and enjoying their breakfast.

At the corner table to my right, Ms. Smith is sitting by herself, scanning a local newspaper for any news worth repeating. If you miss anything in this town, she's the go-to lady. She's like a walking newspaper herself, full of stories.

Next table is occupied by the twins from my building. Their elder sister that sometimes swings by the bar to wash dishes for some quick cash seems annoyed, like always, by the behavior of her eight year old brothers. I never can tell who is who. I tried hard to find differences, even though I feel like I know them while they sit still, I get lost again if they change seats or one of them runs his hand through his hair. Tamara, their mom, looks at me like I'm a total idiot for not being able to recognize them. I used to apologize to her for being stupid, but I've stopped since I'm definitely not the only who can't tell them apart.

I turn to my left and there he is, my lovely Mr. Santiago, sitting with his back to me, sipping his morning tea and eating chocolate croissant. I've seen him eating the same breakfast for the past six years. He confessed to me one morning while we were having breakfast together, that he has eaten the same thing every morning since his beloved wife passed away. And that was eight years before I met him, so the breakfast special has lasted for fourteen years. That's a one hell of a tribute to someone you love, eating their favorite breakfast even though you despise chocolate.

"Hi Nina, how are you this morning love?" The sweet voice of Amanda brings me back to reality.

"Great," I smile at her and grab the cup of coffee she already made for me "And you?" I take a sip of the hot liquid knowing it will burn my lips, like it does every morning.

"I'm great," she extends her left hand to me and

I spot a shiny ring on her ring finger. "Oscar proposed last night." Her face is beaming and I swear it could light up for miles.

"OMG!" I scream, and lean over the counter to give her a hug. "I'm so happy for you, you have no idea." I hold her for little too long, the person next to me clears his throat giving me a signal that they are in need of coffee as well. I give Amanda one more squeeze and turn around only to meet a set of eyes I wasn't expecting. Grey. All I see is grey. Surprised grey. I know my own eyes are the exact image of his. Although, his are pleasantly surprised, whereas mine are full of anger.

"Good morning Nina." His raspy voice hits my left cheek, he's standing too close for comfort. Way to close. You shouldn't feel the breath of the person standing behind you in the coffee line. That's wrong. That's not how you should start your day, being lightheaded from someone's breath on your cheek. Someone that you hate. Someone that you wished to never, ever see again. Someone that, despite all of this, makes you wonder what would happen if he steps closer.

"Dylan." I say passing him and heading for the exit, squeezing the white Styrofoam cup in my hand.

How many deli shops do we have here? There is one on every corner and he ended up here, in *my* deli, drinking the same coffee I drink, standing in the same line. Coincidence is a bitch. I have no tolerance for bitches.

I pick up my speed. I know once I get into the rhythm of my morning routine I will be fine. Free of all these piling, toxic thoughts and situations that I've had to face this morning. First, Gran, then him. Glorious.

He didn't show up at the bar for almost a week. I honestly thought that he left, that he had his fun and headed back home. Wherever his home was. Last time it was California, maybe still is. I don't know, I don't even want to know. He is nothing to me. Nothing. I sigh and I know it's a lie I've kept telling myself for quite some time. A lie I've been telling myself for so long I actually believe it. Believe it so strongly that nothing will ever change that. And no, I will never tell Gran the truth even if she's going to drill a hole in my brain. I will never tell. There is no way anybody will ever find out the truth. I'm not even sure myself. *Jesus, listen to yourself Nina.*

I punch my card in and head for the closet to get my rolling "beauty machine" – we call our carts full of cleaning supplies beauty machines here. Normally it puts a smile on my face to joke about this, but today, I want nothing more than to be out of here, to be done with this kind of life. I want to live in a small town full of friendly people where I can afford a tiny apartment just for Ellie and me. Work a nine to five job and be able to actually enjoy life like I should. Not struggle and barely make ends meet. I'm fed up and today is the perfect day to complain about it.

I look at my assignment card and 405 is on it again. I growl internally, as cleaning his room is the last thing I want to do. I was lucky enough to avoid his room for the past few days. Regina was kind enough to switch rooms with me. I know she's off today and none of the other girls would switch with me since it's against the rules for us to swap rooms.

I head for his room knowing that he's out, that he cannot be here since he was in the deli just moments before. I literally ran here, whereas he seemed like he had all the time in the world.

I open the room and scan the couch with its messed-up pillows. The kitchen with cups lying on the floor like someone just pushed them off the counter out of their way. I step forward and glance at the tangled bed-sheets tangled a red thong is looking at me from the very end of the bed.

A small, totally unexpended knock goes through the middle of my body. It hurts.

The evidence of what has happened here is undeniable. The fact that he was here with a woman. With someone else, shoots a painful dagger through my chest. I know it shouldn't, what am I to him? What is he to me? Nothing. But still, seeing this, looking at the evidence of his pleasure spreads pain all over my soul.

I stand there paralyzed and I don't even realize that he came in until his figure flashes in front of me, going straight to his bed and picking up the red souvenir. But instead of collecting it and putting it somewhere, he walks straight to the garbage and throws it away.

I stand there and watch him walk around the kitchen counter and pick up the cups from the floor. He doesn't look at me, he's acting like I'm invisible. And that's how I feel. I don't exist at this very moment. I'm loafing. Standing still. Not even sure I'm breathing.

"Sorry about that." He grabs the edge of the counter and I can see his knuckles turn white.

I force myself to bring my eyes to his. The look in his eyes confuses me so much that I forget about the anger I was feeling just a few seconds ago.

There are the same grey eyes that looked at me years ago.

They are the same grays eyes that got me lost years ago.

They are the same grays eyes that I got lost in years ago.

They are the same grays eyes that abandoned me years ago.

"There is nothing to be sorry about." I say moving to his bathroom, dreading what I will find. Thank God it looks like there was no game going on here, everything looks to be in its place. I don't turn around to see his face. I spray Windex all over the mirrors and I look at my face appearing clearer and clearer every time I wipe the glass. The face of a sinner, the face of a liar becoming clearer and clearer every time I move my hand.

My jaw clenches at the thought of how pathetic my life turned out. I ran away from my family in hopes of escaping madness, only to step in deeper shit than I could imagine. I put my buds in my ears to detach myself from reality for a little bit. The music calms my erratic thoughts and I can easily do my job without thinking.

"I'm sorry about the other night," his breath is right on my neck, sending chills all over my body and I don't know what I'm more confused about. Him standing behind me, or the fact that I hear him so clearly over the headphones. Only then do I realize I didn't press play. "I wasn't myself." His hand lands on my shoulder and I freeze even though my body is burning from his touch, screaming to be let go off.

"Don't worry about it," I whisper. I try to wriggle out of the little space that holds us together, space that holds all my fear at the moment. He grabs my wrist and stops me right at the door.

"I remember you Golden, don't you dare to think for a moment that I don't." His eyes scan my face, jumping from my eyes to my lips and back to my eyes again. "And I'm sorry that I acted like that."

I didn't expect to hear that. I was sure, so goddamn sure he didn't remember who I was, and now he called me Golden. Golden. I haven't heard that one in so long. No, I haven't heard that one in six years, nobody called me Golden but him. He called me that from the very first day we met. *Golden like one of a kind, the kind you know you will never find, but you search for anyways.* His much kinder voice runs through my memory and I smile a small smile without releasing it.

"So, you remember me as well, right?" His eyes are searching for something in mine and I fight back the tears that are about to come any second, I can feel them right at the rim of my eyelids. They are about to fall, like an overflowing river hitting the dam.

"Yeah, now that you mention it, I do remember you." I spit out and walk right past him toward the exit. I don't care that he will report me for not cleaning his room. I don't care that I will probably lose my job over this. I'd rather be jobless than see him one more time. Than be with him in the same room one more time.

I head downstairs to main room and down a bottle of water, trying to keep my mind off of him. I nod hello to a few girls passing by and force a smile on my face so I don't seem rude.

I know I have to go back to his room and finish cleaning it, I know I have to face him anyway. I take a few deep breaths and stand up ready to face whatever this day is going to bring.

If I only knew.... if I only knew...

"You want to hear something?" Kelly is flashing her white, super straight teeth at me while I put my order in. It's not like Kelly and I are best friends. No we are not. The only friend I have here is Rachel, and she's gone for a month in Spain to visit her sick mother. I hate the fact that we were unable to talk to each other for the past three weeks. I don't have enough money to afford international calls and neither does she.

Kelly is just a pal from work that I got to know. I feel comfortable enough around her to talk about some of the things going on in my life. I find her stories funny and I find her blabbing about every boy she sleeps with interesting enough to distract me from work every now and then, but we will never be in the friend zone. She just doesn't seem like the 'friend' kind of person to me and honestly, I'm way too closed off to share stuff with anybody, especially with my bar colleague.

"Sure." I nod my head while punching the keys for my order.

"He's even more amazing naked than he is clothed."

My finger freezes over an order of a hamburger with American cheese and chili fries. I know exactly who she's talking about but for some reason I refuse to register the information.

"Tell me more." I play stupid, hiding my jealousy.

"OMG Nina, the sex was amazeballs, and he is fucking gifted in that department, like you have no idea!"

Oh, I have an idea.

That almost spilled out of my lips.

"Awesome, what did you wear for that special night?" I don't even want to hear the answer, I swear I don't, but it's like I have no control over it. She looks at me surprised for a second and I see her eyes closing for a moment before she answers me.

"I wore this red set from Victoria's Secret I got on sale last week." I could see her going over memory lane in her mind. As much as I didn't want to study her, at this very second I was like a sadistic maniac, wishing that she would drown with her next mistake.

He fucked Kelly. That red lacy underwear was hers. The kitchen counter, the tangled sheets were all her doing. Her red lacy Victoria's Secret set fueled his hungry eyes, bringing him pleasure. Shit.

"Good for you." I spit out, and I don't care that it came out bitter; it probably came out as venomous as a snakebite in the middle of the desert.

"Oh honey, good is not even close to describing the feeling." I see her facial expression with my peripheral vision and I'm ready to vomit right on the spot.

"Well, I guess you got what you've wished for since the first time you laid your eyes on him, who's next?" I wiggle my brows so I look like my normal self, like my normal self before he showed up. The one that gossips with her about every hot guy that walks in here and listens to her one-night stand stories, living vicariously through them. Yeah, I didn't get those often. Who am I kidding I don't get them at all. The last time I had sex was about three years ago, the day before Marcus got locked up and since then... well, I do what every girl in my position would do. I rely on quick fixes in the shower. Do I miss it? No. Yes. Sometimes. There are days I wish for someone next to me, towering over me, making me scream his name in waves of pleasure. Yes, I have those desires once in a while, but mostly I'm grateful for the little, smooth, plump body with a big bright halo of hair sleeping next to me.

"Actually," she pauses and a smile spreads across her face, "I've been seeing him for the past week."

Stab.
Rip.
Pull.
I can hear my heart slowing down, going silent.

That couldn't be. That can't be.

He is not one to ask for a do-over. He is the type to run away, to replace his flavor every night. I saw it. Years ago, I saw him jump from girl to girl on a nightly basis. For god's sake I was one of those girls. And now he has been seeing Kelly for a week? A week. Seven damn days. Shit.

I look at her from a different perspective while she mixes a drink. What can she possibly have that I don't? A magic vagina? How magic could it be? What is so great about her that makes him come back?

"Nina?" I jerk my head in her direction and as much as I try to see the good colleague from the bar that she was for the past few years, I see a stranger.

"Good for you girl, good for you," I force a smile and head towards the floor.

It's stupid. It's so goddamn stupid to be mad at her. What does she know? Nothing. I'm sure that if she knew she wouldn't even go for him, she would give him a deadly stare every time he showed up in here. But she doesn't know. Nobody knows. There is no logical reason for me to be mad at her. But still, it hurts. The old wounds have been reopened and I have no idea how to stop them from bleeding. Will they ever stop? Will I ever heal?

Dylan

I avoided the bar for a week. Not that I don't want to sit in an old, familiar setting that brings me comfort. Nope, it's not that. I simply can't be close to her. I can't stomach looking at her and not be able to do shit about it. It's clear that she hates me. For what fucking reason? I don't know. God, I wish I knew. But I don't. All I know is that every time she looks at me, she is killing me with her piercing eyes, wishing me death. Slow, painful death.

There is something about her that makes me think of her constantly, that doesn't let me get her out of my mind. Her presence or her eyes maybe. I have no damn clue. But every time she's close I can't relax, I can't be myself. Every time I smell her floral perfume, I'm losing my mind and losing my game. Game that has been working fine with the bartender, Kelly. Yes, she's hot as hell and she can blow like a pro, letting me get lost for a second, letting me forget for a while. Until she talks. They all are able to get me lost, get me in the state of not being there until they speak. So I made it clear and simple for her. We have sex, or fuck rather, and then she's gone. I even asked her not to talk. I made her believe I like silent, no talk sex and it's been working great so far. She comes, we fuck, and then she leaves.

Fuck, I didn't want Golden to see my room like that. I didn't want her to see those fuckin' panties glowing on my bed like a fucking treasure. I didn't want her to see the messed up kitchen, the proof that I fucked someone, raw and hard on the tiny kitchen counter.

Shit!

I wished I smoked, so I could have a few calming, mind clearing minutes to myself before I stepped into that familiar bar. I know I should avoid this place like the plague. I should walk by and choose the next bar, or cross the street and find my poison in different place. But no, the stupid sadistic voice in my head is ordering me to go to the place I should avoid for now.

I walk in and head straight for the bar, Kelly flashes me a megawatt smile and I give her a small nod in return. Geez, I hope she won't turn all clingy. This is not what we agreed on.

"Hey," her smile stretches for miles and her eyes are basically eating me. I hate it.

"What's up? Hit me with some moon shine." I turn around and search for her. And there she is. Golden. My fuckin' Golden from years ago. Scratch that. She's nothing like she was years ago. Back then she was a scared, trusting girl that lit up every time I looked into her eyes. Now... she's far, far from it. Now she's cold, angry, and very much untouchable. Untouchable like Mia. Fuck. Mia. My one. My only. Gone.

I turn around and tap the glass to let Kelly know I'm ready for next round. There is no need to repeat myself as a new glass, full of clear liquid appears in front of me.

"Thanks," I lift the glass to my lips and down half of it in one gulp.

That, there, the simple fact that I compare her to Mia should be my warning in itself. My gut is telling me that nothing good will come from chasing her.

There will only be disaster. And fuck, I'm stressed enough. So ideally I should keep my distance from her. Keep away. But then, just one look at her and the match is lit, burning slowly. I swear to fuck that if I could pour my heart out, everything around me would explode. As if it was filled with fuel and only needed to be lit with a tiny drop of fire.

That's how I feel and I can't find any rational explanation as to what I'm feeling right now. Somewhere back in my head, I have this little smart person trying to convince me that all this doesn't feel right. That there is no way I can have such feelings toward someone while I'm still in love with somebody else. Even though that someone is no longer breathing.

It's like my heart has split in a million different pieces and each has its own mind. A mind I can't control. A mind that slips every time I try to get a better grip on the pieces. Maybe I should just stop controlling every single thing and let myself be. Let fate take control, even though I already got fucked by it once.

I should just to talk her, bring up the good ol' times. That may ease the tension that radiates from her for miles. But the look in her eyes tell me "don't", warns me to back off and leave her alone. Something also tells me that she wouldn't even let me to go back to that time even if this kind of conversation could ever occur.

In my peripheral vision I see her approach the bar and stand in front of the computer, her lips tight, eyes tired, yet sharp. Her fingers work quickly over the screen. The urge to stand up and walk over to her and talk about anything, about the fucking weather if necessary, is overwhelming, but I know better.

I sit on the bar stool, put the cold glass to my

lips and watch her. She's more tense than ever. Her shoulders are pulled up, her hands are gripping the tray while she stands next to Kelly, waiting for the round of drinks she ordered. I squint my eyes and watch them more carefully. They were always friendly with each other, joking and smiling, but today... Right now I can sense a quiet war between them.

"You Ok Nina? You've been acting strange today." I hear Kelly's voice shout over the loud music. I see Golden turn her head to the side and the look on her face is scary, dangerous. She looks like she might jump her friend and beat the shit out of her at any second.

"I'm good, just tired." She turns her eyes toward me and they are tense. Fuck, they are rigid and full of hate.

She knows. Fuck, she knows. I tap the bar and let Kelly know that I'm ready for another moonshine, while keeping my eyes on Golden. The glass appears almost immediately and I waste no time downing it.

"Here, have one on me, relax a bit." I hear Kelly say and I watch her slide the shot glass toward the ice queen. I watch her hesitate for a moment, like she weighs the good and the bad of what might come from this one, single shot. Then she lifts it to her lips, opening them wide, putting her plum lips all over the shot glass. Fuck me, I wish nothing but to be that fuckin' glass, to have her lips on mine, around my now growing cock. I thought I'd seen sexy, but this...this is something else.

"Are we on for tonight?" Kelly's sweet, seductive voice is dancing around my ears as she leans over the bar. Her full tits resting on her forearms staring straight at me. I frown and pull myself together, trying to find something else to focus on beside her breasts.

"I don't think so." I take another sip of the moonshine and watch the confusion on her face. "I'm not a one-women man, I thought I was clear about that." I don't even try to sound like I'm apologizing, cause I am not. I made it clear - we fuck, no strings, no attachments.

"Cool." She swallows and walks to the other side of the bar, pours a shot of something and downs it in a flash.

I stand up without looking at her and I move to the opposite side of the bar. I don't feel like watching her drama go down. I sit down and smile as one of the male bartenders wearing pink shorts comes my way.

"Travis," he stretches his hand in my direction and I take it. "What can I do you for?" I smile. I like him already.

"Your choice," I wave my hand. "Dylan." I add, simply to return the favor of introduction. He smiles and I watch him grab a small glass, fill it with ice and pour amber liquid to the top.

"Shit man, that's my venom." I take the glass from him and take a sip. That shit burns like motherfucking gasoline. Sliding down my throat, still burning, going deeper and deeper.

"It will do you good." He winks at me and I can't help but sigh.

"Nothing will do me good." I take a bigger gulp, this time filling my mouth fully, swallowing the alcohol with a force.

"Bad day?" He leans closer to me, eyes asking, brows raised.

"That's an understatement."

"I have time." He grabs a glass of sparkling water that was sitting abandoned next to me.

"Aren't you working?" I look around the busy bar.

"That's part of it." He winks and grins showing

his Colgate smile. I watch him for a second or two, maybe minute or two, I'm not certain. I can feel the alcohol starting to work, making me more relaxed than I was when I came here. I take a look at this Travis guy and right off the bat I know he's asking questions. He's not just throwing them at me to get a higher tip for being friendly. He seems like a nice dude and maybe saying things out loud, to someone that doesn't know me, will take some of the guilt away.

I haven't really talked about it with anyone for the past six months. All I've done was go over every detail, every little fuckin' detail in my messed-up mind. The mind that drives me crazy, the mind that is set to go off like an explosion any time.

I take another swing of whiskey and I give in. I confess to a gay bartender wearing pink shorts and diamond earrings. I confess everything, I tell him every single thing from the moment she left me hanging with my erect dick in the bathroom, to the first time we met, to the moment I pulled the plug and watched her take her last breath. I also didn't leave anything out about her being my half-sister and how wrong and devastating that news was. How this news and this news only is why she is no longer alive. She wouldn't have been in that tragic motorcycle accident if not for the letters of truth she had discovered on my table.

"How big of a monster am I to fucking end the life not only of my lover, but also my family?" I ask Travis, even though the question is directed at myself. By the time I'm done, my moist eyes see nothing but chocolate, hazel brown. Mia's eyes. Like she is standing right before me.

"Shit, man," he tucks his blond locks behind his ears. "Fuck," he takes a deep breath, "you didn't know. You can't help who you fall in love with man, that's out of our power." As much as this statement is directed at me, I know this is an explanation for himself as well. "Thanks man," I nod my head, and the memory of her sweet face flashes through my mind.

I look at him, or rather through him, and I see Nina taking another shot with Kelly. My Golden laughs at something that a piece of meat sitting behind the bar said to her. She leans closer to him, her facial expression nothing but flirtatious, her hips swinging even though he can't see them for shit since she is behind the bar. It's only for me to see from the opposite side, her arms under her full breasts, pushing them up to the point that he can't possibly look anywhere else but her cleavage.

I shouldn't feel what I'm feeling, I shouldn't be jealous. I shouldn't feel the need to punch the loser right on his nose, beat the shit out of him. She's not mine. Never was to begin with, so why am I getting all hyped up, all fucking worked up while I watch her flirt with some dude?

"I've never seen her flirting with anybody before to be honest," Travis follows my gaze and he scratches his eyebrows in disgust. "I love her voice," he nods his head towards my glass, and as much as I want it to be refilled I shake my head no. I need to be alert. I need to watch her, see her true colors while she thinks I'm not paying any attention to her.

Nina

I can feel his eyes on me right now, just as I felt them an hour ago. I know he is watching me, my every move. My every shot of that disgusting vodka that I continue to bring to my lips and swallow hard.

I never drink. Well, I do drink here and there. A glass of wine here, a bottle of beer there, but I never let loose like this, not since then... not for the past six years. Drinking leads to carelessness, carelessness leads to trouble, and trouble leads to scars that don't tend to fade with time. Trouble is nothing that I need in my life.

But now, knowing he is watching me, watching my mouth wrap around each glass of poison, I think of nothing but putting on a show that I know he is eagerly watching. Each shot that I take, I make special, dedicated for only one observer. Him. Mouth around the glass, tongue swirling to lick the very last bit of liquid, head thrown back while I swallow and enjoy the numbness overtaking my body.

Shit! I'm drunk.

But I will keep on with the show, especially with that innocent dude playing my cards.

Take that! I think while I slide my hand over the muscular arms of total stranger.

Dylan

"Hit me up with another one!" I clench my teeth while I watch her skim her hands over that loser's body. Fuck! That shouldn't be an issue. She is some chick I banged years ago, left naked in a hotel room and never spoke to since.

I want to deny the feeling. I want to push that scary, irritable thought away, out of my brain. But the more I watch her smile and bring her hands toward that pathetic human being that would like to call himself a man, I boil.

That's not how this shit should have ended up. I was supposed to come here to forget everything. Have a hell of good time, fuck as much as I could, drink myself into oblivion and go home clean and ready for whatever awaits me. But shit got out of control the second I recognized her. I know we had a helluva good time together years ago. I know perfectly well that I was the one who pushed her to step on that stage, and I know I was the one who took advantage of her the last night I was here, even though I knew it was wrong. I left her alone, naked in my hotel bed, to wake up to nothing but confusion. Shit!

And now she is flirting with a polo wearing boy like she does it every night. I know she doesn't. Travis just assured me of that, and that eases my fucked up mind a bit.

I look at my watch and it's three a.m., they

revival

should be closing soon. I watch her stand close to the baby blue shirt boy, his hand sliding down her ass, cupping her ass cheek, while he drinks whatever it is that he drinks. I can't help but walk towards them. I can't watch this for another second. I'm next to them within a few strides.

"We should go." I gently wrap my hands around her waist while sending daggers with my eyes to that piece of shit loser.

"She's with me." This motherfucking douchebag is brave enough to talk to me.

"She was, until now." I ignore her open mouth. A mouth that I would most likely cover with mine in any other situation, but right now I push that thought aside and gently push her away from him. Her eyes are like fucking saucers, trying to understand what's going on. Yeah, she's drunk alright.

She doesn't object one bit while I walk her out of the bar, listening to loud complains and threats from the polo pussy. To me it's simple, if you wanted to hang out with her, you wouldn't let her go that easily.

"Let me go." She tries to wriggle out of my grip but I ignore her pleas and keep walking straight, trying to maneuver us between the seas of people. Nothing unusual at this hour, the streets are still packed with bar hopping tourists.

"Which way?" I tilt my head and wait for the answer, as I have no fucking clue where she lives. I'm not even sure if we are heading in the right direction. She stops in her tracks, lifts her hazy eyes to me, and just keeps staring, ignoring me. "Which. Way. Nina?" I separate each word just in case she's *that* drunk.

"I. Understand. What. You. Are. Saying. Dylan," She mimics my tone and I can't help but smile. "You don't have to be an ass about it." She tilts her chin higher and looks alert all of the sudden. Her blue eyes send chills down my spine, in a good way. I scan her face, just inches from mine, way too close for her comfort-I can tell, but she doesn't show it. I can see the tiny freckles covering her nose and part of her cheeks, her lips pressed tightly in a hot as fuck line. I glance at her exposed neck, silky skin asking for attention. My attention. I can't help it. I lift my hand and trace my fingers along her exposed collarbone and up her neck, ignoring the slight shiver that overtakes her body. I slowly move up to her jaw line and I stop at the silver line, two inches long, hidden under the bottom of her jaw. I frown. I don't remember that about her. I know I might not remember much, but looking at her like that and touching her, brings all the memories back. And this scar is definitely something I would remember. She tenses at this, steps away, and takes off in the opposite direction. It takes me a few strides to catch up with her.

"Leave me alone!" Her voice is angry and clear.

"Let me take you home, it's late. Look around, there are drunk, crazy people everywhere. Don't be unreasonable and-"

"And what? You're are not a stranger? Who are you? Oh wait, right, you are Dylan Fucking Heart, so I guess I should know you right? Listen, I am the one that cleans your room after your nightly sex sessions and the one that occasionally brings you a drink, if you are lucky enough to sit at my table. Besides that? Nope you ARE a stranger, like all these people around us. And guess what? I've been walking these streets for a quite awhile, by myself, every night, and I'm still alive, so I doubt that this night will be any different." She takes a deep breath and turns around and walks away from me, shaking her head in disbelief.

I'm stunned. I did not expect that. At all. I watch her get farther away and I start walking after her, close enough to see her, but far enough to keep my distance so she can't see me. I just want to make sure she gets home safely.

You are a stranger. She's right. I am a stranger. We don't know each other. We might have crossed paths years ago, spent some time together, and that's it. But I can't deny that strange, puzzling connection that I feel with her. I run my hands through my hair and exhale a hot breath, equally as hot as the night. I swear to God that I feel like I'm having deja vu from the first time I met Mia. The same unexplainable emotions, the same need to be close, to feel, to touch.

I can't go down that road again. What a fucking pathetic human being I am to think this way about someone, while Mia has been gone for only a few months. How wrong is that, how fucking wrong? A couple of months ago I vowed to myself that I would never let those kind of emotions sneak in again. That I will close the gates to my iron heart and never open them again. For anyone.

Yet here I am, feeling. And there is not a thing I can do about it. Even if I try to not think about her, try to push her out of my mind, she comes back like the wave of tsunami, taking over everything, washing out all the doubts. They say you don't choose these kinds of emotions, you don't choose the person that overtakes your mind and makes you stupid as fuck every time you think about her. They say that you can't choose that, that it's already written somewhere in the stars, that's it's already engraved in your own personal journey, and even if you try to escape it, even if you drift far, far away you will always find your way to one another.

But I already have that person, I already felt these feelings and they got me nowhere. They got me into a dark, dead end.

I round the corner and notice the coffee shop I already labeled as my favorite and I see her slow down and search her purse, for keys perhaps. I don't need to look at the neighborhood to know that this part of town is not the place for a young girl to live, definitely not a woman like her. I watch her disappear into the darkness, the light in the stairway turns on as she enters the building. I walk to the other side of the street and watch her figure walking up. Up to the second floor. The light goes off and it doesn't turn on again, so I assume she's safely home. I wait for the light in her apartment to go on, but it never does. Maybe she's one of those people that move around their place in the dark with the agility of a cat. Knowing every curve, every little corner even with their eyes closed? Maybe. Maybe I don't know shit about her and I'm trying to bring back good memories to make myself feel better?

On my way back to the hotel I pass the open doors of bars, still very much alive, when I hear my phone ringing. I fish it out of my pocket and see Austin's number. I frown, that can't be good.

"What's going on?"

"You are not sleeping." It was a statement not a question.

"No mom, I'm not," I smirk to myself. "I'm in New Orleans Austin, people are basically having their cocktail hour right now."

"Russians are pissed, they want to have the date exclusively to themselves, if we can't give it to them, they're out."

"I thought you said we are all good on this one?"

"We were, until they found out that the Germans are planning to build at the same time, now they are backing out."

"Talk to the Germans then, ask them to wait a few months, I don't see the problem."

"I did, they are set on the same dates and it looks like they want to have the upper hand on this. I don't think either of them will wait, we have to decide which one of them we will let go."

"Bullshit, send Marcus over there, they like him, let him talk to them."

"Marcus said he can't fly for another couple of weeks, something about the surgery he's having, I'm not exactly sure."

"Shit, right." I totally forgot that he is set to have hip surgery of some kind, and needs to take some time off. "Ok, I guess I will go, I'll leave from here. Let them know I'm coming so they are ready for me."

"Thanks for saving me from making that suggestion." I hear him smiling on the other end of the phone, then hear the furious clicks of his keyboard.

"You know you could have waited until the morning to do all of that, right?" This guy is out of his mind. As soon as he thinks of something, it needs to be done.

"Whatever, I will send you all the details as soon as I'm done."

"Sure, which will be in three, two..." I hear the ping of my mailbox notification. "One, I guess I got it, bye." I press end and walk into the hotel lobby, holding the phone in my hand. I take a quick look at my voicemail list and there is another voicemail from Dina. I press play and then press stop immediately. I'll listen to it tomorrow. I will drag out the denial a little bit longer. I know I should deal with this. If she wrote me that strange letter, she probably wants me to read it and I feel terrible for ignoring her wishes, even those from her grave. I'm just not in the right state of mind to face it, will I ever be?

I take a quick shower, and as I'm getting out I hear the ping of a text message. I slide the phone to see who is still awake, or maybe just woke up, and what is so god damn important that it can't wait until a decent hour. It's Kelly.

Kelly: *You in need of company?*

Shit. I wasn't really thinking when I picked her up and brought here more than once. She was just easy, good looking, and within my arms length when I had needs. Mainly to numb myself with mindless fucks whenever I felt like it. Mix that with a decent amount of alcohol and you can call it therapy. One that doesn't help, obviously. But after that little speech Nina pulled off with her drunken lips, I'm not so sure of anything anymore. *I am the one that cleans your room after your nightly sex sessions.* I picture her stunned face from this morning when I got to the room, grabbed those panties and threw them in the garbage. Shock. Disgust. And I might be wrong, but I swear I saw a tiny bit of disappointment, and an even tinier bit of jealousy in her face. What a mix. Full of contradictions, just like her.

Me: *I'm leaving in the morning, heading to bed now.*

She doesn't respond right away, it takes her a few minutes to write me back.

Kelly: *K*

I guess that's all there is to it then. I put my phone on the nightstand and close my eyes in hopes of drifting to sleep. Every night has been the same, except one of the nights when I was shitfaced enough not to think of anything. But even then I could still fall asleep somehow feeling her next to me, in my intoxicated state. There haven't been

revival

many nights that I closed my eyes and drifted to sleep peacefully, to be honest. I don't do well in the numbness department. It's like this guilt, this grief that will never go away. Doesn't want to go away. Maybe because I'm holding on to it like to an air filled balloon, afraid that once I let the string slip from my grip, and I will lose her forever. And I don't want to lose her. I want to have her right here, next to me, her delicate hands wrapped around me. Her long hair spread around, tickling every nerve on my body, legs tangled with mine. Her warm, sweet breath giving me reason to breathe. I want all of that. Want her by my side.

I bring my wrist up and look at the tattoo that I got for her. *And I will never let you go.* Now there is a date next to it. A date I will never be able to forget. A date that will continue to drill a hole in my body, deeper and deeper until there is nothing left to drill.

"I won't, you will forever be mine." I whisper, hoping that she can her me.

Nina

He is gone and I don't know how I feel about that. There is a part of me that is relieved that I won't have to face him anymore. That I won't have to fight with myself while I look into his eyes or stand too close to him. Like few nights ago, when I had slightly too much to drink. Well, slightly is an understatement, I had way too much to drink. The next day was hell on earth, that was probably God's way of making me pay for my mistakes.

For a second there when I was looking deep into his eyes, standing just inches from him, I swear I was mesmerized. That grey. Those damn, grey eyes that are so different now, yet still the same. They are like nothing that I used to know, they are nothing like I remember - they are better. His gaze was so intense, so focused on me and me only that I swear I got even more drunk just looking into them. Thank God I snapped out of it at the right moment. While he touched me and traced a lovely line with his fingers, he woke up a fire that I had no idea existed under my skin, I was seconds from losing it. Until his fingers rested on my scar. That damn scar that reminds me that I don't and never will belong with him. That this crazy fantasy that I let myself slip into sometimes will never be real. And that silver line will never let me forget that this can only be a fantasy, nothing more.

I lift my chin up and trace the faded scar. It will

never disappear completely. It will be my eternal reminder of the poor choice I had no idea I was making.

I look in the mirror and stare at it through my now tearing eyes. Choices. My life is all about choices and so far none of them have been good. They all have put me deeper and deeper into misery. Even though the past five years have been nothing but a pathetic attempt to push my pity away and try to be the best I can be for Ellie. She's everything. She's the only good thing that I have, that I've created. She's the ONLY good thing that ever happened to me.

"Mommy, hurry up, we are going to be late." Her sweet yet aggravated voice puts a smile on my face.

"I'm coming, I'm coming," I put my hair in a ponytail and open the door, only to find her ready to go. "Ready?" The question is more to myself than her, as she's definitely prepared; shoes on, two big boxes wrapped in a blue ribbon with a card sticking out in front of her.

"Duh, I've been ready for like, forever." She rolls her eyes and I laugh at her not-so-five-year-old attitude.

"Ok, ok, door." I push her gently in the direction of our door.

As we walk down the hall to Tamara's apartment, I watch her struggle with the presents for the whole twenty seven seconds it takes to get there, as she tries to balance them in her little hands.

"You want me to help you with that?"

"Mom, please, I can handle it." She doesn't even look up at me, just keeps walking straight, focusing on holding those two Lego boxes in her tiny hands.

We step into Tamara's place. It is the exact replica of Gran's apartment, the only difference today is that there are a ton of balloons floating around in the air, a Happy Birthday sign plastered over the patio door, and a bunch of kids running around, sugar pumping through their veins.

Ellie drops the boxes on the present pile to our right and runs to the boys to wish them a happy birthday. She's gone the next second, playing whatever game they have going on.

"How are you Nina?" Tamara places a kiss on my cheek, hugging me kindly.

"I'm good, good." I return the friendly peck on the cheek as well.

"Wine?" she's already turning on her heel and pouring a glass of yellow liquid into a plastic glass. I take it. Not that I will drink it, considering the fact that I have work in two hours, but saying no to the wonderful hostess that Tamara is sounds impossible.

"Cheers love." She lifts the glass to her lips and raises her eyebrows at me to do the same. Crap. I guess I will have to drink it.

"So, how's everything?" I ask just to keep the conversation going. We have never been good friends, but she's been my neighbor for as long as I can remember so I've talked to her a lot. Especially since she was the one to find me at the bottom of the stairs with a broken jaw.

"Everything's good!" She takes another sip of her wine. "We are moving out of this shit hole." I arch my eyebrows in a surprise. "Yep, we are out of this town, this state to be specific. We are heading to Pennsylvania." She looks proud of herself, like she just accomplished the biggest task of her life, and I can't blame her. Getting out of this place is my main priority as well.

"What's there?" I know she's a nurse, and as far as I know, nurses don't get relocated for job opportunities.

"My fiancé honey, my future." She winks while

revival

sipping some more of her wine, a dreamy look in her eyes.

"Oh, I see." I nod my head, "That's awesome." I give her a tiny smile and feel a small stab somewhere between my stomach and my heart. People follow their dreams, they make them happen, and they make them real. But I've been stuck in this crappy place for so long, way too long. "I'm happy for you Tamara." I hug her to let her know that I really am happy for her. I try to push away the feeling of jealousy that runs over me. *You will get there Nina, you will get there.*

───•●•───

Walking into the bar has gotten easier with each passing day. I would be lying if I said I wasn't pissed at Kelly for everything she told me. Everything that happened with Dylan. I know perfectly well that she has no clue, no idea why I've acted so strangely towards her for a few days. I felt a wash of relief the day after my little drunken stunt, when she told me that he left, and that he blew her off the night he tried to walk me home. Relief came like it was the like gush of a waterfall. Pouring over me, cleansing all of the doubts, all the 'ifs'. God I'm so glad he's gone and my life is going to resume normality. I like normal. Simple. Predictable. I have had enough of complicated.

"Hello Nina," Kelly greets me as soon as I approach the bar.

"How are you?" I put my waitress apron over my head and tie it at my back while smiling at her.

"Well, see that guy at the pool table? That's Max, a new firefighter in town. Do I have to say more?" I shake my head no. She doesn't have to say anything else. It's more than obvious that she is doing him at the moment.

"Good for you girl." I wave my hand and walk to the floor while I hear her laugh. I don't blame the guys that fall for her; even her laugh is packed with sexiness. Not to mention her hot, tight body that she keeps in shape with her daily workouts. I wish I had that kind of determination. I think of the image of myself in my tiny bathroom mirror from the other day. There is always that unpleasant roll when I zip my shorts up. There is always that extra skin that I wish would just disappear, just go away after two or thhere days of starving myself. It's never happened, I can starve all I want and I will never get rid of that pathetic roll above my waist.

I dash through the tables, taking orders, smiling and promising that drinks will arrive in a few minutes. I have my signature, friendly waitress smile on my face until I round the back corner table and see him, sitting with his head down. A wrinkled piece of paper in his right hand, amber liquid in his left. I back out slowly, silently wishing he does not lift his head and see me moving away. I stop at the point where I know he can't see me, unless he knows I'm standing there; a big pole is separating us. I watch him, wondering what could possibly bring a man like that to his knees. He glances at the paper and takes a big gulp of whatever he's drinking. And again. And repeat, over and over again. With each lift of his drink to his mouth he clutches the paper tighter and tighter.

I watch him with a puzzled expression. This strong, independent, selfish creature, crumbling over a piece of paper. A man crumbling over words, black on white, is not what I expected to see tonight. Not ever.

I snap out of it when I hear someone call my

revival

name and I turn around and see a table of regulars waiving in my direction.

"You saw him?" Kelly asks me, and I know who she means, so there is no point in trying to play stupid and deny that I don't know who she's talking about.

"Yeah, what's wrong with him?" I know the question sounds as casual as I wanted it to.

"Who knows? I thought he was gone for good," she turns around and picks up a bottle of Titos. "Apparently not." She makes that duck expression, the one that reminds me of Ellie when she doesn't like something. I giggle.

"What the fuck is funny about that Nins?" She pauses with the bottle of vodka over the glass, scanning me.

"Nothing. Absolutely nothing." I don't hide my smile as I pretend to sound serious.

I keep glancing in his direction every time I'm on the floor. I can't help it. He is sitting in the same position, holding the same piece of paper in his hand. Like he never moves, frozen, stuck in his miserable position forever.

Dylan

The day before...

I gave up. I caved in. I decided in a split fuckin' second after listening to Dina's voicemail that I would pick up the letter on my way back from Germany. The stupidest idea, the most stupid decision I've made since January first. I should have denied it for much longer, forever maybe. I should have lived in hope that she would be the one, the only one to fill my mind for the rest of my days. How little did I know? I should have known though. I should have known, knowing her and her outlook on life that she would ask me to do just that. That sneaky lover of mine knew that I would do whatever she asked me to do, especially after she'd left. She knew I would follow her advice and cave in. Literaly. Cave in to the labyrinth of her sweet wishes for me.

Fuck! I was strong. I was good, getting back to my old self even while I was in Germany. Nailing the deal with the Germans, losing myself in girls that stuck around for too long. The girls that silently asked for permission to enter my bedroom. I let them in. I let that brunette ride my cock while the blonde was sitting on my face. While I felt every single second of pleasure they were giving me, I couldn't shake the fuckin irony of the women I

revival

choose. The hair color, the familiar futures of their bodies, each of them reminded me of either Mia or... Nina. I was imagining that I had them both, both at the same time. And fuckin A, it was intense. It was sick. The high I had was out of this world. Brown mixed with blue, chestnut mixed with blond, both on me. Both riding me at the same time. I imagined Mia clenching all over me while my mouth devoured Nina's pussy. Sick and sad, how pathetic I have become.

That wasn't the highlight of my trip if I think about it, but after that night I was good. I behaved. Concentrated on business. Kept myself out of trouble.

Until I picked up the letter.

Dina was standing in front of her office, with her eyes scanning me like she didn't believe I was who I said I was.

"Dylan?" The question in her eyes was enough to let me know I didn't look like Mia's type of man, or at least not the one Dina envisioned her with.

"Hi Dina, just give me the letter so we can get this over with." I stretch my arm towards her and lower it immediately seeing she has no intention of passing it to me easily.

"Come on in for a sec, Dylan." She walks to the sofa, takes a seat and waits for me to do the same. I don't. I walk in and close the door behind me, then lean back on it.

"I'm good here." Honestly I don't want to sit down, as I already feel like I'm engaged in a therapy session. I don't do therapy. Don't need it.

"Ok, fair enough." Her eyes are scanning me, drilling holes in my brain, looking for something, searching for a crack that will let her slip in.

"How are you?" She takes a sip of the water sitting on the little table between the two black leather couches.

"Couldn't be better." I smirk while taking my baseball cap off and running my hand through my hair. "Couldn't be better." I repeat and I already curse myself for it. The look in her eyes tells me that she doesn't believe me at all and she waits for me to continue. There is a split second in which I consider letting her know exactly how I feel. Letting her know how I struggle each day. How every single day I blame myself. How every rise of the sun starts the same way - with guilt.

But she doesn't need to know any of this, she doesn't need to know the true story, the fucked up truth that would make people turn their faces in disgust. That would make me feel like a monster, make me look like a monster. They will not understand the fact that I simply didn't know, that we didn't know. We had no god damned idea we were related. Knowing that, would change everything. Every. Single. Thing.

Only Mom knows. I remember her little hand grasping her mouth, eyes full of terror the second I told her. For a moment, I thought she would hate me, that she would tell me to leave and never come back. But when I was kneeling at her feet, sobbing like a fucking baby, letting out all the emotions I've held for so long, I felt her arms wrap around me tight and I knew she understood.

"We are only human Dylan," she placed a kiss on the top of my head. "You couldn't possibly know." We stayed like that for quite a while. Me trying to ease up the guilt of killing Mia, and her, trying to comfort me as motherly as she could.

I hear Dina clear her throat and I snap my eyes back to her. "You made the right decision. I understand that you had no other choice, considering her condition." She's waiting patiently, waiting for

revival

me to say something. To agree perhaps, to nod my head and acknowledge the fact that this was the ONLY choice I had. I do nothing. I keep looking at her and I know she is trying her best to help me, to make me open up to her. To let it all go. I know she sees the emotions through my stubborn coldness. But I'm not ready to talk, to go over the details in order to cleanse myself. Maybe one day. Maybe. But not right now. Not here.

"I have a plane to catch Dina." I lie. The plane will wait as long as I want it to wait, but I want to get out of here. I'm done with her all-knowing glare. The simple fact that she knew Mia to the very core, knew every little fear that haunted her since her childhood, it's quite overwhelming.

I see her weighing something in her mind, nodding her head so lightly one may mistake it for a muscle twitch, but I know better. She's thinking. She stands up and walks over to her desk, picks up a white business card and clips it to the manila envelope that she's holding in her hands. I watch her take six steps before she is right in front of me, her eyes full of pity as she looks at me.

I hate pity.

"Here, call me if you ever want to talk." Her arm stretches to me, a yellow rectangle ready to burn my hands. I hesitate. I glance between her and the envelope, questioning if this is what I really want. "You can still wait if you are not ready Dylan." Damn she's good at all that reading people shit, isn't she?

I snatch the paper from her hands in one quick move, and within seconds I'm on the other side of the door. "Thanks." I throw over my shoulder without turning back. I walk down the stairs, clutching the piece of paper in my hand, my knuckles turning white even though there is no physical effort needed. I walk out the door, get into my service car and let the driver know we are heading for the airport. I should have stayed here a day or two, visited mom, maybe stopped by the cemetery and put fresh lilies on her grave. Stopped by the tattoo shop to see how everything is going. But I can't stomach being in Cali any longer than I have to. I was having serious doubts about this short stop anyway.

I take my phone out and text Vince. Since I'm here in Cali it only makes sense to ask him how they are doing with my tattoo shop. Or rather Mia's tattoo shop that I couldn't let go after she was gone.

Me: *Everything alright out there?*

I don't have to wait long for his response, it comes within seconds.

Vince: *Everything is good, you?*

I throw my head back and struggle with the answer, seeing his face in my mind on the day I arrived to look for her. Not knowing why she didn't pick up her phone, why she was ignoring me. His face full of hurt and fear, his eyes teary, letting me know right there on the spot that something terrible had happened.

Me: *All good. Just checking, if you need anything, you let me know.*

Vince: *Sure boss.*

I smile a small but broken smile at his response. Boss. Mia was his boss for so many years and I became his boss by pure accident. The shop was put up for sale after her death, after the truth killed her. It was a split second decision, one that didn't required thinking. I couldn't let this place go to some stranger. I wanted to keep it alive. Make it mine. I wanted to hold on to something that had her written all over. And what was better than her tattoo shop?

I glance down at the mystery letter. The letter that was written before we both knew what would

revival

happen. She could not possibly have known, could she? I have this irresistible itch to open it and read it right now, but I feel like that would be the biggest profanation of all times. A letter from her is not to be opened in the back of a service car, it needs to be opened in a special, secret place. Not in here during rush hour, on a California highway.

Fuck, I wish I were already on that plane heading back to New Orleans, even if I don't understand the need to be there. I should stay here where my home is and have my bike shipped to me. I should forget about the strange discovery that I made by going back to Louisiana. Forget about that blue-eyed girl that stirs something in me every time she's around. But for some unexplained reason, I want to go there. I want to be in the middle of summer craziness even though it's said that the craziest, most unbelievable time is in February during Mardi Gras, I know better. Summer is crazy as hell. And I need that distraction. I need that different kind of crazy to keep me going right now and discover what else is there for me.

I'm about thirty-seven thousand feet in the air, sipping on a whiskey that burns my mouth, as I stare at Mia's letters. I want to read them, but at the same time I'm terrified. What could she possibly write to me? What could she possibly want me to know about her that I already didn't know? How the fuck did she know that her life would end so soon and unexpectedly?

I peel back the clear tape covering the envelope slowly and drop it to the floor. I slip my hand inside and pull out a few thin sheets of paper. I stare at them while I take another sip, just to get the courage to do what I'm about to do. I recognize her handwriting on the white paper and I take a deep breath. A breath that stops somewhere between my heart and my throat. I try to exhale but the damn air is stuck there like a little golf ball, blocking the path. *I can't do it! I can't fucking do it!* I slide the papers back in the envelope and lean back in my seat, trying to calm myself. Trying to get the courage to be a man and read what's addressed to me.

I pick up the rest of my drink and down it in a second before I go for another take, setting my empty glass on the tiny table next to my seat. *I'm ready.* I think as I pick up the envelope and lift it up so the papers are sliding into my hand slowly, like a lazy snail not sure if this is the right way to go. I take a deep breath and read the words.

I know the first question you are asking yourself right now is, What The Fuck? Why?

Fuck Mia, you are killing me with the first sentence. You knew me so well.

And I will deeply disappoint you, as I have no fucking clue why! It just felt right to do it after that little stunt I pulled on the dirt racetrack the other day. I knew I was going too fast, I knew that any second could be my last but that didn't stop me. I kept pushing the gas pedal; I kept pushing my limits until your face came in clear in the front of my mind. And then I thought, what If I was gone now? You wouldn't have a fucking clue how I feel about you, how much you mean to me. What if? And if you are reading this, I guess that IF did happen. Fuck! I don't even want to think about it, as I believe we will live a happy, simple life

together, and nothing, literally nothing will separate us. But IF (it's simply hypothetical), then I have something to say to you.

I assume I've been gone for about six months now, that is if Dina followed my instructions. Why did I choose to wait six months? Don't know. Maybe because it took me that long to finally accept the loss of my father, and then my mother. I don't know. Six seems like a good number, in between, somewhere in the middle. One hundred and eighty days seems like enough time to still remember, but no longer grieve. You still remember me don't you? God, I hope you do. I'm actually hoping that you will never read this. Or even better, that we will be reading this together, holding our wrinkled hands while watching the sun set somewhere over the ocean.

I can't imagine a day without looking into your eyes, eyes that saw everything in me, everything that nobody else could see. I love how your grey eyes twinkle while your lips curl into that sheepish, happy smile of yours. I love how they darken with hunger right before you get close to me, right before your fingers caress my skin. I swear that every single stroke of your fingertips wakes up a volcano in me that is ready to erupt, ready to explode, not caring about the consequences.

I really hope that I will have all that and more, until the very end. But if for some fucked up reason I'm not around, I'm not here, I want you to give the same love, the same passion, the same intensity of your eyes to someone who deserves it. Damn, she will be the happiest person on earth.

Promise me that you won't waste too much

time grieving, wondering, "what if?" There is no fucking way that your grief will change anything. You know as well as I do that it won't Dylan. If I'm gone, I'm gone. And nothing will bring me back. Simple. Shit, now that I'm thinking about it, I won't go as crazy on the tracks as I always go. I want to be next to you for as long as possible. And I believe that we were a gift to each other. You are like my second half, you fill me completely in all the cracks that need filling.

Did you notice we have the same dimple in our chins? How crazy is that? To have two complete strangers that have the same shaped dimpled chin? I never believed in soul mates, but now, with you next to me, I know that this is not just shitty talk. This soul mate shit is real. You and I baby, you and I are the proof of that.

So anyway, IF I'm gone, and you are still very much alive, then it means you are still capable of giving and receiving. Simple as that. Give, give everything you have and fight. Fight if needed, if necessary. Fight until you get what you are after or until you can't fight any more. And we both know you are a damn good fighter and there is nothing, I mean nothing, that will stop you from getting what you want. Look how hard you fought for me. Me! I gave up way too soon and you kept going. Keep fighting baby. Fuck, how I love you for that!

I keep falling in love with you. Yes, I think that's the name of the feeling I get anytime you are around. Every time you touch me, whisper something sweet in my ear. That emotion has a name and I Googled it, it's called L.o.v.e. I have to be honest I used to dread and fight that *tingle, that speeding pulse that made me lightheaded every time you were around. But I finally admitted to myself that what I feel is love, baby, love. I never knew how powerful, how strong that emotion could be, but damn. Love is crazy.*

I can only hope that the look that you have on your face while you search my eyes, my face, is also love. I looked in the mirror once, I was thinking about you and my eyes resemble yours.

If I'm wrong, then fuck me, I'm a fool for writing all this shit. I hope I'm not.

If you ever have to look for someone else, I know that it sounds stupid to even write about this, because let's be honest, it's not like you have trouble finding girls. They gravitate towards you like your dick is made from a fucking magnet, ha!

Ok jealousy aside, I can't be jealous while I'm not around right? So jealousy aside, please pick the one that will give you everything that you ever dreamed of. Everything that you are looking for. Damn, she will be the luckiest bitch on this planet.

Shit, I hope this letter will get buried by me one day. I hope you will never have to read it.

But, if you for some reason are holding this, are reading this and I'm not next to you, I'm sorry! I'm so fucking sorry baby!

There is nothing that I want more than to spend my life with you, next to you. If I can't ... then at least I will be leaving this place called earth knowing I've been loved. Loved by you.

But promise me something Dylan. Fucking promise me right now, that you will never give up in your search for love. Even if you have to

fight, sacrifice, forget your fucking name in the process, promise me that you will never give up fighting for it, that you will never let it go. Cause baby, I promise that I will always guide you to your happiness, that I will always be next to you no matter what, I will always smile down at you and I will always hold on to you.
   Love,
   Always,
   Mia

   Fuck me.
   I'm done.

Nina

I just sang a few of my covers and I'm about to sing something I wrote, which I haven't done in a long while. My own song. My own words. I can't even concentrate on the cover songs as I keep searching for him, and every time my eyes land on him, my heart breaks. Over and over, little by little. It's not often that you see a grown, strong man, falling apart like this. I won't lie, I had a moment of weakness and I thought about walking straight up to him, wrapping my arms around him and holding him. Just holding him until everything that he is facing goes away. I wanted to tell him that it's going to be ok. That no matter what, everything is going to turn out OK. But the smarter voice in my head reminds me that it's none of my business, it's not my battle to fight, not my demons to get rid of. That, in reality, I don't really know him. He is not the same person he was years ago and I am definitely not who I was back then. We are complete strangers to each other.

"I know I haven't done this in a while but I want you to hear something that comes from my heart, from my soul. I hope you all like it." I hold my mic tight as I place it on the stand, taking a seat on the stool and tuning my guitar, playing few notes. Not to check if it sounds right, I know it does, but to calm the nerves that are rising in me.

There is silence, complete silence. The kind that I don't usually get while performing. It gets quiet, but never like this. All eyes are on me. I can feel it. I hear the first notes of the bass guitar from the band behind me. Deep breath. Another strum. Deep breath, my eyes close, separating me from the wall that stands between me and the audience; one listener in particular. I start to play and I escape from everything, I take one last deep breath and I start...

> Coming out of nowhere, unexpected
> Like morning summer rain
> There is nothing good coming out of your presence
> Nothing real
> There is nothing you can nurture with your tender heart
> Everything has withered
> Everything is gone
> The sooner you go
> The stronger I will grow
> The sooner you go
> The deeper I will breathe
> All I see is a tornado
> Heading my way
> Destruction I can feel
> Crushing the walls of my veins
> The walls that you had perfectly stretched before
> Walls you filled with love
> Only to rip them open the very next day
> Leaving me delirious
> Begging for more
> The sooner you go
> The stronger I will grow
> The sooner you go
> The deeper I will breathe
> The sooner you go
> The stronger I will grow

Stronger I will grow

Once I finish the lyrics I open my eyes, my body still swaying to the final strums of the electric guitar playing behind me. All eyes are on me, and once the silence surrounds the room, I can feel its mute energy. I panic, my heart rate accelerates to the point where I can feel it slamming dangerously in my rib cage. Ready to escape. Leaving me breathless.

I stand and turn, readying myself to leave. And it's right there, right at that moment when I hear hundreds of hands clapping. Voices shouting 'woo!', and 'yeah!' I turn around to face them in disbelief, and I have the biggest grin plastered to my face. I'm proud. I'm so proud of myself, of us. Of The Thunder. The approval of the audience is everything, and they are giving me that everything right at this moment. I mouth a 'thank you' over and over while heading for the stairs to the floor. I hear people saying 'great job', 'that was awesome', while they pat me on my back. I smile, no, I grin and thank them while getting back to the bar. I still have few hours of work to go.

"You really hate me that much." A familiar voice is to my right. As soon as the meaning of his statement hits my ears, my happiness disappears. Just like that, my beautiful bubble of ecstasy burst with one sharp sentence. Gone. My smile replaced with shock. For a couple of minutes, I forgot that he was here. I forgot that he was listening. My mouth opens and closes as I think of an answer to a question I never expected. He stated it. He didn't ask me if I hate him, he just stated the obvious.

"I don't know what you are talking about." I manage to blurt out, my mouth feels like it's filled with big, fluffy cotton balls.

I lift my chin higher and meet his eyes. My

mistake. Big mistake. There is a storm brewing in them. There is a hurricane of emotions, none of which are the good kind. If looks could kill I would be dead, even though I'm not sure I'm alive at this moment anyway.

"Your song." He watches my eyes and my eyes only. Like he is trying to find out the absolute truth. I swallow and nervously bite the inside of my cheek, hard. So hard that I get a taste of the coppery flavor of my own blood. I take a deep breath while I try to look annoyed.

"It was just a song, get over it, it has nothing to do with you." That's a lie. And I know he knows it, because his eyes narrow even more while his head cocks to the side and he starts scanning me once again.

"If you want me gone, tell me now. I will go and you will never have to look at me again. I have no fucking clue why you hate me so much. I apologized for my drunken behavior, I apologized for disappearing on you years ago, what else could I do? If you still hate me that much, I will go." He steps closer to me and I get intoxicated by his presence, with his proximity. He's way too close. If I lean forward just an inch I will be able to touch him, and that thought alone scares me. It terrifies me and excites me at the same time.

His face is so close to mine that his breath has become one with mine while he waits for my answer. *What was it that he asked me just now?* I can't think straight when he is this close.

"Tell me," he lowers his head just enough that I can feel his lips touching my earlobe, no, not touching, only his breath warming it, but the sensation is so strong that I swear it feels like a touch. "Do you want me gone?"

My eyes are closed. I must be drunk on his

presence since there is no way I would say this while sober. "No," I breathe out, almost silently.

"No?" The warmth again "You want me to stay then?"

"No." I feel like I'm spinning, like I'm falling down and going back up again, the imaginary rollercoaster ride feels so real. I feel like I've died and I'm born again, over and over in this very second. His mouth hovers over my cheek and up my temple, only to come back to my ear once again.

"I will stay then, but don't treat me like I'm your enemy, I'm far from that." I can't believe what I'm feeling right now. I can't believe the emotions he stirs in me with just his breath on my skin. It's like my body has a mind of its own, it's own system that I'm not a part of. I take a deep breath and I open my eyes, ready to face him and tell him how I really feel about him. But when I open them, I see him already leaning over the bar talking to Travis. I shake my head trying to understand what just happened. I compose myself and head back to finish my shift.

"Whooo Nins that was kick ass!" Kelly is hugging me shouting into my ear. "You killed it girlfriend. You were awesome. You should stop doing covers and just sing your songs."

"Thanks. It feels bizarre. Awesome, but bizarre." I hug her in return and I smile again as I realize that I really was, in fact, awesome.

"You nailed it Nina, but don't quit your job just yet, we need you here." Ritchie's voice comes from behind me and I turn around to give him a hug as well. I wouldn't be here if not for this fat, big and loving guy.

"I'm not going anywhere." I wink at him and get back to work, the smile still on my face while I pass people giving me thumbs up. I forget the cold stare of Dylan's eyes, forget everything bad at the moment and focus on the good. I focus on the support I have from my usual Thursday night crowd and remind myself what it is that I'm here for. Make a few bucks to support Ellie and maybe, just maybe, get recognized one day by someone important in the music business. I know the second part is more like winning the lottery, one in a million chance, but that doesn't stop me from dreaming. That's all I have left after all. Dreams and hope.

Nina

"You are already paid for," Amanda's eyes swing in the direction to the left and I smile thinking Mr. Santiago bought me my morning coffee today. "That GQ model got you a cup, and this." she hands me a chocolate croissant smiling mysteriously.

A GQ model? I step out of the line to the left and see Mr. Santiago waiving at me, but there is also someone else sitting with him at the table. I freeze once I realize that it's Dylan, holding his coffee cup up in a greeting while I have a small, inner battle for a few seconds.

I shouldn't go over there, I should thank him for the coffee and walk away, go to work and let my day start without unnecessary surprises. I should. But I wouldn't be Nina if I did everything that was expected of me.

"Nina, love, come join us." Mr. Santiago's voice is shaky but welcoming. I walk the few steps to the table that I've occupied so many times before, taking the seat across from Mr. Santiago and next to Dylan. The only seat that is available.

"Good morning," I smile in my old friend's direction and place the croissant in front of him. "That's for you I guess." I smile and wink at the same time.

"Nina you are killing me, I already had my share of chocolate for the morning, you eat it." His sheepish smile makes me giggle and I can sense that

kate vine

Dylan is watching us like we are two crazy people.

"That was for you." Dylan nods to the croissant and I bite my lip to stop myself from bursting in laughter.

"She hates chocolate." Mr. Santiago states with a straight face. After looking at me, though, we both burst into laughter. I see Dylan's face go still for a fraction of a second and then he laughs with us.

"I get it." He gestures to the pastry, "That's what you have in common." He shakes his head keeping his smile while looking between me and my partner in crime.

"Pretty much." I take a sip of my coffee, still laughing. I turn my full attention to him now. I haven't seen him laugh. Heck, I haven't seen him smile since he arrived here, and the sight is pretty fascinating. His dimpled chin is even more prominent while his smile reaches his eyes, and his eyes do that crazy, sexy, sparkling dance while his mouth stretches to them.

"You know each other?" My old friend drops a bucket of cold water over me with that question.

"No." coming from me.

"Yes." coming from him.

"Interesting, so he knows you but you don't know him?"

God, that feels stupid, mortifying even.

"Well, we knew each other years ago." I meet Mr. Santiago's eyes and I already regret what I've said. He is eighty years old for Christ sake, he probably saw and heard everything.

"So you don't know each other anymore? That's what you are implying Nina?" He holds my gaze, his still vibrant hazel eyes penetrate me like he is looking for the ultimate truth. And I'm afraid if he looks any longer, he will find what he is looking for. The truth.

revival

I smile my best smile " I don't think so, that was years ago and we have all changed, people change." I take a sip of my coffee and try to slow down my breathing. The simple fact that he is sitting next to me, at the same table, doesn't put me at ease.

"What do you say Dylan?" I jerk my head in his direction and watch him add another sugar to his coffee and stir it with a wooden stirrer while trying to answer Hector's question.

"Well, I think we know each other just fine, isn't that right Golden?" I feel myself getting smaller and smaller while his eyes are focused on me, waiting for me to agree, I guess.

"Golden?" Mr. Santiago seems to have his ears and eyes wide open to everything going on at the table right now.

"My old nickname for Nina." I watch his strong hands bring the hot cup of coffee to his incredibly plump lips. As I watch him take a careful sip, I can't think of anything else but that sensual mouth covering mine.

Get a grip Nina!

"Nickname, interesting." I hear Mr. Santiago mumble. I'm still fixed on something I shouldn't be.

"Yeah, isn't she Golden?" I see Dylan's lips moving and I try to stop repeating Golden in my head, copying the same way it sounds on his tongue. "You see something you like?" I hear Dylan's voice and he is facing me with a tiny smile on his face.

"What?" I can feel the heat rising up all the way to my forehead, I'm sure even my scalp turned red from embarrassment. "No, not at all," I reach for my purse and grab my cup of java, standing up. "I, uhm, I have to go to work. Thanks for the coffee." I point to the beverage "Have a great day, both of you."

I rush out of the deli. Once I'm outside I pick up

speed, heading toward the hotel. I look back once, maybe twice to see if he is following me. Not that he would. Why would he follow me in the first place?

Why am I thinking about him more and more often lately? Why do I let myself get all mushy whenever he is around? That lovely smile and that damn dimpled chin didn't convince me to stay away from him at all. In fact, I feel the opposite, I would love to see him smile like that once again. Or maybe smile like that all the time, just so I can stare at that tiny hole in his chin. God help me and God please forgive me for breaking one of your rules while I think like that of another man. Not that I go to church every Sunday. I don't. Granny makes me go once in a while to clean up my soul from all my sins. What sins? I have no clue, but maybe I will go this Sunday, just to make sure, just to make damn sure I'm clean. All I know is that he is a good reason to visit the house of God and try to stay focused. And I will do anything to stay focused. Anything. I have too much to lose to slip like that. To fall for someone who would leave me once again. No, I'm not doing that again. I simply can't afford to be the irresponsible one. The one that throws all the good things out of the window and jumps head first into something that screams trouble. No, not this time.

And yeah, what am I thinking, going all soft hearted just because he's smiling? He smiled before, he was cute and lovely before, and where did that cuteness leave me? By myself, scared and hopeless. No, that is not going to happen again. There is no amount of cuteness to steer me away from the path I dream of taking. There is no man walking on this planet that will stand between my plan of getting out of this little town and making it on my own. Well, maybe there is one, but I secretly hope he will have no say in it when he finally comes back into our lives. Mine and Ellie's that is.

Dylan

"So, you know each other then?" The old fella is smiling while he takes small sips of coffee between bites of the chocolate croissant I bought for her.

"I thought you hate chocolate." I can't hide the surprise in my voice.

"I do." He takes another bite and it's obvious that I won't get the explanation I'm waiting for.

"Like she said, we don't…" I pause and let my eyes wander around the deli for a second, "We used to know each other, and I think that would be a better statement."

In fact, a much, much better statement. The "we knew each other" part came easy to me, I didn't think about it when he asked that simple yet complicated question.

"I guess I would like to think that we know each other still," I verbalize my thoughts and meet Mr. Santiago eyes. I know he won't say much about her, I can feel his protectiveness for miles, and I don't blame him. Here I am, a guy out of nowhere, stepping into their morning routine. Who does that?

From what I see and feel, I know he and Nina know each other pretty well. Even though he seems like the 'I won't tell you much about anything' kind of fella, I hope that I still can get some kind of information about her.

I want to know as much as I can and since she seems like she doesn't share my idea of getting to

revival

know each other, I will have to find a way around it. And he seems like the perfect connection between us. Between she and I. From the looks of things, it'll never be us but I would like to at least get to know her better, maybe spend some time with her. I remember that we had a good time a few years ago. I remember bits and pieces, here and there. Situations and conversations. I sure as hell remember her smiling in every memory I have, so it must have been good, we must have had fun even though now she looks like I'm the last person on earth that is worth laying her eyes on.

"You here for long Dylan?" He breaks my train of thought. I meet his eyes and ask myself the same question.

"I don't know." I answer honestly as I rub my face, hoping that it will help me find the answer. "I have no idea, maybe a week, maybe two."

"There is nothing that you need to go back to?"

Is there?

"No." I take a deep breath and try to fill my chest with air, exhaling slowly through my nose. Counting to five in my head, a calming technique I looked up online. Apparently Google is the shit, any question you have, it will find the answer. Just type in a question and it can solve any problem.

It works. I meet his eyes again and for a second, I feel the need to tell him everything, to explain why I don't have anything to go back to. Nothing that is worth going back to anyway, but he stands up at the exact moment that my mouth is about to open.

"Nice to meet you Dylan and I hope we will meet again soon," his old, wrinkled hand is stretched out in from of me and I stand up to shake it.

"Same here Mr. Santiago, hope to see you soon." I smile and I'm glad that he got up and saved me from the confession I was about to give.

"Good day, son." He smiles in return and I watch him head outside and put his sunglasses on, a small, gentle smile on his face.

I finish my coffee and try to form some kind of a plan for the day, it's beautiful outside and I miss simply laying on hot sand and listening to the waves of the ocean. I decide to take a trip to that little beach I frequented years ago. I'm not sure if I remember how to get there, but I will give Ritchie a ring. I'm sure he can point me in the right direction.

I enter my room and it looks way cleaner than how I left it this morning, so that means I won't be bumping into Nina. I head to the kitchen counter to grab my bike keys and my laptop and put it in my backpack when I notice something on the counter that doesn't belong to me for sure. An iPod is plugged in, charged to eighty-six percent, as the green battery light informs me. I pick it up, and there on the little screen it says "Nina's property". I smile. I never thought I'd smile at an electronic device. It belongs to her, yes, but still, it's so pathetic that I laugh at the stupidity of it. I keep my fingers over the screen, hovering over it, not sure if I should open it or not. But I have to, no, I want to see what it is that she is listening to. It's not like I'm looking in her private shit or something. It's just an iPod for Christ sake. I also know that music can tell you a lot about a person, and I also know that she loves to express herself through music, so yeah, once I swipe my finger over that screen I may as well have entered the property of Golden.

I shove the thing into my backpack and head down to the parking lot. I send Ritchie a text asking him for the address of that little beach I used to love so much. He responds to me within a minute, I start the engine and head out.

The weather is beautiful. The sun just hit the

revival

highest point on the sky, like it's watching over everything that is going on, here on Earth.

As the hot wind hits my bare face, I fight the urge to close my eyes and let my memory float. It's like I can feel her behind me, feel her small hands on my waist, holding me like she doesn't have a care in the world, but I always knew better. She was never fully relaxed sitting behind me, she always wanted to be in charge, holding her own steer, going at her own speed. Mia.

It took me over six months before I decided that she would never be the person she wanted to be, that she would never be able to breathe on her own or even open her eyes. Six fucking months ago I pulled out her breathing tube, out of her no longer pink mouth and watched her take her last breath. I killed her. It fucking destroyed me. I still feel like I'm a walking zombie.

I check my speed and I'm not surprised to see ninety-eight miles per hour, my hands are white as I try to hold to the handlebars, the only thing I can hold on to right now. The only thing I can control at the moment.

I turn onto a sand road that I remembered well. It was my rest spot. I would come here every afternoon to rest and get reenergized for the night. Yep. Years ago when my life was easy. Sleep. Rest. Drink. Fuck. Repeat. Awesome summer for a twenty six year old. What else could I have asked for? Sounds almost like rock and roll.

The beautiful line of the ocean comes into view and I take a deep breath, inhaling the fresh, salty air into my lungs, I've missed this. I've missed the ocean. I used to hang out at the beach every day, by myself or with her. Not anymore. I stopped going to the beach even though my backyard now has an ocean view. I couldn't stomach leaving my porch and enjoying the beach by myself, without her.

I take out the hotel towel that I grabbed from my bathroom and spread it over the white sand. I take off my boots and as soon as my bare feet hit the warm sand I smile to myself, wiggling my toes like a little child that just discovered the fact that the sand will wrap around your feet like a soft blanket and slip away the next second. Just like life. Just like love. Just like everything that is most valuable to us. It fills us until we overflow with its beauty and then slips between our fingers when we least expect it.

I take off my shirt and slide my jeans down, kicking them to the side. There are only few people here, which is weird since this is one of the best beaches this area has to offer, but I guess locals still keep this place a secret, just like they used to.

I walk toward the ocean and the closer I get, the more memories float through my brain. Memories of Mia. Her tiny body in that hot little bikini, her eyes wide while my lips connected with hers for a split second, and even though she denied my access, I knew that I would taste those lips again, and again.

Shit. Will I ever be free of the memories of her? Do I even want to be? Will I torture myself with her image until I grow old? I know it's sick as fuck to still hang tight to something that is gone and will never, ever be back again. It's not like she moved to another state and might come back any second. She's dead, for fucks sake and she will never, ever, be standing in front of me again. I will never be able to hold, feel or touch her. Not until we meet at last. Not that those thoughts never crossed my mind. Oh they did. Trust me. I had my low, very low point around the middle of January when the only thing on my mind was that I wanted to join her. To be with her no matter what the price was. The only thing that kept my head straight was the thought of my mother being all-alone after I cross to the other side. She wouldn't survive. She would die of fucking pain. I couldn't do that to her. I love her too much. She didn't deserve this. She was too good for that.

I walk into the cool water and splash at the low waves with my feet, getting used to the coldness. Then, just like that, I run into the water and dive as soon as it's deep enough. I stay under as long as my air supply allows, maybe a tad longer, pushing myself, testing. I come up for air and keep swimming against the low waves that are coming at me one by one. I swim and swim until my muscles ache, until my breath becomes short and my legs feel slightly numb. I turn around and I curse, seeing how far I have to swim to get back to the shore. I'm spent. I'm breathless. I turn on my back and start swim back, moving my arms slowly, lazily, saving my energy.

It takes me a long ass time to get back to the shore. As soon as I hit the sand, I walk straight to my towel and collapse on it, passing out.

I wake up few hours later, the sun still shining strongly, looking at me from an angle. I don't have to look at my watch to know what time it is right now. I guess that it's around four. I grab my backpack to take my laptop out, and my fingers touch the iPod I threw inside before leaving. I let the computer slide down to the bottom of my bag as I take out the little device. I search for my earphones and plug them in, hesitating for a second before unlocking the damn thing. It feels like I am entering something sacred, like I'm violating her privacy already. It feels wrong as hell, but the curiosity is much, much bigger than the slight guilt crawling inside me.

I slide my finger to the right and I swear I stop breathing for a tiny fraction of second. Call me a fucking pussy, call me what you want. I. Don't. Care.

I scan the list of artists. I know some of them, but most are unfamiliar. I see that she's not all sugar and sweets, as I scroll through Pink Floyd, Ramones, Pear Jam and Black Sabbath. When I see The Eagles and The Doors, I'm pulled back to the memories of when we met. That was the music we cherished, the music we breathed in the short time we spend together.

I scroll further down and see Jason Walker, Adele, Damien Rice, Susan Jackson-Holman, Ella Henderson and many others that I have no slight fuck about. I touch the first one under my finger. As the strong bass hits my ears and the words start to flow, I recognize the song as the one she was singing the morning I snuck out with my sneakers, without even letting her know I was there. When I listen to the words I start to feel. I feel the pain she's in while singing the words to me, and only me. I can't do anything about the tears rolling down my cheeks, it's out of my control, and there is nothing that can stop them right now.

I can't remember the last time I cried, it was months ago. Sure, I have been sad as fuck. Sure, I was pissed. But the tears never came. It was my invisible armor that kept them in, never, ever, let the tears see the light.

I guess today was the day to break this pattern, as there was nothing I could do to control them. As the next song played and the words came in, I gave up. I didn't want to fight anymore. I want to let it all go. I want all of this to disappear and let me breath. Let me be.

Too bad this shit never went the way I wanted. With the tears came guilt, and guilt turned to anger, and even though my brain is still mushy after listening to this girly shit, I know better. I am still

revival

fucked up. I am still the one that couldn't escape the shit I created. Will I ever?

The craziest idea came to me while I listened to a song by Walker. Pulling out my phone, I text Ritchie and ask him for Nina's number. The answer doesn't come for a few good minutes and I know he must be wondering why I'm asking for her number, especially after that stupid stunt I pulled on my first night here. Fuck, alcohol is not my buddy. Not when I'm that deep in shit.

Me: *Hey man, you going to hook me up with that number or what?*

Ritchie: *I can't give out my personnel's numbers like that Dylan. Sorry.*

Me: *K, I understand, no problem man.*

I know the next person to ask for her number would be Kelly, but since I fucked her a few times and then basically told her to fuck off, it doesn't make her a good option. Fuck.

I call my hotel and ask them for the last name of the cleaning lady that cleans my room every day. They hesitate for a second, so I remind them that I'm the one that has been in their hotel for a few weeks, and that I don't have any desire to leave anytime soon. This is a lie, as I don't have a fucking idea how long I will be staying here. Maybe a few more days, maybe weeks, I don't know. They decline to give me her info, even then, so I hang up and search Nina Lewis in New Orleans on the White Pages. I come up with nothing. I search the phone number to my morning Deli and ask for Amanda, I know she will not disappoint me, knowing that I gave countless suggestions about the business to her soon to be husband. She doesn't hesitate for a second – I have Nina Lewis' phone number. I dial it right away and the answer doesn't come for a minute, two, and then three. Maybe this is a stupid idea. Maybe she really hates me and has no desire to have any contact with me. Shit. I wish there was a way to delete the text like it never happened. I'm a moron. She never talks to me, so what gives me the right to think that she will jump at my text and respond the second she gets it?

I curse under my breath, stand up, and head toward the shining ocean. I enter the cold water that slides lazily over my calves, each wave causing my feet to sink deeper and deeper into the sand. I run and dive in once the water reaches my thighs. I need some distraction. The girly music plus my clinging guilt is not a good combination.

When I get back to the shore and lay flat on my towel, the first thing I do is check my phone to see if she texted me back. She didn't. What the hell is her problem?

I press the call button without thinking, and as I listen to the beeps letting me know that the phone is ringing my heartbeat speeds up, I suddenly hope she won't pick up the phone, what will I say anyway? I'm filled with panic as the rings become louder and louder in my head. I think I count at least ten rings and there is still no answer, no voicemail, nothing. I hang up and breathe out, bringing my hands to my face and pinching my nose. *For fucks sake, what was I thinking?*

My phone pings and I see that Travis texted me to see if I want to go to that pool place we talked about. I text back that I will meet him at the bar, as I have to stop there anyway. I don't inform him that the reason I need to stop by is to see Nina, to give her the iPod back. He doesn't know where I'm staying, nor that she is my cleaning lady during the day.

I'm sure she noticed by now that the thing is missing. That's why I texted her, earlier to let her

revival

know that I will stop by and drop it off. So she can swing her hips and sing her heart out tomorrow in my hotel room.

Nina

I hear the house phone ring as I approach my apartment. I don't usually get a lot of calls to be honest. They are mostly sales calls, or the occasional call from someone at work to ask me something, or inform me about a schedule change. In general, people will call me on my cell, so I don't really rush right now to pick this up. I don't have an answering machine or caller ID, so if I don't get to it, I never know who called.

    I know I should invest in a proper phone, with all the gadgets, meaning answering machine, caller ID, oh and a cordless. Yes, even Gran complains that she can't walk and talk when she's here. Not that she's here often, and honestly I've never seen her using my phone. Maybe it's due to the fact that it has a cord, or simply because she is not here enough to call her friends to talk about the latest recipes for an apple pie.

    By the time I get inside, the phone is quiet and I walk to the kitchen counter to unpack the groceries I bought. Ellie's favorite cereal, milk, some fruit, yogurt, and a pack of Oreos. The last one I will have to hide, as it's something she gets as a treat. I smile as I open the upper cabinet and hide the blue package behind a pile of plates. My daughter has the biggest sweet tooth, and she would probably eat the whole pack in record time if I allow it. I know perfectly well that she is getting a fair share of

revival

sweets every day while she's at Gran's, her little and often sticky hands are shameless in telling the truth.

I hurry to the shower, trying to be as fast as I can so I can squeeze in a little time with my princess before I head out to the bar. I spend so little time with her that it kills me inside. There are moments when I want to quit my job at the hotel, since it is the one that brings me less money, but I know all too well that I wouldn't be able to survive without that cash. So I suck it up and hope that one day soon, I will be able to be the parent she deserves to have. A parent who will be around when she wakes up and goes to school. The one that will be able to pick her up from school and spend some quality time with her. Not the one who steals kisses in between shifts, not the one who watches her asleep, watches her little perfect mouth open slightly while she's in her deepest sleep, dreaming of rainbows and unicorns.

I hate it, and I hate that there is not a damn thing I can do about it at the moment.

I grab my purse and go back to the kitchen to pick up the two Oreos that I wrapped in pink paper with a red bow. I know it's not much, but she will love it. And that little gesture, that little bundle of sugar will put the most beautiful smile on her face.

I knock at Gran's apartment door. The same knock I've been using for the past five years. Just so she knows it's me and not some psycho standing on the other side of the door.

I hear shuffling feet and Ellie's voice in the distance. It sounds like she's singing and I smile, happy that she has another thing that she takes after me.

The door opens and Gran is standing in front of me with a glow on her face. She's holding a small plastic guitar in her hand. I arch my brows and even though I try, I try so hard to stay unaffected by this sight, I burst into laughter knowing that she must have been a part of the band. Ellie's band that is.

"Looking good Gran," I walk past her giving her a peck on the cheek, "Hope you rocked that guitar." I wink as my eyes land on Ellie standing on the couch, holding pink plastic microphone to her mouth.

"Apple doesn't fall far from the tree, my dear." Gran says while pretending to pull the non-existent string of a plastic guitar.

"Nope, it doesn't, whatcha singing, rock star?" I ask my little angel.

"Mooom," she stretches out the word, obviously annoyed at my appearance. Or rather, at my interruption of her imaginary concert. "I'm not a rock star, I'm Sparky and I don't sing rock, it's just a simple twinkle, twinkle." I nod my head and do my best to contain my amusement.

"I see," my tone is serious. "And how is the performance going so far? Is the crowd going crazy?"

"Mom," she plops onto the couch, "We are taking a break right now and if you must know, yes, the crowd is very pleased with my performance." I can't stay serious any longer and let my laugh burst out, earning a deadly glare from my five year old daughter. I take the pink bundle from my bag and put it on the coffee table. "If you ever feel tired or need a extra energy to perform, here is a little something for you." I watch her eyes go wide as she jumps off the couch and grabs the paper with her petite hands.

"What is it?" She squeezes and shakes the package trying to figure it out what's inside.

revival

"You will see, once you finish round two." I give her a quick kiss and squeeze her tight against me knowing that it will be many long hours until I can cuddle with her in bed.

The evening is slow. The usual crowd must be partying somewhere else. The beginning of the month could also be taking its toll on the attendance. I stand next to the bar and browse the internet when someone enters through the back door. I don't have to lift my head to know who it is. Nobody comes through the back door except Ritchie, and he's already here. During the day, there are delivery guys walking in and out that door constantly, but in the evening, nobody is allowed to enter from the back.

That strange little yank in my stomach is present right away. That pull that is trying to tell me something. Something I can't figure out. It's like my head is detached from my body and whatever I think, my body is not even considering following. In my head I know I hate him, I hate him for what he has done. I hate him for the way he treated me, even if it was years ago, I will always remember it. But my heart, and the rest of my body acts totally different whenever he is around. The warm, fuzzy feeling that wraps around my broken heart clouds my thinking, the slight tingle I feel down to my core creates a thick fog around my brain. His presence makes me feel like I'm two different people. Bipolar. One part of me is trying to push him away and the other wishes he would step closer.

"I see you *do* have a phone, and it's actually working." The surprise in his voice sounds honest, and I lift my head in confusion.

"What is this about?" It came out almost like a challenge; I hope that he doesn't take it that way, I already wish I could repeat my question using a different tone.

"Nothing." Simple, short. Not much of an answer. He taps the bar and Kelly is right at his side, batting her fake eyelashes at him, leaning on her folded arms knowing that they will only push her breasts higher, right in front of his eyes. Surprisingly, he doesn't even look down, he doesn't even look in her direction. His eyes are fixed on me. I'm the one watching her failed attempt to stir his cock. I clasp my hand over my mouth and I can't believe I just thought that. *OMG, get it together Nina.* I look past him, ignoring his questioning look. I scan the few tables that are occupied, hoping that someone will call me and I will have a much needed excuse to walk away.

No one.

Not a single person turning in their chair to look my way. Perfect.

"I called you today." His low, husky voice enters my ears and travels down my chest, to parts I forgot that I have. Did he just say he called me? Or am I hearing things?

"You what?" I register what he said after a few seconds.

"I said, I called you today." He repeats slowly, like I'm a little child.

"I get what you are saying, but why?" I answer in the same slow way, stretching the "why" too long. He grins and shakes his head in disbelief.

"You didn't pick up." He nods at my phone on the counter between us and before I know he has it in his hands, presses some buttons and frowns. Then he pushes some more and I hear his phone ring. He takes it out of his pocket, slides his finger over something and puts it back. "Done." He states, and glides the phone in my direction.

I pick it up and the screen displays the call log, his name the last I called. My heart speeds up for a reason I don't understand. Anger? Excitement? I have no idea. I look at his name and I hope my face doesn't show the emotions I'm feeling right now. There was a time, years back, that I wished I had his phone number. I wished I could call him and tell him everything. That was six years ago. Now, I'm not sure having his digits is a good idea. It might lead to a disaster.

"And why do you need my phone number, care to explain?" I tilt my head slightly and look him straight in the eye. Big mistake. The biggest mistake since the one I made years ago. I no longer see the angry eyes I saw the very first day. I no longer see the person I should stay away from. All I see is a gorgeous pair of eyes, a pair of endless steel eyes staring back at me with want and need. I try to think of the reason why I shouldn't be staring at this handsome man in front of me, but I fail miserably. I break eye contact and move away from the bar, grab my phone and slide it into the front packet of my apron, only to be stopped by his firm yet gentle grip on my elbow. He turns my body slowly towards him, he doesn't have to use his strength, since I don't resist. Almost like I need it, like I crave whatever is to come.

"So I can call you anytime I feel like it Golden." My hips are between his muscular legs, my hands hanging in the air shocked at the closeness. I stand there speechless, looking at his chest, afraid that if I look in his eyes again I will get lost. Again.

I feel his fingers graze my chin and the next thing I know I'm looking directly at him. My eyes have no choice but to search his. I can feel his breath on my skin, mint mixed with whiskey. God, I think I will start my mornings by drinking Whiskey right after I brush my teeth, just so I can live this moment over and over again. He leans closer and his lips hover above mine. I can feel the heat of his mouth burning my delicate skin. I close my eyes for a brief second and I lick my lips to make sure they are not, in fact, on fire.

"Fuck." My eyes snap open as I hear him swear and my body feels suddenly cold with the absence of his fingers, his lips not next to mine. I step away from him and without looking back, I walk towards one of my tables, trying to keep my balance because I feel lightheaded. What was that? Why am I affected by him like that? It must be the fact that I haven't had proper sex in over four years. Pathetic. I know. But living with a child in fewer than seven hundred square feet doesn't allow much privacy. I'm not going to lie, I do pleasure myself once in a while in the shower, but that's the extent of my sexual life. So him being that close to me, with his lips almost touching mine and the memories of what those lips did to me years ago, woke up the emotions that I thought were dead inside.

I walk slowly from table to table asking if they need anything, taking my time to pull myself together and forget what just happened. I'm sure that to him it's nothing, he is a player who I assume gets what he wants and I don't blame him. With his looks and that body, it's a no brainer that he gets whatever and whoever he wants.

When I get back to the bar I see that his stool is empty. As much as I feel relief, there is a bit of disappointment that travels through me. Nothing new. Disappointment should be my middle name by now. It happens so often.

As I stand there, I notice my iPod at the bar with

revival

a napkin next to it. I frown. I didn't even notice I lost it.
Check your phone.
I fish my phone out of my pocket and see that I have a new text, and it's from Dylan. I open the message with a slightly trembling finger.
Not ready to let go
Cause then I'll never know
What I could be missing
I instantly recognize the lyrics to a Jason Walker song, but I have no idea how this applies to me. Does he miss me? Is he thinking about me? Did he listen to my iPod while he had it? He must have. I refuse to believe that any man alive would listen to such emotional songs of their own free will. I pick up the napkin and run my fingers over his handwriting, slightly curved, his y exaggerated. I pick up my earphones, pop them in, and press play on "Down" listening to the whole song, which now has a completely new meaning.

Dylan

This is more fun than I thought it would be. I forgot how much I love playing pool, how much I enjoy it. Travis is definitely the best partner you could have, as he is kicking our opponent's ass anytime I hit the wrong ball in, which is almost every round.

"Man, I told you I haven't played in years, so forgive me if I'm making you the Capitan of our pool team tonight." I bring my hands to my chest and do my best 'forgive me' face. He smiles. I smile back and for a second there, I feel like I have a real friend next to me. This is our third time going out to grab drinks, and every time we've had a blast.

"You suck, and you know it."

"I might suck but there is no fucking way I'm sucking you off." I take a sip of my beer and put the bottle in front of me, watching his next move. I can tell he is taking the game way more seriously that I first though he would. He takes his time deciding every move, walking around the table and predicting the track for each ball. I watch him in amusement. He reminds me of my fighting days, when the first thing I did when I entered the ring was to scan my opponent and find his weaknesses. It worked every damn time.

I take a second to ask myself if I miss those days, if I miss that unbelievable high of not knowing what each fight will bring? The unknown of the consequences even though I was the best. And to my surprise, I don't feel like I made the wrong decision walking away from it. It was a phase that lasted way too long, and I wish I had stopped years before I did quit. Before I was somehow forced to quit, to walk in my father's footsteps.

"It's not like I would like your mouth around my dick anyway, Dylan. Don't flatter yourself sweetheart." Travis voice comes to me as my eyes watch the double combo, impossible in my opinion, to play out.

"Holy fuck!" I stand and high five him "You are the best, my friend."

"Tell me about it." He smirks with pride and moves to our table to grab his drink, Sex on the Beach. I laughed inside when he ordered that girly mix.

After winning another game, we sit at the table and sip on our drinks. Travis wraps his mouth around the straw to sip his drink while I take a big swig of whiskey.

"You like her." It is not a question. It's a statement.

I look in his eyes for a second trying to figure it out if he is someone I can really, really talk to.

"I guess I always have." I say casually between sips, then turn my head toward the pool table to watch people play.

"Was she different before?"

Fuck! I bring my hand to my forehead and rub it slowly. "Yes." I hear myself say.

"How?" Fuckin' shit, he will not let it go, I know. I have to answer him honestly. I think I *want* to answer him honestly, so I can finally admit to myself that she is taking up a lot of space in my mind as of late.

"She was young, I was young." I shrug my shoulders, "I don't know." I pause for a little too long. I know I liked her a lot, she was different, yes, but still great. She was this young, innocent bird that wanted to spread her wings but didn't know how. She was shy, but friendly back then. Not like she is right now, cold and closed off for whatever reason. She never looked at me with wondering eyes, like all the girls did back then. She treated me like a friend, someone to talk to, and we did have a ton of conversations while I watched her get the bar ready. But everything changed that one night, that very last night in this city. I remember her eyes asking me, no begging me, to take her home and do things to her. The things that I had imagined doing for way to long. I never pressed her for some reason. She seemed too fragile. Too pure to treat her like any of the other girls I was interested in back then. But, in the end I treated her like all the others. I fucked her and I left. Without a trace, without a goodbye or a thank you. Plus, 'thank you' would have been the most appropriate phrase to have said to her, as she was the only girl back then to stir some kind of emotion inside me. I had wanted her for a few more months. I craved her touch and smell in every girl I fucked. I didn't know what I should have done with that feeling other than to forget it, let it fade with time. I didn't know what it meant. Until Mia showed up. And then I was lost. I was lost in her touch, in her smell, in her presence. Then I understood what the feeling was, and even though I didn't remember Nina by then. Mia got me good, she got me to feel things I never knew I could feel. She got me to say things I never knew I was capable of saying. And in the end I loved her, I loved her so fucking much that it broke me. I loved her so fucking much, and in the end I had to kill her.

"Dylan, you ok man?" Travis's hand is waving in front of my eyes, breaking my train of thought.

revival

I clench the glass tighter and feel my jaw working hard.

"Yeah, I'm good," I take another sip. "Your turn," I nod towards the pool table, seeing that our opponents are standing there, waiting impatiently. I take a quick glance at the table and there is no doubt that we are going to win. By 'we', I mean Travis, he's the one putting most of the balls in. I'm just tagging along for all I know. Jeez, I suck at this game. Big time.

I lean back in my chair and watch him stand up, a look of determination on his face. I know he's got the strategy to end this. Before I know it, the eight ball is in and we high five each other like we just won the world cup. Little things. That's all that matters, I guess.

I check my phone just out of habit, I'm fully aware that there are no new calls or texts, but I'm secretly hoping that she will call me or text me anyway. I feel stupid for sending that text. It wasn't even about her. It was about me. That only proves how selfish I am, how fucking self-centered I can be.

After I part from Travis I head to the hotel and sit down at my computer and attempt to get some work done. There is nothing that screams for my attention, everything is perfectly handled by Austin.

The only thing that's begging me for attention is the wrinkled piece of paper laying on my desk.

Her thoughts.

Her words.

Her.

I shouldn't read it again. I pretty much memorized the whole letter after reading it God knows how many times already. But seeing her hand writing, knowing that she was leaning over this piece of paper, makes me feel close to her.

I think about what she wrote. I know she wants

me to go forward, to find my happiness, to never give up.

But promise me something Dylan, fucking promise me right now, that you will never give up in your search for true love, even if you have to fight, sacrifice, forget your fucking name in the process, promise me that you will fight for it, that you will never let it go.

I shake my head at those words. It's easy to say, to write this little piece of advice when you are not the one that is fighting the demons of loneliness. How could I let it go? How could I love someone as much as I loved her?

Nina.

I know for certain that I don't love her. Sure, I get that wrenching feeling in my gut, and my cock most definitely approves that little tight body of hers. But... I feel like there is more than just physical attraction. I have this feeling deep down in my black heart that there is something more that connects us. And that scares me. I can feel, I can see that she is not immune to my presence. Her eyes dilate like she's on fucking drugs whenever I come close to her. I'm not gonna lie, I stepped close to her a few times just to prove myself right. Just to see if she was in fact reacting.

I almost lost it today. Feeling her hot breath on my lips, watching her eyes close for a fraction of a second, her body angled towards me, inviting me in. That. Almost. Broke. Me. I was ready to kiss her plump lips, run my hands through her hair. To pull that stupid ponytail holder down so her blond waves could cover her shoulders. Run my fingers over every single tiny freckle on her face, and kiss each and every one of them.

That's what I wanted to do.

Not walk away, and leave her the lyrics to some

revival

song, letting her know that I'm not giving up on her even though she keeps pushing me away. Fuck. Smooth. Real fuckin' smooth Dylan.

Once I'm in bed, I get an incredible urge to call Dina. The damn shrink. I don't believe in shrinks, I never did, but I think I need to hear what someone with some knowledge has to say about the way I'm feeling now. As far as I know, she will put some Freud shit on me and make me more confused that I already am. I look at the clock, it shows one a.m., not terribly late for an emergency call. I dial her number and take a few deep breaths, my mind racing as I'm not sure what I will tell her, what will I ask her exactly?

"Hello?" I hear her voice on the other end of the line.

I clear my throat before I speak "Hi Dina, it's Dylan." I wait for her response but it doesn't come. "You told me it's ok to call you whenever I need to talk."

"Dylan?" The surprise in her voice only makes me more nervous. That was a stupid fucking idea. She doesn't even know me. "What's going on?" Of course she knows I'm not calling her to ask about her day. "Is everything ok?" She sounds worried now, and I hesitate for a second.

"Everything's fine, sort of." I state stupidly and keep quiet letting the silence stretch uncomfortably.

"Good, that's good." I hear some muffled voices and I'm sure that I've called at the wrong time. I have the urge to hang up without even apologizing for my stupid call. "So how are things with you Dylan?"

She is not going to give up now, she will drill me until I surrender and I already feel bad for calling so late, so I might as well go on and confess.

I take a deep, long breath through my nose and

look up at the ceiling. "I read Mia's letter." That's all I manage to say. I want to say so much more, but this single, simple sentence is out and it's already killing me.

"Good, good," her voice comes much clearer. "How do you feel about it?"

How do I fuckin feel? You tell me! I want to scream into the phone. I want her to tell me how I should feel after reading a letter from someone I love, telling me that I should go forward. That I should seek my happiness even though the only person that I want to be with is no longer alive! How confused I feel when I look into Nina's eyes and find myself lightheaded when she's close to me. How guilty I feel every time this happens. How I feel like I'm betraying Mia every time I feel this way. You tell me what this is all about!

"That's completely normal Dylan, it's the way life goes. We lose, then we gain. We have to learn how to embrace the things we have during the moment and learn how to leave the memories buried deep in our hearts. They are the perfect reminder of why we should keep loving in the first place."

Shit, I said that out loud. How messed up am I to not know that I said my thoughts out loud? To a fuckin shrink.

"I'm still confused." I exhale out in to the receiver, wishing that she would send me some magic solution that will make me a whole new person when I wake up in the morning.

"It's ok to be confused Dylan. It's ok to not be ok, and it's definitely ok to be hurting, but…" she pauses for much longer than I like, and I have a feeling that whatever she will say is not going to sit well with me. "If new feelings take over, it's your heart telling you to let go and take a step forward. Don't fight it Dylan, just embrace it."

revival

I nod my head and repeat her words in my mind. They sound so smart, so legit, that I start to believe them. I know I can't hold onto Mia forever, I know she's never coming back and that, that simple thought, is killing me. But I also know that I have to live, have to breathe and survive this thing called life.

"Thanks Dina." My voice comes out sad, harsh and tired at the same time.

"You're welcome Dylan, call me whenever you feel like it, remember that."

We say quick goodnights, and as soon as I hang up, I open my Spotify app and search all the songs I listened to on Nina's iPod. I wrote them down, and now I'm searching song-by-song. Adding them to my secret, personal playlist named Golden.

Nina

I never texted him back. Honestly I didn't know how I should have responded.

I cringe a little, seeing his room number on my cleaning list his morning. When I signed up for extra rooms few months ago, the only thing on my mind was extra money. Right now I would easily give up that cash.

I knock at the door to his room and listen for any noise. Silence. Good. I walk in and look around to confirm that the suite is empty. I move to his bathroom, where I always start, and I stop myself from sniffing his body wash or the bottle of cologne standing on the counter. *Don't do it!* I chant to myself as I pick up the bottle in my hands to clean the surface underneath. I stop for a second, and my stupid curiosity wins out when I find myself sniffing the spray I just spritzed into the air. I dive my nose into the mist as it drifts down at the speed of light, and let myself get lost in the scent of him. It's not the exact scent. I'm missing the primal scent of his skin, but it's close. So close that I feel my thighs rub together, my eyes close briefly, imagining a moment that will never occur again.

Jeez, how stupid do I sound? A sex deprived mother standing in a bathroom of a sexy hunk, fantasizing about sexual experiences that will never come. Classic.

I pull myself together, and as soon as I'm done

revival

with the bathroom, I move on to the bedroom. Then to the little kitchenette, spraying and wiping the faux granite counters. Once I'm done, I move to the small office space that is a desk and nothing else. I put together the papers that are scattered all over the desk, and I'm about to move on when I see a hand written letter on top of the pile. Wrinkled, bent in so many places, with a few dark water marks.

I hesitate. It's against the rules to look over anything personal, but he is not here. He is nowhere in sight and he will never know that I've looked.

I pick up the piece of paper and I start to read out of stupid curiosity.

I don't hear the door opening.

I don't hear him stepping into the room.

I don't feel him staring at me as I'm drowning in this heart wrenching love letter.

I put the paper down with my trembling fingers and I can feel tears streaming down my cheeks, I don't bother to wipe them, nobody will see them anyways.

I turn around and meet the set of grey, steel eyes looking at me.

"I...I didn't... I'm sorry." I have no idea what to say. My mind runs into overdrive and I feel something between guilt and sadness. The thought that yesterday's text was about that other girl Mia, slices my heart in half. How could I be so stupid? He has a girlfriend, one that loves him so much and I hope, no scratch that, I fantasize, that he will ever be interested in me.

"Did you read the whole thing?" His low voice is very clear and very disturbing, bouncing off the walls before it hits me.

I nod, not able to vocalize anything that I'm feeling right now. How could I?

"She's dead." The painful look on his face almost

has me running to him, to wrap my arms around his chest that looks so small right now. "I was a big part of why she's no longer alive." I watch him closely and I swear I can see his eyes glistening, tears hanging on the very edge of falling.

Seeing him, this big, tough man with tears about to fall, it's not something that I ever thought I would witness.

I'm stunned.

By the letter.

By his reaction.

By his statement.

I have no idea what to say to him, or how to react. I just read the most heart-breaking letter and now he is telling me the person who wrote it is no longer alive. I know she must have been special to him, that, I'm able to figure out. There are tons of questions rising in my brain, but none of them seems appropriate enough to be asked at this moment.

I tilt my head and try to hold his gaze. Those eyes don't look harsh anymore, they look broken, sad, and there is no sign of hope.

He still loves her, even though she's no longer here.

"Sometimes the hardest part is to say goodbye to something we no longer have." I have no idea where this advice came from, I don't even know if you can count this as advice. I think I was trying to give advice to myself, not to him. There is really no other explanation for my sudden counselor role.

"I'm trying." His voice is suddenly closer and his face is right in front of me. His presence takes all of my oxygen, leaving me breathless, struggling for the tiniest gasp of air. I'm light headed and I'm not sure if his eyes are dancing between my eyes and my lips. Not sure if his hand is wrapping around my waist and bringing me closer to him. I'm pretty sure

revival

I imagine his lips covering mine in a soft, light, feather like stroke, pressing lightly, trying to gain access. I'm more than sure that I imagine his tongue slip in and tangle with mine, dancing slowly, touching every part of my insides, and bringing me to life.

I break away and blink looking at him with wide eyes.

"You scared of me Golden?" His voice is definitely real, he's here, so that's pretty big proof that whatever I felt seconds ago was real. "Think again," his voice is rust and cotton at the same time. "You are not scared of *me*, you are scared of what I may bring into your life. And you are obviously not ready for it. Not from the look on your wide eyes, or that fast heartbeat I can hear pounding in my ears every time I get close to you." His thumb moves slowly over my swollen lower lip that is screaming for his touch. "No, you are not ready for what I might bring if you were in my life." He dips his face into the small crook of my neck and nips slightly, causing a small moan to escape from my lips. "You are already in it, Golden, it's too late to fight it." His lips go up to my chin and slowly trace their way to my lips. "Now the only thing left is to accept it." He sucks my lower lip into his hot, wet mouth causing my knees to buckle. "Let go of your fears and let yourself feel me Golden, let yourself get lost in me like I got lost in you. Let's feel it together."

Hotness covering my hungry mouth.

Tongues dancing together.

Legs losing control.

Strong hands keep me from falling.

I should stop this. I can't do this. I'm taken. I already belong to someone. But this... his lips on mine, his hands exploring my waist, my back, all this clouding every rational decision. God, his touch is even more venomous than I remember.

"I can't do this." I pull away and head towards the door, not even looking back to see in what state I left him in.

I lean against the cold wall of the elevator and lick my lips, hoping that I can still taste him. I arch my back in exactly the same way I did when his hands were sending fireworks through the small of my back, his lips marking me.

Jesus Christ, nothing has changed.

His hands still spark a fire that lives quietly under my skin. And his mouth, shit, his mouth tastes even better that it tasted years ago. And the things he said; *you are not scared of me, you are scared of what I may bring into your life.* Hell yes, I'm scared of him and whatever he brings with his presence.

I should tell him. I should say once and for all why I hate him so much, why I'm scared of him, of his coming and going.

But I'm too much of a coward.

I'm afraid of telling the truth, because then I might get pity. And pity is the worst. I would rather be cut open and bleed to death than tell the truth. Something I vowed to myself years ago, and the truth will go with me to my grave. I'm not breaking.

The letter...

I try to go back and repeat the words that I've read. This wasn't your regular love letter, this was more of a 'what if' kind of letter. And he told me she's no longer alive, no longer with him. Did she commit a suicide? No, she didn't sound unhappy in her letter, the opposite, she was praising life and him in it.

revival

I toss and turn in bed. I feel my heart break slightly for him. He looks so big, so unbreakable on the outside, but today I saw something different in him. The moment he saw me holding the letter, his eyes weren't mad that I invaded his personal space. There was some sort of relief, like he was glad I found out in a way.

I should ask more questions, but then my questions will be followed with his questions, and I'm not ready to answer his.

Before I know it, my fingers type "I'm sorry". That's the only thing that comes to mind. I know it's pathetic as hell. Random and stupid. A phrase that is thrown around when nothing else can be said. I wish I was able to say something else. I wish.

No response comes so I put my phone on my night table and curl up to the sweetest little thing- Ellie.

I shouldn't have let him kiss me, I shouldn't have let him touch me the way he did, even though I enjoyed every second of it. God, I would do it again in a heartbeat if he were standing in front of me right now. I would push the heavy feeling of wrong doing, and dive into him again.

I run my fingers over Ellie's face and brush away her blond curls. She smiles in her sleep and her dimpled chin catches my eye.

I cry myself to sleep.

Nina

He didn't show up at the bar, nor did I see him at the hotel. Funny how he manages to avoid me now, but he was capable of running into me accidentally in his room before.

That's good. I'm not complaining because I don't trust myself with him. I can't guarantee that I will not repeat the same mistake from other day. The memory of him next to me is still strong, still too fresh to forget, and being in his presence would be too tempting.

After I finish my shift, I'm surprised to find a note in my locker telling me that I have been given a Sunday off, upon my request. I hold the slip in my hand and frown in confusion. I did not request such a thing, why would I?

I grab my stuff and stop by the manager's office, entering after Randa calls me in.

"Hello Nina, what can I do for you sweetheart?" She's a plump, soft woman in her sixties, always smiling and treating all of us like her children.

I smile back at her holding the slip towards her, "I didn't request a day off Randa." The confusion must be written all over my face, as she is looking at me then down at the slip of paper, twisting her lips in a sheepish smile.

"No you didn't." She nods her head while her smile grows bigger. "Somebody else did it for you."

I feel my heartbeat speed up and my mind goes

revival

round and round, trying to find a logical explanation.

"I don't understand."

"You know Dylan Heart?"

I nod, unable to say a word.

"He arranged something with me so you can have a day off." She shuffles the papers on her desk almost like she's trying to escape my angry eyes.

"He what?" I ask, my voice so quiet that I'm sure the only person that hears this question is me.

"He was too sweet to say no to Nina. Enjoy the day off." She waves her hands in the air trying to get rid of me. "You deserve it."

I nod to myself, unsure of what I should say or how to act. I walk back to the door and when my hands wrap around the door knob, I turn around and thank her. She returns the smile and lowers her head, going back to whatever she was pretending to be doing, because we all know that sitting behind that desk all day has nothing to do with work.

A day off.

I smile and panic at the same time. What will I do with a day off? A thousand possibilities run through my head. I still have to be at the bar, but my shift doesn't start until six pm, so it's basically a whole day.

Why would he do that? Why would he go so far to do something for me?

I hear my phone vibrate and I swipe to see a text message.

Dylan: *Feel like spending a Sunday afternoon with me?*

I look at the text and I have the answer I was looking for.

Do I feel like spending an afternoon with him? I already made plans in my head to take Ellie to the beach and enjoy much needed mother daughter quality time.

I can do both, I think to myself. Before I know it, I text him, letting him know that I'm free around 2 p.m. His response was to meet me in the front of 'our' morning deli.

Our. Morning. Deli.

We only saw each other there two times, so I'm a little confused about how this can be our deli, confused about how something can be ours in general.

Ours.

I don't let my brain enjoy the sound of it. I know better. He will be gone before I know it, leaving me once again. But this time I'm prepared, I won't be left heartbroken. And this time I will be left alone, no one else will be left behind.

"We are heading to the beach on Sunday princess!" I scream loudly as I enter Gran's apartment.

Ellie's face goes still for a second before she is screaming and jumping up and down in excitement. Gran is standing in the kitchen over what looks like a pot of soup and she freezes with the spoon half way to her mouth, a shocked expression on her face. I want to tell her that she's not the only one that is in shock, but I ignore her and run straight to Ellie, bringing her into my arms.

"We are going to the beach on Sunday?" Ellie's voice is heavenly in my ears.

"You lost your job?" Gran sounds terrified.

I laugh, swirling my little angel in circles, kissing her blond curls, stealing the little moments that I have with her.

"I have a day off." I turn to the kitchen and pray she won't ask me how in the world I managed to get a day off. She only nods her head in approval, her face still full of shock and amusement.

"So, do you want me to go with you?" The hope

revival

that I hear in her voice makes me laugh harder, the hope that I will say no, so she can have a second to herself. I know she is a full time babysitter, one that I can't afford. I also know that she talks about those silly bingo gatherings in our neighborhood that happen right after church.

"I heard there is bingo on Sunday morning, you might want to talk to Lily to get the details." I wiggle my eyebrows and watch her excited face. I watch her eyes sparkle. "I definitely will." She finally tastes the soup on the spoon she was holding this whole time.

I walk over to her and hold her in a tight bear hug. "I love you. Don't forget that I appreciate how much you do for me." She squeezes me tight and kisses my cheek in response, letting me know it's ok.

I go back to the couch and sit down next to a dozen Frozen and Anna dolls and watch my angel. I get lost in something that I should be able to do every day. Watch my daughter play.

Nina

I shouldn't go with him anywhere. That has been my main thought since I woke up. And now, trying to put this damn sand castle together while Ellie is running to and from the shore, trying to bring more water so the sand will actually stick, my mind is in overdrive.

I shouldn't.

There is no logical explanation as to why I agreed to see him today. I blame it on the excitement and the overall feeling of being truly happy for once, when I learned about my few hours of freedom.

Yes, that is to blame.

I hate that there is a storm inside me stirring since I woke up.

Go.

Don't go.

Go.

Don't go.

Go.

I'm more than sure that if I go, nothing good will come out of it. I know if he gets close to me, if I feel his heat and electricity upon my fragile skin, I will be lost.

Lost.

I can't afford to be lost right now, I have living proof of this running around barefoot, her hair ruffled by the wind, a big smile stretching from ear to ear.

I can't get lost.
I can't be broken.
Not again.

I slide my fingers over my phone deciding what are the best words to use to get out of this mess.

I'm sorry I can't make it.
I'm sorry I'm tangled up at home.
I'm sorry I don't feel well.
I'm sorry.

None of it seems right or legitimate. They all sound like lame excuses, and I hate lame. I guess I will do it, I will go and see him and try my best to keep a safe distance from him.

Try.

That's the only word that is actually fitting in my inner monologue right now. Try. That much I can do. If I fail, at least I can say that I've tried. I did. Really, really hard.

I step out of my apartment with butterflies in my stomach. How pathetic am I? I *want* to hate him, but the memory of that little brush of our lips, of the frenzy of our tongues seems to alter my feelings slightly. Maybe more than I care to admit.

I refuse to believe that I'm weak. I'm not. I am a woman who hasn't experienced this kind of feeling in a long, long time. You can't blame me. He will be gone soon, he will disappear just like he did before and I will go back to hating him, like I did for all those years. For now, I will let him show me what I'm missing. What could be my fantasy.

"You look beautiful." I stop short at his greeting, not even realizing that I'm already at the corner. I feel the heat go up to my cheeks. What am I wearing again? I look down, flip flops, denim shorts and flowy orange blouse that I picked up at a second hand store a few days ago. Beautiful? Really?

"Thank you, you are not so bad yourself." I eye him and try not to wonder how he can be comfortable in this heat, wearing long, faded jeans with a black tee shirt. Add motorcycle boots to that, not comfortable at all.

"Do you want to grab a cup of coffee before we go?" He brings his hand behind his neck and rubs it slightly, like he's nervous, something I have hard time believing.

"Go where?" I squint my eyes and curse myself for forgetting my damn sunglasses.

"For a ride Golden, I'm taking you for a ride." The corners of his mouth turn slightly upward and his eyes scan me with amusement.

A ride? I didn't prepare myself for a ride of any kind, particularly one on a motorcycle. I haven't been on a motorcycle in my entire short life, and that thing that he just nodded at screams scary and fast. I don't do fast and I don't do scary.

"I... I didn't expect to ride anywhere." I roll my eyes at how stupid that must sound, yet I follow him to the curb of the street. It's not the bike that scares me so much as the closeness of him.

"Oh, come on Golden, I didn't take you for the scared type."

My brows come together immediately and I jump on the back as soon as he is seated in front. I look behind me in hopes of finding some kind of a handle, but of course there is none.

"You alright over there? You might wanna hold tight." I shake my head "no", but before I can even vocalize my answer, he starts the engine and shoots forward. Immediately, my whole body is pressed to him, whether I like it or not, feeling weightless, like

I'm flying in the air. My hands fly over his chest in a self-protective reaction, which has nothing to do with my twisted fantasy of being close to him.

I keep my eyes closed. I can tell we are getting closer to the ocean as the familiar smell hits my nostrils. I feel like I'm dreaming, hallucinating even, as Dylan's skin pulsates under my touch, the seat vibrating under my butt, not helping this whole situation. The fact that I am riding on a motorcycle with none other than Dylan Heart makes me dizzy.

I thought I would never see him again.

I thought I didn't want to see him again.

I guess we never get what we want, or we simply don't know what it is that we really want.

We stop at the common parking lot, the city beach that is. There is a slight wave of disappointment running through me as I thought we would go somewhere special. Pathetic, I know. How could he know any good, secluded, private spots? He is just a tourist, stopping along. And God, I wish I could keep him as no more than that in my mind. A tourist.

The fact that I just came back from this exact beach, only to shower and get changed makes me smile, and that doesn't go unnoticed by him.

"What's funny?" He takes a sidelong glance at me while he unpacks some stuff from his bike.

"Nothing." There is no way I can tell him that I just visited the same beach few hours ago with our daughter. "I just haven't seen this place in a while."

Lies.

"Why do you work seven days a week, two jobs, full time?" He suddenly stops what he's doing and focuses his eyes on me.

Shit.

"I have goals." It's not a lie. I do. They just include more than myself.

I can see from his raised brows and twisted lips that he doesn't buy it. "I see." That's all I get in return.

We walk to the shore and I stop with him at the edge of the water. "Low tide." He smiles.

I watch him spread the blanket on the sand, take out a bottle of wine and a cheese platter from his black leather backpack, and put it in between us.

I'm stunned. I'm shocked and I'm flustered. I know I should say 'oh wow, oh how awesome', but instead I take the plastic wine glass he filled, and hold it my hands, not taking my eyes off of him.

"Wow," I hear myself say, and his megawatt smile causes me to shake my head. "You are good."

"Am I?" He touches his glass to mine and we drink our wine. I down it like it's water, he just takes a little sip. "Haven't heard that one before." He smiles his beautiful smile that can bring a girl right to the ground.

"I have to be honest I wasn't expecting this," I gesture to everything around us. "Nice." I can feel the wine hitting my stomach, warming it, telling me it's ok to let go for a little bit. I take another sip, bigger this time. I tilt my head back and enjoy the tart drink sliding down my throat.

"You are amazing." His says out of nowhere, and I meet his eyes only to find that they paralyze me. I feel his gaze dancing around my whole body, sliding off my shoulders, stopping briefly on my breasts, right, then left, going down my waist, slowly sliding the length of my bare legs. Back to my eyes again.

Lust is a bitch. Lust is a scary, scary thing that sneaks out of nowhere and crawls under your skin, without asking permission, without seeking any kind of approval. It hits and you suddenly feel full of it, as if drowning in it, not even looking for a way out.

I swallow the gulp that is blocking my throat and

revival

see him watch me shamelessly. Now he knows. Now he knows what kind of effect he has on me, and there is no denying how I feel at this very moment.

He brings his glass to his lips, "Cheers to a second beginning." Without thinking, I lift and drink to whatever he just said.

There is a long pause of silence between us, and I try to look anywhere but at him. Try to calm my crazy voices, my crazy feelings by taking in the beauty of nature.

"You changed, you look different." That took me by surprise. I instantly turn to him and weigh my answer. Do I tell him what made me change, or do I keep it to myself? I'm not going to lie that the wine I've been drinking works like a truth serum, thankfully only in my mind, so far.

"People change, you changed." I keep it simple, even though the truth is hanging on the very end of my tongue, ready to be spilled.

"True." Simple, but burning holes in my mind.

He pours wine into my already empty glass, skipping his.

"Why do you hate me so much?" There it is. The dreadful question I was trying to avoid. The question I was running away from. Do I confess? Do I tell him the truth right here, this very second?

"You left me like a damn whore." This is a fraction of the truth. That part hurt, but it's nowhere near the pain he really caused.

His head hangs low for a second, and when his eyes meet mine, my breath catches somewhere between high and low, heaven and hell.

I sense everything he wants to say, and yet I'm waiting for it to be said out loud.

"I'm sorry." His fingers find mine somewhere between sand and sorrow, "I was a total ass back then."

I laugh. Loud, honest laughter escapes my body and I hear him doing the same.

"Gosh, that you were." I manage to say. When I turn to him, his seriousness catches me off guard. His eyes are pinned to mine and his hand is still intertwined with mine. The feeling between us is no longer fuzzy and friendly, it's charged, dangerous and lethal. Our eyes lock, and neither of us makes a move, afraid of the outcome.

"We should go." My voice cracks and my hand goes back to where it should be, by my side.

"We just got here."

"I know, but suddenly I don't feel well." I lie. The truth is I don't want to answer any more of his questions, because I simply don't know how.

I would like to say that the ride home was less pleasant because we didn't clear the air between us, but I would be lying. Lying big time. It was as exciting as the ride to the beach, if not more so, knowing what he thinks about me, that he remembers me.

Life has a funny way of messing everything up.

Dylan

I'm a fucking fool. A stupid, ball less motherfucker that is way too high up on his own shit to accept whatever is going on right now.

Fuck! I dip my hands into my hair and run them forward and backward. I'm fucked.

I think about Dina. About what she said and it seems legit. It seems like the perfect advice, go forward, she's not coming back whatever you do, get the best out of your life. Yes, it all seems great and perfect.

Easy to fuckin say. I always knew that it's easier to say fuck it to those who never experienced shit like this, to those who never lost someone. The One. Try to live through it and then say fuck it. I dare you.

But Dina seems so right. Nina, my Golden, she seems like an angel fallen from heaven. Heaven I don't believe in. I have no idea what it is about her, I tried to figure that out so many times. I failed. But I know, somewhere deep in my heart that there is something that connects us, something that will bring us together. One day. One day it will happen.

I hate that I have to restrain myself from touching her, from kissing her perfect lips that I swear have my name engraved on them. I hate it. And I hate the scared look she gives me every time I get close to her, like I'm a fucking monster. No honey, I'm the one that's going to save you.

Honestly, I hate that she's working seven days a week. Two jobs, the hotel and the bar. I hate it. I'm willing to pay her whatever she makes in half a day to quit and spend that time with me. I'm thinking about paying for her time at the bar. I hate to see her walking between those tables, asking drunken, often horny fuckers what they want.

But in reality, who am I to make that decision? I know I could, money could make anything possible, and in my case I have plenty of it. But then how would I talk to her about that? *Hey, I really want to spend some more time with you and I don't like the fact that you're working at the bar, so I will give you whatever you make working there so you can hang out with me.* She will never agree to that. I still have a weird feeling that under those layers, under those sweet, cotton like words that slip from her perfect lips from time to time there is a layer of poison that will paralyze me when I least expect it.

I feel that she has the power to destroy me. And it scares the shit out of me, as there was only one person to hold that kind of power before, Mia. And look at the destruction we caused without knowing it.

Fuck. I know I should let go of the thought of Mia, I should let go since there is not one rational thing to hold on to, but I can't. I don't know if I will ever be able to let go like that. To forget.

Life is a bitch.

I've said that before.

I walk into the deli around eight a.m., and as I stand in line I look around at the tables. I spot Mr. Santiago at his usual spot and I smile to myself, knowing I will join him soon. It's the weirdest thing, having someone to actually talk to you. Not about business or fights, like my so called friends used to do when I belonged in the ring. Someone to talk to me about simple things that bring a smile to my face.

I order that fancy latte she drinks and a chocolate croissant. I know she won't eat it. She made it clear that she doesn't like chocolate, but I find it funny to order it for her anyway. She'll hand it to her old friend, who won't refuse chocolate even though he can't stomach it either.

I walk to the table on my right and take a seat across from the old man.

"She just left," he mumbles between big bites of the chocolate croissant.

My inside shrinks for a second, the hope of seeing her this morning is now reduced to nothing. Ashes.

"More for you." I force a smile and push the piece of pastry towards him.

"You're fooling no one, you know that Dylan, don't you?" His chocolate covered teeth are on full display.

"I'm trying to fool myself, don't step in the middle of that." He doesn't say anything to that, he just sinks his teeth into another bite of processed cocoa beans and washes it down with a gulp of black coffee.

That's the only thing we have in common, a black, thick cup of coffee.

"You like her." His eyes are now firmly on me, doing their best to discover my secrets.

"I do." I say unashamed, causing his eyes to flicker.

"But she's not the only one you have on your mind." I pause with my cup midway to my lips.

There is no way that I told him about Mia, there is no way he could know about Mia.

"You need to let go of the other girl in order to fully understand Nina. You have to boy, she's not coming back, and you know that." I'm stunned. I'm speechless. I want to ask him what and how he knows? But I refrain, I put the tepid coffee to my lips and watch him.

"How the fuck do you know all this?" I seethe through my teeth and drill holes in his now averting eyes.

"The little blond bird was singing about it one morning."

Ah, the blond bird.

That means she was talking about me. That thought alone makes my pulse jump. She thinks about me, then.

His eyes are fixed on mine. I don't break the silence that lasts way too long for comfort, waiting for him to tell me something else. Like maybe what she thinks about me. Fuck, I sound like a sixth grader who is trying to find out if the girl that sits next to him at math actually likes him.

"If you hurt Nina again, you will have to deal with me." It's a pathetic statement coming out of a seventy-year-old man with shaking hands, but that short statement sends shivers down my spine. And I'm not one to be scared easily. I nod in understanding and lift the coffee cup to my lips, sipping more than I desire just to buy time. This old, wrinkled man scares me, and I have no desire to piss him off, or to tell him something he doesn't want to hear. My mouth is shut. But my brain is working in overdrive.

You need to let go of the other girl.
Hurt Nina again and you will deal with me.

I stand up from the table and politely end the

revival

conversation. I have to get out of here. There is nothing that I want more than to walk outside and breathe fresh, humid air through my lungs.

I step outside and take a few deep breaths, but that fails to calm me down.

The old man is right about everything.

Feelings, mostly guilt, mixed with some anger are coming to me in big, unstoppable waves. Hitting me to the point where I don't know how to react, how to stop it.

I'm drowning.

In guilt.

In an unknown.

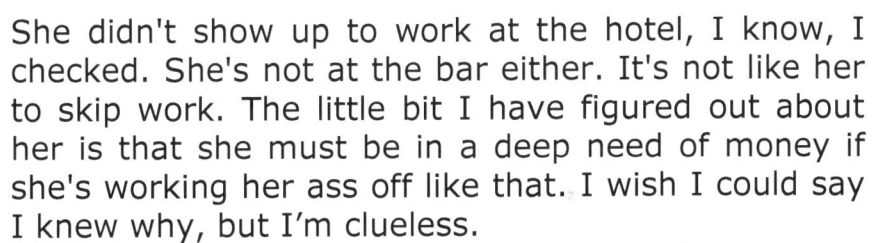

She didn't show up to work at the hotel, I know, I checked. She's not at the bar either. It's not like her to skip work. The little bit I have figured out about her is that she must be in a deep need of money if she's working her ass off like that. I wish I could say I knew why, but I'm clueless.

I order a glass of whiskey, and as I look at the amber liquid swirling over two cubes of ice, I can feel Kelly's eyes glued to me. Shit. She's here, next to me. Standing across from me flashing her soft, double D's in my face. And my stupid as shit, horny mouth waters at the sight of it, my dick on the other hand is still, lying gently between my balls.

My mind needs a good fuck, but I guess my body has its own scenario for tonight.

She is not here.

"Personal issues."

Ritchie, Kelly, and Travis said the same thing.

Although Travis' eyes were trying to escape mine.

Lies.
Motherfucking Lies.

Nina

I run around to my tables, but the only thing on my mind is Ellie. I check my phone constantly for any news from Gran. I'm sure she has had enough of my texts, they are basically the same every five minutes: Did the fever go down? Is she feeling better?

I hate that I have to be at work when she needs me the most. I was able to take off last night only because it was slow as hell and Kelly was able to handle the bar and the floor by herself. Not today though. It is the middle of the week and people are flying in and out of the bar like damn birds.

I can't concentrate and I serve the wrong stuff to more than three tables, probably costing me low ass tips in return. I can't say that I care about that. I don't give a damn. My mind is racing around Ellie. I must look like a maniac, since Ritchie calls me to his office.

"Go home." It doesn't sound like a suggestion- it's an order.

He must see my big, round, saucer eyes "You're useless, and we have a new girl that can step up her game and fill in for you."

New girl. Filling in for me. Taking *my* space.

"I'm ok. I will stay, no worries." I can't lose this job. Not to a new girl who will fill my spot with her long legs and dark curls covering half of her back. "I'm good." I repeat.

"No you are not, go home to Ellie. I'm not asking you if you want to go home Nina, I'm telling you to go. Understand?"

"I... I don't want to lose my job. I will stay, she's with Gran." I can feel the heat in my eyes, and I swear if he lets me stand here for a few more seconds, I will break. I will break with tears that might be unstable. This will be a sob cry for everything, not only this day filled with my daughter's sickness. It will be for the past one thousand, eight hundred twenty five days of sorrow. Of living this fucked up life I live, unable to change anything.

"You are not losing anything." His big hands are around me, bringing me into a friendly hug.

"You are going to be Ok girl, you're going to be ok."

And I do my best to believe that. I am going to be ok. No matter what I will be ok. This, this little hiccup that occurred tonight, is just a tiny bump in the road.

I put my lips to her forehead and sigh with relief that it's no longer hot. She breathes steadily, her arms are wrapped firmly around my neck.

This.

This is what I live for, minus the fever of course. Those little hands wrapped around my neck, letting me know that there is someone who loves me unconditionally, makes my heart swell. The fact that this someone is only five years old, and has many more days ahead to fill with her love for me, makes me a little giddy.

Yes, I'm selfish at the moment.

revival

And I love it.

The second I turn the little nightlight off and pull the covers more tightly around me, my phone rings. I reach blindly for the phone, a big smile on my face as this ringtone is familiar. In fact, I've been waiting to hear it for the past few weeks.

"Hello to you." I say to Rachel with a huge grin on my face, slowly standing up, careful not to wake Ellie. "They don't have phones in Spain?"

"Hello Nins." She's squeaking like a little duck. "They do doll, but things are more than crazy here now." I hear her tone go somehow flat and I immediately regret that question.

"I miss you like crazy." I sigh and plop onto the couch, bringing my knees to my chest and hugging them with my free hand. I really do. I miss her. She left at the beginning of May and I haven't heard from her since. I know she didn't forget about me. That I know. But still, I've missed our phone calls and constant texts. She was, no, she still is the only person that knows the semi truth about me. I feel guilty that I held back telling her everything, maybe telling someone will ease the enormous mixture of guilt and hate, and maybe erase the regret that is sticking to me like cotton candy. I can't tell her now though, not after four years of friendship. What kind of a friend would that make me? What kind friend am I anyway for hiding things from her?

"When are you coming back?" I hold a breath in hopes that she will say that she's already here, or that she's heading home soon.

"I... I don't think I'm coming back Nins." I hear her take a deep breathe, and I know exactly what she's doing. Breathe in and breathe out. Her calming technique. Never works. "I didn't tell you that my student visa expired, I thought I could work something out over here once things with Mom got

kate vine

better, but..." I can hear her tears, don't ask me how, I just know that they are sliding down her cheeks. "They said I can try again in a few years, but they won't give me another visa right now, fucking system."

My mind spins, she won't be coming back, she knew she wouldn't be coming back and yet she didn't say anything. She said she is going to be with her mother during her breast cancer treatment and then she would be back. She lied. I guess I'm not the only one with terrible friendship predisposition. But aside from that the news she just dropped doesn't really register.

"How is your mom? How is she holding up?" I'm just going to pretend I didn't hear the 'I'm not coming back' part.

"She's good, really good. She took it like a pro and the doctors said she will be fine, she's good..." She trails off and I wish she were next to me so I could hug her. "And how are you? I mean, what will you do now?"

"I'm a shitty mess that's how I am." She forces a laugh, and I hear her blow her nose straight into the phone receiver.

"Seriously? You sure you don't need to use the toilet while we are talking, I mean, by all means be comfy, sister." We both laugh. The truth is, she did call me once or twice while on the toilet, that was one of those night conversations where getting off the phone just to pee doesn't seem like a good idea. "Oh God, I miss you and I can't believe that I won't see your sweet face anytime soon."

"We can Skype, I know there is a bitch of a time difference but if you are not tired after your shifts, we can Skype then. I will sacrifice some nights so I can see my one and only child." The thought of how will I break the news to Ellie crosses my mind, she

revival

loves Rachel and vice versa. Rachel always jokes about how she is her daughter, as they share the same curly blond hair.

"Sounds good, we will do that," my tired body sinks deeper into the couch, thinking about how lonely I will be without her crazy, loud, obnoxious personality around. I managed for the past few weeks in hopes that she will be back soon. Sure, there were times when I wished she were within reach more than once since Dylan showed up, but knowing myself, I would probably keep everything to myself anyway, not wanting to answer questions that lead to more questions.

"So," There she is, "Did you at least meet someone interesting since I've been gone?"

I shake my head and I can't believe she can't drop that stupid subject, even from the other side of the ocean. "Cut it out Rachel, we've talked about this enough."

"You are no fun."

"That, I'm definitely not."

"That day will come, and I will swim across the ocean just to congratulate you." I burst out laughing, she doesn't know how to swim. It's kind of funny to think of a twenty six year old that doesn't know how to swim. I used to constantly tease her about it whenever we were at the beach.

"I wouldn't be rushing to swimming lessons just yet."

We talk for another hour or so, until we both keep yawning. We promise to Skype every Sunday unless there is some kind of an emergency, then we would text. She told me to install some kind of app on my phone that will allow us to text for free, even though she's on another continent.

I hang up the phone with a smile, even though the fact that she is not able to come back is disturbing.

I head to the kitchen for a glass of water, putting my phone on the counter and filling the glass with cold water. As I'm half way finished drinking, my phone rings again and this time the ring doesn't sound like the one I use for Rachel. It's Dylan. I put the glass on the counter and stare at the name displayed on the screen. Why the hell he would be calling me? At night? I keep my eyes glued to his name on the display, and let the call go to voicemail. I have no idea if I even want to talk to him on the phone, not to mention talking to him on the phone in the middle of the night.

I reach for my phone and it starts to ring the moment I pick it up. I flex my fingers and let it hit the counter with a loud thud.

I stare at his name on the screen again.

Let it go to voicemail.

Again.

I don't pick it up the phone from the counter, just in case he calls again. The fact that he called a second time piqued my interest and now I'm trying to think of any reason he would be calling.

The phone rings again and I pick it up carefully, curling my fingers around the case, holding my index finger over the green answer strip.

One.

Two.

Three.

Slide.

"Golden?" I hear his voice before I put the phone to my ear.

"Yeah?"

"You ok? I mean is everything ok?" The concern in his voice surprises me and I feel a tiny warmth cover the corner of my heart, warming me in a pleasant way.

revival

"I'm good, it's just E..." I cut myself short. My pulse speeds up and my hands sweat like I've been caught in a terrible lie. "I'm fine, I had some family things to take care of." The lie rolls of my tongue easily, like I am a professional.

I can hear him sigh with relief. "Anything I can help you with?" God, I wish you could. I wish you could have helped me with this long, long time ago. Now, thank you very much, I'm good.

"No, thanks." The line goes quiet for a few moments and I hear him mumbling something under his breath, too quiet for me to understand. Should I end the call? Should I wait?

"Will you be at work tomorrow?" Even though he is trying to sound casual, there is a hint of hope in his question. I smile.

"Yes, and if I don't go to sleep right now, it might be a total waste of money for my boss, as I will be like a zombie."

"See you tomorrow then."
Click.
Silence.
No goodnight, no take care, no sorry to bother.
Silence.

Nina

I swipe the entry card for his room. As soon as the door swings open, I stop in my tracks.

On the small kitchen counter is a tray from room service, with breakfast for two. Untouched. Dylan is standing behind the counter, with his hands gripping the dark granite. His white button up shirt reveals part of his tan chest, his sleeves are rolled up to his elbows, showing his flexed forearms covered in tattoos. I take a step back, as I feel like I've interrupted something, but his voice stops me.

"Good morning, breakfast?" I search his face and I can't help but frown, eyeing his slightly cocked grin.

"Breakfast?" I stupidly repeat his question.

"I didn't know what you would like so I ordered everything they have on the menu, sans chocolate." The wink of his eye doesn't go unnoticed, but I'm still holding the door open, ready to leave. "Close the door Golden, lose that stick up your beautiful ass and come here, have breakfast with me."

Golden. Stick. Ass. That's all I hear. That combination of words alone sends mixed signals to my core. And the day just started.

"I already had breakfast."

"Then have coffee." I watch him pour some of the black liquid into a cup and add some milk.

"I just had my coffee."

"Fine." He growls and walks past me to close the

revival

door. "Then sit with me and watch me have my breakfast, along with my coffee." He grabs my elbow gently and nudges me to one of the bar chairs. I sit. I feel like a puppet, all I have to do is nod at everything he says, let him pull some invisible strings, and I'm sure the applause will come soon.

"I'm here to clean, not to entertain you."

He clears his throat. "I already took care of that, so sit back and relax for a bit, will you Golden?" I look around. My last chance of getting out of this ridiculous situation just flew out the window. The suite is sparkling clean. Everything is in place and there is nothing left for me to do.

"I have to change the sheets." I blurt out and when my own words hit me, I can feel the effect of embarrassment on my face. *Jesus Nina, really?*

"That is something I was hoping we could do together." I snap my head in his direction and exhale with relief that he is chuckling to himself, shaking his head. "Can you at least take a joke without going all stiff?"

"I'm not stiff. And yes, I *can* take a joke." Now I feel offended. I know I can't really relax in his presence, but I'm not some kind of *stiff*, as he seems to think. "I'm actually fun, I just don't have a lot to laugh about." I reach for the cup of coffee he made for me and bring it to my lips, simply to buy time in this ridiculous moment.

"Show me then."

My eyes widen and my grip on that cup tightens. "You are impossible." I roll my eyes and take another sip.

"I've heard that one before."

"I'm sure."

We sit in a complete silence, drinking our coffee, glancing at each other. Me, with serious, stone like expression, him with a smug smile plastered on his face.

"Tell me about her." The smile drops and I watch him swallow, not the coffee, as he didn't even refill his cup, what I see him swallow are his nerves.

"What do you want to know?"

"Everything."

"That's a lot you are asking me for, Golden."

Honestly, I'm not sure if I want to know anything. Now I'm watching him struggle, his face twists in a painful manner, his knuckles whiten on the edge of the counter.

"Sorry for being nosy." I have no idea how to back out of this. I know I have no right to ask him to talk about something that personal and obviously so heartbreaking for him. But there is a part of me that is dying to find out a little piece about this whole situation. I already know what he did for work for the past few years, he told me those facts while we talked on the beach briefly. But this, him talking about his emotions, is something I would love to hear. Maybe he is not the hard hearted, tough, no feelings kind of man that I took him for. Maybe there is more to him than what he wants everybody to see. Maybe he is breakable and fragile just like everyone else at some point of this bumpy road called life.

"I should go." I set my coffee on the counter when he starts talking, his head hangs low, eyes closed, voiced hushed.

He talks about this girl he saw one night when he least expected that anything out of the ordinary would happen. That he would fall in love. I watch his face soften, a small smile on his face while he takes this moment to describe her. She had long, dark hair, a petite but curvy body covered in massive amount of tattoos, perky tits that were impossible to miss in the tight fitting tank tops she wore. His eyes

revival

close as he describes her face, in details so vivid I can almost see her myself. I have no doubt that he truly, honestly loved her. I wish I had someone to remember me in such a way.

When he goes on about her and fills me in on some of the most and least important details of their relationship, I feel like I'm in the theater watching the very complicated rollercoaster of a romantic movie. I can see them go through their happiness but the ugliness is just as visible. Like when she left him for her best friend, only because she felt obligated by an unexpected pregnancy. How she got back to him months after her miscarriage, the same day Jason, the father of her unborn child, asked her to marry her. How they spent the best months together being practically one. Living and breathing each other every minute, every second, of every day.

He is silent for a moment and I'm surprised to feel a tiny pang of jealousy peeking out of nowhere, reminding me that I've never had anything like that. That I never had someone to love me like this. Someone that cherished every second they spent with me.

And then he drops the bomb, face twisting in slight disgust, pain so visible in his eyes that I have to fight the urge to get up, walk to him and hold him tight in my arms until everything gets better. I thought I knew the pain of losing someone, I thought I knew the sorrow of being lonely. I knew nothing.

He takes a deep breath readying himself for what I believe is the hardest part to tell. My mouth opens wide when he confesses that he found out, that she was his half-sister, a sister he had no idea about. A sister he didn't know existed.

Another fact about him that I didn't know. He

was adopted as a baby, unwanted by his biological mother. He entered a family of the most amazing people he could have wished for. He mentions that he never blamed his mother for not telling him sooner that he might have had a sibling somewhere on the other side of the country. He knew how hard it was for her to break the news that he was adopted when the time came, so he could never have imagined that she would drop the news of a sibling on him as well.

Then I listen to him tell me about the accident. She was riding her bike after she discovered the letters saying that they were related. The split second that changed everything in his life. That changed everything in both of their lives.

He turns around and brings his hands to his head, running them through his hair a few times in a slow motion, like he is trying to erase whatever is brewing in that broken brain of his. He puts his face in his hands and I see his shoulders moving up and down.

"I didn't know what to do." I hear him drag out his next breath, "All the doctors told me that there was no chance for her to wake up. That was it."

I keep quiet, there is nothing I can say, even if I knew what to say.

"I had no choice, I didn't want her to lie in that pathetic bed, vegetating. She would have never wanted that, I just know, deep in my heart that she would have never wanted to be *that* person." He turns his face to mine and it takes all of my will power not to break down in front of him.

Tears slide down his cheeks, he doesn't even try to wipe them away. They're there on full display, streaming down a familiar path. A path they must have engraved by now.

I charge from my chair and pull him close to me,

doing my best to hug as much of him as I can manage. He lowers his head to mine and wraps his arms around me.

It feels good.

It feels safe.

We stay like this until his breath calms down and his cheeks are dry. I wish it would take him longer to compose himself. I really do. Being this close to him, feeling his body next to mine, brings me some kind of security.

"I'm sorry." He breathes into my hair.

"There is nothing to be sorry about." I can feel my heart beating so hard and so fast that I'm sure he can feel it as well.

"I broke down like a mental case."

"Aren't we all are mental cases after all?" I sigh into his chest. The fact that part of my cheek is touching his bare skin makes me dizzy and I know we should part. I should tell him how sorry I am and go back to the work that still needs to be done. But it feels so damn good to feel someone else, to feel his strong arms wrapped around me even though I'm the one giving comfort.

I slowly pull away and lift my head to look at him.

He smiles.

Not the cocky smile, not the one that tries to make me swoon and makes panties drop. No. This warm smile that tells me more than his words could ever say.

"Thank you for listening Golden." He brushes a tiny strand of hair behind my ear while he watches me.

Golden...

How I love that forgotten name. The name he gave me years ago that I've repeated a thousand times in my head, over and over but never out loud.

Too scared it will lose its magic if it came out the wrong way.

"I have to go." I step back towards the door. My body feels cold without his next to mine.

I don't turn back.

He doesn't say anything.

I close the door on the other side and push the cleaning cart in front of me to my next room.

Life is back to normal, except for the weird feeling in my stomach that I can't shake.

A feeling that I can't name. I never really loved him, that I'm sure of. Back then I was starting to fall in love with him and I think I'm just starting to pick those feelings up exactly where I left them six years ago. And that scares me, terrifies me to have all of these emotions creep in like that.

Dylan

I'm on my third set of chest presses and I can feel my muscles straining, being pushed to the limit. I focus on taking even breaths, pushing the weight up, down and then up again before resting the barbell on its rack.

I barely slept last night. After I made a few phone calls to check on my business, I tried to fall asleep, but it was pointless. I still don't know why the fuck I told her everything, why I made a confession like it would be my last.

She thinks I'm crazy. She will think I'm one of those people that still lives hung up on their past. That lives and clings to their loved ones like they have nothing else to hold on to.

Truthfully, I feel a shit ton lighter after the monologue I pulled yesterday. It made me realize that what I had with her was great, perfect even, but it's not coming back. I only have those mind-blowing memories, those moments that I can keep to myself, hidden deep in my heart, never to be forgotten.

I should go back home. It's been too long since I left it all in the hands of Austin and I miss my mother.

I put back the weights and grab my water bottle and my cell, heading out of the gym to my room. I search for my mother's face in the screen of my phone and press dial.

"Dylan?"

"Hi Mom." Hearing her voice makes me smile.

"Oh God, I was going crazy but I was just giving you some time, you haven't called in weeks."

"Three, three weeks to be exact. You could have called me you know."

"I know I could but I just... wanted to give you space, time, it seems like you needed it. Isn't that why you took off like that?"

"And who would better understand me, huh?" I smile, as she doesn't even realize how happy that little comment makes me. To have someone who understands you, even though it's you mother, is like lifting one of many bricks from my shoulders.

"I met someone Mom."

There is a second of silence and I don't do anything to break it. I wait.

"Isn't it too soon Dylan? I mean not really too soon to meet someone, but are *you* ready for this?"

I chuckle and shake my head even though she can't see it.

"Not like I fell in love ma, I met her years ago when I was on the run from home. Remember that summer when I found out that I was adopted and I just took off? I met her then."

Silence again. I know I acted like a spoiled, ungrateful brat back then. The minute they told me I was adopted I took off, ran away basically. I told them, no, I screamed in their faces that this news should have been broken to me ten years prior.

"Oh." I know she's thinking, she never responds with a short oh, or ok, so I wait.

"So you still like her after all these years? Does she like you? It has been what, six years since that trip?" I have no fucking idea how to answer any of this.

Yes, I still like her after all these years. She's even hotter and better if you ask me.

revival

No, she seems not to like me that much.
But she kissed me.
Great kiss by the way.
But is that enough? Enough to stay here and hope for something? For what exactly?
"Do you think I should head home?" I know she will give me the most honest answer.
"No"
"No?" I smile to myself.
"I know it will sound stupid coming from me, but if she helps you forget about Mia, then stay. See where that will take you, and if it gets you nowhere at the end of the day, at least you will have moved on from fear of trying, and that's a huge step."
Why do I have the feeling that she is telling me to do what she did after my father died? I thought she loved him too much to let someone else in, even for a tiny second. I was wrong. She loved my father unconditionally but was able to move on once she admitted to herself that he would never be here, next to her. And I only know this because few weeks ago Austin told me that he saw her at her favorite restaurant with some old dude holding hands and sipping wine.
"I love you." I say, and I really mean it. Probably more than all of the other times I said those words to her. I really do love her. For being there for me. All the time.
"Love you too, Dylan, just don't do anything stupid."
"I won't." I assure her, even though I'm not certain I can keep that promise.
We end the conversation just as I step into my room.
She was already here. The perfectly clean room indicates that.
I shower and then check my email, just to be

sure that everything is under control. Everything seems fine until I open an email from Trish, the head manager of the tattoo parlor I own.

Hi Boss!
I hope you are having a blast on your vacation, but we have an emergency. Well, not really the kind that you have to be here for, but Victor just got engaged and he's planning to get hitched at the end of this month. Everything is great, we all are happy for him, but she's from the East Coast, New York to be exact, and he is moving in with her after the wedding. He knows I'm writing this to you, you know how big of a pussy he really is. Honestly, I have no idea how any woman would commit their life to him, she must be crazy.
Anyway, we are going to be short staffed in a few weeks and my questions is, do you want me to hire someone, or you want to do it yourself? I know I'm the manger and shit but I feel weird to making this kind of decision.
Let me know,
Trish.

I read it twice and I smile to myself. There is no other person on this planet that is sweeter than Trish. I rub my eyes for a second trying to make a decision. I know I trust her. I know she will never hire some douche bag to work in there, but what would Mia think of that? What would she think of me letting her staff run her business?

I can't. I fucking can't live in the past like this.

Trish,
It's up to you who you hire- I trust you will make a good choice. Tell Vince I will be there if

revival

I can manage. If not, tell him that I'm so fucking happy for him to have found the other half he was always searching for.

P.S. You're the Boss, so stop calling me that, otherwise you are fired.

I smile to myself just imagining Trish's face when she opens this email. Busted.

I approve all of the emails Austin sent to me and then I do something I haven't done in a long time, I put my Bose earphones on and listen to music. I close my eyes and let the words penetrate my broken soul, let them heal whatever is broken, and formulate hopes for everything that is yet to come.

I take a seat at my usual spot in Travis' section, I've been avoiding Kelly's spot for weeks now. She's too much of a tease and I'm way too lonely. Besides, I don't want to give the wrong impression to Nina. Kelly is nothing to me, always has been. I kept her as a distraction from everything because that's all I knew. All I knew until I brushed my lips over Golden. My Golden. How pathetic that sounds when she is nowhere near mine. She might never be mine for all I know, but the thoughts of her being mine swirl around like a tornado.

I watch her deal with her tables and I can tell that the little smile she has on her face is fake. I know this much about her. I watch all those guys wave their hands at her and I die a little every time she goes over to their tables, smiling and being super friendly. I know it's her job, I know she is here to make money, but why the hell does she work two jobs back to back? She's only twenty-seven for

Christ sake and I have never met a twenty seven year old who works so much. Sure, they work to cover school, but she definitely is not attending school. Sure, they work to help their parents, but from what I remember, she is here alone.

Questions.

No answers.

I gesture to Travis to give me a pen, and as soon as I hold it in my hand I write.

"Can you put it somewhere she will find it?" I ask him, and the eyes I meet are not the eyes of a friend anymore.

"What are you doing?"

What am I doing? I can't even answer that question myself so why the fuck does he think I will answer him?

"Can you?" I repeat holding his stare.

"Sure." He grabs the napkin and heads over to the second bar. I watch him place the piece of paper next to her computer.

"Happy now?"

"Thanks."

"You know you will be hunted by every person in this club if you hurt her, including me, right?"

Everyone is being so fucking protective.

"I know." I swallow whatever I have left in my glass, looking at the napkin lying next to the computer.

I watch her pick up the white folded napkin, the slight frown on her face turns into a smile, although she is biting her bottom lip slightly.

I smile.

Then she turns around and everything stops. Suddenly I feel stupid for sending that note to her. Suddenly I feel foolish for asking her to come to my room.

But she is still smiling and there is something

revival

else radiating from her eyes that makes my smile spread wider.

And then I breathe. Blowing all the anxiety away.

She will come. She will knock on my door and once I open the door, she will step in, forgetting everything and knowing me.

Only me.

———•●•———

At 1:47 am, I hear the soft knock at the door and I jump out of bed, rushing to it. She's here. She is really here. I wasn't sure she would really come.

I take my time and look through the peephole, her big blue eyes wide, her expression unsure. She runs her fingers through her hair to put it in place.

"You came." I open the door wide and let her in.

"Wouldn't you?" She takes the napkin from her pocket and puts it between us. "Stop by my room." She read it loudly.

"I forgot to add please."

"No you didn't," she gives me a wicked smile and heads right for a minibar. She opens the door and points to bottle of vodka. "Can I?"

"Be my guest." I nod and put my hands in my pockets in order to keep them out of trouble. She is trouble. She might look innocent but I know she will be trouble soon.

She takes a few, long gulps of whatever liquid was inside and then she puts the empty bottle on the counter, looking me straight in the eye.

"So, you wanted me to come here, huh?" Her words come out way too easily. She was never that easy with her words. Not towards me. I look at her and her eyes are blazing hot, dancing all over my body.

"Are you drunk Golden?" I raise my brows in disbelief.

I watch her smile grow and her body rises from the stool she was just sitting on. Fuck me. Those eyes are pinned on mine and that perfect body swinging my way is too much. My dick twitches and my balls tighten at the thought of her doing anything to me.

"Yes," she is standing close enough to make my heart pound hard and fast in my chest, "I'm drunk on you." Her fingers trace my cheek, traveling to my mouth and I can't help but to touch her in return. Her tiny hand slides from my shoulders to my pecks, tracing a path over my abs and popping my jean button open faster that I can register what is going on. "What do you say to that?" Her hand slips lower, brushing my already glistening head.

"No underwear," she moans in my ear, "I like."

Fuck, that gets me even harder.

Her hand is now gripping my cock. I watch her close her eyes while a slight moan escapes her now parted lips. Her hot breath sends chills to every little cell in my body.

She's beautiful like that.

Her hand slowly slides up and down my shaft, making it almost impossible to fight the urge to throw her up on my counter and get deep inside her.

I shouldn't. She's slightly drunk, and I believe that the alcohol is responsible for her sudden bravery.

Her hand moves faster, my breath matches the strokes of her hand while I watch her. Watch her give me the hand job I've been fantasizing about ever since I first saw her.

I would kill for that mouth to wrap around my dick.

I grab her by her waist and pick her slightly up,

revival

take a few steps, and place her on the counter. Her legs are wrapped around me, her hand is still, eyes pinned to mine.

"What are you doing Golden?" As soon as this comes out of my mouth her hand leaves my cock, her eyes fill with regret.

"I... Shit I don't know, I'm sorry." She wiggles and I know she is trying to get out, but there is no way that I'm letting her escape right now.

"Don't be sorry, just tell me. What are you doing?" She looks at me like I've lost my mind, like I'm talking nonsense.

"I don't know." I can see her eyes well up with tears and the last thing I want is to see her cry right now. I watch her drag her teeth over her bottom lip and I instantly bring my hand to her face, running my thumb along her lips.

She stills. There is a tension between us so strong, so dense that you can almost see it.

"I can't." Her words are so quiet that I'm not sure they are meant for me.

"You can't? Or you wont?" I watch her eyes close, her face molding into my hand.

"I ca..."

That was what I wanted to hear. I don't let her finish, my mouth is already covering hers.

I dip my head down and brush her lips gently, just a tiny little touch. She sighs into me, causing me to press my lips harder to hers. I have thought about this for quite some time now. I've fantasized about tasting that mouth again, showing her what kind of power she holds over me. But being here, right now, touching this velvet like mouth, there is nothing that can compare to the kiss I have brewing in my mind.

I press my lips harder against hers, demanding access and she doesn't refuse. Her hands are now tangled in my hair, bringing me closer to her. Our tongues are dancing together in perfect rhythm, like they were made for each other. My head feels light and I don't feel the guilt or sorrow that I thought I would feel touching another girl like this. No, in fact, it's the total opposite. I feel like I've been waiting for this all along, like her mouth was made for me, and only me.

I break the connection slightly – not because I need to catch my breath, I don't. Breathing the same air as her is enough for me to live in his moment- I break the connection to simply look at her.

"Golden." I whisper into her mouth. It just feels good to say her name, my name for her, like that.

"Dylan." The whisper I get in return is louder than thunder.

Our eyes are lost in one another. As if we are trying to find out everything about the other within their depth. I could stare at her eyes forever, fascinated by their magical shade. Like the bottom of the ocean, or the sky just before night fall. Mystery.

Her hand curves at the base of my neck, bringing me back to her. I don't hold back this time. I go full force, showing her how I feel about her right now.

Nina

I shouldn't be here and I shouldn't be doing any of this but it feels so good, too good to stop right now. His hands, his fingers send jolts of electricity through my entire body, waking me up in a way nobody has for so long. Too long.

His hands slide down my back and dive under my shirt, tracing my ribs, going higher, hooking under the lace of my bra. I arch my back and push myself firmer against him, hoping he will proceed. And that he does.

My shirt slides over my head, silently landing on the floor.

My bra frees my breasts and I watch him suck in air while his eyes roam over my naked chest.

"Jesus Christ." It's all he says before his hands cup my breasts and his mouth covers my right nipple.

I lean back, propping myself up on my elbows, head thrown back. My mind swirls, making me dizzy. The sensation is too much, it's growing like a balloon, pushing on every nerve of my body, expanding but having nowhere to go.

His hands slide up my bare legs, hiking up my skirt in the process. As they reach the top of my thigh, they don't stop. They travel higher and higher. Slowly. Over the thin lace that is now the only thing between us. I don't even breathe anymore, I forget that simple necessity the moment he touches me.

"Oh God." There is nothing between us now. His fingers are part of me now, exploring my secrets. His mouth is sucking my needy breasts, one by one, giving them equal attention. The heat in my core is unbearable, as I start to feel a familiar tingle overtaking my body. I can't help but repeat his name over and over. "Dylan." Over and over. Waves travel through me and I get lost in the sea of pleasure.

"Thank you." His voice is suddenly next to my ear, his rigid body hovering over mine, eyes dark, yet gentle.

"Thank me?" The surprise in my voice is evident.

"For this." He presses himself to me while covering my mouth with his. My fingers work fast over the buttons of his shirt, then his jeans. I don't dare break the connection of our lips. When I grip him in my hand and feverishly guide him towards my entrance, he stops, his eyes dark, breath fast and shallow.

"Is this what you want?" I nod, not wanting to waste time with unnecessary words. "Tell me."

"This is what I want. I want you Dylan." Honestly, I would say whatever he asked me to say at this very moment. I hear him growl and the next thing I know, he carries me into his bedroom, laying me gently on his cold sheets.

"You're beautiful Golden." His hands trace a path along the sides of my body. His eyes drinking in every inch of me, like he is trying to fill up for days to come.

"So are you." He is. His tanned, toned body is made for moments like this. Moments of pleasure.

His lips mark every inch of my body, spreading a path of fire along my skin.

His hands are busy on me and mine are busy exploring him.

"There is much more to you than just your

revival

beautiful body, Golden. I want you to know that I'm becoming addicted to every single thing about you." His mouth traces a line down my ribs and I shiver at both his touch, and his words.

"Please..." I beg him, "I need to feel you."

He leans over his night table, foil crinkles and seconds later, his head is teasing me, a little preview of what's to come.

"Are you as ready for this as I am?" I don't get a chance to respond as he starts sliding inside me, causing my breath to stop, my hips to buckle. My legs wrap around him, asking him to go all the way.

Our bodies dance together in the most intimate way possible, skin, mouth, hands. Altogether bringing me closer to the top, the high that might be the end of me.

And soon I let go, fireworks dance under my eyelids, my body erupting like a volcano, exploding with so much force that I can feel the earth shaking. I never thought this moment would come again, but here I am, having the best orgasm I've had in years, from someone I tried to erase from my life for so long.

My body is limp and spent under his, my breath slowly comes back to normal, and a smile spreads on my face.

He lifts his head from the crook of my neck, kissing the tip of my nose, smiling down at me, turning me to the side next to him. His arms wrap firmly around me and I scoot closer, burying my face in his chest.

"I have to go."

"Stay." His fingers tease my naked body like a feather.

"I can't."

"Why not? You work here in a few hours anyway." His lazy voice is quiet, yet it hits me like he is talking thru a megaphone.

Shit. Panic. Guilt.

"Shit." I slide out of his arms and rush towards the clothes scattered on the floor.

"What's going on?" He is right next to me, standing buck naked, watching me get dressed. All I really think about is to be naked again.

"I have to go, I'm sorry. I... I have to be somewhere before work and I can't go like this." I gesture to my wrinkled outfit. I walk to the bathroom and try to fix my hair. I'm doing my best to avoid looking at my flushed face and sparkling eyes that only remind me of how great the last hour was. I step out after making myself decent at last, and see Dylan standing next to the exit door, fully dressed, ready to go.

"You didn't for a second think that I would let you walk out by yourself, did you?"

"I was kind of hoping for it." Crap, that was too harsh. "Really Dylan, I can walk by myself. No big deal."

He shrugs. "There is nothing I have to do anyway so..." He opens the door and gestures for me to exit. I step out in the hall and he is right next to me, walking by my side. He presses the elevator button but I head for the stairs.

"Let's use the back door, I don't want anybody to see me here." He nods like he understands although a tiny wrinkle on his forehead makes an appearance. It's true though, I know most of the people who work here and what would I say if I stumbled across someone at such an hour? That I just had sex with one of the guests? Oh gosh.

"Are you ok? You look nervous."

Terrible. Ashamed of myself. Like a cheater. Like the worst mother on earth.

"I'm fine, just tired." His hand wraps around my

shoulder and he places a quick kiss on my head as we exit into the hot night. That feels too good, so good.

"So when are you leaving?" I ask him while we walk down the street.

"Nina, just because I acted like an asshole years ago, doesn't mean I will do it again." He takes my chin and lifts it up so I have no other choice but to look at him. "And to answer your question, I don't know. I haven't given it a single thought yet." He kisses me gently and we resume our walk.

While we pass our regular coffee shop, he leads us to the right and my senses pick up, panic swirls over me as I realize he knows where to go.

"You know where I live?" The anger that laces my words must be more than visible, as he takes a deep breath without even looking at me.

"Yeah, that night you had a few too many shots, I followed you home to make sure you were safe." He shrugs and I say nothing.

He knows where I live. That means that he could have seen me, he could have seen more than me. He could have seen *us*.

"Relax Golden, I'm not a stalker."

I should be relived, but I'm nowhere near that feeling. I stop at the bottom of the stairs.

"See you around." I turn to walk away but his hand finds mine, and before I know it I'm standing next to him once again. His finger traces my face, stopping at the scar under my chin. I turn my head slightly to the side, letting him know that this makes me uncomfortable.

"Where did you get that?" There is nothing but pure curiosity in his voice. Still, I don't like it. This is going too far. So far that I keep losing track of what I can and can't deal with.

"Goodnight." I break the connection and head to

the door, fishing out the keys from my purse.

"Or good morning." He chuckles and I look at the sky that is no longer dark. Rays of sun slip in between the dark expanse.

"Or that." I step inside and take two stairs at a time, rushing to granny's apartment. I stop right before I knock and decide that I will pick up Ellie in the morning. I already regret tonight in a sense, and form a plan to explain myself to Gran.

My alarm buzzes way too soon. I swear I just closed my eyes and I have to get up again. I stretch in my bed and panic when I don't feel Ellie's little body next me. I sit up, and last night's memories come back to me like a tsunami. My body aches in places I didn't know it could ache, reminding me that what I did was wrong, very wrong.

I get up as quickly as my body will allow and drag my ass to the shower, letting the water wash everything away.

Why does everything seem so easy at night?

Why do we feel like everything is possible when the sky is covered in stars and the moon is shining at us?

Every single idea seems like a jackpot. And that damn confidence that pumps in our veins makes everything happen.

And then the sun comes up, washing everything away, leaving us with nothing but shame, guilt and foolishness.

The night is a sneaky bitch and we fall under her spell every time.

Over and over again.

I dress quickly and head to Gran's. I'm nervous,

revival

which is an understatement. My hands are sweating as I take slow steps up, trying to come up with a legitimate explanation as to why I didn't pick up Ellie last night.

Her door opens before I even knock.

Crap.

"Is everything ok?" Her tired but very sharp eyes scan my face quickly.

"Yes, sorry the shift ended really late I didn't want to wake both of you."

"Mommy!" I bend over so her little hands can wrap around my neck. I lift her up, kissing her like a maniac. "I slept with grandma and she was telling me this story about a little princess who lost her puppy, but then she went to the forest and found the puppy, and his mommy and she took them both to her castle. Can we get a puppy mom? Please, pretty, pretty, please?"

"We will see about the puppy sweetheart." I kiss her forehead and send a piercing look towards Gran.

"She likes dogs." She shrugs and turns around to head to the kitchen. "So, are you planning on stopping by after work today?" Her voice is mocking. I've never heard that tone come out of her mouth before.

"Yes." There is nothing more that I can say to this.

After I play with Ellie for a little bit I head out, sending a short "see you later" towards my grandmother. I know she doesn't buy that lame explanation about work being late. I always stop and pick up Ellie even at the latest hour. Another lie that I told her. Lies are devious things, covering the truth, making everything easier, until it's not anymore.

My heart feels heavy while I walk down to the coffee shop, thinking about how selfish my actions were last night. I lacked judgment, went to him, compelled by the impulse that was bigger than me at that moment.

I will never make that mistake again.

Nina

I haven't written anything for weeks, the last song I wrote was driven by hate. It doesn't seem like a good one to sing tonight, even though there is this tiny part of me that still dislikes him, there is a bigger part of me that gets completely, undeniably lost in his presence.

    I sit backstage with the boys and try to decide the final songs for the night. We didn't shake up much in the past few weeks, so we need to step it up to keep the crowd excited. We add a few songs that we had practiced, and just before we end the meeting, I add a Jason Walker song.

    "We've never practiced that, Nins." Oscar's voice is full of concern.

    "I have, and I'm sure that since you are geniuses, you will be able to pull it off." I'm met with their surprised eyes and I know I went too far. "Sorry, I'm just exhausted, you know you can do it, we still have hours before we hit the stage. I believe in you." I add putting my hand on Oscar's shoulder.

    Travis's eyes are fixed on me as I head to the bar. The expression on his face is unreadable and I frown, looking him straight in the eyes. Strange. I know his looking at me has nothing to do with trying to catch my interest. I've seen him speak with Dylan a few times, but I know the drill. All of the bartenders make conversation with costumers hoping to get higher tips. All except for Kelly, she hopes for far more sometimes. Most of the time.

"Hi Nina." Travis calls to me in his slight drawl.

"Hi." I call back and try to remember where it is that he comes from.

"You kicking it tonight?" He nods toward the stage.

"That's what the schedule says." I round the bar and pour myself a cup of soda. I bring the drink to my lips, watching him as I slowly drink.

"Cool, I love it when you hit the stage, quite the entertainment." He winks at me and heads in the opposite direction, ready to serve someone who just walked in. I frown and head back to the floor for my round, plastering a smile on my face.

I really hope Dylan won't be here tonight, not that I don't fancy seeing him, but I'm afraid that his presence will bring the back the sweet memories from the other night. The memories that will bring want, and that want will bring action. This vicious circle could be the end of more than just me.

Four hours later, at the end of the second half of our show, I hear Oscar tuning his guitar, indicating that Jason Walker is what we will play next. I search the crowd in a slight panic, hoping he is not here, that he will not listen to this performance.

I close my eyes. Deep breath. Mic to my mouth...

I don't know where I'm at.
I'm standing out the back
And I'm tired of waiting.
Waiting here in line
Hoping that I'll find
What I've been chasing
I shot for the sky
I'm stuck on the ground
So why do I try?
I know I'm gonna fall down.
I thought I could fly

So why did I drown?
I'll never know why
It's coming down, down down.

I do my best to hold back the tears that are pushing their way out, trying to free themselves from the prison of my eyelids. Doing my best to finish my performance.

The applause I get at the end was worth the soul baring, heart wrenching performance.

I high five each member of the band and head down to the floor to resume my shift.

In this second I'm hit with deja-vu, a moment from six years ago, as I see Dylan standing with Ritchie next to the bar, both looking in my direction.

"You never disappoint Nina." Ritchie puts his arms around me, giving me a friendly squeeze. I return the gesture, my eyes fixed on Dylan.

"You did awesome, if you had balls I would say you kicked ass." Dylan's voice is now hovering above my head. His lips touching the top of it.

"So you say vagina can't kick ass?" I call back.

"You know what? In your case, it can happen." His hand grabs mine while he sends me one of his pantie melting smiles. I take a quick look towards Ritchie and find him looking around the bar completely ignoring both of us. Good. The last thing I need is someone aware of my affection towards this random tourist standing next to me.

"I still remember your taste in my mouth, Golden." His voice is now loud in my ear, his breath warming not only my earlobe, but my whole body.

I swallow the lump in my throat. "Do you?"

"I do, and I can't fuckin' wait until I taste you again."

Oh my God, did he just say what I think he said? My legs tighten and my heart skips a beat while the memories that involve him run through my head like kaleidoscope.

"I have to go." I withdraw my hand from his and head to grab my apron, meeting Kelly's eyes. She obviously saw everything. I put my apron on, take my notepad and pencil out of the pocket, and head out on the floor.

"What is going on Nina? Huh?" Granny's voice is hushed as we sit in the kitchen, eating the spaghetti she cooked earlier. I keep my head down, eyes pinned on the fork, trying to swirl a noodle over it. I knew this question was coming but I never put a logical answer together.

"Nothing, what do you mean?" I put the fork full of spaghetti in my mouth and suck in the rest like a five-year-old.

"I thought you agreed to be honest with me." She sounds disappointed. There is nothing that breaks my heart more than making her feel like that. But if I reveal the ultimate truth I will break her. If I confess to something that I've kept from her all along, I know I will lose everything that we have shared.

"You have been different since the last time you were *too tired* to pick up Ellie. Something's happened, should I worry about it?"

"Nothing to be worried about." I scrape the rest of my plate and head over to the sink to rinse it off before placing the plate in the dishwasher.

"Ellie, let's go princess." I call into the living room while I gather my stuff, ready to leave. I try to ignore Gran watching my every move, making me uncomfortable.

"I hope it's nothing Nina, I really do." Her voice is

quiet but I register every single part of it.

"See you tomorrow, Granny." Ellie places a kiss on her cheek as we head out the door, down the stairs to our apartment. To the little heaven that we call our own.

Dylan

I step into the deli wearing my gym clothes, I don't really stress about the fact that I'm probably smelly. I need breakfast and this deli serves the best damn coffee and egg sandwiches around. Plus, I hope she will stop by for a java fix and I will get a glimpse of her in the daylight. I hate that the only places I can see her are at the bar and the hotel. She has little, if any time off between her jobs. I don't even try to ask for the time in-between. So the few minutes before she heads over to the hotel are priceless to me. Sometimes she seems like a different person when I see her at the bar, distant, unreachable.

In the morning sun she shows a totally different side of herself. Real, raw, genuine. The side I admire so much. The side I want to explore.

I order my usual and Amanda smiles at me with her mega watt smile. She hands me three coffees, two chocolate croissants and a bacon and egg and cheese sandwich. I return the smile and head to Mr. Santiago's table, placing everything in front of us.

"If you keep feeding me extra chocolate I might never fit in that door again." He chuckles but reaches for the treat. "How do you know she's coming?" He gestures at the extra coffee on the table.

"I don't." I answer simply and sink my teeth into the hot sandwich. I avoid his eyes, they are watching me carefully and he has a slight smile on his face.

We spent the next half an hour talking about my

revival

work, and I'm surprised how much he knows about international investments. Honestly, if he were younger I would hire him, right on the spot.

"Good morning, Hector." A sweet, yet aged voice greets my companion. Hector? I smile a little, finally able to discover his first name. I turn around to see an old lady standing next to me, holding hands with a little girl.

"I know you." The little voice speaks to me before I'm able to realize that I remember these two from the beach the first or second day that I arrived.

"You do indeed." I stretch my hand toward her, "I'm Dylan." Her little hand tries to get a grip on mine, and a big smile spreads across her face.

"Nice to meet you Dylan, I'm Ellie Price." I feel her little hand shake mine.

My heart skips a beat as I look into her eyes, eyes that resemble mine. I raise my eyebrows and turn my attention to the woman standing next to her, her grandmother, I believe.

"Simone Price." Her eyes are stone cold, penetrating me like I'm some kind of convict. A shudder goes down my spine. I turn to the table and pick up the cup of coffee, trying to busy myself.

"Simone, I haven't seen you in ages." Hector's voice is sweet, lovely even. He seems hypnotized by her presence. Holy shit! This old man, sitting here, eating chocolate every day even though he hates it, has a soft spot for this old lady. The one that just took a seat next to me, her granddaughter next to her.

"Oh stop it Hector, you know I'm busy." She answers and I see that she's blushing, but she keeps her eyes on me. Penetrating my every cell.

"So did you find more of the white ones?" Ellie questions me while biting into the croissant Hector pushed her way.

"No I didn't, I didn't really look for any to be honest." I can't stop staring at her face, she looks so familiar, with her grey eyes and that little dimple in her chin when she smiles...

My mind goes into overdrive while I look between the little girl, her grandmother and Hector. They look at me with the same amount of disbelief, like they just discovered something on their own.

"How old are you?" I ask the little girl, but my eyes are set on Simone.

"Six." She says while biting into her croissant, trying to get as much chocolate as she can, "No, five really, I will be six in May. I know that is almost ten months away, but I can't wait to be six!" I quickly do the math and it fits perfectly. Pregnant for nine months, I left New Orleans in August six years ago. Fuck. I look between the two old folks sitting with me, and I can see the shock on their faces. Shit. At least I'm not the only one feeling dizzy right now.

"And this here is your mommy, I suppose?" I question her grandmother, even though I already know the answer. But I need to hear it, I need to hear her name out loud to be absolutely sure. To be able to accept this fact.

She giggles at that. "No silly, my mama's name is Nina, she's at work. This is my Gran, my great-grandmother." I see her great grandmother sigh loudly while I run my hands over my face. Hoping this is not real, that I'm somehow dreaming.

I hear Hector clear his throat. "How is that chocolate croissant of yours honey?" He points to the croissant. I take advantage of that second to steal a look at the expression on Simone's face. Stone cold. Nothing. The surprised expression is gone, she is sitting here like this is not the biggest news of all.

I put my hands in my pocket fishing for my cell phone, but I pull them out right away. Calling her is not the right way to find out about this. I want to see her face when she tells me that this is real.

"Excuse me," I stand up. "I have to go." They both nod their heads in understanding but when I look at Ellie, she seems disappointed.

"We just got here." The frown on her face is killing me.

"I'm sure we will see each other soon." I tell her, and I believe it. I fucking believe that I will see her soon, very soon.

As I enter the hotel lobby I try to come up with a way to approach Nina in my head. Should I play stupid and ask her if she has kids? Should I play stupid and tell her that I've met this sweet grandmother with an adorable granddaughter at the coffee shop? A few options spin through head and I stop short at my wide open door, her cart parked outside. I walk in slowly and find her changing my sheets, her ears plugged by earphones, her mouth singing the lyrics.

God, she is fucking perfect like that. I'm suddenly brought back to that night when she gave herself to me, and my dick screams for attention. My balls tighten. The only thing I want to do is grab her from behind and fuck her senseless over my bed.

But I have to do something first.

I walk behind her and reach for her headphones, pulling them down as gently as I can. Her wide eyes meet mine as she turns around.

Fuck me.

Stick to the freakin' plan Dylan.

"You scared me." I watch her mouth move. The desire to kiss her overtakes me. I lean down and brush my tongue over her lips.

"Is it true?" I ask teasing her mouth with mine.

"Is what true?" Her breath comes faster on my lips, her hands grabbing my neck, bringing my face to hers.

"That we have a daughter." She freezes. Her lips, her tongue stops moving. Her hands dig into my neck instead of teasing it.

"What did you say?" Her words are slow, venomous.

"Is Ellie mine?" I keep my lips on hers, and I feel her breath speed up, her mouth closes while pressed to mine.

"How did you... how?"

"I saw her." I move my lips to her forehead, where I place a small kiss. "There is no denying that she is mine."

I feel her tears hit my t-shirt and I pull her closer to me. All I want right now is to give her comfort, to make sure she knows that this didn't freak me out. Or maybe all I really want is to bring comfort to both of us, to make sure that this discovery didn't freak both of us out.

Because in reality it did. I can't even gather my thoughts. I couldn't even think straight when I saw those little grey eyes looking at me. The thought that those eyes are mine, that they are from me, that her genes carry the best and the worst of me, hopefully best, is terrifying.

How could she keep this from me for so long?

"I'm sorry." Her tears are now all over me, her shoulders shaking, her hands gripping my shirt.

I let her cry even though I want to know every single fucking detail of her past. Of their past. Of my past.

Theirs.

My daughter.

revival

The word doesn't register yet, I know I'm a father. I know I have a daughter that is the splitting image of me. I know she is already a little smart ass like me, but my stubborn brain is not letting it register fully.

When her shoulders stop shaking, I bring her face up and force her to look in my eyes. "Tell me."

I don't have to say anything more than this, she knows what I want her to tell me, she knows what I want to know.

"I..." She takes a deep breath. "I didn't know she was yours until she was born."

I nod my head and try to calm my ragged breath. She didn't know until the baby was born? That only means she was with somebody else, maybe more than one after me. I know I have no right to be upset. Not a single fuckin' right since I left her the moment the sun started to rise, but still. This shit stings.

"It's alright." I rub her back and repeat the words to myself, hoping I will start to believe it. *It's alright.*

Honestly, I have no idea where this news will take me, where this will take both of us. Anger and surprise it is not a good mixture. I'm doing my best to keep somewhat calm while standing next to her. But my mind is fucking racing.

A noise comes from the front of the suite and we both turn our heads to find another cleaning lady standing in the middle of my living room, her eyes wide, staring at our entwined bodies.

"Nina?"

She breaks away from my arms and heads for the exit. "Everything's alright Regina." I hear her saying with trembling voice. "I'm done here."

And then they walk out. Like nothing happened. Like we just didn't have the most important conversation. Just like that.

Ohhh honey we are not done. We are not even close.

I try to busy myself with something. Try to get my mind of this life changing news. I open the computer and stare blindly at the emails that await my attention. I don't reply to any of them, leaving all that to Austin.

A thousand thoughts slide through my mind. The fact, that she was so distant towards me makes sense. The fact hat she was trying to protect herself from getting too close to me makes sense. The fact that she is working so hard makes even more sense. Fuck. She is working almost 24-7 trying to support herself and her daughter, my daughter. The daughter I should have been supporting all these years.

Six to be exact. It's like I was living in a fucking coma, not knowing there is a part of me, a beautiful part of me that was growing up without knowing me.

I wonder what Nina told Ellie when she asked about her daddy? What she said to her about being the only one to raise her? I hope to God she didn't paint a dark picture of me. I hope to God that I'm still welcome and that I still have time to make everything right.

I want to make everything right. I don't mean just making everything right with Nina, although I'm not gonna lie, I would love to give it a shot. At this moment, the only person that I want to make it right with is with my daughter. *My daughter!*

I. Am. A. Father.

I'm a father to someone who doesn't know me.

But I will change that. Really soon.

In fact, I will begin this change right now.

"We have to talk." I stand in front of her few hours later, as she is exiting the bar.

"There is nothing to talk about, you know the truth now." She walks past me and I walk behind her, trying to keep pace with her.

I rub my hand over my forehead trying to relieve the tension. Doesn't work.

"Why didn't you tell me?"

"There was never a good time, besides why would you care?" Her words sting like a giant jellyfish.

"Why would I fuckin' care?" My voice is now loud, causing a few pedestrians to turn their heads in our direction. "She's my daughter for fuck's sake Nina! That is exactly *why* I care!"

I watch her eyes dance around me, never landing on me. As if she is doing her best to pretend I'm not here. I swear to God, I'm trying to remain semi-calm. I clench my jaw and stand patiently, waiting for whatever she might or might not say.

"Why, Golden?" The words cut my throat as I try to push them out. I watch her take a deep breath, then blow the air out.

"You left the minute you fucked me Dylan, you didn't care about anything after that! Is that enough to refresh your memory?! Is that enough to give you the answers you are so desperately looking for?!" She is screaming in my face now and I have nothing to say. It's true. I left her in the morning. I didn't know. How could I?

"How the fuck was I supposed to know I got you pregnant that night? How? You should have called me! You should have let me know, you should have let me be part of all of this!" Now I'm moving my hands all over, running them through my hair, waving them in the air and then landing on my head again. I'm a fucking ticking bomb that might explode any second. I can feel the explosion is coming soon, I can't take it anymore. My emotions are not going to calm themselves down, just like that. Not anytime soon anyway.

"Well, I would gladly have done that if you had ever graced me with your phone number, but I guess at the time you didn't share your private info with every girl you met."

"You weren't just some girl, and you should know that." I hate that she thinks that way.

"Guess you changed your ways. It seems that every girl has your phone number this time." The malice in her voice is slowly penetrating my skin, making its way into my veins, causing my heart to convulse. "So yeah, Dylan, I think it's fair to say that you can pretty much blame yourself."

The blame is on me. All of it. She is more than right. I left, I never gave her my phone number. I disappeared, leaving her with all the problems. Our problems. Sure, I had no goddamn idea about any of this, but still...

"You should have tried harder." I spit and turn around, fire raging within me. I know I can't stay here a second longer, I will say things I will regret forever. I have to go. I cross the street and walk back into the bar that I just walked out of. I walk inside and order a Jack on the rocks, triple. The redhead that was trying to hump my leg earlier sends me a sheepish smile and comes closer, and this time I let her. I let her grind her pussy all over my leg, let her move her sloppy, drunk mouth over my skin, let her slide her hands over the length of my cock. I let her do all of this. Because I'm pissed. Because I don't care about a single thing at this moment, and because there is nothing and no one that can make me stop.

"What the *fuck* are you doing?" My head snaps

up and the redhead stops moving her hand, her eyes lazily landing on my face, waiting for my next move. I reach down and push her hand back down, letting her know that she needs to keep going while I look at Travis, standing next to me. His eyes are fixed on the hand pumping my cock slowly. "You have to be fucking kidding me! Get the fuck out!" He screams at the cute redhead, tearing her from me, leaving my cock hanging out like a fucking homeless person.

"What the fuck Travis?" I yell putting my business back in place.

He looks at me for a few seconds, his pointer finger swinging in front of my eyes. "I fuckin' told you, you mess with Nina, you will have a ton of enemies on your tail. I'm one of them."

I bring my head in between my hands and shake it slightly.

"You don't know shit." I can't tell him the truth, as far as I know, nobody knows that I'm the father of Nina's child, and I will not give away the secret she kept for so long. She obviously has her reasons. Reasons I hope to find out soon.

Nina

I watch him walk away and my heart breaks into a million pieces, pieces I'm not sure could ever be put back together. There are simply too many of them and they are scattered all over the place. My heart has been broken so many times that putting it back together seems like an impossible challenge.

He walks into the bar across the street, the one that is filled with hookers and easy girls. We used to be like that a long time ago, I heard, but Ritchie kept his policy strict and blocked every single girl that was looking for a good time. Not the bar across the street though, they grew bigger every second we closed the door to the sluts, giving them the chance to stick their mouth somewhere else.

He walked right in there, probably getting a blowjob by now.

I'm furious. I'm livid. My emotions range from hate to lethal destruction. I barely talk myself out of walking into that shit hole and dragging him out. But he does not belong to me. He is not mine, and I have no business saving him.

In a way, I'm glad that he knows Ellie is ours, mine and his. But he doesn't know the most important part. The one reason I cannot get close to him. Yes, I slipped once, but that can never, that *will* never happen again.

He will hate me the second the truth comes out. That's why I don't want him close, I don't want

revival

feelings developing in either of us. Me, him or Ellie. It's much better, much safer when he is out. Out of our lives. We've managed for five years, we will manage in the future just fine.

———•●•———

"I saw him." Gran opens the door and looks intently into my eyes, keeping me in the hallway.

I don't say anything. I know exactly who she's talking about.

"He is Ellie's father, isn't he?"

I nod, the words are too hot to pass through my throat without burning me in the process.

"I can't believe you never told me, I should have known. She's nothing like Marcus."

Tears stream down my face and the next thing I know, I'm in her arms, feeling safe. For a moment I'm able to forget the mess I'm living in. My sobs are loud, I feel like they will never end. Her hands gently pat my back, she runs them through my hair, makes me feel like a little kid again. A little girl who would run to her every time things were falling apart. And yet here I am, twenty years later, doing the same thing.

"I'm sorry, I was so ashamed. I didn't know until she was born. I thought she was Marcus' baby the whole time. I would never have been with him if I knew the truth." I can't stop the sobs that are escaping me right now. The same tears that ran down my face almost every night as I watched my daughter fall asleep, every damn night since she was born.

"Honey, we are given the road we need to take to find the right turn, there are many curves along the way. There are many tempting signs that we want to follow, but remember that they will always bring us to the same place, no matter how much heartache we've been through, no matter how many dead ends we step into, we are always destined to find the end. And maybe this is your destiny, your ending Nina. Maybe this is it." She rocks me back and forth, like she did when I was little girl, running to her every time I felt lonely. "Don't try to fight it, don't run from it, run to it. If it doesn't work out, it means that you are still on the road, looking, searching. And remember sweetheart, that I'm with you no matter where you go," her arms tighten around me, "I'm always with you."

I allow myself to cry until I no longer have the power to produce a sound. It felt so good to let it all go. Years of guilt and years of keeping a secret that blew up in my face.

I wish I had the balls to ask her what the heck to do right now. How should I proceed from here? Should I tell him the whole story, or keep him in the dark until there is no other way, but to tell him?

Just follow your heart Nina, don't do anything stupid, I know what you want, but think twice before you make any kind of decision. Grans voice is ringing in my ears when I step into my apartment and put Ellie in bed

A tiny, soft knock on my door makes snaps me back to reality. A slight chill goes down my spine as I think of whom could it be. I don't get visitors. Ever. And I definitely don't get visitors at this hour. So this, someone knocking on my door, is more than suspicious.

I walk to the door on my tiptoes, my bare feet

revival

leaving nothing but silence in my wake. I get to the door and put my left eye to the peephole, my breath catches in my chest as panic runs over me. I grab the doorknob but hesitate to open the door.

"I know you are standing on the other side of this door, Nina." Dylan's muffled voice is quiet on the other side.

I don't move, knowing the reason for his visit. I'm not sure if I'm ready for this conversation. I'm not sure if I ever will be ready.

"Just open the door so we can talk."

I watch him through the hole, his eyes stare straight thru mine, even though he can't see me. My eyes wander over his face, admiring every inch of it. From the short cut hair, the tiny scar on the right corner of his lips to that cute dimple on his chin. That damn dimple.

"Golden, we can stare at each other like this the whole night, I'm game, but I'm not sure that doing this will solve anything."

Shit, he's right, the sooner I get this off my chest the better. I slide the three bolts I have on my door one by one before I turn the handle. I open the door, letting him in, as I take a few steps back.

"Is this neighborhood that dangerous?" There is a frown on his face and his thick eyebrows are pulled together, his eyes focused on me.

"It's necessary." I blurt out, moving to put my hands in my pockets, only to realize that I already changed into my pajamas. Great. Now I'm standing in front of him in my flannel Spiderman PJ's. Kill me now.

"I like that." He smirks, looking at my outfit. I roll my eyes but my lips twitch.

"Makes me feel special." I shrug.

"You are special Golden, you don't need a superhero costume to prove it." God, why is he always like this? Every time he opens his smart mouth my stomach does this weird somersault and I get weak in my knees. I swear he says this stuff on purpose, just to see me embarrassed. I clear my throat loudly.

"Why are you here?"

"You know why I'm here."

I know. I know it all too well.

"I told you everything that needs to be said." I walk to my sink and grab an empty glass, filling it with water and drinking while watching him walk my way.

"Actually," his eyes don't leave mine, making me pause with the glass half way to my lips, "I believe there is way more we need to discuss."

"There is nothing more." I regret the words as soon as they are out of my mouth. The painful look in his eyes makes me wish for a redo. "What do you want to discuss?" I put the glass down and cross my arms over my chest. I haven't forgotten that he walked into that slut hole and I'm still fired up about it. My thoughts are going wild just imagining what happened in there.

"I'm Ellie's father," he starts slowly. "That is something I learned less than twenty four hours ago, and surprisingly, not from you." His eyes narrow and I see his nostrils flare. "Would you ever have told me? Did you even consider telling me?" He walks closer to me, invading my personal space. His broad chest lingers over me, his eyes pinned on mine, and I'm not sure what emotion I see in them. There is a mixture of hate, hope, anger, and lust. I could go on and on listing them, but I'm too busy formulating my answer. Answer that I don't have actually. Would I ever tell him? No. Was I planning to? No. Never.

I created a perfectly happy family with me, Ellie and Gran. For a little while, I was mourning the loss of something incredible for my little girl. The loss of bond, loss of blood ties, but I got over the fact that she will never know who her real father is.

This secret was never supposed to peek its head out in real life, this was supposed to stay with me, be my little black secret until the very end. Be buried with me and never, ever be brought in the sunlight.

I never in a million years, in my wildest fantasies imagined him coming back here, stepping his foot in the same bar. Much less that he would recognize me.

Never.

I was so confident in my little fantasy that I never thought of a moment like this. I never thought about the explanation I would have to give to him when he found out.

He was never supposed to find out.

He shouldn't know.

But now he knows.

"That's what I thought, you would never fucking tell me." He steps away, his hands moving furiously through his hair, almost ripping it out with each swipe. "You would never have contacted me, you would keep this fucking secret and be fucking happy about it."

I stare.

There is nothing to say because this is exactly what I intended to do.

"Fuck, you would!" He smashed his hand on my kitchen counter and I was surprised it didn't bend under his punch. "You would." He repeated quietly this time, his head hanging low, his breathing shallow.

I know he's hurt.

I know I would be too.

To be honest, I didn't realize how powerful this information would be to him until right now.

I watch him lift his head and focus his red, bloodshot eyes to me. "You just killed me, and I thought I already knew what death was." He straightens up and walks out the front door, leaving it wide-open, the bright fluorescent light seeping into my apartment from the stairway. I don't really care that I stand here, in my kitchen, vulnerable, my door wide open for anyone to walk in. My cheeks sting from the tears rolling down, my heart aches.

For him.
For me.
For Ellie.

I cover my face with my hands and slide down the cabinets, letting out all the emotions of the five years where I tried to keep everything intact.

I lost him.
Again.
But this time he knows what he lost as well.

Dylan

"Book me a flight as soon as possible." I order Austin while hurrying to pack my bags.

I can't think. I can't process what is going on. All I know is that I need to get away from here. Far, far, fucking away.

"There is one in forty minutes that I can get you on, coach, one stop," he waits until I answer and I'm sure he's anxious, but I don't care what class I fly or how many stops I will have on my way. I just want to get out of here.

"Fine." I head to the kitchen and drop my stuff into the duffle bag. "Arrange a pick-up for my bike. I will put it in a monthly garage for now." I stop at the end of the counter.

"You gotta be shitting me." I murmur to myself.

"Christ, what now? You want me to unbook the flight?" Austin's annoying voice says in my ear.

"No fucking way." I spit as I grab the pink iPod and shove it in my bag. *I will listen to every single song on her iPod. Every single one.*

"Good." He breathes in relief and hangs up.

I taught him well. So well in fact, that he knows me like no one else.

I grab my stuff, call a cab and head to the airport. I know I'm escaping. I'm probably running like a fucking coward but she left me no choice. It's obvious she doesn't want me in their lives. I am a stranger, an intruder, a fucking thief that was hoping to steal some of her memories and make them my own. Memories of my little girl.

My little girl.

Fuck.

She looks just like me, only prettier, with blond curls falling around her cute face.

She has my eyes, my nose, my chin, and that damn little dimple that I was always ashamed of when I was younger.

She is mine all the way.

I get in the taxi and give the driver the airport as the destination.

I don't even know how I feel about all of this.

I'm happy and pissed at the same time.

Happy to have a daughter, someone who shares my blood and who is mine in a sense. The little human being that might inherit all my good characteristics. God forbid the bad ones.

Pissed, as I should have known about her the day she was born. The day Nina found out she carried my baby. My baby.

Pissed that she is working two fucking jobs to make ends meet. Now it all makes sense why she works that much, and I could, I should help her but I have no fucking idea how. She will never accept money if I offer it. I know this much about her.

Fuck.

I exit the cab and head to the security gate, walk through it and head straight for the bar.

I know I should stay away from booze, especially since I'm a father, that's what father's do, don't they? But fuck me, I need some booze to get me through the flight so I don't jump out of the exit window.

I take my assigned seat in coach, and even though the space seems tight, I'm not in the mood to complain. Instead, I ask for one of those little

revival

bottles of whiskey, getting a surprised look from the flight attendant and I decide to wait until we take off.

———•●•———

"Oh my God, Dylan." She brings her wrinkled hands to her face to wipe away the tears. "Oh my God." I watch my mother break down under the news that she is a grandmother. I told her everything, so she is well aware that she might not meet Ellie anytime soon, or ever. The possibility of that last part is more realistic.

"You have to make this right." She looks me straight in the eye. Shit. I know this woman and I know that this look, this particular one I know not to mess with.

"I did what I could, she hates me Ma." I've repeated the same thing hundreds of times today. "She doesn't want me in her life, in *their* lives." The last part is still hard to swallow.

"Bullshit." My mother spits out the words like venom and my eyes go wide at the 'curse' word she just said. I say nothing though. I just listen, sensing there is more she wants to say.

"That is BS Dylan, you obviously didn't make it right." I feel her eyes on me. "Did you pledge to be the best father you could be? Did you promise to never leave them again? Did you ask her to be with you for Christ sake? Because from the way I'm hearing it you are pretty fond of her. Did you ask her to give you a chance? Did you ask *them* to give you a chance to make this right?"

My mind skips all the curse words my mother just said and it goes straight to the questions about Ellie and Nina.

No.

I didn't ask them any of this, in fact I didn't even consider any of this.

I walked away and left them to themselves.

Just like they always have been.

Shit. Fuck.

Just like they always were.

I'm changing that. I will go there and make this right. Make it real and make them both know that I want to be in their lives. Day by day. Everyday.

I. Want. To. Be. Present.

I walk into the studio and Trish's eyes go wide. I laugh, she looks like a fucking fish that just saw a shark.

"OMG, boss you are here!" She cries and I hug her, I've truly missed her. "It's you right?"

"No Trish you are fucking stoned and I'm just one of the things you dream about." I squeeze her tight and step away, heading over to Vince.

"Fucking dream." I hear Trish mumble playfully. I smile, shaking my head. I've missed this crowd. This shop is probably the only place that feels like home.

"Hi Vince." I bring my arms around him and bring him close to me. "Fuckin' missed you man."

"Good to see you Dylan." He says back. I don't have to look at him to know that he is still thinking about the day I stormed out of here, when he was the one to break the tragic news to me.

"By the way, congrats." I wink at him, watching his smile almost tear his face apart.

"Thanks. You good man?" His eyes are scanning mine and I know, I just fucking know that he knows that something ain't right.

revival

"Yeah, good." I answer, even though my mind is a thousand miles away. I watch Vince tattoo his client, the light buzz of the needle calming my nerves, even though the needle is not diving into my flesh, yet.

I wait patiently for Vince to finish both of his clients. I don't waste time though. I sit back and draw my tattoo stencil. It comes out perfectly.

As soon as the customer walks out of his booth I step in, handling him my project.

He looks at it.

He smiles.

He looks at me.

His smile disappears.

"You sure?"

"Yes."

The needle buzzes on my chest and I feel butterflies in my stomach.

They will be engraved on me forever.

Both of them.

"There is no way you are not going back there, Dylan." My mother's voice is quiet, but demanding. "You owe them, God, what am I saying? You are the father, so there is no question that you will go back there, beg her to take you back, beg her to let you spend some time with my granddaughter, and then you will be good enough to bring them to me. Stat."

Stat? I shake my head in confusion, checking if I did in fact meet *my* mother for dinner. She just doesn't seem like her old self. There is something different about her, way, way different.

"Mom," I rub my forehead with my left hand and bring my drink to my mouth with my right. "She doesn't want to see me, I'm not going to stalk her in order to be close to my daughter."

"Why not?" Her question is light, spontaneous.

"What?" I take a big gulp of scotch. This is getting more interesting than I thought it would.

"Why the heck not Dylan?" My mother sips her martini; God knows how many she's had. My gut clenches at the question.

"She doesn't want me there. She erased me years ago and she made it clear she won't let me back in." I repeat again.

"Bullshit." I her my mother swear. I watch her walk inside the house. She comes back within a minute. She sits back at the patio table and reaches for the candle between us. My eyes expand as I watch her light a joint. A fucking joint.

"Ma?"

"Unhmmm?" She asks me, sucking on the joint.

"What is that?"

"Oh, please Dylan, cut me some slack. I was living like a nun most of my life, let me live." She winks at me and turns her head back while inhaling another drag.

Fucking joke!

I watch her finish the joint, even offering some to me, but after I declined she just frowned and kept going.

There is something wrong.

I can feel it.

She never acts like this, ever. Sure, she's had some cocktails here and there, but smoking weed?

"Mom, what's going on?" I keep my eyes on her and see her eyes water, her smile fading.

"Nothing, son." She looks into the distance.

"Don't lie to me, Mom." I press on, sensing that she is hiding something big from me.

"Just make everything right and bring my

granddaughter to me so I can have a chance to meet her before..." Her voice breaks and I watch a single tear travel down her cheek.

My heart rate picks up and my hand is wrapped around the glass so tight I might crush it. "Before what?" I make sure to keep my voice in check, but there is no denying the amount of pressure in it.

I watch her take a deep breath and turn her face to me, a sad smile on her tired face. "I just finished my last round of chemo, nothing major, I will be fine. That's what the doctors says anyway."

I don't hear anything after chemo, I can feel the blood pounding in my ears, blocking all other sounds.

"Chemo?"

"You know, treatment for cancer, the one when you get tons of poison injected to your body in hopes that it will kill that sucker called cancer, the one.."

"I know what fucking chemo is Mom!" I lose control over my voice the second my mouth opens. "Why don't I know about this? What kind of cancer is it?" Now I'm pacing on her patio, trying to go back in time and figure out how I could have missed all of this? How could I not see that there was something wrong? Am I that deep in my own shit that I became blind to everything that has happened with my loved ones?

"I found out in February, I couldn't tell you, not with everything you have been going through. You had so much on your plate already and after I found out that there was a one hundred percent chance of survival, I thought, I won't even worry you with this." I kneel next to her, my hands wrapped around her waist, my head resting on her knees.

"You should never keep things like that from me. Ever."

"Everything turned out fine, I will be fine."

"What kind of cancer are we talking about Ma?" I relax a little when her hands run over my head, in the exact way she used to when I was little boy. It feels good. Comforting. It feels like home.

"Lymph nodes, but they found it early so I will be ok," she takes a deep breath, "For now."

Guilt.

Once again, guilt is all I can feel.

It's like this emotion is stuck on me and doesn't want to leave anytime soon. Like it's engraved into my heart not planning to fade ever.

"And the pot?" I hear the smile in her voice. "It helped me get through the toughest part, and now I'm using it as my little escape. You can't blame me for it, you know?"

"It's ok Ma, just don't go crazy with it." I hug her gently and I already know my next move.

I already know that I will bring my ass back to New Orleans and do everything in my power to be the dad I want to be, and maybe more.

"Will it be ok if I leave for a while Ma?" I ask lifting my head to see her face.

"Only if you come back with my granddaughter."

"I promise you that." I take her hand and kiss it lightly, not really sure if I will be able to keep that promise, because it's not entirely up to me.

Nina

"How many birthday parties did you promise her in a year?" I ask Gran as I put the Cinderella decorations around my apartment.

"As many as she wants." By the sound of her tone I know she is not kidding. Great.

"Awesome." Her birthday was in May, the 30th to be exact, and now three months later we have another celebration since my lovely grandmother cannot say no to Ellie. She wanted a birthday party in the summer, before she starts Kindergarten in a few days, so she is having one. If only my own wishes were granted so easily.

It's been three weeks since Dylan disappeared, again. Three weeks since I walked into his room to do a final clean after his check out. To say that I was surprised would be an exaggeration. I knew he would be gone in the blink of an eye once he learned the truth. He seems good at this disappearing act.

Gran was more optimistic than I, telling me that this is typical man behavior and that he needs time to think, to digest the bomb that was dropped on him.

First of all, nobody dropped a bombshell him. He discovered the truth by himself, point for that.

Second, he shouldn't have run away, he should have stayed here no matter what to fight for what's his.

No, now I'm being a hypocrite. I pushed him

away this time. I didn't even offer him anything he could take. Not a single suggestion to hang out with us, with her. To get to know her, to get to know us.

I blew it.

"Ok, Gran, please promise me that when she asks you for another birthday party, you will remind her that her birthday is actually in May and that's when we will celebrate, alright?" I fill the bowl with freshly made popcorn and turn around. Gran's face is right in front of mine.

"I can't swear on it." She gives me one of her sneaky smiles, the one that says that she will probably agree to another party as soon as Ellie asks her.

I sigh and head over to the kitchen to grab more juice boxes for the kids.

"Did you have a good time?" I bring the covers up to Ellie's chin and tuck the rest tightly around her.

"The best," she mumbles half asleep. "Thank you, Mommy." Her sweet voice is the best thank you I could get.

"You are welcome, sweetheart, Happy Birthday." I kiss her cheek and curl up next to her, exhausted.

Once she is fully asleep, I reach for my phone and send Rachel some photos through that app she told me to get. Honestly, it's a life saver. We can talk like she is here, around the corner whenever we want, except for the annoying time difference when I'm awake and she is asleep. But for the most part, with my work at the bar and my going to sleep late every night, we manage to text every night.

I still can't bring myself to tell her about Dylan. I mean, what's the point now? He is not here anyway, and he won't be here anytime soon. He ran away.

Ran.

Away.

I don't think I should bring up this whole mess of a situation now. Not really.

She texts me after few minutes, saying she is heartbroken that she can't be here to celebrate with us.

That makes two of us, because I'm missing her more and more each day. It's been three months and the idea that we might never see each other again makes me sad. Yeah, let's face it, I will never be able to afford a trip to Europe and from what she has said, she cannot come here for ten years, so that puts our friendship on hold for quite some time. A very long ass time.

Dylan

I jerk awake as I feel the plane touch down. I open my eyes and peek out the window, not seeing anything except the few lights of the airport. My headphones are slightly crooked on my head, plugged into the pink iPod I was carefully holding, but that is now is laying on the floor. It must have slid after I drifted to sleep.

I'm nervous. I don't know if anything I have planned will actually work. I hope it will. I spent hours going over my plans with my mother. I won't take no for an answer. But right now I'm anxious. Nina didn't seem like she wanted me anywhere near either of their lives for some reason. A reason I would love to find out. Reason she guards so much, reason that stands in the way of my possible happiness. Of our possible happiness. All I know is I want to see my daughter. Get to know her. Let her get to know me. Make her aware of the fact that I want to be in her life, that I care.

I leave baggage claim and head for a taxi. This time my destination is not a hotel, but an ocean view home that I've rented. I don't want to meet Nina in a hotel room anymore, I know that limits my ability to see her as much as I'm hoping for, considering the fact that she works almost twenty four hours a day. I figure that will give me plenty of time with Ellie though, if they both agree to it. I fucking hope they will.

revival

I arrive at the house around eleven o'clock. After a quick shower I head over to the bar. There is no point in hiding my presence, delaying my announcement that I'm here. In fact, I want to get on with my plan as soon as possible.

I pay the taxi driver and exit the cab. I stand in front of the door and hear people going wild inside, clapping and applauding. And it hits me that it's Thursday, I'm just a step away from hearing Nina sing.

I walk in and suck in the air of the bar, familiar yet forgotten. The smile on my face disappears quickly once I lay my eyes on Travis. His eyes are stone cold, definitely not the welcome I was expecting. But I get it.

I left.

Again.

It seems I'm really good at that.

"Hey Trav." I stretch my hand over the bar and watch him hesitate to greet me.

"You are a piece of shit, you know that?" His palm meets mine and I shake it, just like we have countless time before.

"Heard that one before." I don't even force a smile, as it's pretty obvious the he has an issue that I don't have any intention of resolving right now.

"Sure you did." He turns around and I have a glass of whiskey sitting in front of me.

I turn my attention to the stage and there she is. Mic in her hand. Her round, sweet butt resting on the stool, eyes closed. Her hair loosely rests in front of her shoulders, stopping right at her breasts. Breasts I still remember the taste of. Breast that fit in my palms like they were made for me.

We were walking on the moonlight
And you pulled me close
Split second and you disappeared

And then I was alone.

I know that song. It was among the songs on her iPod and I've been listening to it for the past three months. Meghan Trainor. That's who it is.

I feel a heavy hand slap my shoulder and I see Ritchie as I turn around.

"I can't believe what I'm seeing, twice in a year? We should definitely put that on the wall of accomplishments." His voice is definitely not happy or welcoming, and that confuses me. Why are they all acting like I'm an intruder in this place?

"What can I say? I missed this place." I grin, bringing the glass to my mouth. I can sense some kind of tension and honestly, I don't get it.

"Is that so?" He eyes me wearily, his eyes flicking between the stage and me.

I think I know what his concern might be, but I won't be the one to bring it up first.

"Need to talk to you." He points his finger at me and heads towards his office, and I nod my head, following him inside. I'm not even inside before he starts talking.

"She's like a daughter to me Dylan, you think you can come here, have your fun and leave whenever you please? This shit ain't working like that in my club, not with Nina." His eyes send the message more clearly than his words.

"It's not what you think." I try to explain but I give up. Any radical explanation will involve telling him that Ellie is my daughter, and I definitely wouldn't share that info before I have Nina's permission to share it.

"You think I don't know?" His question makes my eyes focus and my jaw tighten.

"What do you mean Rich?" I frown in confusion.

"I know that Ellie is your daughter Dylan, I would have to be stupid not to see the resemblance. I know the two of you, you both are fairly close to me."

"You know? You knew it this whole time?" My jaw is clenching and I feel like a ticking fucking bomb.

"Not right away. I noticed the resemblance when she was about two or three, something like that." He lowers his head and I watch him take a few deep breaths, deliberating about something. "Anyway, you don't know shit about her and you have no idea about the life she leads, so be smart, take my advice and go home. Leave her alone. That's the best thing you can do."

I nod my head in a steady motion and try to gather my thoughts. He knew. He fucking knew and he didn't try to reach me, to give me some kind of heads up that I have huge, life changing responsibilities waiting for me.

"Sure Ritchie." I head to the door but turn around just before I twist the knob. "You have nothing to worry about."

"I mean it son, go back home."

Now I'm facing him again. I can't put this puzzle together. The pieces are somehow mismatched in a way I don't understand.

"I have a daughter Ritchie, I can't just go home and pretend she doesn't exist." Those words hurt me as they come out. Why wouldn't he want me to make things right? Why is he so eager to get rid of me? He always says that Nina is like a daughter to him, everybody knows that. So why wouldn't he want me to stay and fight for them? Instead he's pushing me out the door and trying to send me back where I came from.

"I don't get it." I cross my arms over my chest not ready to leave just yet. "You of all people should be on board with what I'm trying to do here."

I watch his head drop down once again, resting on his palms. There is a long pause, the only noise is the loud applause coming from the bar, the indication that Nina is probably walking off stage. An exasperated sigh escapes me. I so wanted to see her. I wanted her to walk down and see me waiting for her, just like old times.

Ritchie lifts his head, his blazing eyes drilling into mine.

"Go home Dylan, that's my best advice. You had your chance."

"I can't fucking believe the bullshit coming out of your mouth." I sneer, still standing next to his desk. He gets up and our eyes are on the same level, his full of anger, and I'm sure mine are nothing less.

"Get the fuck out boy, I mean it."

"I see." I nod and walk away from his office. I have no clue what his goddamn problem is and I don't think I really should care. He is one protective sonofabitch who is certain I'm unable to step up to the plate. That I can't take responsibility the way I should. That everything I touch turns to disaster. He is definitely right on some of that stuff, especially the last one, but I'm going to prove him wrong this time

As I step away from his office I think of how appealing it would be to head across the street and get shitfaced so I can stop thinking about all this nonsense. But then I will act like an asshole again, running, and I don't want to run anymore. Not when something as big as this is at stake.

I round the bar and meet Nina's cold stare. Her face doesn't really say anything. Nothing. Just a little scowl around her mouth that indicates that my presence is definitely not welcome.

"How are you doing?" I ask, coming closer to her. I fight the urge to lean down and kiss her. I nod instead, greeting her like I would greet an old pal. Fuck. That is not how I imagined things. Not at all.

"Listen, once you're done here, can we talk?" I

revival

watch her face closely, hoping for some kind of a sign that she is happy to see me. Instead, her face is like stone.

"There is nothing we need to talk about Dylan." She looks around the floor, pretending to check for anyone who might need something. "Why are you here?" Her lips curl and my eyes are focused on them. Remembering the taste, remembering the velvety way they felt. "Why. Are. You. Here. Dylan?" Her words are full of with hate, but her eyes betray her mouth in an undeniable way.

"You know why I'm here." I lean closer to her, her scent hits me like the morning breeze off the ocean. "Let's talk later." I push as soon as I see her eyes soften.

I watch her take a deep breath, her head going from side to side, checking our surroundings. "Talk." Her chin is raised high and I can see the challenge in her eyes flashing brightly at me.

Just by looking at her reaction I know I've lost this battle. I know she won't agree to talk in private and I get it. I do. It's just that I didn't really see it going this way. I thought she would be happy that I'm ready to step into their life and that I'm more than ready to be with them, now that I know they exist.

I wasn't ready for this. To talk inside a crowded bar surrounded by strangers.

But if that's her game, I will play it.

"I want in." It's all I need to say. Those three words make a powerful combination that states how I feel perfectly. I want in. I want it all and even though she is putting up walls, making it harder for me to go forward, I will break those walls down.

Because I want it badly.

Because I need it badly.

She raises her eyebrows like she doesn't

understand what I'm talking about. "I want to be a part of Ellie's life. I want to be present as much as I can. I want you to move to L.A., I will get an apartment for you. I will take care of you, of both of you. I don't want you to work two jobs, twenty hours a day to make ends meet. I'm here now, I got it." I watch her eyes grow big and I smile as soon as her lips form a smile. But mine quickly fades when she bursts into laughter. Right in my face.

I narrow my eyes and watch her carefully, not sure if I should join her or not.

"You want in. Now. You want Ellie and me to move to L.A. and you will turn our life into a little, happy ending, fairy tale story. Wow! Sounds awesome Dylan. I would say I'll think about it but since I don't want to keep you waiting, I will give you my thoughtful answer right now. No. Thank you. We've managed for so long without you that it's pretty clear that we will manage in the future as well. And who the hell do you think you are, to walk in here, and plan out my life like I don't have any say in it? You weren't here. You weren't even aware that you had a daughter just a few short weeks ago and now all of the sudden you feel responsible? Wow. Good for you. But please feel free to go and leave us alone."

"I had no idea, which you know well enough. Cut me some slack here Golden."

"Don't call me that." She hides her face in her hands and I see tears hitting the shiny surface of the bar. "Don't ever call me that again."

I walk around the bar and wrap my arms around her, bringing her close. "I love calling you that. You are, *my* Golden." I whisper to her ear.

"I'm not anyone's Golden. If you think, that just because you can make my heart race every time you are around, and make my stupid legs wobble

revival

whenever I feel you touch me, that it gives you the right to call me that old nickname, then you're wrong. You are so wrong."

I watch her in shock. I can't believe that she just admitted what I thought all along. "I knew all of this already." I smile. "And I mean it when I said I want you both in my life."

And I mean it.

I really do.

I've thought about this long and hard. I had my mother and Dina convince me that this is the best thing that could ever happen to me. I truly believe that *this is* the best thing that could have ever happened.

The second I laid eyes on that little blond angel I knew that I couldn't let her go, that I don't want to let her go. I knew deep in my heart that I wanted to have her close to me. I want to be next to her every second of her journey.

Nina pushes away from me and locks her glossy eyes on mine. "Go away Dylan. It's for the best." I feel her soft lips brush mine quickly before she goes. Maneuvering between the tables, not even looking back my way.

I know she wants me gone, but I also know she wants me to stay. I can feel that she wants me to stay.

She doesn't have a clue how stubborn I am once I make up my mind.

And my decision has been made.

Nina

He is back.

The moment I saw him walking out of Ritchie's office I panicked. Why is he here? I don't want him here, not now. I wanted him next to me years ago. I dreamed of him coming back, showing up on my door step like a prince in shining armor. Saving me. Saving us.

But not now.

Now is the worst time.

I know I have to tell him to go back, to never look back. Never to search for us and to just forget. That should be easy, considering the fact that he easily forgot about me the first time.

There is one little difference this time around though.

He knows Ellie is his daughter and I know how stubborn and demanding he can be when he wants something. I also know that there is something slightly different about him. I know it's been years. We were young, free and wild back then and I completely understand that we changed over the course of these years. Life changed us, threw challenge after challenge at us. Leaving scars in the process.

Now we are facing each other again, two complete strangers and yet it feels like we are somehow connected.

But that connection doesn't matter. There is no

revival

hope for us to move forward. There is no hope for him to call Ellie his daughter.

And all of this is my fault.

My weaknesses, my pathetic need for someone at the time. My desperate need to create a picture perfect family was much stronger than than my rational thinking.

Now I have to pay for it.
We have to pay for it.
Me.
Ellie.
And Dylan.

Dylan

I waited four days, four fuckin' days to try and talk to her again. It kills me to wait this long but I wanted to give her some space, to let her warm up to the all the things I said. To think about the possibility of moving away from here. To start a new chapter, to move forward and do the right thing.

Monday seems like a good day to start again, and I want to set some things straight with Ritchie first. It bothers me that he thinks I'm a douchebag. That I'm here just to use Nina and head back home again. I want to, no, I need to make this straight.

I drive to the bar around noon. Straight from the dealership where I purchased a new Jeep, because getting around in taxis wasn't really up my alley.

I pull into the back parking lot like I've been doing since I started hitting this place and look around in surprise at the construction trucks parked in the back as well. As far as I remember, this place was reserved for delivery and personnel only. I'm a little taken aback that Ritchie lets other people park here as well.

I push open the double swinging doors and all of the vehicles make sense. There are about ten guys working inside on what seems like a big hole in the middle of the celling. I see Ritchie sitting at the bar talking on his cell phone. He is not happy, not at all.

"Hey man." I wave a hand towards him and he gestures for me to wait a second.

revival

"Can you fuckin believe this? I had a leak overnight and the roof collapsed." Ritchie is next to me. I turn around and scan the ceiling above the seating area. Even though I know nothing about construction, I know that it is bad.

"It doesn't look good?"

"Does that look good to you?" He points to the big hole above us.

"No."

"There you have it." He walks to the construction workers, probably to give them some directions on how to do the job they are perfectly capable of doing on their own.

"So how long will it take to fix this crap?" I hear him ask the guy whose clothes are the cleanest, so I assume he's the boss.

"Few days, a week at the most." The construction guy rubs his beard and looks up, scanning the damage.

"Jesus Christ!" I see Ritchie running his hands over his head. I know that he is worried. A week. Seven days with the bar closed means he will be losing a lot of money. Loads of money. And on top of that, losing clients. Once they get accustomed to a different bar, it might be hard to bring them back in. And there are tons of bars around. I know exactly where his concerns are coming from.

"Put a note that you are renovating, this way they will want to come back here as soon as you open. They will want to see what you had done, but that means you have to actually change something." I look around, thinking of any way to improve this place. "Maybe add some light over the bar, change those used seat covers." I see his head snap in my direction and I can tell he is considering my suggestion.

"Thanks Dylan." The expression on his face

softens.

"Sure, see you around." I say as I head toward the exit, smiling to myself. Thinking about the idea that I have. The moment I step out of the bar and get to the car, I call Austin.

"What's going on?" He gets to the point, like always. I smile at that.

"Find the best restaurant design company and send them to Ritchie, you have the address right?"

"Yeah, I do."

"Pay them. Make sure that they use their best. It needs to be done ASAP, but not faster than a week." I don't care that I'm manipulating the situation. I will pull any trick I can to have some time with her, and if she doesn't need to be at the bar, it means she will have free afternoons and evenings.

"Sure Dylan, will do." There is a pause, and a pause is not a good sign.

"What is it?"

"Germans pulled out of the deal."

"Really? After everything I promised them if they held back a few months?"

"Just got a call thirty minutes ago, was about to buzz you."

"Fine then, sell the hotel to the Italians, I think they were next in line for the project. Contact them, ask if they still want it, even though they will have to wait a few months. If they are good with it, go ahead."

"Yep, that's what I thought, will call them right now."

"No, you will call the people I asked you to call first, they can wait."

" Ok, shit, you can be demanding sometimes."

"Tell me about it." I smile and hang up the phone. I don't know if I smile because I did something great for Ritchie, or because I don't give a

revival

fuck that Germans backed out of this project, or the fact that the bar will be closed for a week which means Nina won't be working nights, and I can actually try to see her and Ellie.

If she wants to see me that is.

I drive towards the rental house and I bring up her number a few times before I actually press call.

She picks up on the fifth ring, just before I was ready to hang up.

"Hello?"

"Hi Nina." I smile. I'm sure she can sense it, her response is comes way softer than when we last spoke in the bar.

"Hi Dylan." Her soft voice is like a balm to my soul.

"Listen, I really want to see both of you, and please, before you say no, just listen to me." I rush my words hoping she won't be able to cut me off, "I rented this awesome house on the beach, with pool and ocean access. I did this for you and Ellie to come and enjoy it with me, what do you say?"

There is a silence on the other side, and I take a deep breath, waiting for the rejection that I'm sure is about to come.

"Listen Dylan..." Silence again. "I don't think it's a good idea."

Shit.

"Of course it is, you don't have an excuse. I know you're off from work at the bar for a few days, so... What do you say?"

"I don't know..." Her voice is sad which makes me sad in an instant.

"Come on Nina, if you have a terrible time and you girls decide you don't want to see me again, I will back off. Promise."

"Promise?" Her voice changes to playful and I feel a ray of hope.

"I said that, didn't I?"
"Where is the place?"
"I'll pick you up in fifteen."
"Ok, see you soon."

That went well. I think as I make the first possible U-turn. And now I'm nervous. I have no idea what I'm doing.

I don't stress about seeing Nina. No, I'm anxious about being close to Ellie. I have no idea how I'm supposed to talk to children, much less my own child. Especially one who doesn't know that you're her father.

I park the car right in front of their apartment entrance and contemplate calling or texting her, when I see them walking down the steps.

My eye catches what seems like a perfect picture. Nina's head turns towards Ellie, her hair piled up in a high, messy bun that looks sexy as hell. Her yellow sundress flowing in the wind as she moves. And Ellie. Her face smiling an honest smile. One that's only seen on children's faces. Her tiny body jumps the stairs while her mother's hand tries to keep her balanced.

I'm transfixed in this moment.

I've never looked at women this way, and I'm sure I've never looked this way at a child.

Any child.

Except mine.

Mine.

That thought in itself puts a smile on my face.

I get out of the car and run around to open both doors quickly, meeting Nina's surprised eyes.

"Get in my ladies." I watch Ellie jump into the back seat and greet me quickly as she sits on the booster seat and puts the seat belt on.

Nina stops for a second before getting in, I wish I could see her eyes but they are covered with the

revival

black wall of her sunglasses. From the look of her pursed lips I can only imagine how her eyes look in this moment. She turns around without saying anything and gets in the car, shutting the door. I walk around and take a deep breath to calm my nerves. I have no idea how to do any of this, its freaking the hell out of me.

"So where are we going?" Nina's nervous voice cuts the silence that is growing with each mile that passes.

"I want to show you something that we talked about earlier."

"Surprise? I love surprises!" I look in the review mirror and smile as I see Ellie's eyes shine with excitement. Then I see Nina's hands clutching her purse closer, bringing her hand to her forehead and rubbing it like she's trying to send a headache away.

"Yep, a surprise sunshine." I smile.

"I'm Ellie, sunshine is when the sun comes up and it's high in the sky, like during the day, you know?" I watch her purse her lips slightly.

"And you are exactly like that." I think of all of the moments when I thought about her in the past three months. Her face shines in my mind like sunshine, warming my heart, telling me to believe that there is a reason for everything in this world.

After countless talks with my mother and few visits to Dina, Mia's former shrink, I found the courage to finally visit Mia's grave. I haven't been there since the day she was put to rest and I vowed to myself to never visit it again. At the time, I didn't want the pain of standing there, looking down at the gravestone.

This time I stood there and was kind of thankful. I know how stupid it seems and I know how cruel it might sound, but it's what I felt.

Mom and Dina wanted me to get closure, some

kind of peace that they both knew I needed, and both knew I would find once I acknowledged that she is no longer coming back. That she's gone forever. That the only thing I can do is keep those sweet, lovely memories tucked somewhere inside my heart. Bury them deep like she was buried there.

Dina still doesn't know the truth about Mia being my half-sister. That we shared the same blood in our veins. So she has no fucking clue that I was mourning two people at the same time.

A lover.

A sister.

Now, looking back, I know how sick that might sound. I know that people will never understand, they will turn their faces in disgust and try to judge. But fuck them, they don't have a clue about what we had together. Even if it was wrong.

Here in New Orleans the only ones that know are Ritchie, Travis and Nina. And surprisingly they do not send me a single sign that they are thinking of it as an act of sickness.

Shit happens.

Life happens.

We go on.

Or try to.

I remember how I stood there, looking at her name engraved in white marble, her pretty face smiling at me from the little picture attached to it. I was trying to find the perfect words to say to apologize to her. To say how sorry I'm that I didn't leave her alone when she was pushing me away. How sorry I am for not seeing the similarities in us that were so obvious, so prominent, yet we missed them.

I did apologize for all of this.

And then I thanked her.

I know thanking you for what I might have found

at the end of all this is a paradox, it sounds stupid as fuck and it might be wrong. But all this, me, you, everything that happened has lead me to something incredible at the end. Something I might have never known about if not for this. And even though I'm struggling every day with the thought that you are not here, I hope that you are in a good place right now. I hope that you are surrounded by people that love you like I love you. I do Mia. I will always love you and I will never let you go. I will never let you escape my heart, but I know I have to close that chapter and keep going, especially now that I have someone that I have to keep going for. You have no idea how fucking' happy I am knowing that I have a daughter and that she looks just like me. Although I swear to God her eyes are shaped exactly like yours even though they are the same grey color as mine. To say that I'm scared of all of this would be understatement. I'm freaking out big fucking time. I have no idea how things will turn out. I have no idea if I can be a father, if I can step up and be someone's role model, a little girl's role model. I really don't, but I know that I want to try. I want to give everything that I have in me to make that happen. And I'm so driven Mia, I'm so fucking driven right now that I will break down every wall standing in my way just to make that happen. I will always miss you, I want you to know that. I will always love you, I want to you know that as well. We will always be together. In our hearts. Forever.

"Are we there yet?" Ellie's voice cuts off my flashback.

"Few more minutes." I take a left turn and drive on the sandy road, leaving a big cloud of dirt swirling behind us.

"Are we going to the beach? We are going to the beach! I love the beach! Mommy, mommy, we are going to the beach!" Her little sweet voice is the only excited thing in this car. Nina is sitting next to me looking nervous, her face pulled tight and her hands white from squeezing her purse.

"Something like that." I wink in my rear view mirror and Ellie winks back at me, her face getting serious all of the sudden, like she is on a mission.

We drive for a few more minutes before pulling into the parking space in front of the rental house.

"We're here." I announce as I get out of the car, heading to the other side to open the door. Before I get there, Nina is out of the car already and taking Ellie out.

"What is this place?" Nina asks, eyeing the surroundings.

"My house for now, I rented it so you can come over once in a while."

Her face shows nothing but fear.

It makes me feel stupid, maybe this wasn't a good idea after all. Maybe I should have just gone easy and started with phone calls. But fuck, I want it all and I want it now. I don't want to wait any longer to have my daughter next to me.

"For how long?" She almost whispers that.

"As long it takes." I keep my eyes on her. I set the statement free, I'm committed. "As long as it takes." I repeat and turn around, walking to Ellie who is waiting for us on the top of the stairs, eager to get in.

"You ready to see paradise, sunshine?" I ask and open the door, listening to the sound of her laughter as she runs inside without looking back.

"Mommy, mommy come here, look! There is a pool and the ocean is right there, it's like he has his own beach!" She screams and jumps up and down, her cheeks flush and my heart swells.

Little moments.

revival

Little steps.

"Awesome honey." I watch Nina walk slowly to her, looking at the exceptional view in front of her.

"Let's go to the beach." I rush to the door leading to the patio and open it wide, waiting for them to walk through it. Ellie runs through first, Nina walking behind her. Her eyes catch mine the moment she passes me in the doorway.

"You should go, this won't change anything." Her voice is hushed and painful, and I don't understand it.

"What are you talking about? I'm here, I want to be *in*, I want to be in your life, in her life, from now on." I try to stay calm. I try to keep my voice steady but I'm boiling inside. I don't understand why she keeps pushing me away like this. She sees that I really want this. That I am serious and committed to be here and to get to know them both the way I should know them.

"It's a tad too late Dylan, things are complicated." Her eyes are not focused on me. They are focused on the little girl, our daughter, leaning down to the water and picking something up.

"Look at me Nina," I grab her elbow gently and turn her to face me. Her expression is killing me, almost like she doesn't want me to be here, like she wishes I would never show up again. That look sends prickles down my spine. "I am not going anywhere. I'm here to stay. For her," I nod in the direction of the ocean, "And for you." The need to bring her closer is hard to tame. "If you let me." I add, fixed on the petals of her lips.

Her blues are now shining like the brightest stars, looking at me with disbelief. Then she turns away from me and walks toward Ellie.

I go back in the house and grab a blanket and few sand toys that I picked up earlier, thinking they would be something the little girl would like to have while playing on the beach. I feel stupid that I just made an assumption about her, that I don't really know what little girls her age are interested in. I catch up to them when they are ankle deep in the water, looking for shells.

"Looking for white ones?" I ask Ellie smiling.

"You bet, they are the best." She doesn't even lift her head from the surface of the water. Unlike her mother, who is looking at me with narrowed eyes and pursed lips. Fuck. I prefer those lips spread apart.

"How do you know she likes the white ones?"

I scratch my stubble for a second and try to formulate my answer.

"I saw her at the beach once, she was with her grandmother I believe, we had a little chat."

"Is that so?"

"Yep, just talking about the shells. I had no idea she was mine at that time." I say directing my attention to the water where Ellie is still diving in to pick up some shells. "I should have known right then though, the story she told me should have been the tell-all. I guess I was just so tied up in other crap that I missed the clue."

"Story? What story?" She frowns, but I know I have her full attention now.

I step closer to her, careful not to touch her, not to make her uncomfortable. Close enough to smell her perfume, and close enough to feel her heart beating fast next to me.

"The same story I told you one morning on the cove beach." I watch her face blush, her eyes escape mine by traveling to the safest point, her daughter.

"Who can forget that?" She asks quietly, not looking at me. I feel like I just won the lottery. She remembers. That's what matters. She remembers.

revival

"It's a great story, worth passing on for generations." I lean closer, brushing her bare arm with mine. She shudders.

"Definitely is." She walks to Ellie and bends down to fish shells out of the water.

I watch them both, standing right next to the shore and I fantasize about the shore being my home in Malibu. I know it's way too soon to think about shit like that. I know, but having both of them there with me, would be the top of my dreams.

I spread the blanket over the sand and take a seat, watching them bend over the water and fish out shells, only to inspect them.

I think of all the possibilities. I know Nina is strongly against any involvement between us at this moment, but I also feel and see how she reacts every time we are close to each other. That is not a behavior you get from someone that doesn't care about you. I know she cares, but at the same time, there is something holding her back. I want to find out what it is. I *need* to find out what is it.

I watch her walk towards me, her dress flowing in the light breeze, her hair slightly curled from the humidity of the ocean, forming sexy waves around her face. She takes a seat on the far corner of the blanket and doesn't even look at me.

"Why are you so distant? I'm here, I want to make things right. I want to be here for both of you and it seems like you want the same thing. Except, different things keep coming out your mouth. What's the problem?"

She doesn't turn my way for a few moments and I feel like I've lost another chance, another battle.

"You don't understand." Her voice is quiet, laced with a pain that is written all over her face. I watch her and wonder if maybe this time I will get some kind of explanation, some kind of clue as to why things can't be the way they should be. I move closer to her and put my arms around her to comfort her. Comfort her in what? I have no idea. I hope she will tell me that soon.

"I won't understand until you explain it to me, Golden." I lean over her shoulder and breathe the words in her ear. Shitty move on my end, I know her earlobes are her weak spot.

"I don't know how." She tilts her head back and inhales deeply through her nose, like she is trying to ready herself for something "I don't know how to even start this."

"From the beginning?" That brings a small smile to her face.

"I... I don't know where the beginning is..."

"Mommy! Look, I found more, they are all white." Ellie screams from the shore. I move away from Nina slightly.

I watch her run toward us with a bucket, half full of white shells.

I smile.

"How many you got there sunshine?"

She narrows her sparkly eyes at me and starts to count all of them. She carefully takes them out of the bucket and places them on the blanket. I watch every single move she is making. The smile I have on my face while she does this doesn't leave my face for a second. I can feel Nina's eyes on me from time to time but I don't look at her. I'm focused on watching my little girl count shells.

"Twenty three." She proudly announces after she's done. I know there are really eighteen, as she skipped a few numbers along the way, but I don't intend to say anything.

"Wow!" Me and Nina say at the same time. We both look at each other and laugh.

"That's the most I've found in one day, can we

come back here Dylan? Can we? So I can look for more?"

"Sure, whenever you want Ellie."

"Thank you, thank you!" She wraps her small arms around me and I freeze for a fraction of a second. I'm not used to little hands around my body. I don't even look at Nina, I don't want to see what she is thinking right now, not that her expressions are easy to ready anyway.

"You are welcome." I bring her closer, closing my eyes. I want to remember this moment, to put it in my heart so I can have it whenever I need it, whenever I want it.

Nina clears her throat, "I think we have to go now. Tomorrow is another school day." I watch her stand up and gather her stuff. I do the same and follow them to the car, wondering how little I know about their life. Ellie is in school now, kindergarten I believe, and I missed the first day of school already. I've missed so many firsts it hurts.

We get in the car and head back towards the city.

"So how do you like school Ellie?" I take a quick peak in the visor.

"I love it, my teacher Ms. Quincy is the best. And I already made a friend. Her name is Shelly and we've been sitting together and we sit at the same table at lunch. She made me this card with BFF on it so I think we are really close friends now."

"That's good, friends are important." I quickly glance at Nina. "Should I make you a card with BFF on it? Would you treat me like a friend then?" I whisper to make sure she is the only one that hears me. I take another glance at her and feel good about the smile that covers her face, even though she keeps silent.

The rest of the ride I ask Ellie about her school and her friends, about her favorite activities and her favorite TV shows. I want to know all of this. To be able to say that I know, like really know, what my daughter likes.

I park at the street next to their apartment and while Ellie runs up the stairs after saying a big thank you to me again, I hold Nina's hand. Silently asking her to stay with me for a second.

"I want to see both of you again. Soon. " She doesn't look at me. Instead she searches the street like she's afraid that someone will see us. Like she and I sitting in near the car is something worth gossiping about.

"Yeah, sure." There is no hope in her words.

"Nina, I mean it."

"She doesn't really know you Dylan, she doesn't know who you are and I want to keep it that way."

"I understand, I will not tell her anything until she feels comfortable with me."

Her head snaps to me. "No, you will not say anything, ever."

I try to search her eyes for something, but they are not giving me anything back.

"Sure, for now I will keep quiet about the fact that she is *my daughter* and that I am her father, are we good?" I take a deep breath "When can I see her again?"

"I will call." She heads toward the apartment and I head back to my car, driving away and trying not to think about the fact that this phone call might not come soon. Not soon enough.

Nina

"Did you have a good day, bug?" I watch Ellie's little face light up at the question and there is no doubt what her answer will be.

"It was awesome!" She puts her shells carefully in the shoe box, her jewelry box as she calls it. "I wish we could have a house like Dylan's, I would love to live on the beach."

I pause with my cup of tea and swallow the guilt clogging my throat. "Maybe if we dream about it we will have it one day."

"You really believe that?" She keeps piling her treasures.

"Of course I do." I take a sip of the tea and let my mind drift away for a second, imagining the way my life would look if I could actually live in a house like that. Waking up and falling asleep to the calming sound of the ocean. But my dreams are not over yet, so things like that might actually happen.

"Time for bed Ellie." I stand up and head to the bathroom, turning around, making sure she is following behind me. I watch her as she brushes her teeth and I can tell that her mind is elsewhere, wandering somewhere in the la-la-land she created. La-la-land I wish was my reality.

We head to bed. Once I tuck her in and kiss her goodnight I close my eyes and go over every detail of today, every word that was said. I see Dylan's warm eyes, his kind smile, its killing me. I know he is hoping for some kind of relationship with Ellie, but I'm not sure I can allow it. I'm not sure this is the smartest thing to do, and honestly, I'm terrified that in the end, we will end up the ones getting crushed. That me and Ellie will be the ones to piece our hearts back together. And her little heart might yet be too fragile to handle such a break.

Mine is already wrapped up in steel armor, but hers is still soft as a sponge, taking everything in. That's what I'm afraid of. That he could easily fracture her little heart and then leave, not thinking about the holes he created.

I wake up before the alarm goes off. It's a stupid habit of mine to wake up at five thirty, no matter what. The bar is closed for a week so I decided to ask for a week off at the hotel as well. I know I will lose the pay, but I haven't had a break in years and the idea of having some time to myself is appealing. To my surprise taking a week of vacation wasn't a problem, in fact, my manger asked why on earth I've never taken any days off in the past five years, and all I was able to do was shrug.

So here I am, drinking coffee at quarter to six, trying to kill the half an hour I have left before I wake up Ellie.

I browse my computer for nothing in particular when the Skype window pops up. I see Rachel's name on the screen and I press accept right away.

The first thing I hear is laughter, then Rachel shushing someone next to her. Next I see her face pop up on the screen.

"Nina, I have the biggest fucking news to tell you." She smiles for miles and then I see this big, diamond rock take up the whole screen. "I'm engaged!" She squeals and brings her hands to her face.

"Wow, congrats!" I'm shocked. She was never into any relationships, short term hookups were the only thing she was good at. So this, her being engaged, is a kind of a shock. In a good way.

"You have a full year to plan the trip here, and don't worry," her hands are waiving in the air, "I will help you cover the cost of the flight and you will stay with us, so there is no money to spend on the hotels. OMG, can you believe it?"

"I actually can't. How did this happen?" I wink at her and her eyes go wide and she takes a glance to her side, giving me that signal to keep it quiet. I nod, letting her know that I understand. I suddenly feel like a secret agent, James Bond on a mission. The mission to keep my friend's hookups as private as possible.

"Ok, that's enough, what's up with you? And please don't tell me you're still working those two jobs back to back, without any time to see anyone?"

"Still the same story here." I smile thinking about Dylan.

"Wait, what is that face? I need some sort of explanation to the face that I just saw, please rewind." She leans closer to the screen and now her nose is the main future that I can see. Not that it's a bad nose, not at all, it's just disturbing looking at my friends nose while I'm about to confess something.

"Rachel? Can you sit back a little, like a few inches so I can see your eyes?"

"Go on." Now I feel like I'm actually talking to her.

"You just want me to say it, right?"

"Do you want to write it down and then hold the paper to the camera?"

"You're annoying." I sigh and try to quickly sort how much I can tell her. I know it sounds stupid, she is my best friend and we don't have any secrets between us. Well I do have one, but this one is different. At least that's what I've been telling myself.

"So there is this guy Dylan," Even saying his name feels good, bringing smile to my face.

"Do I know him, where is he from, what does he do? Is he the one that drives the delivery truck that always breaks down in the bar parking lot?"

I take a sip of coffee, patiently waiting for her assumptions to pass.

"No, he is new to town, I mean not totally new. He was here a while back, but new as of now."

I see her eyes narrow, "I see."

I let that slide, she doesn't see shit as far as I'm concerned. "Well, we saw each other, it got a little intense in the room."

"Wait what room?"

"The hotel room."

"You fucked a guest in a hotel room? Oh you're bad, you are the kind of bad I never thought you could be. I love it."

I roll my eyes and take a sip of my coffee again.

"Well technically yes. I mean we did it, but we knew each other from long ago, so technically we were two people that know each other. It just happened to be my work place." I cringe a little. Once I say it out loud, it does sound like a kind of stupid thing to do.

"Tell that to whoever the hell you want, to me you fucked a guy, a hotel guest to be exact. The hotel you are working at. That's kind of cool Nins."

"He kissed me first." I try my best to take the blame off my shoulders, so I don't sound like a slut, even to myself.

"What?"

"I said he kissed me, not that I kissed him."

"Oh, so you're saying you just stood there and he kissed you, dragged you to bed and fucked you senseless while you were lying in his bed like a blow up doll?"

"I can't win with you, can I?" I sigh and wait for her imagination to calm down.

"Does he like you?"

"I don't think so."

Now I see her eyes close up on the screen.

"You are looking at me right?"

"Straight in the eye, don't have any other choice if you ask me."

"You would never fuck a guy just for the sake of having sex, so cut the crap Nina, I'm your friend."

"I think he might like me, yes." I remember the feel of his lips on mine, his tongue dancing with mine like we were trying to become one.

"If I weren't in love like I am right now, I would say the look on your face while you were going over that fuck or whatever it was, is pathetic. But since I do it myself few times a day, I say welcome to the neighborhood sister. Finally."

"Thanks for making that clear to me Rachel." I keep looking at her and I see her face freeze in the middle of something she wanted to say, and its obvious that our connection is lost.

"Until next time." I mumble while staring at the screen.

I watch Ellie walk inside the school. I stand there trying to think of something I can do with my free time. I could go shopping, except my budget is super low and I don't really need anything. I could go clean the apartment, but to be honest there is nothing to clean, as we don't really spend much time in it and I try to keep it tidy on a day to day basis.

I head over to the deli. I will make a plan for the next five days over breakfast.

"OMG Nina, I have something for you," Amanda reaches down under the counter and hands me a pink envelope. "Our wedding invitation." She announces proudly.

"Oh wow, I didn't expect it to be so soon." I open it and hold the perfectly designed paper, my eyes go wide at the date, October 2nd. Two weeks away.

"I know it's kind of on fast forward but we have something cooking in the oven." I watch her place her hand on her flat belly and I can't contain my happiness for her.

"Oh my gosh, congrats!" I lean over the counter and hug her, feeling extremely happy for both of them. "I'm truly happy for you guys. This is the best news."

"So will you be there, can I add you to the yes list?"

"Of course." I say even though I'm not sure I will get off from the bar easily after a week of renovations.

"I can't wait, it's going to be fabulous, you will see."

"I'm sure it will be Amanda, if you need any help just let me know."

"Nope, everything's covered."

"Good. Good, see you soon."

"See ya."

I see Mr. Santiago sitting at his table but I don't feel like talking to anyone. I have so much to think about that I would rather sit by myself and just get

revival

lost in my thoughts. I send an apologetic smile toward Hector and sit two tables down. I carefully open four packets of sugar and pour them into my black coffee, stirring it carefully so the spoon doesn't really touch the cup. In other words, I'm doing it quietly so nobody will look at me or notice me.

I hear the bell ring and I take an involuntary look to see who is walking in. My heart skips a beat as I watch Dylan walk through the door and stand in the short line, ordering coffee from Amanda. I watch her hand him the same pink envelope she just handed me and I frown. It's not like she's known him long enough to invite him to her wedding, as far as I know. So why is she doing this? Is she trying to set us up? How would she even know? I watch Dylan pick up his order and walk to Mr. Santiago table, both of them smiling at each other. I look around in confusion. Who else is he friends with? Is he trying to get my circle wrapped up in him so they can convince me to do the things he wants?

I walk back to the counter not really caring about being invisible anymore.

"Why did you invite him to your wedding?" I ignore the two people staring at the glass case displaying baked goods and I look Amanda straight in the face.

"Who are you talking about exactly?" She tilts her head and there is a pure confused look on her face.

"Dylan, that's who I'm talking about." I seeth trough my teeth, trying to keep my voice at the level of a whisper.

Her eyes widen and her lips turn upright, "Nina, he helped Oscar so much with his real estate business it would be rude not to invite him. Do you have a problem with him being there?" I know this is not really a question, and even if it is, it's not the kind you can answer.

"No, not a problem, just wondering." I walk back to the table and I know his eyes are on me. I know he probably heard the whole stupid conversation and that makes me embarrassed even more.

"I don't have to go if that means you will have a bad time." His body slides in front of me, his knees touching mine under the table and I freeze. I know I should pull my legs away, but where? I don't really know as I'm sitting in a tight corner, but I should pull them back.

I should.

But I don't.

Instead I keep my face straight and try not to make any movement, not even a tiny one. Even a little movement will cause friction; his body touching mine, caressing me, and I don't know if I can handle that. Definitely not over morning coffee.

"Just say it if you don't want me to go." He leans over the table, closer to me. Now I look into those gray eyes like they are the ocean that I love. Endless. Surprising, dangerous and ruthless.

"I don't want you to go."

"Ok, I won't go then." His eyes are on me, and they are covered in clouds so dark it scares me.

"I just.... I don't know if me being around you is a good idea Dylan."

"I thought I made it clear that I'm not going anywhere. I'm not going to leave Ellie's life and trust me Nina, I would love to stay in yours if you would just allow me to show you who I really am. Why am I feeling like I've said this thousand a times already?"

His statement is simple, yet powerful.

Let me show you who I really am.

And he's right. I don't know who he really is. I have this image of a bad boy or a young man from

revival

years ago. Someone that came here for a summer break to live a little and that's all. Somewhere under this thick cover of dust and way too many bottles of scotch, there is a boy, a man, that is fully grown. Carrying his own baggage, diving head first into being a father even if he doesn't have a single clue what that means.

"Ok, then I guess I will see you there." I close my eyes and sip my coffee for a few seconds. Simply enjoying the taste.

"You are the most complicated creature that I have ever met, and yet so beautiful I can't stop looking at you, you know that?" His bluntness pulls me out of my coffee coma.

"Hmm, if you were the kind to live in the desert most of your life and just right now were let out of his cave, I would totally believe you. But since you're come from Cali, the state of the most beautiful women, I think you're a liar. Have a good day, Dylan." I didn't even open my eyes while I said this.

"Impossible." I hear him say at the same moment as I feel his knees brushing my legs under the table.

I know I can't open my eyes just yet, see him like this. To see him close to me is not going to do anything good. I know he can probably sense the stupid little sensations that move between us every time we are close, but I don't care. Let him feel. Too bad he can't act on anything. It won't get him far.

Nina

"Why are you asking me this three days before the wedding?" Ritchie is definitely not happy and I don't blame him.

"I wasn't sure if I wanted to go," it is the truth. I was struggling with the decision. "I didn't want to hurt Amanda's feelings by not showing up but I also didn't want to see or be around someone." I watch his face and he nods at the last part.

"So Dylan is going to be there?"

"He got the invite so I guess he will." I shrug.

"If you really want to go then go, we will manage here."

"Thanks Ritchie." I head for the door but stop when he calls my name.

"Nina," there is a tiny pause, like he is not sure if this should be said or not. "Don't make any stupid mistakes."

I look in his eyes and I know that he really means it. He is always looking out for me and that's exactly what he is doing right now.

"It seems like I am a pro at that, but I promise to be on my best behavior." I wink and head out to the bar. I take in the awesome changes that he made over the week the bar was closed. New lighting gives the place the edge it was missing. The fancy lights dangle above the bar, making it look cozy and inviting. New booth seats, the black leather giving the place the kick it needed. Since we opened on

revival

Monday people have been flowing in like this is the only bar in town. Making us busy like we haven't been in years.

"Will you do me a favor?" I ask Kelly while putting the drinks on the tray.

"Sure will."

"You don't even know what it is yet." I smile and shake my head.

"Nina, you never ask for anything so whatever it is, it must be important." True.

"Will you take me shopping for a dress for this wedding I'm going to Saturday?" I watch her eyes go big and she nods her head with excitement.

"Sure will, when do you want to go?"

"I have a little time off tomorrow around four, two hours are enough I guess, right?"

"I will pick you up at four then."

"Thanks." I smile at her and walk to the floor to serve the drinks and take more orders. I haven't been shopping for myself for God knows how long. The last time I did, it was school shopping for Ellie at Walmart. That is the most I can afford and I doubt I will find the dress in Walmart, so I definitely need Kelly's help in that department.

I know I'm going on stage in less than an hour. I also know that there is new equipment that Ritchie got for us, and new stage lighting. Simon texted me earlier that he was more than stunned to find new stuff when he got backstage. I don't know what made Ritchie do all this but I'm excited to see how the show will turn out with all this new stuff around.

The hour passes quickly and before I know it, I'm standing with the boys on the stage, looking around at all the people gathered on the floor and sitting at the tables. It's definitely a full house tonight and that makes me slightly nervous. We decided to go with our best covers tonight and finish with the song I'd written a few weeks ago.

We start off with a bang and the crowd is on its feet from the first song, I can feel the energy flowing around us, inside me, and bouncing off the walls that can barely contain the atmosphere.

We decided not to take a break like we used to. I can feel myself wearing down after the first forty five minutes so I let the boys know that we need to slow down for a bit. I hear the guitar playing the familiar chorus to my song.

"This piece is mine, I try to write something once in a while and shake it up for you guys." The lights dim and I can feel the spotlight on me. I close my eyes and feel the music before I let the words flow. As I get to the end of the song I know that he is here, I can feel his eyes on me even though mine are closed. Even if they were open I wouldn't be able to see him because of the lights blinding me. But I know. I feel.

The sooner you go
The stronger I will grow
The sooner you go
The deeper I will breathe
The sooner you go
The stronger I will grow
The deeper I will breathe
The sooner you go

I keep the mic to my lips and now, with the music gone, the only thing I can hear is my hard breathing. The crowd goes wild and we pick that moment to hit them with good old "Satisfaction" and they love it. I let myself loose with Michael, standing next to him and letting him sing with me, big smiles on our faces as we put our faces together. Having the time of our lives. It's been a while since I've let loose like this and I can tell the band is feeling it as well, their faces beam with happiness and pride.

revival

"That was something," Michael high fives Oscar and then brings me for a spin. "We kicked ass tonight like we haven't kicked ass in a long time baby." He kisses my forehead and puts me slowly on the floor, his hands still around my waist. The sound of a clearing throat makes us turn around in the direction of the door.

"You did awesome." Dylan is standing with his arms crossed, leaning on the door frame, his eyes focused on Michaels hands around me.

"Thanks." I smile and try to figure it out why he is here. He's never come backstage before. Ever.

"Do you mind letting her go?" He sounds calm but I can hear a bit of jealousy in his tone.

"She didn't ask for it, so why would I?" Michael smiles, bringing me closer to him and I don't dare to look in Dylan's direction.

"Because I'm asking you nicely and if I have to repeat myself, it won't be as nice." I step away from Michael, his hands going slack against his legs. The puzzled look on his face is evident but I don't feel like saying anything, so I just make an apologetic face and head toward the door, Dylan letting me pass him before following me to the bar.

"Bossy much?" I ask, putting on my apron, "And what exactly was that? Can you explain since I don't have the slightest clue why you think you have the right to act like you are my father or something."

"Just protecting what's mine, and the hands on your waist weren't mine so that means they didn't belong there." I can see the vein throbbing in his neck.

"Is that so? You are pathetic." I let the aggravated sigh escape, "and I'm not yours, we share something together but I'm not yours Dylan, don't confuse those things." I take off for the floor and leave him standing at the bar. How can he even think like that? I never, ever gave him any indication that there is something going on between us. Except that one night, that moment when I let myself slip. I can't say that I'm sorry for it, it was something I will remember for quite some time.

I come back with more orders and see him standing in the same spot, watching me with an expression I haven't seen before.

"I want to take you and Ellie out for ice cream, maybe tomorrow after school. You have two hours in between jobs, what do you say?"

I give him a side-glance as I'm punching the orders in. We spent almost every day last week seeing each other, the three of us. Doing fun stuff every day. I can't deny that he is falling for Ellie and he is not fooling around when he says he wants to be in her life from now on. His eyes while they are together say more than his mouth ever will. And surprisingly, I don't feel uncomfortable while I listen to Ellie's blabbing about how awesome the time with Dylan was. A few days ago she told me in secret that she likes him a lot and that he's her best friend.

"I can't tomorrow."

"Why not?"

"I have something to do."

"I can go with you guys, it will be fun."

I can't believe this guy. He really is persistent when he sets his mind on something.

"I'm going shopping with Kelly, Ellie is staying home with Gran, we can go Friday if you want or we will see each other on Saturday, at the wedding."

"I can take her when you go with Kelly." The simple statement flew of his lips like that was the most normal thing to say. I pause and turn to him, looking into his eyes and trying to figure it out if he is serious.

"I'm serious, I will take her and I will have her back around six so you can see her before you go to work."

"I will think about it, and call you tomorrow."

"I can do this Golden, you know I can, give me some credit here."

I know he can. I see how great he is with her. I see how caring and responsible he is whenever we are together but leaving them alone, just the two of them, is something that never crossed my mind. I've never left her with anybody other than Gran and the idea of leaving her with him for two hours scares me.

"I don't know," I watch his face fall and I immediately feel guilty for somehow hurting him. "I leave at four, pick her up around three thirty, and you need to drop her off before six."

"Thank you". He leans down and places a kiss on my head before leaving the bar. From the corner of my eye, I see Kelly watching me with a puzzled expression on her face. I walk to the nearest table to check if they need anything, as I don't feel like answering any questions, especially not the ones about him.

———•●•———

"Are you sure about this?" Gran is sitting at the kitchen island, her eyes don't leave me as I get Ellie ready.

"I'm not sure of anything, but I'm sure they will have fun together." I walk to the window and see Dylan's car coming to a stop in front of our building. "You ready love? Dylan is here." I try to appear normal even though my nerves are through the roof.

All of a sudden, none of this seems like a good idea and I have the urge to call this stupid thing off. But I can't do this to her, her face is all lit up and I can tell she is excited for a few hours with him.

"Yay! Dylan's here and we are going for ice-cream. This is going to be the best day ever." She rushes to the door and puts on her shoes in a hurry. There is a soft knock on the door, and she waits for me to open it.

"Dylan!" She shrieks, and he brings her up for a spin.

"Are you ready for some fun, Sunshine?" She nods her head and giggles while he keeps spinning her. "Ok we are off then, I will bring her back before six." He waves at us and heads out, I can hear them laughing even with the doors closed.

I look at Gran and she looks at me. We both stay quiet as we listen to their voices fade down the hall.

"That's the right thing to do." I assure myself and head to my room to get ready for the shopping trip with Kelly.

"You will never decide on a dress if you keep looking at your phone every few seconds." Kelly throws another two dresses on my arm and I can't help but smile. Dylan keeps sending me selfies that he is taking with Ellie and I can tell just by the look on her face that she is having a great time. That makes me wonder, what if...

"Nina, we have less than an hour and you haven't tried on a single dress yet, I'm not even going to mention shoes."

Shoes. Shit. I will need those as well. Thank God that this past week was extremely busy. Surprisingly, I received a check from the hotel for my time off. It stated that since I've never used any of my vacation days, I had accrued enough paid time off to cover the whole week.

revival

"Try this first." She hands me a hot pink dress and pushes me toward the fitting rooms.

I get in and fail miserably trying to put all of the hangers on the door, there are way too many. Instead I pile them on the bench and change into the dress she asked me to. No, told me to try on first.

"You gotta be kidding me Kells." I groan while I look in the mirror, it's hot pink and I'm sure when they turn off the lights I will be glowing.

The doors swing open and I see Kelly scanning me from head to toe, handing me pair of nude heel sandals. I put them on without saying a word.

"You look hot. Like *damn girl* hot. Like banging hot. Like every head will turn your direction hot, like.."

"Ok, I get the idea." I cut her off.

She looks at me with approval and I can tell she likes the way I look. I do like the dress as well, from the thick straps that sit on my shoulders to the deep v-neckline, the upper part a little loose while the rest hugs my body in the right places. It is a great, sexy dress but I'm not sure I'm brave enough to wear it.

"I look pink." I state with a serious face and we both burst into a fit of laughter.

"Hot pink." Kelly says while pointing her finger at me.

"I can't wear this." I cover my face with my hands feeling embarrassed at the way I look. This is just not the way I dress, even though I have to agree with Kelly that I do look hot.

"Yes you can, and besides we don't have time to try anything else, it's five thirty already."

"Shit." I groan and quickly change into my clothes, not caring that she is still standing in front of me.

"Damn Nins, your body is banging." I give her the "are you serious" look and walk out of there holding the damn dress and shoes in my hands, heading toward the register.

"You didn't really help you know and I'm going to look like a Barbie in this hot mess of a dress." I smile at her.

"Yes, I will take care of your hair and makeup as well, thank you very much, and if you don't bring him to the floor with that look, you can fire me and never speak to me again."

I look at her with my mouth ajar. I don't find it necessary to add stupid comments or pretend I don't know what she is talking about. I just keep quiet and pay for these damn clothes.

"Thank you," I give her a kiss on the cheek "Really, you are the best."

"It's about time you noticed that." She follows me to the exit and I can't believe we've never hung out like this before. She's been working at the bar for three years and not once did we see each other outside of our work place. But then again, I never have time to see anyone, so that explains everything.

Dylan

We're sitting at a red light when she fires a question at me.

"How do you know my mommy exactly?" I glance back at her in the rear view mirror and see her looking back at me, waiting for an answer. I hesitate a moment trying to think of the best answer I can give. There is definitely no reason to lie to her about how we met.

"I met your mom years ago when I was here on vacation and we became...friends."

"How come I never saw you before? Friends come by often, Rachel used to stop by often and she was mommy's friend. Now she is in Spain so she can't come to our house, but she was visiting us when she was here, how come you never visited before?"

"I was away, just like Rachel is right now, but I'm here now Sunshine and I promise that I will visit every day."

She takes a bite of the oatmeal raisin cookie we picked up at Starbucks and her smile grows big.

"Good, I like when you visit." Her bubbly voice reaches my ears and in that moment my heart pulses through my chest, I feel a lightness of happiness that I've never felt before and for the first time in a long, long time I feel hopeful. Hopeful that my life is not over, maybe it's just begun.

We walk to the door and Ellie knocks on it in

some kind of rhythm that sounds like a signal knock. I can hear Simone opening the door and I take a quick look at my daughter.

"I will see you Saturday, Sunshine." I bend down and bring her into a hug placing a quick kiss on top of her head the moment the door opens. Simone eyes us, her eyes dancing from me to Ellie.

"Did you have fun, love?"

"Sure I did, bye Dylan." She rushes inside and I see her jump on the couch and open the book we just bought at the bookstore.

"Good to see you Simone. I will see you soon, take care." I rush down the stairs not even waiting for her response. I have to say, that woman scares me. There is this protectiveness that she is not afraid to show and I know that if I mess anything up, she would beat me up. She would probably leave nothing or very little of me and I respect her for that tremendously. I have a feeling she doesn't really approve of me being here, doing what I'm doing. I know, I feel that in the air every time we meet. And today was no exception.

I arrive at the Southern Oak Plantation few minutes late. I get out of the car and hand my keys to the valet rushing toward the ceremony area, I don't want to miss anything. Truth be told, I want to see my girls as soon as possible.

I walk around the huge house where I know the ceremony is being held. I've been here with Oscar a few times, it was his idea to have the wedding here. He said it will be Amanda's dream come true. And he wasn't kidding, she was in tears when he showed her the place to get her approval.

revival

It is beautiful, but I didn't expect it to be this beautiful the day of the wedding. Lights are everywhere and they look phenomenal, the whole place has a magical feel to it. I know this sounds like pussy talk, but I see what I see and can't deny it.

I take a seat at the very back as all of the front chairs are taken. I take a minute to scan every single seat for Nina and Ellie. I find Golden sitting in the very front row, her hair pinned in loose curls, some of them hanging around her face. I see her smiling at the women next to her and I can't help but smile to myself. I quickly scan the rest of the crowd in search of Simone and Ellie but I don't see them anywhere, and I feel tiny stab of disappointment. I thought I would see her tonight.

The music starts flowing from the speakers and everybody turns to see the bride walk down the aisle. I catch Nina's eye before I turn and I nod in her direction, receiving a smile in return. God, she looks stunning. She has no idea that she is the most beautiful woman in this crowd.

I watch Amanda walk with her father. There is no question that she is the happiest person here right now. I turn my head back to see Oscar walking to join her. The ceremony begins and I listen to their vows, see their eyes set on each other.

I wish I could have this kind of moment with someone I love, I wish I could be so committed that I would declare my love in front of people. I glance at Nina and see her bring her finger to her eyes, wiping something that I believe are tears.

I know I have feelings for her, I know that whenever she is close to me, it's hard for me not to think about touching her or covering her lips with mine. I know I crave every second to be around her. And I miss her presence whenever she is not around. But is that enough?

I watch the couple kiss and there is a big applause from the crowd, everybody claps their hands, shouting congratulations into the air. I stand as well and bring my hands together, smiling, feeling happy for the newlyweds.

The party moves to the other side of the house, to the outside garden. I walk to the table with the nametags and find mine with the table number 13 on it. I smirk, coincidence? 13 has been my lucky number ever since I could remember. As I walk toward the table, I know that it is still my lucky number, as I find Nina already sitting at the same table.

I take in her breathtaking appearance. Her hair and makeup is perfectly done, in a way that I haven't ever seen on her before. It's dark and sexy, yet still classy, emphasizing her navy eyes perfectly. The pink top of her dress covers most of her shoulders but goes low between her breasts. I feel my dick react to that visual right away. She is a sexy little thing.

"Nina." I nod in her direction and take a seat next to her.

"You look *fine*." She looks me up and down and winks. I frown, this is not how she normally behaves. She is a distant, closed up person that never shows her emotions unless I push her to the fucking limit, demanding to get something out of her.

"Thanks, you look beautiful." I lean down and kiss her cheek and I sense her freeze for a second before she pulls back slightly. "Where is Ellie?"

"Oh, Gran didn't feel well so I decided not to drag them here. I promised her a piece of cake though." She lifts the Champagne glass to her lips and suddenly I know where her courage is coming from. As far as I know, she is not a big drinker. Even few sips of alcohol can make her a little tipsy.

revival

"She missed a perfectly wonderful ceremony then." I gesture for a waiter to come. I order a scotch on the rocks but I know that this will be it for me tonight, I have a feeling I will have to take care of someone.

"It was beautiful, wasn't it?" She looks at the newly married couple sitting a few tables from us and she smiles, sipping her bubbly.

"It was." I watch her profile and I can't help but stop at that little scar under her jaw that extends to her neck. I lift my fingers and run them gently over the silver on her skin. She stills, keeping her head straight forward, sipping her champagne in little sips, as if she is in a hurry to finish it and grab another one.

"Will you ever tell me?"

"Not today." She gestures for the waiter and grabs another flute of champagne from his tray. I watch her bring the glass to her mouth and wrap her full lips around the edge, letting the liquid slide through. I reach for my own glass and take a small sip myself.

It's going to be one painful night if I have to watch her act like this, sitting next to me.

We sit in silence for a while, watching the guests arrive and take their seats at our table. Some couples I recognize from the deli, the guy I've seen working behind the counter few times, and a red headed girl that usually sneaks out from the small kitchen window whenever I stand in line. I lean back in my chair and watch everyone interact with each other, and I have to say, that even though they only know each other from those fleeting moments, they treat one another like they have been friends for life.

I watch Nina smile and talk with all of them, her smile stretches from ear to ear, her words flying easily, freely. This Nina reminds me of the Golden I knew years ago. Happy, free. Not the girl I've been seeing lately.

The band is singing the "Stay with me" cover and I place my hand on her knee under the table. "Dance with me."

I meet her confused eyes but I stand up anyway and hold my hand for her to take. She looks at me with uncertainty but stands up. *Fucking hell*, now I have the full visual of her in front of my eyes, her hot pink dress is short and hugs her curves in the right places. She is sexy as fuck and I can't take my eyes off of her.

I guide her to the dance floor and bring her body close to mine, putting my hand on the small of her back, pressing my body closer. Breathing her in as much as I can, so I can remember her for many days to come. I can feel her chest rise up and down while our bodies are close to each other. I can feel her hot breath on my chest.

"You look incredible." I lean down to her ear. I feel her shudder.

"You said that already."

"I will repeat it a few more times tonight, so get used to it." I place a small kiss on her neck and bring her closer, I can feel her body melt into mine and I can't slow the frenzy going on in my head right now.

"Please do." She brings her face up and looks me straight in the eyes. Begging me for something I've been dying to do. I dip down to reach her mouth. Slow, a feather like touch at first, just enough to feel her, to feel her hot mouth on mine. But I can't hold myself back for long and I dive in with full force, demanding entrance, my tongue slipping in and finding what I was looking for. I forget that we are on the dance floor, that there are people who might look at us, I forget all the surroundings in this perfect moment and enjoy her next to me.

She pulls away slowly and her sparkling eyes meet mine.

"Dylan," her voice is quiet and unsure. I brace myself for rejection, for her to tell me that this was stupid and should never happen again. "Let's get out of here." Her hand slides down my shirt and stops at my waist. "Just you and me."

I close my eyes for a second just to make sure that when I open them, she will be still standing here, to make sure this is real. And holy fuck, when I open them she is still here, her eyes hooded, looking at me hoping I will grant her wish.

"The party hasn't even started yet Golden, don't you want to wait for cake?"

She looks around and I can tell she already regrets what she just asked for. I grab her hand and walk toward the hall, bringing her with me.

There is no denying that I would love nothing more than to get her out of here and fuck her brains out, but I know she will regret that she didn't stay until the end of the party.

I walk through the hall, passing some of the rooms, and head straight for the dark wooden door. I quickly turn the handle and pull us inside. I know from the tour that this is an extra party room. I know it's empty, Oscar said we wouldn't need the extra space.

I close the door and she leans on it, unsure of what's going on.

The room is dark, the only light comes from the dim glow outside. The patch of light places a little spot of light, just enough to hit her face in a beautiful way and make her eyes sparkle.

"Where are we?" She doesn't even look around, her eyes are set on me.

"At the wedding." I run my fingers over her face, sliding them lower to her neck line, following the low cut on her dress, arriving between her full breasts.

"I know that but wha-" I don't let her finish. I can't take her standing in front of me like this any longer. I have to feel her. I need to feel her as the throb in my cock makes it painful to talk right now. I press my mouth to hers and her hands immediately dive through my hair, pulling me closer, deepening the kiss.

I slide my hands down her body and trace my finger at the hem of her dress, slowly bringing it up to her hips. She whimpers right in my mouth, her fingers tight around my neck, giving me a definite go ahead.

I trace the lace of her panties and I will be damned if she is not wet already, the delicate material soaked. I slide the fabric to the side and spread her wetness around her. Feeling her soft and wet like that is fucking unbelievable. I groan and go down to my knees pulling her little piece of lace with me as I go lower.

"Dylan," She breathes out my name in the sexiest way imaginable and there is no stopping me now. There could be a war going on outside and I wouldn't give a damn.

My mouth travels the length of her legs and without warning, I bring them both around my shoulders, her sweet pussy lands straight in front of my face.

"You're mine Golden and I'm about to taste that sweet pussy of mine." I lap my tongue over her clit, her legs laced around me, bringing her deeper, closer into my mouth.

She tastes like fucking heaven and I know in this very moment that I will never get enough of this. There is no way I could enjoy anything more than having her legs around me like this, her sweet pussy in my mouth.

Her hands are all over my head, her short breaths are the only sound that fills the room, and they are better than the most beautiful music I will ever hear.

I plunge my finger into her and I can feel her body still for a second, then sweet moan fills the room.

"Dylan, I.."

"You what Golden?" I can tell that she is close. I smile with my lips on her clit.

"Are you smiling?" She whispers but it sounds like an accusation.

"I wouldn't dare." I drag my finger out slowly and add one more, just to feel her pulse around my fingers.

"Holy fuck." She cries out and I stop for a second, shocked at the words flying out of her mouth. "Just keep going Dylan, for fucks sake don't stop now, just keep doing what you're doing."

And I do just that, I lick, suck and rub her, pumping my fingers in and out of her until she screams my name in the quiet room. I can feel her coming all over me and I can feel the precum leaking out of my steel hard cock. I take her legs off my shoulder and put feet back on the floor, bringing my mouth to hers. Letting her taste herself, I'm sure she doesn't know how great that taste is.

"That was incredible." She mumbles over my mouth, her voice drunk on the ecstasy.

"It was indeed, and that was just an appetizer, so let's go back to the party. Don't you dare stop thinking about my mouth on your pussy for a second."

"That won't be a problem." She smiles lazily and traces her fingers over my jaw.

I can feel.
She can feel.

I know.
I can't let this woman slip.
I can't let her get away from me.
I should do everything in my power to keep her close.

Nina

I sip another glass of champagne even though my head is slightly spinning already. I'm not sure if the spinning is associated with the alcohol or the fact that I just had one of the best orgasms, from a man I wish could be mine.

I keep thinking about what just happened, and I know he knows I'm thinking about it. He smirks at me every time I rub my legs together.

He said that this was just the beginning. If beginnings look like that, I'm not sure I can survive the main course.

I take a glance at him while he talks to Shelly, the deli's chef. I take in his strong features, his profile that reminds me of a Greek god, with a sexy shadow covering his face. And when he smiles, that damn dimple is smiling right at me, making me even happier. He is handsome. There is no question about it. Most women in this room would definitely agree with me on that. Their eyes flick to him when they think their husbands are not watching.

I see it and I just smile to myself, knowing that it's me that just got totally, completely undone by his skilled mouth. Take that bitches. I sip on my bubbly and I know this should be my last one, everything seems too easy right now, everything seems so doable and there are no limits. No rules that I should follow tonight, even though I'm still sober enough to think I might regret this tomorrow,

I simply don't care.

I think I need just one more drink so the reflections about regrets won't be visiting anytime soon. I will deal with this in the morning. This and the headache.

I catch Dylan's eyes on me as I grab another glass of champagne from the passing waiter and I smile to him lifting the glass to my mouth.

I watch him smile at me as he places his big hand over my bare knee, making me shudder slightly. "Are you sure you can handle that?" He points to the glass.

"I think it is too late for that question." I put my own hand on his thigh and slide it higher, feeling his slight bulge under my palm. I grin at him and I'm about to say something when the lights dim and they announce cake.

"Just about fucking time." Dylan growls, and I giggle.

"Uhmm..." I rub his pants under the table and keep my eyes on the new couple. I don't really know what is going on around me, I can feel the heat spreading all over my womb, my nipples harden. The only thing that is floating through my mind is getting out of here to finish what we started in the other room.

I would be lying if I said I haven't been thinking about our getaway. I would be lying if I said I hadn't thought about his mouth covering my pussy while we were dancing together, while his legs were rubbing mine, sending chills down my spine and making my head spin.

That would all be a lie.

So I watch the cake being cut and I clap with everybody else, bringing my hands together and leaving him semi hard under the table. His eyes have not left mine, full of amusement and desire. Yes, he definitely wants me, which only gives me more courage to go ahead and finish my *meal.*

The moment the music starts to play and people swarm the floor again I grab his hand wordlessly and head for the exit. He hands the ticket to the valet and we both stand outside, looking at each other without saying anything. There is nothing to say. Our eyes say it all. Our hands say even more.

When the car arrives, he opens the door for me and I get in. Excitement rushing through me like I'm about to do something very big and very important.

I watch him rush around the Jeep and take the seat behind the wheel. "You want me to drop you off at home or do you want to stop by my place?" He asks me, his face turned toward me.

"Do you need to ask?"

He just smiles and leans forward to brush my lips with his.

I watch him as he drives and I see him glance at me from time to time. But when he does, I just look straight ahead with a happy grin on my face.

He puts the car in park and turns toward me, "Should we get out?" He leans over me, brushing my body with his hand, and sets my seat belt free. I feel the need to be close to him right this second, have his body pressed to mine, making me his once again.

I get out of the car and he does the same. I take in the beautiful night as I lift my head towards the sky, not noticing that he is already waiting for me at the door.

"Golden," His husky voice is low right now and I can tell that his mind is running on the same tune as mine.

I walk to the door and as soon as I close it behind me, I reach for the straps of my dress, sliding them down my arms.

One.

Then the other.

I know he can't see it as he is walking towards the kitchen, with his back to me, throwing his jacket on the couch and loosening his tie, throwing his shoes in the corner.

I don't say anything. I don't move. Then he turns around, and by that time I'm standing next to the door, wearing nothing but my fancy white lace bra and matching panties. High heeled sandals on my feet, my hair loose, falling freely around my back and my breast.

"Holy fuck," his hands fly to his head and he licks his mouth like he is about to have the best meal of his life. "Golden." He's next to me in few strides and I can feel his hands covering every part of my body. His touch is gentle, slow, like he is being careful not to scare me.

I lift myself up and cover his lips with mine, I can't stand this. All this is too much and I know I'm not acting like my usual self, but I can't help it. The need in me is much, much stronger than the rational Nina that normally lives in my head.

"You have no idea what you do to me." He murmurs to my neck, nibbling and kissing my scar. "No fucking idea." His mouth tastes every inch of me. "This has been my dream every night. This, you like that next to me, my mouth on you, exploring."

I reach down to his pants and undo the button on his slacks, dipping my hand inside. I cover his cock with my hand and slide my thumb over his head. God, he is ready for this as much as I am. He lets out the most incredible sounds, from deep within his chest, and picks me up, carrying me out on the patio. He places me gently on one of the couches. It's dark and the only light shining on us is from the moon. I don't really care that we are outside and that someone might see us. All I want is him close to

revival

me, inside me, being one with me for this short moment.

Within seconds I'm stripped to nothing, his eyes roam over me like he is trying to memorize every inch of me, his hands stroking my body gently. His lips dance over my skin, tasting me, nibbling on me and licking me in places I want to be licked. I bring my hands to him and unbutton his shirt, letting it fall to the patio floor. Then I push his pants down with my feet as his mouth covers the sensitive flesh of my nipples.

"I need you right now Dylan." I breathe out, bringing his tip to my wet entrance.

"Not so fast Golden, let me enjoy this view." He slides his fingers inside me and I close my eyes, leaning back in search of more.

"Dylan, please." I spread my legs wider and pull him closer to me so I can feel his body on mine.

"Who would have thought Golden." He growls and sucks my nipple like he can't get enough of it.

"Just stop talking and fuck me already." I push my hips upward to grind in his hardness "Please."

That does it. He looks into my eyes and presses himself inside me, inching slowly like he is afraid to hurt me, I buckle and force him to go farther and further until I'm full.

Full of him.

Our breathing is out of control, I close my eyes from time to time, but I have something so beautiful in front of me that I force myself to keep them open. Watching this man get lost in the pleasure we share.

"You feel so good, I could be buried in you and the world could end. I would die the happiest man." He thrusts into me harder and I feel myself losing it. My body overheating while my mind goes blank. Nothing but an intense feeling of pleasure fills up every part of me. I can feel his hips rotate and he picks up speed, his eyes hooded, looking at me and getting lost in me, like I got lost in him.

"I...I can't take it anymore." I pant between each thrust.

"I'm right behind you."

And I let it go.

I let go hard and loud, calling his name into the night. My body goes still and then relaxes under him. The he pulls out of me and the warmth of his cum touches my stomach.

I smile.

I force my eyes open and I see his spent face smiling at me as well.

There is no way I'm going to regret this in the morning.

Nina

My alarm beeps and I stretch my hand to shut it off, giving myself a few extra minutes to get used to the idea that I have to go to work in a little bit. I turn to the side, opening my eyes in shock as I feel something I shouldn't.

Dylan is sleeping next to me. In my bed. His face looks peaceful and I can see his chest rising and falling, indicating that he is deep in his sleep.

What the heck?

I try to piece last night together and I sigh when I realize that he drove me home. I invited him to come upstairs and cuddle me to sleep. Of course, the cuddle came after another round of orgasms that were nothing short of incredible, but none of last night seems so incredible right now.

I panic thinking that last night shouldn't have happened at all. Damn alcohol. Damn the bubbly liquid that somehow took over my brain, told me that everything is possible and that nothing was going to be stupid or reckless.

I lift the covers up and try to get out of the bed as quietly as I can, but Dylan's muscular arm wraps around me, bringing me close to him.

"Morning, Golden." His voice sounds like cotton candy, sweet and thick, something I can't get enough of even though I know it's not good for me.

"Morning." I lay still, not sure if I should wrap my arms around him or tell him to get up and leave.

I can feel him watching me, I can feel the burn of his stare on my face while I focus on a non existent spot on the ceiling.

"Don't tell me you regret any of this." He lifts himself up, playing with a few strands of my hair. He rubs them together like he is trying to figure out what my hair is made of. "I enjoyed every second of it and you sounded like you were on the same page, so what is going on in that beautiful head of yours?"

I can't look at him. And I definitely can't tell him what is going on in my head.

"I'm good," I lie "And last night was incredible." That's the truth.

"So what's with the face then?"

I say nothing. Get out of bed and head to the kitchen to start a pot of coffee. Then I head straight for the shower, hoping that when I get out he will be gone. I don't want him gone but I need him gone.

I get out of the bathroom and he is standing next to the counter, sipping his coffee. Wearing black sweat pants that are sitting low on his waist and a grey shirt that shows off his incredible body.

"Coffee?" He points to the second cup sitting on the kitchen counter. I walk over slowly, grab the cup and take a few sips, trying to think of an easy way to tell him that this can never happen again.

"Can I take Ellie to a movie after school? I will pick her up and drop her off before six."

"Sure." My answer comes easily, automatically and somehow natural. He is awesome with her and she loves to spend time with him. She even said herself that there is nothing better than spending time with Dylan. I have to be honest, it stings a little bit because I don't get many chances to do activities with her. Who Am I kidding? I just place a kiss here and there, running between the jobs and cuddle her to sleep at night. That's what I get. So yeah, I'm

revival

jealous of the time they have spent together, having fun, enjoying each other.

Honestly, I don't know what I'm doing. I shouldn't allow this almost every day interaction between the two of them. They will have to stop soon and I know Ellie will be hurt, and so will Dylan.

And so will I.

I know I should stop this before everything gets out of control, but I don't know how. How do I tell my daughter that she can't hang out with her favorite person? How do I tell Dylan that seeing his daughter everyday is not going to bring anything good?

I can't.

"Ok, I have to go." I grab my stuff and wait for him.

"You want me to drive you?"

"No, I'm good." I head for the door when he's ready and we walk down the stairs in awkward silence. He heads for his car, hugs me and places a soft kiss on my lips before I walk in the opposite direction, heading to work.

I have to tell him the truth. There is no way that keeping this big of a secret from him is a good idea. But I also know that the second he finds out, he will run away.

And I won't blame him.

After all, there is nothing that I can promise or give to him. I belong to someone else.

———•●•———

I walk home from the hotel job smiling, looking at the pictures Dylan sent me while he was out with Ellie. She is grinning from ear to ear in each and every one of them, surely enjoying herself. My heart sinks. I set my mind on telling him the truth. Once he knows, there is nothing that will keep him close to us.

I thought about it long and hard while at work today. Day after day I see Ellie get more and more fascinated and attached to Dylan. I don't blame her. She never had a father figure in her life, except her first year. I'm sure she can't remember, and even then he wasn't really around. So Dylan being a caring and loving friend, as she calls him, is the perfect father figure. I can feel it in my bones that I let things go too far.

I also considered my feelings for him. The constant want and craving to have him around. The need to have him close. Last night felt like the best night of my life, which proves that I'm weak, that I'm not strong enough around him. I melt every time he looks at me with his hungry eyes, I crumble every time he touches me or comes close.

That cannot happen.

I chose a different path for myself and this is not the road I should be heading down.

I stop short as I get to the door of Gran's apartment. I hear laughter coming out of the apartment. I knock and fidget nervously while I wait for her to open the door.

"It's open!" I hear Gran shout, so I press the handle down finding it indeed open. *What the hell?* I storm into the room ready to go ballistic, but I stop when I see the three of them sitting on the floor, playing what looks like UNO.

"Hello Nina." Gran greets me like there is nothing wrong with the door being unlocked.

"Mommy, I'm winning." Ellie is a bundle of excitement, sending me one 'hello' glance before diving back into the game.

I hold my tongue and I smile at her, trying to

revival

catch the eyes of the two adults in the room, but they seem to be preoccupied with the game so much that they can't even look at me.

I sit down on the couch and watch them play. I take in the flushed face of my angel, the serious face of Gran and playful face of Dylan. They all seem to be having fun.

"Ok, I'm going to join in for one round and then I have to run." I plop on the floor next to Ellie and they all cheer while setting the new cards on the carpet.

"You're never going to win with me, just so you know." Ellie's hard stare meets mine and I do my best not to smile.

"We will see." I put my best game face on and focus on my cards.

We play for a little while before my phone chirps, letting me know that it's time to go to work. I see Dylan look at Gran, and then she nods her head like she knows what his stare means.

Confusing.

"I was just asking Simone and Ellie if they want to visit California for Thanksgiving." Dylan's eyes meet mine. It took me more than a second to register what he was saying to me.

"We are going to California?" Ellie's excited voice cuts in. I glance at her and she doesn't need an extra warning. She starts to bring all the cards together and shuffle them the best way she can.

"We have no family in California, so I don't see why we should go there?" I spit out. I know in an instant that the words came out too harsh. But what did he expect? That I will say 'yeah, sure, sounds good let me get my family together with yours and have one Happy Thanksgiving party'?

"You have me, and my mom is waiting to meet you, both of you." His eyes land on Ellie and I try to find the best excuse to escape from this ridiculous situation.

"We can go. We don't have any big plans anyway." Gran says this without even looking at me, shuffling cards with Ellie.

Is she serious? Is she really implying that we should go to California and meet Dylan's mother? I'm already trying not to face the fact that she is seeing her father without knowing he is her father, and now I should bring her to meet her other grandmother? The one that is definitely forbidden?

"We will talk about this later." I glance at Ellie, watching her face fall.

"Sure we will." Gran doesn't even look at me, instead she glances at Dylan and they both nod their heads in agreement.

What is going on?

Neither of them will look at me, so I have to repeat the conversation in my mind to make sure it even happened.

———•●•———

"What is going on? Huh?" I fire right after the door closes behind Dylan.

I watch Gran walk around the kitchen counter and put a pot of water on the stove. Then she turns to me and watches me in silence, her wrinkled forehead scrunching even more and her mouth twists in an unhappy manner.

"She's Ellie's grandmother, and she invited us over. I simply think we should go. I know that you are far from telling the truth to Dylan but honey, you can't keep this from him. You should see him around her, he is acting like the father she never had, he acts like someone you want to keep around. I know that you think you made this vow years ago, but Nina, that was the biggest mistake of your life and you know it. We both know it. Look at me and tell me right now that you will be happy once he shows up at your doorstep. Tell me that you will get your happily ever after once he is here."

I can't. So I kept quiet and let the tears fall.

All of a sudden I feel like I've never done anything right in my life. As if all I did was make these pathetic mistakes that lead to more mistakes, leaving me alone, here, dreaming of a life that will never come.

"What are you saying?" I know the answer but I need to hear it. I need it to run through my ears so I can be sure of the answer.

"We should go." She states.

"And do what? Act like the family we are not?" I can't even imagine how she could suggest something like that. "Pretend that we are one big family? No. We are not going anywhere." I lean over Ellie who just got back from the bathroom, place a kiss on her cheek, and head to my apartment to get ready for work.

I'm furious while I walk up the stairs, taking two steps at a time, rushing to my door and stopping short when I see Dylan leaning on it.

"What are you doing here?" I snap.

"Did you talk about it?"

"Talk about what?" I know I'm playing dumb, but there is no way I will talk to him about all this nonsense right now. I have a less than an hour to get ready.

"Golden." He steps closer to me while I pretend to look for my keys in my purse. His hand lands on my waist and he tries to bring me closer to him. I wiggle out of his arm and open the door, lock by lock. I swing it open and rush inside, and he is right behind me.

"Just go away, Dylan." I throw my stuff on the kitchen counter and head to my bedroom to grab a change of clothes. I can hear him walking in my direction. "I need to change." I send him a glance while putting my hands on my hips.

"Then change," he smirks. "I don't mind seeing that gorgeous body of yours."

"Get out Dylan and let me change." My chest is rising and falling. I'm not sure if it is from anger, or the fact that his hungry eyes are challenging me. I am done with keeping all my emotions in check, and I'm done with doing the right thing, so I let it happen.

I reach for the hem of my tank top and slowly bring it up over my head, my eyes on him, watching his pupils dilate when my bra comes into view. I reach back and unclasp my bra letting it fall to the floor, leaving my breasts on full display. My nipples shrink at the memory of how his mouth felt on them.

As he steps closer, I see his Adam's apple rise up and down as he swallows, his eyes taking me in.

I pop the button of my jeans, making a statement while sliding the zipper down. My own breath catches in my throat. I have never done anything like this. I have never even thought about doing anything like this, but there is something about him that makes me brave enough to push myself out of my comfort zone.

I dip my hand inside my pants, sliding my finger over myself. God, that feels good. The fact that he's rubbing himself over his jeans is an obvious indication that he likes it as well.

"You've gotta be kidding me." He growls and sits down on the bed behind him. I lean on the closet door because I'm not sure I can stand on my own any longer. I slide the jeans down my legs and kick them to the side. As soon as I'm standing naked in front of him, I suddenly don't know what to do with myself. Bravery is much harder when I'm naked in front of a fully clothed man.

"Touch yourself Nina. Show me what you do when you lay in this bed by yourself. Show me how you get yourself off when there is nobody next to you to help you with it. Show me how your fingers dance around when I'm far away." I hear the sound of his zipper and I watch him take his cock out of his jeans, stroking it slowly.

My mouth waters, I would do anything to taste him right now. Instead, I reach for my breast and start to play with my nipple while dipping my fingers into my wetness.

"Don't close your eyes Golden, I want you to look at me. I want to see everything that is about to happen."

I look at him as I play with my clit, circling it the same way he did the night before. I slide my finger inside as I watch his hand move faster. I moan and pinch my nipple harder with each and every stroke of his hand.

"Fuck!" He licks his lips "Whose fingers do you have inside you Golden?"

"Yours." I fight the urge to close my eyes. Hearing his voice like that, watching his hand moving over his massive shaft, having my fingers inside me, it's too much.

"That's my girl, now spread your legs so I can see how wet you are for me."

I pause before I obey. All I want is to move my hand faster and shove my fingers deeper as the sensation is getting unbearable. I slide down the closet door and spread my legs as much as I can. My pussy opening for him, on full display.

"Jesus," I can see his shaft glistening from the

pre-cum, his large hands sliding over his length, up and down. His eyes bounce between my pussy and my face. "I want nothing more than to lick the fuck out of you right now, but seeing you like this is worth the wait."

I move my fingers faster, sliding them deeper and deeper each time. I can feel my muscles clench and I know I won't last much longer, but neither will he. Our quick breaths are synchronized while we both chase the orgasm.

"Ohhh God..." I close my eyes and let the feeling flow though me like an earthquake, shattering me from the inside out.

"Fuck, Golden!" I see him lean down and grab my tank top, coming all over it.

I laugh. Not a crazy laugh but a lazy, 'I can't believe you're doing this' laugh. He does the same after a few seconds.

"You want to keep the shirt? Just in case?" I'm sure he doesn't appreciate the joke but I know if I allow a second of silence, I will be embarrassed more than I can imagine.

"Souvenir." His eyes are relaxed. The smile on his face is nothing but genuine. "Guess now you can get dressed."

I get up from the floor, my legs a little wobbly, and I pick new tank top from the closet. I don't have time to shower anymore so I put the clothes on my body, hoping I don't smell like sex. "I gotta go." I spin around to look at him and he is now lying down, leaning on his elbows, his eyes watching me closely.

God, those eyes are capable of hypnotizing every female, and I'm no different. I can get lost in them the moment I look at them. I don't think about the consequences, I don't think what's going to happen tomorrow. Scratch that, I don't care if tomorrow even comes.

And here I am. Losing myself once again. If I think about it, I don't know if I ever found myself these last six years. I was lost, searching for the wrong answers, wrapped up in the wrong people, choosing the wrong road and stopping at the wrong station.

The part of me, that, *I have had enough of doing the right things,* part is looking at this man and believes, hopes, that me and him could be something more.

Then reality hits and I feel like a slut for breaking the vows I once gave. For betraying someone, even if that someone is worth the betrayal.

"I have to go. " I repeat and head for the kitchen, grabbing my bag. I stand next to the door, waiting for him to join me.

"I will drive you." He offers while we walk down the stairs.

"Thanks, but I'll manage." I suddenly feel so stupid for spreading myself in front of him like that. What was I thinking? I wasn't. Obviously.

"You're impossible." He growls and pulls me close to him, placing a soft, but deep kiss on my mouth. "I will call tomorrow and see if Ellie wants to do something."

"About that..." I look at my phone and see that I have 10 minutes before my shift starts, so that doesn't give me enough time to start the conversation I need to have.

His brows meet at the bridge of his nose and he waits for me to finish.

"Nothing, I will talk to you soon." I wave him off and hurry to the bar.

Dylan

I watch her rush down the street and I rub my face in shock. She surprised me today. I didn't know she had it in her, and I was more than sure that she would stop that little game of hers when her bra came off. But she didn't, she kept going and it was the hottest thing I've ever seen.

I jump in the car and head for my rental.

I can't believe how my life took this spin and I end it up here, finding something to look forward to, after losing something that was so important to me.

I still feel that knot in my stomach while I think briefly about Mia, but it's getting more and more bearable. I'm very, very close to accepting that whatever we had would never have gone any further. I would still give everything to have her here, but I understand that none of it was my fault. I know it was one of those stupid, tragic accidents people get into, and maybe that was something that was in the stars for her. She knew she was living on the edge, she even said that in her letter, the letter she wrote way before anything had happened.

She will always hold a piece of me no matter what.

But Nina...

She is waking up something I thought would never be awake again. She is making me feel, want and desire in the way I thought I would never be able to again.

revival

I don't know if I should be scared or should I let the emotions take their course? What are the chances that I will be left shredded to pieces once again?

That was, and still is, my biggest fear. That was the main reason why I always kept all those girls at a distance, never letting them get too close, never letting myself get too close to them. But Mia, she broke that pattern the minute I laid my eyes on her. And now I know what it feels like to have someone and I sort of crave that feeling again.

I know there is something Nina is not telling me. I can sense her being careful, trying to keep her distance. Until she melts in my arms, and then none of it matters.

She already shocked me by hiding the fact that we have a daughter. That I'm the father. I understand though, I do. I know she couldn't contact me, but it kills me that I have lost five years of my princess' life. Five fucking years.

I see the Walmart sign and I make a sharp turn, parking in the first available spot.

I will at least try to make it up to her.

I jump out of the car and hurry inside, pumped with the brilliant idea that just popped into my head. I rush to the cards aisle and browse the girls section, picking up the card for ages 1 to 5. One card for each birthday I've missed.

I stop short for a second when I realize I don't even know when Nina's birthday is. I will have to ask her the first chance I get.

Then I head toward the toy aisles and start picking gifts for a one year old, moving up each year until I reach five. It might be a silly idea, but it feels right.

I grab wrapping paper and some pens before heading towards the cashier. I hope Ellie will love the idea as much as I do.

I wrap the presents in the car, taking my time to write birthday wishes on each card, my hand twitches with the need to sign them *Daddy*. But I know I can't do that just yet. I know she doesn't know, or she pretends she doesn't know. It took me by surprise when she said how alike we look when we were looking at one of the selfies we took.

Look at that Dylan, we have the same eyes and we have the same hole in the chin.

Yes.

And you have eyes shaped exactly like your aunt Mia. This I never said out loud.

Daddy.

I feel tears pricking to my eyes as I realize that this will never be taken away from me. No matter what happens between me and Nina, Ellie will always remain my daughter, and I will always remain her father.

I finish wrapping and head back into town, parking my car next to their apartment and heading up the stairs. I know this could be the stupidest idea I've ever had, and maybe they will both look at me like I've lost my mind. I don't know.

"Oh my gosh, what is that?" I can hear Ellie's voice coming from the living room.

I pass Simone standing in the doorway, her eyes big as saucers. "What is it Dylan?"

"You know how I missed those five birthdays you had?" I meet her mischievous smile and her eyes sparkle and grow big while she nods her head.

"Well, this is to make up for all the years I've missed, sunshine" I put all the presents in front of her and she is rushes to them, ripping the closest one open.

"Gran, look, it's like having my birthday today."

"Sure is honey." Simone is smiling at her,

sending me sideways glances full of approval.

I can't stop watching her pick up the toys and arts and crafts boxes, gasping at every single item, saying thank you every time she holds something in her little hands. She runs to me and wraps her arms around my neck, placing a kiss on my cheek.

"Thank you, Dylan!" Her face is flushed from excitement and her eyes sparkle. I promise myself in this moment that I will seek more moments like this. More days like today, and I can't wait for the day when she will finally call me Dad.

I know Nina doesn't want to drop the bomb on her just like that, that's what she said anyway. She insisted that I take it slow and see how I feel about it. But I don't want to take it slow. I want to dive in and stay because this incredible, soul filling duty was given to me.

I say goodnight to Ellie and Simone before heading out to my place. I know Austin will call me around 9:00 to talk about a new real estate opportunity. An opportunity I'm not even excited about. Honestly, I never really thought I would have had to take over the company, I thought my father would sell everything when he decided to retire. He talked about it few times, so I never thought that this might be something of my concern.

I didn't have a choice, the moment he passed away, the moment when I saw my mother's body hunched over him, and saying her goodbye, I knew that I had to step up. There was no other choice.

A year later and countless closed deals, I still feel like I'm doing the right thing. That this is the only thing I'm doing *is* the right thing. But the truth is I don't have a passion for this profession, I never have. I never felt truly happy after closing a deal, any deal, even the ones that would financially set the average person up for life. I've never felt the pride that my father did when he came back home with good news. The whole thing has more to do with doing the right thing, than with fulfilling my life dream.

What is my life dream exactly?

All I've ever done was fight. That was the only thing that pumped my blood with excitement, but I'm too old and I'm too worn out for that shit now. It was about time to walk away from it and my father's death was a good excuse.

So what is it that I want now?

I do have a few ideas, but first I need to talk with Austin and my mother. I know she said that I don't have to stay in the company, and whenever I feel like this is not for me, she won't have any hard feelings about it. But I also know that this is something that is close to her heart, and if I decide to sell it by myself she might feel hurt.

I call out my mother's name to the car phone and listen to few dial signals before she picks up.

"Hi Dylan." Her voice sounds fresh and surprisingly upbeat.

"Hey ma, how you doing?"

"I'm good, just heading to the club for a poker night."

I chuckle, knowing how she loves the game. "Good, good, hope you win all the fake money."

"Oh, stop it, it's about fun, not about the money, you know that."

"I know, I know. Hey listen, about Thanksgiving, I don't think they are coming."

There is a short silence on her end and I know she is disappointed. I know she was counting on meeting Nina and Ellie.

"Did she say no?"

"No... Well, kind of. She made pretty clear that she feels it's too early for this type of thing."

revival

"I see." Shit. Now I feel bad that I didn't try harder, but one single look in her eyes and I knew there is no way I could change her mind. Nina is a lot of things, but when she sets her mind on something, she didn't back out. I know she has already decided and no matter what I do or say, her decision will stay the same.

"Don't worry if you want to stay there, I will go to the club. Burk has already invited me to the annual Thanksgiving, so I will definitely not be alone. You can stay and enjoy the holiday."

"I'm coming home Mom. I have things to do anyway and have a few meetings scheduled on Wednesday. I will go with you if you need plus one."

I secretly hope that she will say we can stay home since I'm coming back.

"Great, then we will go together. Richard will be pleased to see you there. Ok. I'm just pulling onto to the club parking lot so I guess I will see you soon, take care son."

"See you soon Mom."

I press the end button on my steering wheel and cringe. The Thanksgiving Gala thrown by the Burk's. The famous Susan Burk, daughter of Richard Burk, will surely be there. She has wanted to drag me to bed ever since I can remember. I've always found a perfect excuse to say no. She is what many would call a whore, yet she is praised on the gossip magazines like a fucking' princess. Shit. I hope that she is married by now and she grew out of her slutty ways.

I turn off the Jeep and walk inside. It's quiet and the only thing I can hear are the waves crashing into the shore. The sun is low on the horizon and I wish for a second that I had someone to share this view with.

Will they want to share this with me? Will they

ever, no, will she ever forgive me and accept the fact that all I want now is to be with both of them?

My phone rings and I pick it up without looking at the screen.

"Dylan?"

"Who else do you think you're calling?"

"Funny," Austin voice is short of humor. "We have a problem."

"Ok. I'm listening."

"Both the Germans and Russians backed out of the deal."

"To tell you the truth, that saves us tons of headaches. You know there were about ten others on the line and they won't care about the dates and who opens first."

"Fuck. I thought you were completely out of it and I was doing all the work. You asshole, you are staying on top of it, I see." He chuckles and I just shake my head.

"Watch it boy, this is your boss you're talking to."

"Yeah. So, the Italians are ready to buy two properties. They are opening one hotel on New Year's day and the other in June."

"New Year's? That's like six weeks away. Are they fucking crazy?"

"I said the same thing, but this one is already built. They need to finish the interior, but still... Anyway, if they think they can do it, let them. They are just waiting for the 'go ahead' from you."

"They can start, but if anything goes wrong, make sure our hands are clean. I don't need them on our asses when they will hit a wall."

"Covered that in the contract already. Ok, so I'm done with you and I'm going to call them. See you soon I guess. And I can't wait to meet those girls of yours."

"Sorry to break it to you, but you will have to

enjoy my pretty face and my face only, they aren't coming."

"And that's my shitty luck right here. Later."

"Sure."

I put the phone on the table and walk to the fridge, grabbing a few bottles of beer before walking out to the porch. I sit on one of the lounge chairs and watch the view. It reminds me of my view at home. The only thing that is different is the house behind me and the fact that I'm closer to my happiness here than I ever was in my own house.

I'm sipping the third beer, trying to figure out the best way to break the news to my Mom, to Austin and to Nina, when I hear the sound of car tires on my gravel driveway. The only visitor I ever get is Oscar, so I just wait for him to walk in. I'm sure he will figure out that I'm sitting on the porch, just like he has many times before.

I take a long sip of my beer and take a deep breath, trying to relax my mind.

"Dylan?" I hear Nina's curious voice coming from inside the house.

"Here," I let her know that I'm outside and I hear her heels clicking on the wood floor in the living room. "What are you doing here, has something happened?" I scan her and my eyes stop on her low cut top, emphasizing her breasts perfectly.

"I need to talk to you."

I watch her walk closer to me and the look on her face indicates that I won't like this conversation.

"Everything's ok with Ellie?" That is the first thing that comes to my mind.

She nods her head, "She's fine." I watch her walk to the opposite seat, grabbing a bottle of beer before she sits.

"I have wine if you want." I know she hates beer.

"That would be great."

I stand up and walk to the kitchen, grabbing the wine glass out of the cabinet and fetching the bottle of red I bought, just for her. While I pull the cork out, I sneak a peek outside. Watching her sit on the edge of the chair, fidgeting with her hands nervously. Something is wrong. I can feel it in my bones.

"Here." I hand her the glass and watch her take a deep sip while I sit back in the chair. Her eyes are looking everywhere, except at me. I try to keep my face still, unaffected by the emotions that are swirling in my head.

"What's going on?" I press after she is half way through her glass. Her eyes are focused somewhere over the ocean, her tongue slipping out once in a while to lick her lips, like she is trying decide if the moment is right.

Fuck me.

"I need to tell you something." Her glass is once again close to her lips.

"I'm listening."

She snaps her head in my direction and looks straight into my eyes. Her eyes are glistening with tears that will come any second.

"What's going on?"

She turns her face toward the ocean, "I don't need you in my life, in our lives."

That is something I didn't see coming.

I try to take a breath large enough to supply me with the oxygen for what is to come, but I fail.

"I just got in." That is all I manage to choke out.

What is she saying? That I will no longer be able to see Ellie? That I will no longer be able to spend time with my daughter?

"You can't say something like that." I will fight for her to my last breath, I will fight until I get what I want. What I need. What is mine.

revival

I watch her fidget in her seat, she twists slightly in my direction. Her face shows nothing but pain and regret.

"Come here." My voice is direct. She doesn't hesitate while she walks toward me, stopping right in front of me. Her face is full of worry, her eyes trying to escape mine.

"What's the problem Golden? What's going on, huh?" I can't help it, I bring my hands to her bare legs, rubbing them gently. I try my best to stay calm and get to the bottom of all of this. I watch her eyes close, her teeth covers her lower lip in a gentle bite. I bring my hand higher and earn myself a sigh, a slight shiver of her muscles, something that tells me that her skin is in sync with my touch. If her mind would be as responsive as her body, I would be the happiest man on Earth.

"The problem is that I don't know if you are any good for her and..." My lips swallow her words keeping them in, not letting them ruin this moment.

Our tongues find each other in a frantic tango and I feel her body melt into mine, her breath becomes short. I feel her hands cover my neck and I bring mine to her back, "Something you wanted to tell me?" I breathe into her mouth, still pressed to mine.

"Later," she pushes her hands down my shirt, "We will talk later."

I know I should stop her and let her tell me what the problem is, but I'm too selfish. I want her right now, at this moment, as much as she wants me. Any regrets, any explanations that we shouldn't be doing this right now, are not something I want to take into consideration.

I swipe my hands under her shirt and bring them to her full breasts, finding her nipples hard, ready to be sucked. I tease her bra and slide my finger in, reaching for her most sensitive part. I hear her suck in a breath as I repeat the same action with my second hand.

Now, both of my hands are covering her breasts as my thumbs rub her nipples gently. I feel her body shudder under my hold and I take it as an invitation to go further.

"Are you sure? We can talk about it right now. I can stop right now." That's a lie. I won't be able to stop, not right now, not ever.

"Don't stop," her voice is rushed, exactly what I was hoping for.

"Don't stop what Golden?" I place soft kisses all over her.

"Touching me like that, keep touching me like that and stop talking." Her head is thrown back. The second my fingers find her wetness she moans the most beautiful sound a man's ears could ever hear.

I plunge deeper and push her gently to lie down on the chair, my hands all over her, in her.

"You sure you want this Golden? Because right now, I don't feel like being gentle with you. You came here to tell me to get the hell out of your life, so I'm pretty pissed."

"Yes," she breathes out, "I want you in me. I want you to fuck me hard and make me feel you like I've never felt you before, can you do that Dylan?" Her eyes are focused on me. I stop for a second to make sure she is the Nina, the Golden I know. Her words don't match the quiet, good girl she seems to be.

But yes, that is still my girl, only with a dirtier mouth.

I will take it all of it.

All.

Of.

This.

Is.
Mine.
Mine.

My hands are exploring her body while hers do the same. I slide her shorts down, taking her panties with them. She reaches for the zipper of my jeans but I stand up and slide them down myself, my cock standing alert and ready. I take the condom out of my back jean pocket, rolling it down, not able to take my eyes off her.

"Turn around." My voice is laced with a lust I'm unable to control. I watch her roll slowly to her belly and I can't wait any longer to slide inside her. I grab her hips and bring her ass up, entering her in one quick move.

"Jesus Dylan," Her words are short. She sounds out of breath. She has no idea I haven't even started yet.

I grab her hair in my hand gently, turning her face to mine, placing a hungry kiss on her swollen lips. I'm fucking her mouth the same way I'm fucking her pussy right now. Rough, fast and angry.

I find her throbbing clit and rub it as I plunge into her, again and again. I can feel her body start to tremble and I rotate my hips to get even deeper inside her.

"You feel so good Golden, I wish I could feel you like this every fuckin' day for the rest of my life." I feel her muscles pulse around my shaft and I bring my thumb to her ass, rubbing the hole gently, pressing the tip inside. She is becoming undone, her body shaking under mine. I listen to the moans escape her mouth as she orgasms, and I feel mine hit me like a cyclone.

"Fuck." I lean down, kissing her neck gently, caressing her body with feather like strokes.

We stay quiet for a while, our breath slowly

coming back to normal.

"There was something you wanted to tell me?" I ask, though I hope she will never answer my question.

"I think we ruined any chance of having a serious conversation the moment you put your hands on me." She giggles and I relax.

"So there will be no conversation?"

"Not tonight, no."

I take a deep breath and brush her blond hair off her face, kissing her lips gently. The moon shining above us makes her body glow, revealing the perfection next to me. I can't get over how beautiful she looks right now. Her naked body is tangled with mine, it fits perfectly.

"I meant what I said."

I see the surprise in her eyes, but I know she understands what I'm talking about.

"I really wish I could have you next to me for the rest of my life, Nina."

I see her swallow whatever nervousness she is trying to overcome, and she brings her head into my chest, hiding herself from me, in me.

Nina

It's been over a week since I pulled myself together and decided to tell him the truth.

It's been over a week since I failed in that decision. I lost my bravery the moment his hands landed on me. Every time he is close and looks at me like that, I lose myself in him more and more. And that is exactly why I made big damn mistake when I decided to put the conversation on hold, choosing his closeness instead.

I saw him almost every day this week while he stopped by to spend time with Ellie. Every time he looks at me my heart melts, and I keep pushing back the conversation that we need to have.

Now he is leaving to go home for Thanksgiving, and he won't be back until Monday.

"I will see you on Monday, Sunshine." He hugs Ellie and glances at me over her shoulder.

We haven't really said more than 'hi' and 'bye' for the past week, and it's all because of me. I know I act stupid and childish, but I can't let anything like that happen again. I know that I'm not strong enough to keep myself at a safe distance when he's around. I tried, and failed miserably every single time.

He says his goodbyes to Simone and I watch him walk out the door. I watch Ellie walk towards Simone, helping her cook. Without a word I sprint out of the door. I don't know what I will say exactly.

I had the whole conversation rehearsed before, but right now I don't remember a single word.

"Dylan!" I call after him, just before he gets into his car. He turns around and smiles.

Damn it! I have to do this. There is no way I can have what I want. There is no way I can untangle myself from the web I built over the years. I have to do this.

"I knew you wouldn't let me go without a proper goodbye," he stretches his arms out to wrap them around me, but I step back. His brows form one, straight line. "What's going on?"

You can do this. You can do this. I chant to myself. I take a deep breath and look past him.

"I can't do this anymore."

I see his mouth open and I bring my hand up to stop him from whatever he is about to say. "It's really confusing for Ellie to go without a father for so long, and then have someone like you around every day. I can't tell her who you really are Dylan. I just can't. I've managed to live just fine without you for the past six years, so I'm pretty sure I can keep doing it."

"Are you talking about yourself? Because I don't see how Ellie can be confused about anything if you refuse to tell her the truth. Why are you so afraid to tell her the truth Nina? Why are you keeping me such a big secret? You do realize that she is smarter than you think. You think she doesn't see the resemblance that we share? Anybody can see that, her included." I watch him step closer to me, his face so close to mine I can feel his warm breath on me, making my head spin. "So tell me Nina, who is more confused? 'Cause I'm sure as hell Ellie is not the one that is afraid or confused here."

"You don't understand."

"Explain it to me then, because I don't

understand what is so damn terrible about me that I'm not good enough for both of you." His words are clipped, his eyes are cold and unyielding.

"I can't have you in our lives Dylan, I'm sorry. Don't make me say it over and over again." I try to push back the tears that are welling up in my eyes. I know they will slide down my face any second, and then I will look like a liar.

"Don't give me that bullshit." He snaps, running his hands over his face "Fuck." He turns around and walks to his car, leaving me standing on the sidewalk. Leaving me alone, like I deserve. I watch him open his door, looking up at me over the hood, before he slams it with a huge force, rushing over to me again.

"Why are you taking everything away from me?" He shouts, not caring who is around.

"I'm not taking anything. I'm letting you go before it's too late. Then none of us will know how to walk away."

"I don't want to walk away. Don't you understand that, goddammit? I'm falling for you or maybe I already fell, but I just haven't realized that yet, and you are telling me to go away?"

I don't say anything to that. I focus on keeping my face straight and unaffected by the fact that he just told me a second time that he is falling for me. That he feels something for me, just like I feel for him.

He grabs my face between both of hands and tilts my head up forcing me to look at him. I close my eyes trying to hide the truth they will probably tell him.

"Look at me Golden," I shake my head no. "Tell me you don't feel this, tell me that the reason your breath catches every time I'm next to you has nothing to do with your feelings towards me. Tell me that the way your chest rises up and down like you can't get enough oxygen to breathe, has nothing to do with me next to you. Tell me that you don't feel the world swirling around every time our lips meet." He brushes his lips over mine "Tell me."

"None of it has anything to do with you Dylan." My voice cracks somewhere in the middle of the sentence and I have to force the rest, feeling like I'm making another huge mistake in my life.

"You are a bad liar Golden." He dives in for a kiss and I fight the urge to let him in. His tongue is seeking access that I deny. Tears slide down my face, their weight is no longer something I'm able to hold.

"Open your goddamn eyes, Nina" He growls in anger.

And I do.

And the second I do, I see the most beautiful eyes staring back at me. I know that I have hurt him beyond repair.

We stand like that for what feels like forever.

He runs his fingers over my cheeks, wiping the tears away. "You are terrible liar Golden, but if this is what you really want then, I'm gone."

I watch him walk towards his car and when he speeds away, I let everything out. I can't see clearly through my blurred eyes. I walk slowly towards my apartment. I know I just destroyed something that could have been a second chance in my pathetic life.

The moment I enter the apartment I get in the shower, hoping to wash everything away.

While I dry my hair I send a text message to Rachel. I need a friend so bad, and I think today is the day I need to tell her the truth. Maybe when I get this off of my chest I will feel lighter, better. I need someone to tell me that I made the right decision. That this is the only rational decision that I could make.

I see her respond with just one word *Skype* and I run to my computer to power it on.

———•◆•———

"You are out of your mind, Nins!" She screams at me after I let everything out. "I wish you could see your face while you talked about him. You fucking glow like I've never seen you before. And I will bitch about the fact that you forget to mention this whole thing for all the years we have been friends, later. Right now, I'm just going to call you stupid."

"Thanks." I blow my nose and throw the tissue at the big pile on the couch next to me.

"I know that you feel that you can't do this, I understand. But honey, you need to be selfish sometimes and this is the exact moment to think about yourself and what do *you* want. Do you want this Nins? Can you see yourself happy with him and Ellie down the road?" I nod my head, as I'm not brave enough to say it out loud. "There you have it, I don't think I have to say anymore." I see her head turn to the side and she gestures something with her hands. "I have to go Nins, but let's talk soon. Love you."

"Thank you Rachel. Love you." I wait for her to end the call and I fall back on the couch, looking at the ceiling, hoping to find some answers.

My thoughts are rushing one after another. In one second, I see myself happy with Dylan and Ellie by my side. Then I shake my head at the pathetic fantasy when reality hits in.

I just told him to go away. Even though he didn't look like he bought what I said, he walked away. Tomorrow he's leaving for California, and most likely he is not coming back here after the holidays.

I blew it. Big time and I'm not sure I know how to undo everything.

I stop by Gran's apartment on my way to work. She eyes me from the moment I step in.

I ignore her and talk with Ellie for a little bit before heading to work. I can't talk about all of this right now, not with her. Besides, he is gone. There is nothing to talk about anyway.

I walk into the pub and see the boys from the band sitting at the bar. Kelley and Travis are working at the same side of the bar, which is weird because they haven't worked together since the huge fight they had a couple of months ago.

I look around and I don't see a single person, the lights are dimmed and music is playing much softer than usual.

"What's going on you guys?" I round the bar and reach for my apron, when Michael's hand stops me.

"We're closed today." He places a glass of wine in my hand.

"Closed?" I can't hide my surprise and I glance at the door to Ritchie's office. "Does he know that?" I joke and take a sip.

"He was the one to get everyone out of here about an hour ago. He told them to go to a different bar." Kelly shrugs, letting me know that she doesn't know what's going on either. I look over at the boys and notice the glances they are passing between each other. Something is not right. We never close just for the heck of it, not during the holidays at least.

I hear the door of the office squeak and I turn

revival

around and see Ritchie walking toward us.

"I see the whole gang is complete." He places a kiss on my cheek and shakes hands with Michael, Oscar and Simone. He takes the beer that Kelly poured for him and sits next to Michael. He nods toward him giving his permission for something.

Interesting.

"So, Nina, remember when we told you that Oscar and I have plans to move to Cali someday?"

"That was ages ago. I thought you gave up on the idea?" I smile, but I know there is something more to whatever he is getting at.

He nods his head and glances at Oscar nervously. "Well, we never gave up, we were just waiting for the right time."

"So I guess the time is now? Is that what you trying to say?"

"It is," he rubs the back of his neck, clearing his throat. "We are leaving on Friday."

I try to wrap my mind around what he just said to me and why all of this is such a big deal that they closed the bar for it. And then it hits me. This means the band will no longer exist. I won't be able to do the one thing that lets me escape the dullness in my life. They know that. That thought breaks me. Not the fact that I won't be able to perform, but the fact that they care so much about me, knowing how I love the two hours of mental freedom.

"Nins," Michael is next to me, wrapping me into a hug, "You know that we don't want to leave, but we have a great opportunity over there. There was an audition for the bass and drummer and we both got placed in the band. It might come to nothing in the end but we have to take this shot."

"No, absolutely, I understand," I sniff right into his blue shirt. "I'm not mad, I'm just happy you thought about me." I smile through my tears. "And

God, this is awesome news." I wipe my face with my apron, free myself from Michael, and walk to Oscar to congratulate him.

"California, huh?" I tease him, I know this has been his dream for quite some time.

California.

That brings another train of thoughts to my mind, but I push them away quickly. This night is about something else.

We sit down at the bar and spend the most of the night sharing stories from the years we played together. We laugh. When there are a few moments of melancholy I feel Michael's arms wrap around me, more than normal. His gorgeous eyes land on me more than necessary, making me uncomfortable.

"I can't believe you closed the bar just for this." I lean toward Ritchie, bumping his arm with mine.

"Nina, we all know how much you love playing with the boys, you guys brought this place to life every Thursday."

"I guess we had our last performance a week ago." I sigh heavily, thinking that I won't be standing on that stage anymore. Even though I'm sad about it, it's not as bad as I thought it would be. I mean, when I thought about the band breaking up, I always thought I would be devastated. Surprisingly, I'm not. Hell yeah I'm sad, but everything has to come to an end, and this is one of those things. We had six incredible years playing together, having fun in front of crowds that came here just to listen to us.

I hear the sound of a guitar coming from the, stage and I notice that none of the boys are sitting next to us.

"Come on Nina," Michael's voice says through the speakers, "For old time's sake."

I smile and jump to the stage, grabbing the mic and standing next to them. As the first notes of my

revival

very first song float in the air, I smile and start singing.

They play our songs one after another, laughing and drinking between songs. I know I should stop drinking. I already feel light headed and dangerously happy despite the fact that my life went to hell this morning, but there won't be a night like tonight anytime soon. There won't be a night like tonight ever again. So I let myself go and soon enough, we all end up dancing and singing to our favorites covers.

"God, I will miss both of you." I salute to Michael standing next to me, and let him kiss my cheek while he says that he will miss me as well.

"We will visit soon, I promise." His breath lingers around my face and I know he is too close, way too close, but I don't do anything to push him away. I just smile and turn to Kelly, who has been standing next to me, talking about some kind of creepy customer she had last night.

Ritchie is the first to go, and he leaves the keys to Travis since he is the only one that is not drinking. Simon, Oscar and Kelly follow soon behind him.

"I think it is time to go." I rise from my seat and sway slightly, Michael's arms preventing me from tripping over nothing. "Shit, I'm ok, I promise." I giggle to myself.

"I will walk you home." Michael stands next to me, taking my hand and lacing it with his.

"I'm good, I can walk home by myself."

"I'm sure you can Nina." He chuckles under his breath and I join him.

"Who am I kidding?" I giggle and walk out to the street.

"Just walk her and head home Michael." Travis' voice sound serious and I laugh like this is the most hilarious joke I've heard in my life.

"Don't worry man."

We take a turn down my street and I get this weird feeling that I'm being watched. I shudder and take a quick look around, but I get distracted by something Michael is saying.

"Come again?"

"I said I will really miss you Nina" We stop at the top of the stairs and he brings me close to him. So close that I can feel his heart racing in his chest and I'm not sure what all this is about.

"I will miss you too, but God you are heading out for this big, incredible adv..." I'm not able to finish because his mouth is on mine and it feels good. Soft, warm and just what my drunken brain thinks I need at this moment... So I open mine and let him in, joining him somewhere in the middle. I bring my hands to his hair and I stop short when I feel the long curls in between my fingers. I hear tires catching the asphalt somewhere close, and I open my eyes in shock.

"I'm sorry." I break the kiss and cover my mouth with my hands.

"Don't be, gosh Nina I was wondering for way to long how you taste, and this is beyond my imagination." He leans in for another kiss, but I hold my hands against his chest.

"I'm sorry Michael, I can't do this," I back away and open the door to my apartment hall. "I hope California will be everything you ever dreamt of."

"Nina," he steps closer, "I'm sorry. I..."

"It's ok, I still like you." I wink at him and he smiles back.

"I like you too, just not like that."

"I know, I know."

I watch him walk down the stairs and wonder for a second what would happen if I ever acknowledged the fact that he has always liked me. He's never tried anything with me until tonight, but I always knew that he looked at me in a way that got my body to tingle, just not enough for me to look back at him.

    I guess I will never know.

Dylan

I was supposed to leave tomorrow morning, but I'm sitting in the airport, waiting for my plane to arrive any minute now.

I wanted to talk to her.
I wanted to talk sense into her.
I wanted to beg her for another chance.
I wanted to make her see how much I love them and that I'm in no matter what obstacles we would have had to go through.

It didn't take me long after I talked to her to admit to myself that my feelings for her are far from attraction. I craved every single moment we had together, I got intoxicated on every single touch we shared and the time we spent apart was torture. I missed her face the second I turned away. I wished for her presence the minute she disappeared from my eyes, and God, if that's not love, then I'm lost.

So I waited for her until she got back from work to tell her how I really feel and what I really want. Three hours in the car, looking at every person walking down the sidewalk, hoping it was her. I was patient. I know how hectic work at the bar can be, and that sometimes the night gets much longer than she wishes.

And then I saw her. Walking hand in hand with Michael, the band member. My hands tightened on the door handle, but I waited to see. I shouldn't have. I should have gotten out of that car and called

revival

her name, not caring that she was leaning her body on some other man. I should have done that instead of letting him walk her up the stairs, placing his lips on hers. Watching her hands rise up to his head, bringing him closer.

That was all I could take. I sped down the street and ran through the closest red light, not thinking about consequences. I managed to call Austin from the car and asked him to send the jet right away.

So I'm sitting here now, drinking *who the fuck cares* which glass of whiskey, and thinking that whatever she said to me earlier in the day, she probably meant it. I was stupid enough and blind enough to refuse to believe it. But now, I saw it. With my own eyes.

Fuck!

"Mr. Heart the plane is ready for you." A pretty blond girl in a blue uniform stands next to me, waiting for me to follow her. I could fuck her. I could ask her to show me the exact way to my plane and take her in the very first seat we walk into. But I look at her and I don't see *her*. I need to see *her* for my dick to have any movement.

"Thanks." I stand up and head over to the gate she just pointed out to me.

After I take a seat in the plane and get the bottle of Jack I asked for, I look beyond the window and wonder how the fuck I ended up like this.

A few months ago I was sure, I was positive I wouldn't be able to look at any girl the way I looked at Mia, and definitely I didn't count on loving someone again.

And here I am.

Loving.

Two people at once.

My daughter and her mother.

Drowning my sorrows over someone I can't have

and someone that doesn't want me. This I might get over. It might take me some time, but I might get it out of my system eventually. But the fact that I had access to my daughter denied, that I was told to stay away, that I was told I'm not welcome and that there is no such a thing as making up for all the years I lost, is pissing me off more than I could ever imagine.

I know that I could fight for Ellie. I could. But I would never do that to Nina. Never. I would rather live my life knowing that they are both happy than break something incredible that they share.

She fuckin' kissed him. That thought keeps coming back to me even though I push it out far as I can. Was he the reason that she pushed me away? Was he the reason she couldn't go further with me?

"Mr. Heart, we are going to land in fifteen minutes anything you need?" I shake my head no and look at the almost empty bottle of whiskey sitting in front of me.

I watch the sexy stewardess as she walks away, her ass swings side to side in that tight, short skirt. I could fuck her, I did in fact. I've fucked her before. She would need nothing more than one look from me, and she would know what I need.

But there is no one else I want to bury my cock in than Golden. Fuck. She got me good.

"You want *me* to be the boss?" Austin looks at me with an expression I can't quite place. It's a mixture of surprise, worry and excitement.

"You're already the boss." I state the obvious.

"That I am."

"Don't get ahead of yourself." I tease him, even

though I know he is declaring the truth.

"Ok, so you want me to be the CEO of this company on paper until I get enough money to buy you out."

"Something like that, yes."

"Dylan, this company is worth millions and I don't know if I will ever be able to buy it from you."

"You will," I cock a smile and I know I have his attention. "I will give it to you in full, but I will receive a twenty percent royalty from every transaction you make. You will be the sole CEO, and I will not have any impact on any decisions you make. So basically, if you decide one day to bankrupt the company I will be left with no profit as well."

"Is that even legal?" I smile at that. Who asks questions like that when they are offered the head position in an already well-established business?

"It is, I checked. Are you in?"

"I have to think about it man."

"What do you have to think about?" I can't believe he is hesitating with his answer, "You will be the boss, and as far as I know, this company needs a boss like you. You already know that you are the one to make all the decisions here anyway. I just nod like a bobble head."

"Sort of, yeah. But man, that's a huge responsibility to take on."

"Please. You sound like a pussy right now."

"Maybe I am."

"That doesn't change anything."

"What doesn't change anything?"

"You being a pussy. I think that your pussy, in particular, can handle all of this."

"Fuck you, Dylan."

"You're still talking to your boss, so pick your words wisely."

"As far as I'm concerned, I just became a CEO few minutes ago." I raise my hand to high five him. There are no regrets to my decision, and I know he will do amazing things with this company, this has been is his passion from the day I met him.

Now I only have to convince my mother that this is the right decision.

I look at my mother sitting next to me in the limo, and I swear I haven't seen a more beautiful person her age. Her hair is pinned perfectly in a low bun, and the dress she chose is nothing but spectacular.

"Mom, I need to talk to you."

"I'm listening." She turns her head toward me and watches me with her aged, yet sharp eyes.

"I gave away all of the company rights to Austin." I see her lips turn in a slight smile, "I'm still the owner on paper, but I'm only taking twenty percent of the profit."

"Its about time Dylan." She brings the flute of Champagne to her lips and smiles at me. There is nothing else I need to say. I know she understands, and she's more than ok with my decision.

"I assume you already have some sort of plans, otherwise you wouldn't do it?" She sort of states, sort of asks me.

"I do."

"Do they include Nina and Ellie?"

Shit. I don't feel like talking about this right now, and the fact that we just pulled up to the entrance to the gala saves me from answering that question.

I jump out of the car and walk over to her side to open the door. I offer her my arm and we walk the black carpet, smiling at the flashes of the cameras hitting us from time to time.

Yeah. Thanksgiving Gala it is.

We walk to our table and I put on a fake smile

when I discover that Susan is sitting right next to me. Great, that was the last thing I needed.

"What a coincidence," she purrs grabbing my arm and pinning me down to my chair.

"I wouldn't call it coincidence, we both know that." I give her half a smile and turn to the rest of the guests to greet them.

I feel her hand caressing my legs under the table. I don't even look at her when I brush her hand away, hoping that she will let it go, seeing that I'm not interested in her games.

"So Dylan. I hear you are doing a great job in making your father proud." One of the fellas across the table asks, while Susan's hand gets dangerously close to my crotch, again.

"I hope so, I really do. I gave the company rights away to one of my colleagues."

"What do you mean you gave it away? There is no such thing."

"Oh, there is," I smile when I feel her hand sliding farther away from me, "as much as I love my father and I have nothing but pride toward his achievements, that wasn't for me. So I made my assistant the primary CEO."

I see the confused faces of the businessmen sitting at our table, and I can't contain the smile that is spreading over my face. I take a quick look at my mother, and I see her smiling as well.

"Dylan was never made for that kind of business to begin with." My mother's voice sounds bored, like this is old news and we should move to the next subject.

"How can you say that? He worked so hard to achieve that status and now you're letting Dylan throw away all of it, just like that?" Richard's voice is laced with disappointment and I don't blame him.

"That's Dylan's choice to make." My mother is

stern in her response and that's enough to stop all the judgments.

I smile to myself and lean down to my mother to place soft kiss on her cheek, letting her know how grateful I am to her for sticking up for me.

"I love you, Mom."

"I know son, I know."

Somewhere between the prize announcements and charity sales, I step outside on the patio overlooking the bright lights of the city. Before I can take my first breath, I sense someone walking up to me. I turn and see the famous Susan Burns.

"How did you find you way over here, there aren't any dicks to fuck as far as I'm concerned."

"I see one and I can tell that he is horny as fuck."

"You haven't change a bit, have you?" I can't hide the amusement in my voice, she is the cockiest girl I have even known.

"Why would I?" Her hand is already traveling down my slacks, resting in between my legs. "I'm perfect the way I am." Of course she is. I feel myself getting hard. But, who wouldn't with a hot blonde moving her hands all over their balls?

"I grew up, I guess." I push her hands away, taking step back, "I found the one I love and then I stopped looking at the random chicks like you."

"Oh Dylan, why are you making this so difficult? Maybe your mind is telling you the right thing, but I'm sure that this hard cock is telling me the total opposite."

"You haven't seen my cock hard yet darling, what you're holding in your hand right now is me thinking about someone else."

"I don't give a fuck as long as you put that thing inside me and fuck me senseless." She is next to me again, sliding her hand between my waist and my bare stomach, reaching for the tip of my shaft. "And

revival

besides, I don't see that love of yours around here anywhere. I'm here, right next you."

Fuck, that she is. I feel her hand slide up and down my cock, and I know it's only a matter of seconds before my cock is sliding deep in her pussy.

"Go away." I step away from her, fixing my slacks and I walk back into the club. *What the fuck was I thinking?* She was digging into my pants and I was more than eager to let her do just that because I was lonely. Just because I am lonely.

I have Nina.

Do I?

She told me to get lost and then I saw her kissing that boy, so do I really have her?

I stop at the entrance to ballroom and turn around, looking at the hot body that might do just fine for tonight.

"Come here," I gesture to her. I don't have to say it twice, she is right next to me within seconds. "You like the thrill babe?" I push her flat to the wall and bring her dress up, finding her wetness. "Or do you want me to take you some place private?"

"Here is fine." She is already unbuttoning my slacks, my zipper flies free, my cock is in her hands while I try to tell myself that Nina doesn't want me, and this is not cheating. She doesn't want me.

I feel Susan's hand sliding slowly over my shaft and the moment I cover her lips with mine, I'm hit with the realization that this is wrong. So wrong.

"Sorry." I back away from her and put my cock back into my pants, backing away from her.

"You fucking kidding me?" I hear her desperate voice. I only shake my head at this.

"I guess we were never meant to fuck, Susan." I don't even turn around while I walk back inside the party room.

A few minutes pass by and as I sit at the table

with all of the guests she, comes storming in with her dress ripped and her face covered with mascara. I see her father rush over to her, making all guests turn around to see what's going on. I try to make sense of the situation. I barely stepped off of the patio two minutes ago, there is no way that something tragic had happened in the one hundred and twenty seconds since I left her outside.

"You are piece of shit Dylan, I thought that your father raised you well. Even though your genes were always a big unknown, I thought your parents did a decent job in raising you. But this, trying to rape my daughter, is something you will never get away with!"

I'm speechless. I see my mother turn her head towards me and I see the pain in her eyes.

"Mom, trust me, I had nothing to do with it." I rise from my seat and walk to Susan, but her father stops me before I can come close enough to tell her what I need to tell her.

"You really that desperate to fuck me that you would fake a rape after I refused to fuck you on the patio? Really? I'm sorry Susan but there is only one woman that has a special place in my heart, and you are far from being her. And if you think you can stand here with the clothes you ripped by yourself and a face that only your father is stupid enough to believe, then you are much, much lower that I thought you were. It's no secret that you have been trying to fuck me since you were fifteen, and it is no secret that I denied you every time you put your hands on me. But this," I wave my hands pointing at her bare chest that she didn't even bother trying to cover, "Is the lowest low you could go. Look at yourself. You're standing half naked in front of hundreds of people only because I refused to fuck you."

revival

I turn around and grab my mother's arm and lead her out of the room.

I gesture for the valet to call our limo and I keep silent, there is nothing I have to say.

"I always knew she had her eye on you." My mother giggles. I chuckle knowing that she understands the torture I just went through.

"You know, she is seeing tons of men according to the gossip magazines. She is a whore, and I can't believe her father can't see it."

"Nina said she doesn't want me in her life anymore." I blurt out not even knowing why.

I meet my mother's concerned eyes as we get in the car. "Did she mean it?"

"I don't think so, but then I saw her kissing one of her band members while I was waiting outside to talk to her."

"I see," she scans me as I lean over to fill my glass with whiskey. "Make one for me." She demands. So I take another glass and pour the alcohol over the ice, listening to the warm liquid crackling the ice-cold cubes.

"What makes you think that she doesn't want you around?"

"I told her how I feel and how being close to her makes me feel, how important Ellie is to me. But she was saying the same thing over and over."

"That she doesn't want you around?"

"That, and that this will never make sense, that we will never make anything of each other."

She doesn't answer immediately, she just sips her drink, looking out the window.

"She's hiding something Dylan."

I laugh at this, there is nothing she can hide from me. Sure, there was a thing she was hiding from me which I discovered by accident. Ellie being my daughter, but that was it. She is not one to have secrets. She is too pure, too honest to hide anything.

"No, I don't think she is hiding something, I believe she is just too scared to move forward, to acknowledge the fact that I want to make a life with her and Ellie."

"You think so?" My mother's eyes stop at mine, and I question her without saying the words.

"When I was about twenty six and your father proposed, I refused. Not because I didn't love him, I loved that man more than you can imagine. He was everything to me. But I knew I couldn't give anything back to him but my love. I knew then that I couldn't have kids, Dylan. I was so ashamed to tell him, that I felt safer telling him that I didn't love him. I remember that day like it was yesterday, him walking away from me with a broken heart. My heart was broken as well. But at the time, I thought that was the best thing, the best decision that I could make. Two years had passed before he showed up at my doorstep once again, and the first thing I told him was that I can't have kids. I will never forget his face when he realized that that was the reason I pushed him away. I know he never forgave me for the two years we wasted, but he was more than ok with the fact that we would have to adopt. He was more than ok with it, but he never forgave me for the time we wasted over such a stupid thing."

I listen to her, and I try to erase the image of Nina kissing that loser. I try to remember the words she said to me, trying to find the message buried under them, but it comes back to the same thing every time. *I don't want you in my life.* She said that loud and clear, although her eyes were telling a different story. They were asking me to stay, and to fight for what's mine.

"Maybe you're right ma." I lean over to her and she embraces me in the loving hug I haven't felt in

revival

so long. "Maybe you're right."

    The limo parks in front of my mother's house and we both get out, walking together. Even though we have different memories playing in our heads they come to the same end – our loved ones.

Nina

He called me a few times a day, he texted me more than few times a day.

I never answered the phone and sent simple OK when he asked how Ellie is doing.

It's been two weeks.

December is around the corner and I'm not even close to being in the Holiday spirit. I go through the days in a fog, constantly thinking about the way I screwed up something that was important to me.

Gran asked me a question the other day, and it's still unanswered, running through my head. *What do you want Nina? Until you answer yourself, it doesn't make sense to look for anything, how would you know which direction to go? You will only get lost.*

What do I want?

Something I've been asking myself since he showed up few a months ago.

What do I want?

Happily ever after sounds like too much of a cliché, so I will skip that answer. My daughter knowing her father, having him close to me like he said he wants to be, that is what I really want.

But I feel like my wants don't matter anymore. I blew all of my 'wants' the day I let somebody else into my life.

Somebody I don't care about anymore.

Someone I don't even have feelings for.

Someone I'm terribly scared of.

That's the price I pay for taking unnecessary detours in my life when, I should have stayed straight.

The price I pay because I'm too scared to face the difficulties by myself and desperately searching for someone to face it with me.

I sigh and recall the conversation I had with Gran a few days ago.

"I don't know what I want Gran," I hid my face in my hands and let the tears fall freely, let them burn my cheeks so I could feel how badly I screwed up.

"You do know Nina, you do, and you are just too scared to say it out loud."

I don't even look at her. I was too scared that if I lifted my eyes to hers, the answer would come easily.

"Just say it Nina, just say what you want." Grans voice drilled in my head and my mind was spinning like a goddamn carousel.

"I want him to be around and I want Ellie to know her real father, not some fake junky that I made the mistake to be with." I whisper under my breath.

She smiled.

"Now you know." She sipped her tea while looking at me with her soft eyes. *"Sometimes facing your biggest fears is best way to approach life. Going easy and living the shadows won't get you anywhere. Being in the spotlight and screaming for what you want might get you a spot that is bright and worth fighting for. Fight for it Nina, I'm always on your side."*

I cover my face with my hands and think about how I will explain to Dylan the whole father-daughter situation. I know I should have been honest about it a long time ago. I know I should be straightforward and tell him how things went back then. I know. But

I'm ashamed. I'm ashamed of my weakness, of my lack of belief in myself.

I let myself down more than I let down anybody else.

I have to think of the best way to reach out to him now that he is gone, and I'm sure he is not coming back. The whole situation is out of my control and I'm drowning in it.

I want him to see me as the girl he met years ago, the girl he felt something for. Not as the loser that is trying to make ends meet each and every day.

Definitely not that.

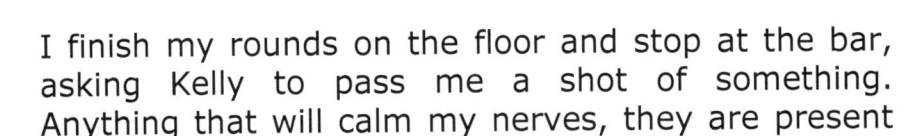

I finish my rounds on the floor and stop at the bar, asking Kelly to pass me a shot of something. Anything that will calm my nerves, they are present every day now.

"Well, well, well. I can't believe I'm hearing that from your little mouth." She teases while pouring tequila in a shot glass. "Drink it up girlfriend." She pushes two shots in my direction and brings one to her lips waiting for me.

"Cheers." I down one and head for the second one right away.

"Cheers to you." We drink the second one and slam the glasses on the bar like we just completed the best challenge in the world.

I pull the phone from my apron and search for Dylan's name in my contacts.

I need to talk to you.

I look at the screen for a little too long before I slide the phone back, my heart sinking at the lack of response.

revival

I turn around, ready to head for the floor again and meet a pair of hazel eyes staring right at me.

A stare that can bring me down to my knees.

No!

One that I wished I would never see again.

"Hello, Nina." I literally hold back the bile rising at the sound of his voice. "Haven't seen you in four years, sweetheart, but you look just fine. Better than I could have imagined." He walks closer to me and brings me to him, placing his mouth on mine. I keep my lips sealed tight and try to calm myself by counting to ten in my head, reassuring myself that everything is going to be alright.

I swallow hard, feeling the gulp blocking my throat.

"What are you doing here?" I look at him and wish my voice wouldn't crack like that.

"Wow." His brow furrows and he cocks his head to the side. An old habit of his when he starts to get pissed at something. I hide my fidgeting hands in my pockets and look around. I'm safe here. There are too many people and he will not make a scene in front of everybody.

"I have to say this is not the welcome I was hoping for, baby. I got off early for a good behavior." He winks in a way that always makes me cringe. "They let me out a few days ago. I thought you would be happy about that." His big hands reach to grab my face, and this time I don't hesitate to give him what he asks for. I'm too scared not to obey him. I close my eyes and as soon as his lips touch mine, I check out. Thinking about nothing else but the dirty glasses of beer waiting for me to pick them up from the tables.

"That's my girl." His voice penetrates my ears and I shudder. I feel like I'm in a slow motion movie, that everything going on around me right now is taking forever. I look to the side and see Kelly and Travis eyeing me carefully. They don't know who he is. The only person that knows is Ritchie, and he is not here tonight.

"Nice to have you back." I blurt and head back to the floor, taking my time and making sure I don't come back to the bar anytime soon.

While I punch the orders into the computer I see a familiar form walk up to the bar. My heart races and I can't believe he is here. Why on earth he didn't let me know that he was back? I would have met him right away, and this awkward situation wouldn't have to be so awkward. He sends me a small smile and I just nod my head in his direction, praying he doesn't sit on Kelly's side. *Please, please sit at Travis' section.*

It doesn't work. He is takes a seat right next to Marcus, ordering a scotch sending me a smile like we are best buddies.

Please don't.

I watch him take a few sips, his eyes are fixed on me.

"Can we talk?"

Hell just froze over. Every single drop of blood drains from my face and I curse under my breath, remembering the text I sent him earlier.

I watch Marcus' expression go blank, his eyes blazing with something so familiar it sends me back to the night I was at the top of the stairs in my apartment building, years ago.

I watch Dylan's eyes watching me, full of hope. He isn't even registering what is going on.

"What you wanna talk to my wife for?" I see Marcus focus his eyes on Dylan, his hand is frozen midair, drink in hand, eyes bouncing between Marcus and me.

"Your wife?" He asks with a smirk on his face.

revival

Oh God please help me!

"Yeah, that's my woman, you have a problem with that?" I watch as Marcus shifts in his chair, turning his body toward Dylan, who doesn't seem to be intimidated by him at all. He brings his drink to his lips, which are curled slightly in disgust, his eyes now glaring at me.

"Why would I?" His low, husky voice sounds careless and that puts a needle in my soul.

"That's what I thought. So why the fuck you looking at her like you wish you could fuck her?" Marcus' voice is filled with malice.

I hear glass break and I look around before I realize that Dylan's glass is shattered in his hands.

"Maybe because I did."

Everything freezes.

Everything.

Dylan.

Marcus.

The whole bar freezes for a second.

And my mind freezes as well.

Everything is in slow motion as I watch Marcus fly out of his chair and charge at Dylan. Dylan is much quicker though, and his fist connects with Marcus' jaw, sending him to the floor. He sends me a quick look before he brings him back up by his shirt.

"You shouldn't reach for me like that." He seethes between his teeth before sending another blow to Marcus' face. This time he doesn't fall down, but fights back. I watch them punch each other, blood splattering all over the place.

I know I should react. Do something. Say something. But I just stand there, watching them fight, silently wishing that Dylan would beat his ass.

I hear Kelly scream for them to stop but I know it's pointless. Dylan's face is raging with anger, he sends blow after blow to Marcus' body, he is beaten so hard he can't defend himself anymore.

I have no intention of calling the police, from what I can see, Dylan is not in danger.

Justice.

I hear sirens outside the bar and my only thought is to take Dylan out the back door and protect him from what's to come. I don't care that Marcus is lying on the floor, blood dripping from his face and that he is barely moving. He deserves that. He deserves that for all the times his hand connected with me. Dylan doesn't know that, if he knew, I'm sure there would be nothing left to pick off the floor.

I walk to Dylan and see his chest rising up and down, his fists clenched together like he is still ready to fight.

"Lets go, cops are here."

"Good." He seethes toward me. "Let them in."

"Come on Dylan, you don't want to be here, you don't need trouble because of this." I plead touching his elbow and he jerks right away.

"Oh honey, I want to be here, trust me." His words cut me like a sharp knife. Slice me in half. I know he is not talking about the stupid fight he just had, he talks about much more than that.

"Dylan, please," I feel the tears welling up in my eyes and the last thing I want is break down crying in here, in the middle of this stupid scene.

I feel his body shift and before I know it, I'm in front of him, heading toward the back door. Once we're outside he pushes me up to the wall, his strong body on top of me, pinning me to the cold brick.

"So you are one of those people that sweep

everything under the rug, huh?" His intense gaze is grilling me, his eyes jump between mine. "Aren't you?" He takes another step closer to me. Now I can feel him all over me, everywhere. His heartbeat right next to mine, furious, like galloping horse that doesn't want to be stopped.

His breathing is fast, his eyes still angry from what just happened.

"And you are one of those people that wear every single problem right on their sleeve? Can't you just let it go Dylan?" I break the eye contact as his stare is too much for my already shuddering soul.

"I can't let it go, not when I have so much to lose." His intense voice makes me look at him again, just one look in his eyes and I'm lost. I think I know what I want, I thought I knew what I wanted, but there is a small voice somewhere in the corner of my mind that tells me that I can't do it again. I can't lose myself in those greys, those promising greys that will be gone before I know it, even though they promised me forever. Even though my whole body is screaming for me to give up, to turn around and leave my past behind as it is, I can't move my feet and I can't force the words of rejection out of my mouth.

"You have nothing to lose." I breathe out while trying not to inhale his signature scent, his own, personal cologne of naughty and nice.

"Oh, I have everything to lose and trust me Golden, I'm not losing it. Again." His statement goes straight to my heart, forgetting to stop in my brain and it's hitting hard, big and powerful. I feel his hands grab my chin and lifting it up so I have no choice but look at him. Oh God, what I see makes my knees wobble. He's not kidding. He's not fooling around this time. His gaze is serious, hard. It means business. I try to swallow the rising fear it is taking all over my body as he holds my chin between his fingers. I try so hard not to fall for his tricks, I've fallen for them once and I was the one that paid in the end.

But this feels different.

"Are you in love with him?" His question throws me off guard and I have to think for a second who he's taking about. "Do you love him?" He repeats the question.

"No." There is nothing more I want to say right now, there is nothing I want to talk about to be honest. I'm fired up with his body pressed close to mine, the only thought that is flowing in my mind is to get him out of here, get him inside of me, and get him to be whole with me. Once again.

"Is he the one Ellie calls her *Daddy*?" The way he said Daddy brings me back to reality.

"Yes."

"Why?"

Questions. Explanations.

"I'm so tired of this." I let my thoughts slip out.

"Tired? I haven't even started yet Golden, I thought I knew everything. I thought I knew what I was coming back to, but this... that piece of shit that my daughter is calling a father, when I'm her real father, it's fucking ripping my heart in half. I thought you were better than that. I thought you could at least do better." I watch his eyes wander to the side and now I'm the one grabbing his face and bringing it straight to mine.

"You weren't here. I slept with you and you were gone, I met Marcus and I was sure the baby was his, I was positive. Til'... until she was born, then I knew she was yours. I could remember your face even after a year; I would never forget your eyes and this goddam dimpled chin that is your fucking trademark. But I was married by then, what should I have done?

revival

Get divorce because I thought my baby looked like someone I fooled around with once? Raise my child as a single mother because I felt like it was the right decision? And you know what? I should do that, I should have divorce the lady puncher right then, but I was scared. I was so scared that my little baby would be without a family, so I stayed in that sick relationship and–"

"What did you say? Lady puncher?" I watch his eyes flare and his body go still against mine. His finger traces the little line under my chin and then he is off, running inside the bar before I can process what is happening.

By the time I hurry into the bar I see him hovering over Marcus, his fists connecting with his face over and over. Four cops are trying to get him off with, no result. Then one of them brings a taser to Dylan's side and before I can protest, he crumples to the floor. Convulsing and holding his side.

I didn't even have a chance to say thank you.

Dylan

Thirty-seven hours.

I've been locked up here for that long.

Normally I would flip out that nothing had been done in order to get me out of here but right now, I don't mind. I don't care that I called Austin thirty five hours ago. That someone should already either have made a call or showed up here to release me.

I have time to think about everything that has happened. And it is a lot. It is a shit load of information that I have trouble processing.

She's married.

To the biggest douchebag and lady fucking beater, and *my* daughter calls him a father.

HIM.

Fuck.

I think that is the biggest bump in the road, one that I don't know how to approach.

Shit. I don't know how to make anything right anymore. I only know that I want to be present in their lives, in Ellie's life in particular. It would be great bonus if Nina was willing to let me in a little more as well. But I don't know if any of that is possible right now.

My fists clench over the edge of the bench that's supposed to be my bed. I can't stomach the fact that my daughter, my blood, my soul, calls him dad.

Fuck!

I lean back and touch the cold wall behind me,

revival

flinching slightly as my swollen skin presses to the concrete. They must have shocked me pretty good if there is swollen and painful patch.

It was worth it.

The second I heard her say, "lady puncher" I thought about the scar under her chin. The one that shines at me every time we are close. I couldn't help myself. There was nothing and no one that could stop me. I didn't want to be stopped. I wanted to smash that motherfucker's face to pieces. Show him how fucking easy is to punch someone that can't actually defend themselves.

My heart squeezes at the thought of Nina being hurt. I can't believe that someone would actually be violent towards her. She is a beautiful thing to be around and an even more incredible thing to look at, why would you want to damage something that is perfect?

I know I need a plan.

A big fucking good one.

I know that he will be around from now on and I have to find out a way to sneak my time in with them somehow.

I want as much time with Nina as I want with Ellie.

I saw.

I felt.

She definitely doesn't want me to go away and I can tell that her heart is winning the battle she is having within herself. I just need her to realize that I'm not going anywhere for Christ sake.

I hear someone approaching and the cell door opens.

"You're free to go Dylan." The guy in the khaki suit calls me out.

I stand slowly and see Austin standing outside.

"I'm sorry it took so long, it's not my fault,

honestly. I did my best but it seems you chose the wrong night, everybody was unreachable for some reason."

"It's all good. Don't worry." I follow him to the discharge desk and grab the things that were taken away from me when they locked me up.

"What the fuck happened man?" Austin looks at me curiously while I walk toward the exit doors.

"I have no idea, I guess I lost my shit."

He looks at me with more caution than disbelief. "You must have lost it pretty well if you pulled your signature move on this fella. He was unconscious when the paramedics took him, and from what I've heard, he will need a major dental job to smile anytime soon."

"Good." I smile, and glance at Austin's smiling face.

"I guess you can never take a fighter out of the ring, huh"

"I guess not."

We get in the car and I don't have to say where we are going, Austin was the one to book the house for me.

"What's in it for me?" I ask during the silent drive.

"Not much. I believe nothing. He on the other hand, is a different story. I did some research on your boy Marcus. He just got out of jail few nights before you smashed him like a fucking tomato. He was doing time for some drug bust. The fact that he was in possession of a gun at the time didn't help his already shitty record."

"Fuck." All I can think of is this man around my daughter, around Nina.

"He got out early for some good behavior shit, but since he was on probation and he was in possession of a gun and had some drugs on him, it looks like he is going back there to finish his time. I think a few more months."

Few more months. That is definitely way more than I was hoping for. That is definitely enough for me.

"So he is not getting out for those few months, huh?"

"Nope."

"Good."

"How long was he in for?"

"Three years and eight months."

I do the math and I'm relieved. Ellie is five, so he went to jail when she was a little over a year. This is definitely a win for me.

I exhale with relief and fish my phone out of the zip lock bag. The message light is blinking repeatedly so I check that first.

I hope you're ok.

I'm sorry for everything.

God, I hope you are ok, the silence is killing me and the fact that they didn't let me say anything while they were putting you in that car is destroying me.

Call me once you get this.

All are from Nina.

I smile.

I'm ok, will call you soon. I press send and lean back in my seat.

"Thanks man, I really appreciate you coming all the way here and saving my ass."

"No problem, I will treat this like the vacation I never had."

"You never wanted to take them, maybe you should start with that."

"Don't have anybody to go with, how about that?"

"I can't help you if you have fucking trouble in

that department, you know that everybody in the office thinks you're gay."

"What the fuck?"

I keep a serious face as I nod, "Yep, even that hot assistant to the assistant that I caught watching your ass once, thinks that."

"No fucking way, why wouldn't you say something?"

I can't take it anymore and burst out in a terrible fit of laughter.

"You're kidding right?" He sounds relieved. "You fucking bustard, you are kidding right?"

"About which part?" I watch him shake his head while he laughs along with me. "Actually, people are wondering, nobody has seen you with a girl, like ever."

"That's not true." He cuts me off.

"I know that, you know that, but they don't. She was really checking you out, that, I saw." I bring my fingers to my eyes and point them from mine to his in an 'I'm watching you' gesture.

"Shit."

"Mhmm."

We pull into the driveway and get out of the car.

"Wow, it looks much better than it did in the pictures."

"Wait until you see the rest."

We head inside and I show him to the guest room he will stay in, "Make yourself at home, I'm off to get some stuff done."

"Thanks."

"Thank *you*."

I head straight for the shower, washing off the shitty last two days. I have no idea what I will do, or what I need to do. But there are things that I need to know before I take any further action.

Once I'm on the patio having an early lunch, I

pull out my phone and call Nina.

"I'm sorry." She whispers.

"Hi."

"Hi."

"We need to talk, can you meet me tonight before you head over to work?" There is a long pause on her end. "Nina?"

"What do you want to talk about?"

"Things."

"What kind of things?"

"Stuff I need to know" I sigh.

"What kind of stuff?"

"Jesus Nina, stop fucking around and tell me you are going to meet me. I will pick you up from the hotel around three. See you then."

I hung up. She is impossible. I always knew that women are complicated creatures, but this, her acting like she has mood swings bigger than anything, is beyond everything.

"Give her a break Dylan. I think she has enough shit going on already." I turn around and glare at him and that is enough to shut him down.

I pull up to the hotel entrance and I see her standing there, waiting for me. Her head turns in my direction a tiny smile appears on her face, one that she quickly hides.

I can't help myself, my eyes wander all over her long legs. They go for miles, especially in those shorts, they leave little to the imagination. I would kill to have those legs wrapped around me once again.

"You look beautiful." I watch her climb into the seat and I swear that she is blushing.

She smirks, "Beautiful huh?"
"That's what I just said."
She shifts in her seat like she is uncomfortable.
"You hungry?"
"No, I just ate."
"Coffee then."
"I thought you wanted to talk." Her head turns to me and I watch her eyes narrow.
"We may as well do it over a cup of coffee."

She nods and I lean over her to plunge the seat belt in place. My arm rubs over her breast and I hear her hitched breath. I pull on the belt to stretch it out and click it. There is nothing that I want more than to push her to the back of my jeep and fuck her to oblivion. And from what I am seeing, her mind is not that far off as well.

But instead, I put the car into drive and head for the coffee shop down the street.

We drive in complete silence. Glancing at each other from time to time.

I am nervous. The closer we get the shakier I get. I don't know if I can ask the questions that have been brewing in my mind for the past few hours. What if her answers are not the ones I want to hear?

After we order our coffees, we sit outside on the little bench in front of the deli.

I see her glance at me and I try to get my thoughts straight so I don't say the wrong things.

"I'm really sorry." She blows the words out like they have been heavy on her chest for way to long.

"Sorry for what exactly?" I need to hear her say it. I need to hear what she is sorry for.

Her chin quivers and she looks around like she is searching for the answer.

"I should have told you that I'm married." She takes a deep breath "But I was so ashamed about who I am married to."

revival

"Why did you marry him in the first place? Sorry Golden, but he looks nothing like someone that deserves to be with you."

"I was..." I watch her tears slide down her face. I set my coffee to the side and bring her closer to me, wiping her tears slowly. "I don't know why. I thought that I was pregnant with his baby and that it was the right thing to do."

Shit.

I can't stop blaming myself for the fact that I should have been around.

"What now?" I ask while stroking her hair gently.

She doesn't respond and I can feel the cold sweat starting to cover my body. She should be saying without hesitation that she is leaving that piece of shit.

"What now, Nina?" I repeat the question.

"I don't know." Her answer is quiet, like she is unsure of anything.

"You don't know? You're telling me that you don't know what you need to do to make your life better for you and for my daughter? You're telling me you have doubts about leaving that piece of shit you call your husband? Are you telling me this is not the right time to tell Ellie who her real father is?" I know my voice is way too loud and a few people are watching us as I stand up and run my hands through my hair. "I can't fucking believe this."

"What do you want me to do? I don't know what I want Dylan. I haven't thought about what I want in so long that I forgot what it is that I really want. Until a few months ago I knew that I wanted to work my ass off and move away from here, divorce that pathetic husband of mine and actually make something of myself."

"What changed? You don't want to divorce him anymore?" I swear I don't understand a single thing she is saying to me. She sounds like she is mumbling and I can't make out a single word she is saying.

"That, I do."

I blow my breath out at her response, that just took away the only thing that was keeping me on my toes.

"You don't want to move out of here anymore? Are you telling me you decided to stay here and work two fucking jobs, seeing your daughter for about an hour a day just because you are too proud to get any help from me? Is that what you are saying? Are you saying I don't have any say in this?"

She doesn't say anything to that. I see her look down at the sidewalk and I know that I just said out loud exactly what she is thinking.

"Fuck Nina. I don't know how you can deny anything that is going on between us. I have no fucking idea why are you trying so hard to push me away. But I've told you this a thousand times already and I'm going to repeat myself once again. I'm not going anywhere, and the fact that I'm beyond the point of falling in love with you because I *am* in love with you, only proves to me that my place is here, and here only." I kneel in front of her, wrapping my arms around her waist, bringing my head up to look at her. "I can't stop thinking about you for a single minute. I can't stop craving you next to me, the way you make me feel and how you and Ellie make me a better person, is something I never thought I would have. I thought I had my chance with someone, and that I would never again feel my heart race so fast that it might burst out of my fucking chest. I know you feel the same Golden. I can feel this, and I don't want you to fight it anymore. Don't." I feel her tears land on my face as she looks down at me.

"It doesn't feel right." She shakes her head "It doesn't feel right to have any feelings towards you while I'm married to someone else."

"For fucks sake Nina. Listen to yourself." I can't take it anymore. I can't stomach that she is trying to live by the fucking rules when she should be running away from them. "Maybe I'm wrong then, maybe you should stay with that beloved husband of yours and live happily ever after. But I'm not giving up Ellie just like that. I'm her father and there is no way you will take that away from me."

I walk to my jeep and drive away, not even looking back at her.

I can't believe that after everything that happened, after everything I told her, she is denying herself.

There is no way she was faking any of her emotions while we were together. There is no way. But I can't wrap my mind around the fact that she can't make a rational decision about her life.

Fine. She doesn't want me in, I will survive. There are far worst things I've had to overcome. I will be fine.

"Cancel the rent and call for the jet. We are going back home." I inform Austin as I head to my room and throw my stuff into the suitcase.

"You're not serious are you?"

"I'm fucking dead serious. I'm done here."

Dylan

Two months later...

"You send the money?" I ask Austin right after we order dinner.

"Like I have every week for the past eight weeks."

"Good." I nod and smile at the waitress that just placed our glasses on the table, filled with whiskey.

"Did you talk to her?"

I take a big sip of the liquid and let it slide slowly down my throat. Did I talk to her? I tried. I tried calling her and sending her tons of messages asking her to think about giving me a chance to be a part of their lives. What I got in return was *I need time*. Fucking time. The thing is, I've lost so much time with her that I don't want to lose anymore.

"She needs time." I say exactly what she told me.

"How much time? Another five or six years?"

"Jesus Austin, what the fuck do I know? That's what she said. What do you want me to do about it? Go there just to face another rejection? No, thank you." I tap my finger on the table. "Maybe she doesn't want anything to do with me."

"Sure she doesn't." I scan Austin's face and I swear there is something he is not telling me, but I just don't have it in me to find out what it is.

"So I found the perfect guy to train the evening classes." I change the subject.

"I thought you were going to do it yourself?"

"There are way too many people that signed up, we had to add another class."

"Who is he? Anyone good?"

I smile thinking about how good he is. "Jake Donovan." I watch his fork hang mid air.

"No shit. How did you manage to get him to teach?"

"I have my ways." I smile and think how easy it was get him to work with me. Not work for me, because he doesn't even want any money for it. When I met him and told him that I opened a gym that specializes in youth training, and that I'm in the works of giving free classes to the less fortunate, he asked if he could take the position. I had no other choice, but to say yes. He is a legend and an old friend of mine, I'm happy to have him around.

"You don't miss the office?"

"You are kidding me right?"

"Just making sure I won't be kicked out of my position anytime soon."

"Nothing to worry about."

I recall the shock on his face when I broke the news to him. He sat there, saying nothing for a few minutes and I started to get nervous that the whole plan was going to backfire on me. Of course, he agreed because he loves his job more than anything. I explained to him how I am staying in the shadows by keeping a royalty, and I keep the rights to make the final decision if the company is ever to be will be sold or closed for any reason. I wanted to keep that small tribute to my family by not giving away something that my father worked so hard for. My mother actually asked me to put that clause in the contract, and it was the least I could do in exchange for her understanding.

"Good. I like the way my name looks on your door." He winks and I just laugh.

I drive home and while I pass my old house, Mia's face flashes in front of my eyes. It was just four weeks ago that I visited her, bringing her a dozen lilies. It was a chilly but sunny day and I spent way too much time talking to her, wishing she was around. I can't believe it's been a year already. I can't believe how time does heal. When I heard that popular phrase years ago, I was ready to punch someone. Today, I truly believe that everything is possible with time. Time it's like your best friend. Walking you through the good and holding your hand through the bad. Making sure that you heal and rise up to new challenges.

Time.

That's what she says she needs.

She needs time.

How much time?

Time for what?

She never said.

That was the only response I got from her. Like a fucking riddle, those three words are swimming through my head trying to make sense.

I wait for the gate to open and I park the bike on the newly redone driveway. I step through the garage door and glance up at the Jeep that I haven't driven since it got here from New Orleans. I didn't feel brave enough to drive it, as I'm sure her smell still lingers on the leather seats. That was just another painful thing that reminded me of what I'm

revival

missing.

I turn the lights on and glance around the empty house. The house I bought hoping that she will come around, that she will change her mind. That she will quit with that stubbornness of hers and accept the fact that she wants me as much as I want her. But as the weeks go by, I slowly start to believe that maybe I imagined all of this. Maybe she was just lonely and I showed up at the perfect time to fill that empty hole.

I miss Ellie. I miss her every fucking day. Missing her is the worst in all of this. Her giggles and smart comments brought a smile to my face every single day.

I wanted to fight for her and fight for my right to see her, to visit. But it felt wrong to disturb something that I wasn't even part of for so long. Sure, the way they were living as a family wasn't ideal, but there was no denying that they love each other. She has the most loving mother and the most caring great grandmother by her side, and I would only shake the harmony they worked so hard on.

I grab a beer from the fridge and walk outside, stretching my body on one of the chairs facing the ocean.

Four more months and that worthless husband of hers will be free. He'll probably walk back to her apartment and share the bed with her. Fuck. And there is not a single thing I can do about it. She made it clear that I'm no longer welcome. I need to respect that even though it's killing me inside.

I grab my phone and call her without thinking about what I want to say when she picks up, *if* she picks up.

She doesn't. I hear her sweet voice asking me to leave a message. I press end and throw my head back in frustration.

She just needs time.

Nina

My phone rings and I see Dylan's number flash on the screen. I cringe inside. My fingers twitch to answer and tell him how incredibly sorry I am for acting like a lunatic. But I have to take care of a few things first. I need to finish what I started and maybe then, if he still wants us, we can start something new.

I watch Ellie play on the beach, shuffling pots of sand from one place to another and I know that the decision I'm making is the right one. There is no question that she needs to be close to her father, even if we won't be together as a couple.

I close my eyes and let the sun warm my skin, the weather is pleasantly warm for the end of January, but the cool breeze that is blowing the scent of the ocean gives me chills once and a while.

I miss him.

I think about him every day. Our last conversation is still vivid in my head.

I'm beyond the stage of falling in love with you because I am *in love with you.*

I smile at the fact he actually declared his love for me, just like that, in the middle of a fight. As if it was something obvious he was stating. I wonder if he even realized he said it.

"Mommy, I want to go home." Ellie is standing in front of me and I nod, taking a second to look at her, finding him in her with even more evidence now that his face is so fresh in my mind.

"Let's go, we have some packing to do." I pick her up and tickle her while she giggles and wiggles, trying to free from my hold.

We get to our apartment and I see Gran packing some of my stuff into the big boxes I got from U-Haul this morning.

"You don't have to do this, really, I can do it. It's not like I have tons of stuff anyway."

"I know I don't have to Nina, but I want to help." I watch her and wonder if she really isn't as sad as she is telling me. Since I told her about my decision, she has not once looked sad. The exact opposite in fact. She is cheery and smiling all the time.

"You are more excited about this than I am. It's like you have tons of weight lifted off your shoulders, I guess." She turns to me and sighs heavily, her brows forming one line.

"You were never a burden, not for a second. You have no idea how happy all of this makes me. Being with you, watching Ellie grow was something that some people my age can only dream off. So no, Nina, I'm only happy because watching you making the right decision makes me happy." She comes closer and gives me the warmest hug imaginable.

"God I'm going to miss you." I feel the tears swelling in my eyes and I let them fall freely. There is no need to hide them.

"It's not like you're moving on the other side of the world."

"So why does it feels like it?"

It really does. I know it's a less than four-hour flight, and she promised to visit soon, but still, I'm heading out in the unknown. And that's scares the hell out of me.

"Oh, there is mail for you." Gran walks to the kitchen counter and hands me few envelopes. I

revival

recognize one immediately and just shake my head.

"You take this." I hand it to Gran and she looks at me with surprised eyes.

"No, I can't, this is for you and Ellie and you have enough expenses to land you in debt."

"Please Gran, take it." I plead with my eyes. She shrugs, putting the envelope on the counter.

"You are a terrible granddaughter you know that?" She chuckles under her breath.

"Heard that one before." I wink and shuffle through the rest of the mail. I hold my breath when I see the letter from the court. Gran watches me and she instantly knows what it is as well. I slide my fingers inside the envelope and tear it apart. Taking out the papers with shaky hands, I walk to the kitchen island and lean on it, reading the first few lines stating in black and white that I am a single person once again. Single mother, with full custody. Plus a restraining order from my ex-husband for life.

"Oh my god, this is it." I wipe away tears of happiness and laugh at the same time.

"There is sure a lot of crying today so let's celebrate." She hands me a glass of wine out of nowhere. "To new beginnings, Nina."

"To new beginnings." I take a sip of wine and for the first time in forever, I feel like I'm doing something right. "Ok, now let's finish packing."

It's Monday morning and we have to be at the airport around noon, so I still have plenty of time to get ready. I check my phone and smile at the text I receive letting me know that everything is set for us at the new destination. I watch Ellie still sleeping peacefully and walk through the apartment to see if there is anything left that needs to be packed. The boxes are gone. We had the moving company pick them up and they are already waiting for us at the new place. The only thing I have to take is one suitcase.

Funny how little we need to make a change.

I hear a familiar knock on the door and I know it's Gran. Our secret code that we had used for over five years.

"You ready sweetheart?" She glances around the place and gives me one of her warm smiles.

"I guess." I look around nervously.

"Ok then, I'm not the one for big goodbyes so let me hug you and kiss the princess before you break down."

"Am I the princess today?" A sleepy voice calls from the bedroom.

"That you are. Come here and give me a hug, I won't be seeing you for a while."

I watch Ellie run to her and give her a big squeeze. "You said you would come visit soon."

"I will, but I need this hug to last me for some time, so you better make it a good one."

I walk over to them and wrap my arms around both of them.

"Thank you." I kiss her cheek, "For everything."

"Ok, now you go get ready. I'll go and enjoy some old lady time." She winks and I know she means a trip to the deli to have a breakfast with Hector.

"Live it up Gran." I laugh and she walks out the door smiling.

"Call me when you settle in."

"I will."

After the door closes I make Ellie's breakfast and head for the shower. In a few hours I will be two thousand miles away, starting a new life. And I

revival

swear I will make it a good one this time.

After we claim our baggage we step outside and wait for a taxi to take us to the new place. I listen to Ellie ramble about how awesome the plane was and that she really wants to do it again. I try not to think about the fact that this might be the stupidest decision I've ever made. The four hours on the plane did nothing good for me, I only had more time to doubt all of this.

"Where to?" I hear the rushed voice of the taxi driver, and give him the address of our new apartment. He gets out of the car and throws my suitcase in the trunk while we get in the car.

"Coming back from vacation?"

"Not really."

"We are going to live here now." Ellie announces proudly.

He nods his head to the beat of the music that is playing loudly from his speakers.

"You an actress?"

"No."

"A singer?"

"No."

I have no idea what all his questions have to do with the fact that we are moving here, he must see my surprised expression as he is glances at me in the review mirror.

"Sorry, I just see those girls all the time, so I assumed you were here for the same. I mean with your looks, you can easily pass for either."

"Oh." I don't really know what to say so I just keep looking out the window.

After an hour drive, he parks at the front of the

apartment complex. I can't believe what I'm seeing. I know I had no say in the apartment choice, the primary thing was safety and comfort. But this, this is way more than I can afford. I find the apartment number and I pick up the key from under the mat, just as I was told.

"Oh my gosh mom, this is awesome!" I hear Ellie's voice from far away as I scan the place.

"Yeah it is." I reach for my phone and dial Austin's number.

"You already here?"

"Yes, I'm here, but I'm afraid I won't be able to afford this. If you can tell me which hotel I can stay at and help me look for a new apartment tomorrow, I would really appreciate it." I hear him sigh.

"You don't like it?"

"I do, but I can't afford it."

"Jesus Nina, you scared the shit out of me. I told you that you don't have to pay a cent more for this place than you were paying for your old apartment."

"I'm not a charity case Austin."

"And I'm not saying you are, I thought we talked about this."

I close my eyes and I can't believe I'm about to agree to this.

"Fine."

"Good. Oh and that car in space 206 is yours, the keys are on the kitchen counter. You'll need it here." I hear the line go silent before I can respond.

Great. Just great.

I walk into the kitchen. It is one of the most beautiful kitchens I have ever seen, and notice the car keys placed on the top of a piece of paper. I look closer and I see Dylan's name with the address underneath. My heart speeds up at the thought that I am so close to him. The person responsible for this mess is no one else but Austin. He was the one

revival

waiting for me on a Thursday afternoon. He scared the shit out of me when he said he needed to talk to me and that he is a friend of Dylan's. I thought he was some kind of lawyer that was there to tell me that Dylan was going to fight for custody of Ellie.

But within the next five minutes he told me the most radical idea, told me to sleep on it and call him, handing me his business card before he walked away.

I called him a week after and said that his proposition made sense and that I was willing to do it once I had my divorce finalized. He was the one to help me speed up the process so I could move here faster. And here I am. Standing in a luxury apartment that I will call home for now. I'm not even sure if anything will work out the way I hope it will.

Dylan

I watch Jake as he teaches the teenage boys, they are determined to do something more than hang out on the streets. But I can't stop thinking about the weird encounter I had this morning. I swear that I saw Nina driving in a black Honda a few minutes away from my house. I know that this is just my imagination playing stupid tricks on me, because I miss her terribly. I even told Austin that I'm thinking about a quick visit to give it another shot, maybe see if she's had enough time on her own already. But he told me that I should wait. I hate waiting. Especially for something that I care so much about. Not to mention the case of blue balls I get every time I think about her. Honestly, I think I broke some kind of Dylan Heart record. I haven't had sex in about two months. None of the chicks I see come close to her. None of them.

    I hear the phone buzz on the counter and I check to see who it is. My heart skips a beat when I see Nina's name flashing across the screen, but then I frown as I realize it's not my phone. Its Austin's and he is showering right now, he just had his evening spar session. What the fuck? I slide the answer button but it's too late, she already disconnected the call.

    I can't fucking believe that she is calling him. For fuckin' what? I charge into the locker room, ready to break every bone in this assholes body.

revival

"What the fuck Austin? What the fuck is this?" I hold the phone up to him, with Nina's name displayed on the missed call screen.

"Shit." He walks out and grabs a towel, putting it around his waist.

"Shit is not an explanation."

He rubs his face and looks up to the celling blowing out a big breath.

"She's here, alright?"

"She's here?" I repeat his words and get the meaning of it after few seconds. "What do you mean she's here? Where here?"

"If you shut up for a second and let me tell you the whole thing then you wouldn't have to ask so many stupid questions." He sits on the bench and I tower over him. My mind is on overdrive thinking about the reasons of why she could be here, and why I don't know anything about this. How the fuck did Austin get a hold of her when I could only get one single text over the past two months?

"I went there to see her after I saw how miserable you were without her, without them both to be exact. I made a proposition to her. I offered her an apartment, I offered to find a great school for Ellie and a job that will pay her well enough to have some free time and still be home at dinner. She thought about it and she called to say she agrees, but only after she was no longer connected to that piece of shit."

"So she is divorced now?" He nods his head and I smile, knowing that she is now free of that junk of a man. "How long she has been here?"

I see his worried eyes and I know that this won't be good.

"How long?" I press and he looks everywhere but at me. "How long has she fucking been here for, Austin?" I swear, friend or not, if he keeps playing

with me like this, he will get what he is asking for.
"Three weeks."
Fuck.
I could have seen her three weeks ago. I could have held my girls in my arms three weeks ago.
"And you didn't care to tell me a damn thing about it?" I slam my fist into the locker door, I don't even care that it left the marks on the wood.
"It's not my business to tell, Dylan. She said she would find you when she is ready. She knows where you live. I gave her the address. I guess she just isn't ready yet."
"Give me the address."
"Fuck Dylan, I don't want to be in the middle of this –"
"You're already in the middle of this so stop fucking around and give me the damn address." I cut him off.
I storm out of the gym as soon as he tells me where she lives. I can't believe that he went behind my back like this, and I can't believe that she didn't even make an effort to let me know that she is here. I just don't get it.
The good thing is that she is here, and that means that I can see my daughter whenever I want. I can actually *be* a father, not just think about being one.
The bad thing is that if she was putting off meeting me for three weeks, it can only means one thing; That she does not share the same feelings towards me as I feel towards her, and that is definitely not good.
I enter the apartment complex and I curse under my breath that she has been less than ten minutes away from me. All this time, three weeks to be exact, and she is right around the corner from my house.

revival

My heart is pounding so hard in my chest that I'm afraid it's going to explode while I knock on the door. I hear some shuffling on the other side, I'm standing so close to the door that my nose is touching the wood.

The door opens and the set of the most amazing eyes is looking at me, but the terrified look in them makes me confused.

"Hi."

"Hi." The sweet sound of her voice is enough to put me over the edge. I step closer, bringing my hands to her waist; it fits perfectly in my arms. I watch her run her teeth over her lips and I push into her. My head swirls with all kinds of emotions but I know for sure that she missed me as well because I get a hungry, passionate kiss in return.

I break the connection for a second and take a look at her face, which is now smiling.

"I believe your time is up." I place another small kiss on her forehead.

"Dylan! Dylan!" I hear Ellie screaming as she runs down the stairs.

"Hello, Sunshine!" I pick her up and I feel the happiness tearing me apart. I bring Nina into a hug with us and kiss the top of Ellie's head, closing my eyes and sending silent prayer to the angel that I'm sure is watching over me.

Thank you Mia.

Dylan

One Year Later...

I sit on the oversized beach chair with Nina's body pressed against mine, and watch Ellie fish the shells out of the water. She screams with excitement every time she finds a white one. I guess the story will go on, she will pass it to the next generation.

My hand slowly caresses the growing bump that holds Ellie's sibling. I smile and press a soft kiss to Nina's ear. I'm about to say something that I know will get her off, when I hear Ellie's voice, "Daddy, Daddy, look! This one is the biggest I've found yet."

I still get super soft inside every time I hear her call me that. I remember the day we sat with her, struggling to find the right words to explain to her the whole *Daddy* situation. She looked at us and made that annoyed face of hers.

"I know you are my Daddy, so if this is what you're trying to tell me then I already know." I remember Nina's shocked face as she looked at me for some kind of help, but I just shrugged and laughed. "Everybody says I look like you, so I think you are my dad, aren't you Dylan?" Her big, sparkling eyes were looking right at me.

"I am Sunshine, I am. And I'm the happiest Dad in the whole entire world"

That was about seven months ago. Right before we decided to get married. I wanted them out of the apartment, to have them live with me at the beach house. And every day when I hear her call me that, I swear I get all mushy.

I look at Ellie and Golden, thinking how lucky I am to have everything in place right now. It wasn't easy at first, we basically started backwards. Having a child together then getting to know each other, then getting married. I still remember the day when she walked down the sandy aisle wearing a white lacy dress, hair slightly curled and flowing in sync with the ocean breeze. Her face was the best part, the smile and confidence that made me sure that she was truly happy, that was priceless. I remember that I pinched myself to make sure that all of this was real. That me, taking this beautiful woman, inside and out, was not just a dream I will wake up from.

I brush her hair away from her neck and place soft kisses on her skin, warm from the sun. "I love you, Golden." I whisper to her ear and watch her shudder slightly.

"I love you too baby." Her soft voice is music to my ears. "Just don't get me all worked up right now." She teases me wiggling in front of me. "We have people coming over in a little bit."

"What people?" I watch her head shake in disbelief.

"You're impossible."

"That I am." I take a look at my daughter building something in the sand. "I can't believe she's seven." I know I've missed a few years but I'm making up for it every damn day. I do my best to be the best father I can be, and I'm pretty confident that I do my job well.

"Ok, I'm going in as we have a party to throw." Nina stands up and heads inside. I watch her now wider hips swing from side to side and my dick twitches, just like every time I look at her.

I walk over to Ellie and we play together until it's time to go inside, when the first guest arrives.

"Let's celebrate the best number in the whole entire world." I bring her up into my arms and walk to the house. "Happy birthday, Sunshine." I kiss her cheeks and tickle her until she is wiggling like crazy.

These are the moments that I live for. These are the moments that are worth the struggle I needed to survive in order to have them. These are the memories that will be forever engraved in my heart. They will keep me going no matter what.

Thank you Mia, for showing me the path to love. I lift my eyes to the sky and smile, knowing she is watching over us.

kate vine

The End

Thank you for reading Revival.

If you enjoyed it, please consider leaving a review at your point of purchase and on Goodreads. It means a lot you me to hear what you think!

Keep up to date with new releases, promotions, and giveaways, become a newsletter subscriber!

Playlist

Jar of Hearts-Christina Perri

I won't let you go- James Morrison

Break my heart- Sara Jackson-Holman

Say you love me-Jessie Ware

I'm a mess-Ed Sheeran

Stay-Thirty Seconds To Mars

Try-P!nk

In love with a boy-Kaya Stewart

One time-Marian Hill

Nina-Ed Sheeran

Lies-Sunset Sons

Lost-Michael Buble

Do You remember-Jarryd James

Bleeding love-Leona Lewis

What do you mean?-Justin Biber

Everybody lies-Jason Walker

What A feeling-One direction

About me

I'm a mother, a wife and a friend. I'm a chauffeur, a cook, and everything else that my kids ask me to be by day, but I put my magic hat on at night and become what I cherish most-a writer.

I'm a hopeless romantic that still believes in a fairy tales, even though not everybody gets them.

I'm an owner of dirty mouth that often gets me in trouble.

I think boundaries are there to be broken, and I definitely broke more than one and I plan on breaking them as I go forward. YOU should try it sometimes. It's fun!

I've been avid reader since I can remember and always had stories in my head, till I decided to put them on paper and share them with you, so you can take a glimpse inside my head and join my ride!

Made in the USA
Middletown, DE
23 July 2016